Exposed
Indecision's Flame
Book Four

by JS Ririe

Jan Hill Books

Betrayal - Indecision's Flame
Book 4, by JS Ririe
Publisher: Jan Hill Books
ISBN: 978-1-7326612-4-0
Cover Image by: Yurly Shevtsov/123RF.com

Praise for: Exposed - Indecision's Flame - Book 3

"JS Ririe is definitely in top form as a storyteller with her *Indecision's Flame* series. What will happen between Brylee and Jake? The greatest pleasure in her next installment will be in learning the answer." - Reta Cloward

"Every family has challenges, many different kinds of members, and moments that give glimpses into heaven. Brylee Hawkins' story proves that 'family really is everything." -Denys W.

AUTHOR'S NOTE: Since the setting for this novel takes place in the Australian Outback, certain colloquial words like "bloody" instead of "very" have been used to set a more authentic flavor. These are deliberate changes.
Please join my mailing list and stay updated with my latest releases and more. The link

----

Dedication:

To my amazing granddaughter, Ellie, who at age seven, loves to write and illustrate her own books. She's amazing! May she always have that passion for creating.

~JS Ririe

Chapter 1

I waited for what seemed like the longest time on the veranda looking up at dark, cloudy sky and wondering if Jake would reemerge from the bunkhouse. It had been one of the strangest days of my life with all the rain, the destruction and the battle with the spiders in the outhouse. But what had kept me going through all the unpleasantness was knowing that the man I had sworn to detest would be returning at the end of each long, lonely and work-filled day.

That seemed very strange in light of our past interactions. I liked that he was beginning to understand—or at least accept—that my future was with Ben. I was committed to him, our marriage and our future children, but there was still something about Jake Johnson I couldn't shake. Maybe we had simply been through too many unsettling experiences together or perhaps I had just gotten used to our constant wrangling, but I relied on him to bring a semblance of normalcy to our otherwise scattered and unsettled lives.

I brushed my teeth with the smallest amount of water I had ever used for that purpose and then slipped into a clean t-shirt and pair of pajama pants. My little brother might be able to sleep in his boxers, but I didn't have that luxury. I needed to be fully dressed and ready to move at a moment's notice. Last night's storm had taught me that.

Since there was little else I could do to prepare for bed without running water, I made my way cautiously down the staircase to the dining room where Trevor had set up our sleeping bags. I knew he was still asleep from the sound of his rhythmic breathing and was just about to lie down and turn off my flashlight when I heard a rustling beside him. It caused me to jump with fright.

"It's only me," Jake whispered. He was lying on the sleeping bag nearest the door. He had extinguished the lamp, and the smell of kerosene suddenly invaded my nostrils. It was strong and pungent but almost a pleasant change after the musty, earthy smell outside. "I didn't mean to scare you."

"You didn't!" I said as my heart slowed to a more normal pace. "I just thought you had decided to sleep in the bunkhouse tonight, that's all."

"Maybe I should have. I know it is not the best situation having the three of us in one room together, but with everything that has happened the past few hours, I didn't think it was wise to leave you alone either."

The beam of light I was shining in his face made him look almost sinister, somewhat like an aborigine's native mask with hollowed-out, black eyes and lips curved into a sardonic smile.

"And would you mind shutting that bloody light off," he continued. "You are blinding me."

"I'm sorry," I said as his image disappeared into the darkness. "My nerves are a little ragged."

What I wanted to tell him was that we would be fine without him. But the truth was, I felt much safer with him around. My body was bushed, and I felt like I could sleep standing up, but I knew I wouldn't be able to stop worrying about Trevor and what might happen in the next few hours without him close enough to reach if the need arose.

"Whose aren't?" he said, interrupting my conflicting thoughts. "It has been one bloody hell of day, and tomorrow isn't going to be any better."

"You're still going out at first light?"

"I have to, Brylee, much as I would rather stay here with you and Trevor. I know today wasn't easy for either of you."

"We managed!" I told him. "And even had a few laughs in the process."

"I wish I had been here for the outhouse incident. I could have used a little humor today."

"Then I am sorry you missed it, even though it was not one of my finer moments. There is always strength in numbers during both good and bad times."

"Strength in numbers," he reiterated in a lazy, quiet voice. "You are a very tactful woman when I am more than certain you would prefer me being half way across the country right now."

"That's not true," I replied as I lay down on top of my own sleeping bag in the dark, grateful that Trevor separated us, and that the expression on my face was hidden from view. I no longer understood my feelings for him. They were all over the place like marbles from a dropped jar that scurried so fast I couldn't begin to catch them. "I trust you with my life, Jake, and Trevor's too."

"But not with your heart."

"That is already taken as you well know. We can't control what happens when it comes to love."

"I suppose not," he admitted. "A woman would be crazy to get involved with a bloke like me anyway. I am not exactly the most honorable man in the world, at least you have certainly told me that often enough."

"I never meant to criticize. I have enough skeletons in my own closet."

He laughed and it wasn't comforting.

"We all have pasts, Brylee, and the majority of it we would like to forget. But life would not be worth much if it wasn't filled second chances."

His words caused added confusion. That's exactly what the gospel was—an opportunity for second, third and forth chances. We would get as many as it took for us to learn the lessons necessary to get back to our Heavenly Father—as long as we never quit trying.

"I guess we never know where life is going to take us," I said, wishing I didn't need him so desperately right now. He was not a man a woman could take lightly, even if she was engaged to someone else. "And I have come to the rather sad conclusion that true friends are nearly impossible to find."

"So have I," he replied. " But every relationship has to start somewhere, and we never know where a new day might take us."

I allowed my body to relax just a little before responding. "The past few months have certainly been different than I ever thought they would be."

"And I suspect the next few will be the same." He rolled over on his sleeping bag and I sensed he was facing me now. "Have you ever wondered why things happen the way they do?"

I shook my head in the darkness. This personal conversation was making me uncomfortable. Perhaps our brush with the possibility of death had caused him to reflect on something more than the present, or the women who were such an important part of his life away from the ranch.

"I think we all wonder that," I finally said. "But I believe that nearly everything that happens is part of a bigger plan."

"You said 'nearly'. Is this one of those 'nearly' situations? I can't imagine what plan would include all this destruction."

"I was thinking more along the lines of personal choices that take us away from where we want to be."

"And I suppose you want to be back in Los Angeles."

"Part of me does but I also want to be here with my family, helping them continue the Hawkins' legacy for generations to come."

"So you really are caught between the proverbial rock and a hard place," he said. "Can't say that I envy your position since there is no way you can have a life here and one in America at the same time."

"It does sound rather impossible," I admitted. "But I have faith that Ben and I will be together and I will still be able to help my family. Don't you believe in God just a little bit, Jake?"

"I don't know," he said. "When you have seen as much of life as I have, it's hard to believe any higher power exists. Why would a merciful God allow good people to suffer as much as they do?"

"Maybe they need to learn just how strong they really are. I know we will never be given more than we can handle, as long as we put our faith and trust in God."

"I tried that before. It doesn't work."

I looked out the open front door at the navy blue sky overhead. How could anyone not believe God existed? Evidence of his reality was everywhere from the depths of the oceans to as far into the universe as eyes could see and beyond. People couldn't live forever, and tragedies had to happen or they would never learn to depend on the God who had created them.

"I know you've had a lot of disappointments, Jake."

"Don't go feeling sorry for me," he promptly retorted. "It is a waste of time and energy. I have learned to deal with whatever comes my way."

"That sounds like mere existence to me."

"Well, it's worked this far, and I don't intend on rocking the boat, but you could answer me one thing."

"What's that?" I asked.

"That little song you were singing to Trevor about God and parents and being led. Don't you think it is a little presumptuous to encourage his belief in something his parents would not approve of?"

"I never meant to be disrespectful, but the words of that song are true."

"Only in your world, Brylee."

His words saddened me, but they couldn't stop the warm feeling that had started in my heart and was gradually traveling to the extremities of my body. I would try to express the deepest feelings of my heart, even if I failed miserably.

"We were sent here for a reason, Jake, and we were placed in families that could guide us in becoming the kind of people we were meant to be."

"Guide us towards what—poverty and loss? That doesn't sound much like help to me."

"But it is part of the earthly experience. We needed to gain a body and be tested."

"You're losing me," he said.

"I don't mean to be vague, Jake, but truth is truth no matter where it is found. I simply no longer believe that life is a free ride or simply a happen-chance. What would be the purpose of Christ's sacrifice and atonement if another human could forgive our sins and automatically send us back home to God?"

"You do know what you are saying would be considered blasphemous among certain religious leaders? I would love to hear Father Frederick's response if you told him he didn't have the right to absolve sin."

"I respect Father Frederick, but that doesn't mean I have to agree with him. I know where I came from, why I am here and where I will be going some day if I follow Heavenly Father and our Savior, Jesus Christ. Father Frederick can't answer those questions."

"Have you asked him?"

"Not directly."

"So you found your answers in some religion that has only been around for a few years. LeAnn told me you had joined a new church and it had Jack worried. Seems like a rather irresponsible move since Catholicism is the oldest Christian religion in the world."

"I don't expect you to understand, but the Bible talks about many truths being lost, a falling away and the need for a restoration. I don't have all the answers, Jake. I just know that what I believe feels right. I wish I could explain it better."

"It's no big deal," Jake replied. "It's not like what we believe is going to help us out of the mess we are in anyway. A little bit of luck, and a whole lot of backbreaking labor and money are the only things that will restore all that has been lost. But if it makes you feel better, then I say go for it. But I wouldn't indoctrinate Trevor too much. LeAnn wants him to grow up Catholic like us."

"And I respect that. I was just trying to help him feel better. He is very confused and discouraged right now with both of his parents gone, and he certainly doesn't understand why this flood happened."

"I don't think religious nonsense can take away any of the troubles in his life. Will they bring back his father, or make his mum come to her senses, or undo all the destruction and loss of the past twenty-four hours? Those are the things that really matter to him, not some little song that makes life sound simple. Reality just isn't like that."

"But it should be," I thought as I drifted off into a troubled sleep. Teaching Trevor the truth was what God wanted me to do, but maybe I was going about it the wrong way. Was LeAnn's absence from home enough of a reason to teach him things she didn't believe? I was his sister, not his mother, and he was supposed to honor and respect her, even if she didn't know the real reason for our existence like as I did.

Jake was gone when I opened my eyes the next morning. He had taken a few of the supplies on the dining room table with him and had left a note in their place.

"Be back early. Be careful when you're looking for the well. It has likely been covered with a board or something else that could be rotting. If you take a shovel and dig around a bit you should be able to find it. Hopefully, it hasn't been filled with rocks or soil. Your ancestors had to know it might be needed again some day."

The clouds had dispersed, and the sun was coming up when I walked to the open window and looked out. If the trees had not been stripped of their leaves, and the mud and small pools of water still in existence most everywhere, it would be easy to believe that the past 30 hours had been nothing more than a ghoulishly bad dream.

"Is Uncle Jake still here?" Trevor asked me as he opened his eyes and stretched. He had barely moved the entire night he had been so tired.

I turned from the window and smiled at him. "I'm afraid not, but he will be back tonight."

"Oh," he said, and his disappointment was evident as he sighed and lay back in his sleeping bag on the floor. "I was hoping he would take me up in his plane."

"He is going to be very busy helping other people today. I'm not sure he would have room anyway. He took some of the supplies we gathered yesterday."

Trevor looked over at the dining room table and frowned. "Which ones?" he asked.

"Well, I haven't had time to check that out yet, but he did leave us a note. Would you like to read it?"

"No," he said. "If Uncle Jake isn't here, what are we going to do today?"

"We are going to look for a well as soon as we eat something and finish the chores."

"What's a well?" he asked.

"A deep hole in the ground that helps people bring water to the surface, only this one has likely been covered up by something, so we will have to look hard and be very careful."

"Do you know where it is?"

"Your uncle said it was out by . . . ."

Suddenly, the words would no longer come. I wasn't sure I should be taking Trevor anywhere near the cemetery. We hadn't talked about the place where our father had been laid to rest since it happened. What if the water had disturbed the graves as it rushed over the ground? I didn't want him any more traumatized than he already was.

But he was not about to be deterred from an adventure. He jumped to his feet and then remembered that he was only wearing his boxers.

"Don't look at me, Brylee," he said with childish embarrassment as he raced from the dining room and up the stairs.

I put my hand over my mouth so he would not see my smile. Modesty was a virtue few young people possessed anymore, but Trevor had certainly learned that lesson well.

After we had eaten some bread and jam and finished off the rest of the milk, we headed to the barn to feed the horses and Trevor's animals. Poor Copper had to be left in her kennel in the house again, and we could hear her whimper until we were on the far side of the driveway. But I still felt better knowing she was safe while we were working outdoors, and Trevor didn't argue with me.

Locating the well proved to be an arduous task. I thrust the tip of my shovel into the soggy, dank earth and dug soppy holes all around the shed that stood outside the white picket gate leading into the cemetery but found nothing that resembled a covering to a well. All I uncovered were large rocks, some tin cans and a few pieces of rusty scrap metal.

It was hot and muggy after the heavy rains with flying insects swarming around our heads, and our shoes were caked with heavy, stinky mud from walking through soil that had yet to dry out. It was disheartening that so much work produced nothing of value, but that was how it happened sometimes. Nonetheless, had there been a dry place to sit I might have thrown my shovel aside and given in to a good cry. But I didn't want my little brother thinking hope had been lost since that was all we had going for us right now.

Trevor soon grew tied of watching me dig. I didn't see him leave or even know that he was gone until I looked up and saw that he had wandered into the small cemetery that I had religiously avoided until my mother was killed. I felt a moment of panic. I should have taken time to check out burial plots before commencing with my digging. What if one of the graves had been disturbed? Trevor was no more inclined to hysterics than I was, but the remains of a human corpse would freak anyone out.

I tossed the shovel aside and while calling his name ran into the enclosure. I didn't see him at first, but as I sloshed my way past headstones that were now completely visible I found him crouching near the place where our father had been buried, looking more sad and forsaken than he had the day of the funeral.

"What's up, little brother?" I asked as I gently lifted him to his feet and wrapped my arms around his shoulders. This place was filled with nothing but gloomy and unsettling memories, and I should have been paying more attention to him than to my pointless digging.

"I was just wondering what father was doing. I miss him so much." He wiped his eyes, leaving streaks of brown on his cheeks. He had been crying but didn't want me to see.

I cleared my parched throat. That was not a question I had expected him to ask. Most people would wonder where a loved one who had passed on was, not what he or she was doing. Children certainly had more insight than adults at times.

"I am sure he is helping people just like when he was here. Father was a wonderful man and I know you will grow up to be just like him."

"Does he know mum isn't here, and that I miss her too?"

I fought back my own feelings of sorrow. "I believe he knows exactly how we are feeling, but he is very busy. Do you know what I do when I start missing father and my mother?"

He shook his head.

"Well, I close my eyes really tight and picture a time when we were happy together—like Christmas—and concentrate on that until I can actually feel like I did when it was happening. I remember father's smile and the way it felt when he hugged me. It is not as good as if he was here, but I don't feel quite so lonesome."

"I don't think I can do that," he said.

"Come with me," I told him, taking his hand and leading him to the iron bench that still stood under a now leafless tree. Unbelievably, it had not been swept away and the mud on its decorative curves was no longer wet so I pulled him down beside me. Everything around him was in turmoil, and he was too young to understand why any of it had happened. He needed something solid to cling to.

"Now, close your eyes really tight and think about your birthday," I instructed. "Can you picture Copper when you first saw her?"

He nodded his head.

"Okay! Now you are carrying her to the carriage. How does she feel?"

"Soft and wiggly," he laughed. "She is trying to lick my face."

"That is a good feeling, isn't it?"

"Yes," he said. "Her tongue is wet."

"Can you see father waiting for you in the carriage?"

Another nod.

"How does he look?"

"Happy! He is holding hands with mum."

I felt an unwelcome burst of jealousy. Why couldn't my father have loved my mother the way he loved LeAnn? But now was not the time to fixate on past disappointments. Trevor needed to know that not everything in his life had changed just because his father was gone and his mother had decided she could not be around any of us right now."

"That's because they love each other. What was father doing after we eat lunch?"

"He is sitting in his chair talking to mum."

"An what are you doing?"

"I am sitting on the blanket in front of them playing with Copper and listening to them talk."

"How does that make you feel?"

"Good. Father told me he loved me."

"Do you believe him?"

"Of course! He is my father."

"Then remember how that feels and every time you start to miss him, think about the times he told you how much he loved you. I know he can feel it when we miss him, and he will let us know that he hasn't forgotten us either."

Trevor opened his eyes. "Don't ever leave me, Brylee," he said. "Not ever!"

He put his arms around my neck and embraced me. I felt my heart explode because there couldn't be any better feeling in the whole wide world than being wrapped in the arms of an innocent child. In that moment, I knew there was nothing I would not do for my little brother.

Chapter 2

Jake came back early as promised, but he wasn't alone. I heard Uncle Ned's deep voice penetrating the stillness of the late afternoon before I actually saw him, and I nearly flew into his open arms the moment he stepped onto the veranda.

"I have been hearing some pretty amazing things about you, Brylee," he said.

"And I have been worried sick about you and Aunt Nora," I told him as fresh tears rolled down my cheeks. I didn't bother brushing them away. They were part of what separated humans from the rest of God's creations.

"Well, we are not pushing up daises quite yet," he said with another roar of laughter.

"We," I looked over his shoulder. Jake was helping Aunt Nora across the driveway. She looked grimy and bush tired, but she was smiling too.

"Are you okay?" I asked as I left my uncle and ran down the steps to greet her. I didn't step onto the muddy path leading to the house. Water was scarce, and I could not afford to ruin another pair of shoes.

"I'm fine, but remind me never to ride in the cargo hold of Jake's plane again," she responded. "I'm not sure I will ever walk upright again."

Uncle Ned took her arm and helped haul her up the few steps to the veranda.

"Nora's just mad because I wouldn't let her spend another night at the ranch. She wanted to be there when her laying hens came back."

"You, hush!" she retorted. "You are just as concerned as I am about all the animals, but I still don't see why I had to be the one to sit in the back."

"Because you are the smallest, love," Uncle Ned told her.

She snorted her disapproval, and I decided it was time for an intervention. The only thing that mattered right now was that they were both safe. We would talk about everything else later.

"I'm just so glad you are here," I told them, the relief on my face and in my voice more than evident. "I was worried sick when Jake told me about your house and not being able to find you. I just kept praying that you would be okay."

"You don't have to worry about us," Aunt Nora said, leaning heavily against the porch railing. "Ned and I have been in worse situations, and we do come bearing some good news. As far as we can tell, the sheep and cattle are safe, for now anyway. We have spent the past two days on horseback looking for them."

"So," Uncle Ned broke in. "There is nothing to worry your pretty head about."

Oh, how I wished that were true. Jake had already told me about the water running through their house. They had spent their entire life together building what may have been completely lost in one act of Mother Nature's fury. But they both looked so tired and dusty, I didn't want to bring up anything more until they were ready to talk about it.

"Come on in," I said as I propelled them towards the front door. "I can't offer you anything cold to drink, but we still have some semi-fresh water and some warm sodas if you would rather have that."

"What I could really use is a stiff drink," Uncle Ned responded. "I don't suppose there is any of that good whiskey in your father's den?"

"I haven't looked, but you are more than welcome to anything you find," I told him. "I am just so glad to see both of you."

"I hope that is not going to change when I ask a certain favor."

"Anything you want is yours, Uncle Ned. You don't even have to ask. We are family."

"That is mighty hospitable because Nora and I need a place to stay. Our home, or what's left of it, is still flooded with water and there is no telling how long it is going to be until we can resume residence there. We would go into town like a few of the other ranchers have done, but we don't like being that far away."

"You can stay here forever if you want to."

Aunt Nora gave me a hug. "How is Trevor doing? I thought he would be out here to greet us."

"He is in the barn with his animals. They seem to bring him comfort."

"That's good," she replied. "Jake updated us on the situation with LeAnn. I still can't believe she has run off like that again."

I shared her concern, but now was not the time to belabor it. We all needed something to eat and a good night's rest.

"Trevor's doing amazingly well," I told her as she removed her muddy boots and left them outside to dry. "He seems to understand that his mother will be home when she is well enough."

"What an absolute God-send you have been," Aunt Nora responded. "I'm not sure this family would have survived the past couple of months without you."

"I think I am the lucky one. I could have been turned away when I came home so unexpectedly, but instead I have been reunited with my family. It's just a little larger than when I left."

"I'm glad you feel that way, love, but it doesn't keep me from wondering when you will leave us and return to the man you want to marry. It will be incredibly lonely without you."

"No reason to be concerned about that quite yet, Aunt Nora. There is no way I will be going anywhere until things get back to normal around here."

I had Uncle Ned and Aunt Nora move what few things they had with them into the master bedroom. LeAnn wouldn't need it until she came back, and the upstairs bedrooms were too small and too hot for company.

After they were settled, Uncle Ned, Jake and Trevor went out to keep looking for the hidden well while Aunt Nora and I headed to the kitchen to see what we could prepare for an evening meal.

"Do the twins know you are okay?" I asked as she started pulling things out of the refrigerator and dividing them into two piles—things that could be salvaged and things that needed to be thrown out.

"Jake called them for us while he was in town earlier. They wanted to drive back home today, but they wouldn't make it through to the ranch. More than just a portion of your lane has been washed away."

"Is it really bad out there?" I asked as I got a garbage bag out from underneath the sink and started throwing the food items that were no longer edible into it. "Jake hasn't said much, except that your house had six feet of water running through it, but he thought most of the animals were safe."

"That's a pretty fair description of where we are at, but I don't know about anyone else. It's not like people live just down the street. Ned and I spent last night with the horses and cows since it seemed absolutely pointless to go back to the house, even though the rain had stopped. I suppose we could have slept upstairs, but you never know about flooding. It can weaken floor boards and support beams as well."

She started to cry and I put my arms around her in what I hoped was a comforting way. I had never seen her emotional before, even at my parent's funerals.

Within moments, she sniffled and straightened her back. "I'm acting like a silly, old fool," she said, taking a tissue from the box on the kitchen counter and blowing her nose. "I know we should be grateful to be alive, but I really loved my home. Ned and I spent years building it together. You are probably too young to remember, but we lived in a tent until we got the house closed in. We didn't want to go into debt for it, so it kinda grew around us. The kids remember when the upstairs was one big room, and we all slept there. It's going to be hard on them when they see what has happened."

My heart went out to her. She had sacrificed so much to have a home of her own—filled with family heirlooms and artifacts she loved—and now the lower level had been completely submerged and everything not nailed in place washed away.

"I can't imagine how you must feel. Losing something you worked so hard to build. We will help you all we can."

"I know you will," she said, giving me a motherly smile. "And I am not afraid of the hard work it will take to rebuild once the water has receded, but the personal things we have lost can never be replaced. The photo albums, my grandmother's crystal and Afghans, and her treadle sewing machine. You can't put a price tag on things like that."

Saying I was sorry again seemed pointless. Aunt Nora needed time to mourn what was no longer there and decide how she was going to survive without even the most basic comforts.

"Maybe some of those things are still in the house and can be fixed," I said in a feeble attempt at reassurance.

"That's what I have been praying for, but the truth is, I don't hold out much hope of there being anything left by the time we get back. The sheer force of the water running through the house broke out all the windows. The whole thing could collapse."

She stared out the window above the sink. "Do you think we will see the sun again tomorrow."

"I sure hope so," I told her, but the sun would not take away the devastating losses people had suffered. It would only make them far more apparent.

The men returned to the house just before dark. Uncle Ned was laughing. "You won't believe it, Nora," he said. "Great grandfather was a bloody amazing man—mot much shy of being a genius. He constructed the gardening shed right over the top of the well. When we got to really looking, it was as plain as the nose on your face. All we have to do is take down a couple of walls and attach a bucket and rope. With a little luck we should have fresh water in no time at all."

"No wonder I couldn't find it when I was digging around out there today," I said, feeling a little foolish myself for not thinking about the shed being a possible covering for the well. I had really wanted to be the one who found it.

"That was my fault," Jake admitted. "If I'd had any idea it might be disguised, I would have found it myself much sooner. I always thought the rock walls of that shed were odd considering where it was built, but I figured it must have been easier to use rock than haul in lumber."

"It really is cool, Brylee," Trevor interjected. "Uncle Jake said I could take you to see it in the morning. We get to haul water up in a bucket."

Uncle Ned ruffled his hair. "Now, don't get ahead of yourself, young man. We haven't tested it out. There could still be rocks or something else in it."

"But you found it. That's what is important," Aunt Nora said, giving her common-law husband a warm smile that proved once again how much they cared about each other. "Now wash up all of you. I won't have dirty hands at my table."

Aunt Nora was as amazing as any ancestor without modern conveniences could be. She had thrown more lamb chops on the grill and had an iron pot filled with all the salvageable food from the fridge boiling beside them. The meal she created was delicious and a hundred times better than anything I could have come up with.

I might have felt another stab of pain over all my inadequacies, but how could I when my relief was so great because my uncle and aunt were safe and would be staying with us until LeAnn came back, or at least until they were able to inhabit their home again. I wasn't prepared to make wagers on which would happen first, but at that moment I didn't care. I was just grateful to have them with us.

Now that Uncle Ned and Aunt Nora would be staying, Jake returned to the bunkhouse to sleep. That relieved even more anxiety since his presence made me skittish, and I had never been able to explain why it did to either Ben or me. How I missed my knight in shining armor and the constant source of strength and comfort he brought into my life. But there would be no way to contact him until power was restored, so worrying about where our relationship might be heading was futile. I had to believe that God still meant for us to be together, and this was just another test to see how strong our love for each other really was.

Jake and Uncle Ned spent the next two days in his plane offering help and assistance wherever they could. While they were gone, Aunt Nora, Trevor and I rode horses into desolate parts of the country I had never seen before to drive the cows to our ranch so it would be more convenient to milk them twice a day and make sure there was still enough feed for the sheep and cattle still on the open range. It was good having fresh milk, although I still couldn't drink it without triggering my gag reflex. After five years of living on the fat free kind, it was hard ingesting rich lumps of cream, but I did love the cottage cheese and sweet whipped cream she made. She was even curing milk curds and cheese. There was so much I could learn from her, and I was enriched by the time we spent together.

In due course, she asked me about the remaining supplies that were still sitting in the dining room. I told her about the preparedness fair I had attended, and how Trevor and I had gone through the house and donated everything we could to the relief efforts. It was our way of trying to help others when we needed to stay at the ranch to take care of things there.

I would have said more about the church and its part in worldwide relief efforts, but after hearing Jake's take on my recently accepted beliefs, I decided it would be better to leave religion out of our conversations for now.

Aunt Nora was just as Catholic as everyone else in my family, even though no one seemed to take attending church or doing things any different on the Sabbath seriously. I had been the same way until Becky and then Ben brought the true way to happiness into my life. Now, I missed the change in routine Sunday brought. It was a time for reflection and good works. I could still keep part of it holy without causing waves, but I didn't want her thinking I was straight on my way to hell like everyone else in the family did simply because I had turned my back on decades of religious preference.

So, I read my scriptures, prayed in private and tried not to do things on Sunday that I didn't feel right about. It was pleasant having my uncle and aunt around, and I almost dreaded the day when they would decide it was time to return to what was left of their home.

We soon discovered there was water in the old well, but the waterbed was nearly seventy feet down and getting the precious liquid to the surface in a bucket was hard work. Trevor wasn't strong enough to turn the handle by himself so Aunt Nora and I took turns helping him. Copper followed him from the well to the barn many times each day once the ground had become dry enough that she wasn't getting covered with mud every time she went outside. She didn't like cold baths, and Trevor didn't like giving them to her either, so it made it easier on both of them.

Once fresh water could be obtained, Uncle Ned began riding over to his ranch each morning and staying there most of the day. He discouraged Aunt Nora from going with him. The water had eventually subsided, but it had left a six-foot water line throughout the lower level of their house, and what wasn't ruined had been swept away. Jake went with him whenever he wasn't needed to carry supplies to the people who would not leave their ranches.

No lives had been lost, and the destruction was localized—affecting few ranchers outside a hundred mile radius. Most people agreed it was real miracle, despite the destruction, and I was one of them. I was equally thankful that my father had not lived to see it happen. It would have cast a tremendous shadow of darkness over his final days.

The economy was generally poor for everyone who still lived in the outback, with the exception of the corporations who had bought out most of the smaller ranches. They were large enough not to be wiped out by a single act of nature, but the ones like us were taking a tremendous beating. We just wouldn't know how bad things really were until we were able to move about more freely.

The power company was restoring electricity as rapidly as it could, but roads had to be rebuilt before repair trucks could travel as far as we needed them to. Jake and Uncle Ned hauled enough dirt from one of the pastures to fill in the hole in the miles-long driveway leading to the main highway. But so far, no one had tested it with anything other than the tractor that had been used to make it passable again.

I would have liked to see more of the countryside but didn't want to ask Jake to take me up in his plane. We had become a society that thrived on the misfortune of others, and I didn't want my interest to be interpreted as anything other than a desire to help. I had quickly realized that my role in cleanup efforts would be limited to our ranch and Uncle Ned's until both of them were fully operating again.

Trevor and I were with Aunt Nora the day she decided it was time to return home and see for herself what had happened. She had been humoring Uncle Ned since their arrival at what I now considered our place. But it had been six days since the heavy rain came and with all the heat brought by the sun most of the ground was already beginning to crack open again. Uncle Ned and Jake were already gone, and we left by horseback after morning chores were done.

Rupert was glad to be out of the pasture again, but Thunder didn't want anyone on his back. I almost insisted that Trevor ride a different horse, but he was adamant. After being fed an apple and a few carrots, Thunder calmed down considerably and my little brother was able to mount him without any issues. He rode between Aunt Nora and me. That way he would be close enough that one of us could grab the bridle if Thunder became spooked by anything.

Like we had already been told, all the windows on the lower level had been shattered so the water could run through the house unobstructed, but seeing it with my own eyes made my heart ache. Mud lay everywhere—filthy brown and thick. A six-foot ring of dirt encircled her house on the outside assuring us that everything would be just as bad when we stepped through the front door. Her chicken coop was gone, and the shed where they kept their four-wheelers and lawnmower had been pushed over by the force of the raging water.

Her vegetable garden had been destroyed, as had the pigpen and all the flowers she had been so proud of being able to grow in the unrelenting heat. Remnants of her once-beautiful furniture had been placed on the muddy front lawn: sofa and chairs, dining room table, piano and books—hundreds of them.

Uncle Ned and Jake came out of the house wearing heavy boots when they heard us approach. They both looked exhausted.

"I told you to wait for a few more days," Uncle Ned told Aunt Nora. "You shouldn't have to see things this way."

"Ned Hawkins," she emphatically declared as she climbed off her horse and planted her feet on the barren soil that had been stripped of all life. "This is my home. I helped build every inch of it, and if it needs fixing up, I will be here for that too."

Then she reached out for his hand in a show of affection and trust that made my aching heart feel like it might explode with compassion it was so gentle and unpretentious. That was what being together as a couple really meant, sharing both the good times and the bad. I wondered if Ben and I would be that way after we had gone through a few of life's heartaches together. There was no doubt in my mind that they would come after all I had experienced since coming home.

Together, they walked towards what had once been their home.

"We are in this together, Ned Hawkins," she continued. "We always have been and that isn't going to change. Now, stand aside while I see for myself exactly what is left."

But instead of moving away so she could pass in front of him, Uncle Ned squeezed her hand and went inside with her. I knew in that moment that I could never return to Ben until everything was set right in their lives again.

"How bad is it?" I asked Jake who was leaning against the porch railing out of the direct heat of the brilliant sun. I was surprised he wasn't smoking one of his ever-present cigarettes.

"Let's just say that it is not the worst I have seen, but they will have to gut the entire lower level. As for their furniture," he indicated with a nod of his head towards the mud-covered items on the front lawn. "This is the best of it. We can clean up anything that is made from wood as long as it hasn't warped, but everything else is a lost cause. Ned and I have been hauling all the stuff that cannot be salvaged to the back yard. The only good thing is that the bedrooms upstairs are okay."

"Can I see?" Trevor asked.

Jake looked at me to gauge my reaction to his request.

"I suppose it's okay, as long as it's safe," I said. "We can't very well help out if we don't know what needs to be done."

"The house appears structurally sound, but we have been tearing things up and there are nails and pieces of flooring everywhere. Just be careful where you step and don't try to pick up anything that is too heavy for you to lift."

"But I want to help too," Trevor said as his eyes filled with tears. He was a sensitive child who loved his family dearly, despite the way his mother had treated him lately. "People think I am too little to do much, but I can carry things."

"Of course you can," I said, climbing down from my horse at the same time he did. "We are family and stick together, no matter what."

The mud covering the inside of the house had dried, leaving everything a dirty-looking brown that made touching anything without gloves distasteful. Furniture had been removed from every room on the lower level, and Uncle Ned and Jake were in the process of tearing up carpet and hardwood floors, leaving pressed wood exposed to see if it would dry out without buckling. If it didn't, it would have to be removed as well.

"We will start on the wallboard next," he explained as Trevor and I followed him from room to room. It was hard seeing so much damage and knowing it would be months before the lower level of the house was habitable again. We were so lucky that our own home sat high enough that water hadn't made it past the front veranda.

"It looks pretty awful, but I think there is a chance for complete restoration," he continued as we paused inside of Uncle Ned's den. "We haven't seen any sign of mold, but that's because the water receded pretty fast and the sun came out without hiding its face for a few days after the storm. Did you really mean what you said about sticking together no matter what?"

I looked around to see if I could measure Trevor's reaction to the question his uncle had asked, but he had gone ahead to the kitchen where Uncle Ned and Aunt Nora were talking.

"How can you even ask that after what we have been through since I got back? I think I have proven my level of commitment to my family."

"You have," he admitted. "But I know this isn't the kind of life you signed on for. There isn't anything easy about living in the outback."

"Maybe not, but I am not afraid of hard work. Sometimes it even helps to be so busy there is no time to think."

"But if you had the time, you would still be thinking about that bloody bloke back in the United States, wouldn't you?"

"I can't help that I want to be with him. He is the man I have chosen to spend forever with."

"Forever is a long time. How do you know you won't get tired of him and want someone else? That has happened in nearly every relationship I have ever known about."

"Ben and I are different."

"Sure you are," he said, running his hand along the spines of the books on the very top shelf that had not been damaged by the mud and water. "You really think this Ben is going to wait forever? How long has it been since he heard from you?"

I bristled at his implication. We hadn't had electricity for ten days, and I couldn't exactly drive into town since LeAnn had the family Land Rover and there was no way Jake would allow me to drive his truck even if the roads were repaired.

"That is not my fault," I said, wriggling my lips to keep from crying. Why couldn't he just let things go? I would be with Ben if I could. "I had nothing to do with the flood or the power outage."

"This golden guy of yours might not know that. He might think you have found someone else."

I looked up at the few family pictures that had missed the assault of water as it rushed through the house. "Never! Ben knows I love him and always will."

Jakes shrugged his shoulders. "I hope you are right. I only know it isn't easy being away from the person you love. Someone else is always available to swoop in and take advantage of the situation. But then I suppose we have talked about all of this before, and it is a mute point since fate seems to make most of our decisions for us anyway."

He turned around and walked through the doorway leading to the front entry as my chest heaved with emotions I had tried so hard to keep hidden. I knew he was only thinking about Wendy, but his comment brought home the fact that Ben was spending more and more time with his old girlfriend. What if she was beginning to replace me in his heart? I hadn't been able to write to him for what seemed like forever, and I doubted the news he listened to would cover what was happening in a small part of the vast Australian Outback.

Chapter 3

Over the next few days, things changed again. Uncle Ned and Aunt Nora moved into the upstairs of their house so they could work on making it livable during any free time they might have. The cows were herded back to their ranch and most of the chickens were now living in the barn, making it harder than ever to find their eggs before they spoiled. The pigpen had been rebuilt and the majority of the pigs had returned home. It was too late to worry about the animals that had not been accounted for. They had likely met their fate at the jaws of wild dingoes whose natural hunting grounds had also been disturbed by all the rushing water.

I didn't like thinking about death and destruction all the time, but it was hard not to when that was what I faced from the moment I arose in the morning until I crawled into bed completely exhausted at night. Without power, we were still hauling water from the well, cooking what little we did on the grill, and taking sponge baths with the small amount of water allocated for that purpose. A hot bath or shower would have felt heavenly, but I dismissed it as a luxury until everyone who needed help had their way of life restored as much as was feasibly possible.

Trevor, Jake and I rode over every morning after our own chores were done to help rebuild Uncle Ned's and Aunt Nora's home. It was a tiring and filthy job, but no one complained when walls were taken down, often in broken sections so the studs behind them could dry out. We found a few dead mice and other small rodents in the process, but I tried not to think about them. We would likely find far worse if our own home was the one being renovated. Parts of it had been standing for nearly sixty-five years.

Trevor worked as hard as the rest of us carrying the smaller pieces of wallboard to the ever-growing pile of debris in the back yard. I did what I could but mostly helped Aunt Nora go through drawers and cupboards sorting out items that could be restored or cleaned up from those that had to be thrown away. Her china and silver that had been displayed in the cabinet Uncle Ned had built and nailed to the wall just in case had been mercifully preserved. All it needed was a good cleaning, but that would have to wait until later. Most everything else in the living area of her home was gone.

As the days progressed, we began hearing stories about other rancher's experiences. Most of them had lost as much, if not more, than Uncle Ned and Aunt Nora. But they were no more inclined to sell out than they had been before the flood came.

There was a grittiness and determination in the soul of the outbacker that defied description. I was beginning to appreciate it. Sometimes traditions and the sacrifices of ancestors meant far more than modern luxuries or anything else money could buy.

It took nearly three weeks for the roads to be cleared of debris and repaired so power could be restored. I was more than grateful when that time arrived but still felt a certain amount of pride knowing that I could survive without twenty-first century conveniences. I had hauled water in a bucket, learned how to cook over a campfire, gotten over my fear of the outhouse and washed my hair with dish soap when my shampoo ran out. My skin was red and chapped, and my blisters had blisters from doing work I wasn't accustomed to, but I felt oddly pleased with myself anyway and wished Ben had been there to see my grit and strength of character grow. I had certainly done unaccustomed things and would never take fresh water and electricity for granted again.

I luxuriated in my first real bath with shampoo, conditioner and body wash. And I didn't mind doing a mountain of laundry or vacuuming the carpets. I didn't even complain about scrubbing the floors or the bathrooms. It was just so nice to feel normal again, and Jake had made most of that possible by taking a special trip into town in his plane to pick up the things I requested, along with most of the other items we had run out of.

The first afternoon I could power-up the computer in my father's den, I did. There was so much I needed to tell Ben. I hoped he had continued checking out the local Edna news like we had started doing before I came home. If he had, he would know exactly what had happened and why I hadn't written. If not . . . . Well, I would just have to make him understand.

Three messages from him were waiting for me. The first two expressed his concern about the flooding and told me that our names had been placed on the prayer role at the temple again. He assured me that he thought about me many times each day and wished he could be there to help, but it was the third email that caused my pulse to race and my stomach to knot.

"Dear Brylee," it began. *"I know you likely still don't have power, and I hate dropping this on you, but I have been sitting on some information for a couple of weeks now and it is driving me crazy because I don't want to believe what I heard with my own ears. I hope you won't take this wrong, especially after all you have been through, but I need you to*

explain why you kept something I should have known from me. Jennifer and I went to a party at UCLA a few weeks ago. She enrolled there to get her master's degree, and we met a guy you used to date by the name of Jon Mathews."

The words were swimming in front of my eyes, and I felt my hands grow cold as ice. I wanted to stop reading but couldn't. Jon Mathews had raped me. He should have been prosecuted for his vicious attack, only I had been too frightened and ashamed to tell the authorities. I figured they wouldn't believe me. After all, I was nothing but a penniless girl from Australia trying to put herself through college, while his father was a powerful political figure with connections in all the right places. He had certainly told me that often enough.

"We were just talking and I told him I was engaged to a girl who used to go to the university. When I told him your name, he got this funny look on his face. He said that was interesting because he used to date a girl by the same name— a beautiful girl with long, brown hair and the sexiest accent ever. Then he wished me luck and said that you had not only dated, but your wildly, crazy, sexual relationship had gone on for months."

"That's a lie!" I cried out in hopeless misery as every nerve in my body pulsated with hurt and betrayal. I was glad Trevor was in the barn with his animals and Jake was at Uncle Ned's. I wanted to scream out in wretchedness and break anything I could get my hands on, but I didn't seem to have the strength to move from my chair. So, I just sat there staring at the computer screen without really seeing it while visions of that horrid night resurfaced causing me almost as much pain as when the violation first occurred. I should have told Ben. Now that option had been taken away from me.

But why would Jon lie about our true relationship? We hadn't been lovers. We had barely been friends. Certainly he had to believe that I had told the man I was going to marry what had happened, even if I hadn't reported it to the police. Was this just his sick way of covering his tracks by turning everything into a "he said, she said" scenario that couldn't be proven since there were no witnesses and no evidence left to support my claim? It just didn't make any sense. He was nothing but a perverted, horrid monster who had ruined my life for a second time. I felt like throwing up but forced myself to continue reading.

"He said you broke up because you wanted more than he could give. What does that say about me, about you, about us as a couple? Was everything between us a lie?"

I tore at the tears with the backs of my hands, but it did little good because they were falling so fast. How could Ben believe anything Jon told him? The man was a rapist, a sexual predator that should be in prison. If only I had reported him or told Ben the truth, but it was a little late for regrets. I should never have taken the coward's way out. I deserved what I was going to get.

Ben's email continued.

"We talked about making love as being the most sacred and special part of our lives, and then I hear that you have already shared that with someone else. I need some help understanding how you could lie to me about something like that. I am dying inside, Brylee. I thought what we had was forever, but maybe I am just a naïve fool who fell in love way too fast. Please help me understand why you couldn't tell me the truth. Didn't you trust me enough? Didn't you ever really believe in us?"

That was the end of his email, except for a postscript that read. *"Pease contact me as soon as you can. I still love you, but we have a whole lot to work through if we are ever going to be together again."*

I just sat there with my hands clenched and my body motionless for the longest time trying to figure out what had really stopped me from telling Ben about being raped while I had the chance. Fear and humiliation most assuredly, but I wasn't the only girl it had happened to. Designer drugs were slipped into drinks with regularity on campus, and the morning after pill was readily available. There were even support groups for victims of violent attacks, but I had never admitted to anyone what had happened to me until I was preparing for baptism.

As I sat in the bishop's office discussing the important step I was about to take, he asked me if there was anything in my life that hadn't been resolved yet. The spirit of love and acceptance was so strong that the words just came tumbling out.

He had listened with compassion and understanding but had left the choice of telling Ben up to me. Now it would always be my word against that of Jon Mathews, and it was obvious Ben believed what he had been told. But why had Jon told him such a blatant lie when there was no need for it? Did he really believe he could make a mockery of the laws of the land just because his father would always be there to protect him?

Even if I decided to tell my side of the story now, I had no proof. That had long since been washed down the drain or destroyed. Even personal and family embarrassment would cause Jon little distress since his parents were used to having their private lives exploited in the tabloids. Besides, he was studying to become a lawyer and knew every loophole when it came to prosecuting crimes of passion. I wouldn't have a leg to stand on, so there was nothing for him to prove or lose.

But none of that mattered anymore, and reliving the past would not take away the sorrow and regret I was feeling now. I had lost the respect and trust of the man I loved by withholding something he had every right to know, but why had it happened during the time of the flood when communication between us couldn't occur? It was impossible to imagine the emotions he had gone through since discovering something I should have been strong enough to tell him before our relationship ever advanced to the point of engagement.

"Oh, Ben," I cried out. "Please give me a chance to explain —to make everything right. I didn't have sex with Jon no matter what he said. He raped me! And I didn't say anything to you because I was ashamed and afraid you would never look at me the same again. I will be on the next plane out of here if you want me to."

But that wasn't what I put into words. In fact, I didn't write anything. Ben would try to be understanding when I told him my side of the story because that was just the kind of person he was, but there would always be a hint of doubt because I had not believed in him enough to share my deepest, most heart-wrenching secret when I should have. If I had been there with him—instead of dealing with family issues in Australia—he would never have gone to that party and my secret would still be safe.

I needed to go into town where Ben could hear my voice as I told him the truth. This topic could not be discussed in emails. But I didn't have a way to get there unless Jake was willing to take me, and he would want an explanation for an unnecessary trip. But I didn't want him to know either. He would only look at me with derision and tell me "I told you so."

I pushed myself away from the computer without shutting it down. I was going to lose Ben and then my life would be over. There would be no wedding, no apartment together, no children and no forever with the man I loved.

Why had Ben ever insisted I come back and make things right with my father? If I had stayed in L.A. all of my hopes and dreams would have come true. Suddenly, I was tired, so emotionally drained I didn't have the energy to leave the room. I lay down on the leather sofa and closed my eyes. How could I make Ben understand that what Jon had said was a horrible untruth meant to hide the reality of what he had done? If I had just reported him, but then life had no do-over's and I was left to deal with repercussions that would undoubtedly destroy what was left of my miserable life.

There was a prayer in my heart as I closed my eyes that God would direct me in what to say to Ben. I loved him with all my heart and didn't want to believe that our life together was over. Surely there had to be some way I could help him understand that my silence on the subject was not admittance of either lack of trust or betrayal. I had been robbed of the most cherished gift I possessed—nothing could ever return it—and I hadn't reported the rape because I hadn't believed in myself enough to do so. Even with the best lawyer—that I could in no way afford to hire—it was infinitely hard to convict someone of a crime that could not be proved. It made me wonder if I was the only one he had hurt and gotten away with it.

Jon could tell a very convincing story. Hadn't he persuaded me that he was an honorable, upstanding guy? He played college ball, got excellent grades, and came from a respectable, wealthy family, while I had run away from home because my drunken father had killed my mother. And if they contacted the headmistress of the boarding school I had attended, she would only tell them was that I was an average student who had few friends and seldom dated. I would be considered just another lonely girl from the wrong side of the tracks who cried rape when the brief affair with a man who was obviously too good for her was over.

It was an age-old story that never had a happy ending, even if the assailant was convicted. Being raped changed everything. I hadn't wanted to accept that until now, but I had lost my ability to trust. If I hadn't, Ben would have known what had happened to me before we ever became emotionally involved. Now, he believed that everything about us was a lie. If I were in his shoes, I would likely feel the same way. Maybe he was right not to believe in me. I had always known that keeping secrets destroyed. Even now, I wasn't being completely honest with anyone about my every-changing feelings regarding both of the lives I wanted to live.

I must have fallen asleep. It was still light when I opened my eyes, but Trevor was standing next to the sofa looking at me. He had Copper in his arms.

"Are you okay?" he asked as I struggled to sit up.

I was in the greatest pain imaginable, but it wasn't a sickness any doctor could cure.

"I'm fine," I told him. "I was just tired, I guess."

At least that wasn't another lie. I was tired—tired of heartache and trying to do what was right for everyone else. I wanted my life back, the one I had left behind in Los Angeles where I felt safe and secure and where Ben was always there to help me. I needed his strength, his calm reassurance, his ability to see only the good in me—the person I had become since meeting him and joining the church. But now all of that was gone. I had broken the trust between us by not telling him what had happened to me at the hands of a ruthless man; a man who might be in jail if I'd had the courage to call the police before washing every trace of evidence away in hopes of feeling clean again.

But rehashing the past was futile. I had known from the first that Ben was different from every other man I had ever met. He believed in truth and honesty because that was the way he lived, and I had let my own shame and insecurities blind me to the fact that not being willing to share the most painful part of my past only proved that something important in our relationship was missing.

"Brylee," Trevor said again. "What's wrong with you? Do you want me to get Uncle Jake?"

That question snapped me back to a cold and lonely reality in a hurry. No one needed to know about the email until I decided what I was going to do about it.

"You don't have to call anyone," I told him as I took a deep breath and stood up. My legs were less than steady, but I managed to make it across the room to my father's desk. Two clicks of the mouse and the revealing email was hidden from prying eyes since no one knew my password.

"I'm okay, really," I assured him as I took a deep breath and stepped away from the computer. "I just have a lot on my mind today."

"You look sad. Is it because of father? I am always sad about him too."

"That must be it," I replied as his arms encircled my waist. This was where I needed to be—where God expected me to be. Whatever happened with Ben was out of my control. The damage had already been done. I sniffed back unwanted tears as I returned his hug. I had never appreciated him more. Maybe he could be my reason for going on until I had the chance to make things right with Ben. I simply wasn't ready to give up on us yet.

"I bet you are starved," I said, wiping the moisture from the corners of my eyes. "I think it is about time we ask your Uncle Jake to take us into town for a few groceries. There isn't much left in the house to eat."

Aunt Nora had turned as much of the meat as she could into jerky, but most of it had to be buried in holes on the top of the hill because it had thawed out too rapidly to be eaten. The dry goods, canned food and other essentials in the pantry were basically gone.

It had been twenty-seven days since we had eaten at McDonald's and watched *Toy Story III* at the cinema. I had been away from Ben for nearly four months. No wonder he believed Jon's heinous lie. We had been separated for longer than we had been engaged. It didn't matter that my reasons for staying with my family were valid. I had still made the choice to remain in Australia and not go back to him. That had to hurt, and having Jennifer back in his life at such a crucial moment just made matters worse.

I wished I could stop the circular thinking. It was going to drive me crazy because there was nothing I could do about what had already happened. The best I could hope for was that Ben's feelings for me had not turned to hatred during the weeks he'd had to process what he had heard. Still, I couldn't stop from wondering if Jennifer had known beforehand what my assailant would say about me and that was the reason she had taken Ben to the party. I had been gone long enough that she might be trying to help him forget about me.

Chapter 4

Things changed to a new normal once the repairmen had restored our electricity and the road into Edna had been repaired. According to them, many of the people in the area were calling the aftermath of the flooding a marvel since no lives had been lost. I preferred to think of it as a wake-up call so we would be better prepared for the next time, and there would always be a next time. The only question was when. I had already begun making a list of things we needed to replace and things we needed for survival—things I had never even considered before the rain came.

If I could just keep what Ben had written from invading my every waking thought, I might actually do some good around the ranch. But as the days drug endless onward, I knew that would never happen. I still hadn't returned his emails. He had no way of knowing if I had even gotten them yet. That bought some time for me to decide how I was going to handle the messed-up situation we were in. I tried not to obsess over the fact that it might already be too late. If Ben and Jennifer were attending parties together, what did that say about the possibility of us still being a couple? But I clung to the fact that as long as we had no contact, there was always a chance that things would right themselves on their own.

"Well, what shall we have for dinner, little brother?" I asked Trevor late one afternoon as we stood side by side in the pantry staring at nearly empty shelves.

LeAnn usually kept it well-stocked with canned and packaged foods, but we had eaten nearly everything, and I hadn't wanted to bother Jake by asking if he could take us into town to go shopping, or if he would be willing to do it himself. He was gone every day as it was, and he had already made one special trip simply because I had ask him to, but we were getting to the point of desperation.

"It looks like canned chili and soda crackers is as good as it is going to get tonight. We will have to see if your Uncle Jake is up to a trip to town."

Trevor didn't say anything, but I knew what he was thinking. "This isn't the way my mum does things."

Well, I wasn't his mother! I was his sister who had just had her heart ripped open wide, but I could do better at taking care of him now that I didn't have a future to worry about. For all I knew, I would spend the remainder of my days in Australia while Ben enjoyed the life we had been planning with someone else.

Oh, why couldn't I stop thinking about him? He had basically told me it was over. I wondered if his feelings for me had already begun to change before meeting Jon, and if what he had been told was just the excuse he needed to give in to his past relationship with Jennifer. Certainly she'd had plenty to say after hearing the lie Jon had told about me. And while she might be sympathetic to my plight, if she really wanted Ben back, she would do whatever it took. That had to be infinitely easier since I wasn't around to defend myself.

"I wish we had some of those treats like we made before," Trevor said, and then looked down at the worn linoleum floor. "And I wish my mum was here. Why won't she come back, Brylee? Doesn't she care about us anymore? "

I knelt down and put my hands on his shoulders. "It is okay to miss your mother, Trevor. And I promise, she won't be gone forever."

"But why didn't she come home after the flood? She didn't even checked to see if we were okay."

I sighed and wished I could make life easier for him, but I was having enough trouble holding my own life together. There simply had to be some way to make Ben understand that what he had heard was nothing more than a vicious lie. But for the life of me, I couldn't figure out why Jon had taken the risk to tell it.

"She couldn't come home because the roads were washed away," I told him, trying to stop myself from thinking. "And she couldn't call because the phone lines were down."

"But they aren't like that now!"

He started to cry, and I hugged him even closer.

"I didn't mean to make her leave," he sobbed. "I miss her so much and just want her to come home."

Quite suddenly I realized that Trevor had not talked about his mother's disappearance because he felt guilty. He thought it was his fault she was gone. It was a mistaken belief, but I understood guilt. I had never felt it more powerfully than I did right now. But how could I ever make him understand that he wasn't responsible for anything LeAnn did? She was being both selfish and cruel deserting him right after his father's death. Her indulgence in self-pity had gone on long enough. Somebody had to talk some sense into her before we had another casualty on our hands. Children were resilient and forgiving, but they could only take so much, and my little brother was as close to his breaking point as some of the rest of us.

"You are not responsible for your mother leaving or anything else, " I told him as I sat down on the floor and pulled him into my lap. "I can't explain why she felt she had to get away, but it had nothing to do with you. You are the most remarkable little boy in the world, and I love you with all my heart."

He snuggled into my arms.

"I love you too, Brylee," he said. "But I still wish mum would come home. Things just aren't the same here without her."

Oh, how I echoed his sentiment. Things had only gone from bad to worse since my father's death. LeAnn needed to come back now. We might be able to survive physically without her, but Trevor needed to know that the one person who still mattered most in his life hadn't forgotten him. But how could we convince her of anything when she refused to even talk to us?

Jake was washing his hands at the kitchen sink when we emerged from the pantry with two cans of chili and a stack of saltine crackers. He looked at us and frowned, clearly disappointed by our evening fare.

"I was wondering when we would get around to eating beans," he said, taking the cans from me and putting them on the kitchen counter. "They bring back memories of the nights we spent in the outback herding sheep."

"I wish I had been with you," Trevor said, drying his tears. He was trying so hard to be the man he had promised our father he'd be.

"All in good time," Jake assured him. "It isn't nearly as fun as it sounds, is it, Brylee?"

I didn't know what he expected me to say. It had been two of the worst nights of my life. Just how many more horrible nights would I be expected to live through before I fell completely apart?

"It was an experience only a man could appreciate," I said, wishing I could smile and really mean it, but my heart was just too heavy.

"And a darned good one," Jake said, tossing a can of beans behind his back and catching it with his other hand. He was obviously in a good mood. Then he knit his brows and looked at Trevor. "Did you know your sister snores, Trevor?"

Trevor started to laugh. It was a wonderful sound, even though it was at my expense.

"No, I don't," I addressed the two of them with all the lightheartedness I could muster. "I never snore."

"How would you know?" Trevor asked. "Cuz you would be asleep."

"The boy's got a point," Jake said. "I guess you will just have to take my word for it."

"You're impossible," I replied, turning away from them so I could get three bowls from the cupboard to put on the table. I wasn't in the mood to play games, but it looked like I didn't have a choice unless I wanted to tell Jake what was really bothering me. Since I didn't, I had to play along.

"I'm just telling it like it is," Jake continued. "And even more startling is the fact that she is secretly in love with me and won't admit it, but that doesn't stop her from snoring like a freight train when she sleeps."

His unsolicited remark caused my resolve to shatter. I didn't care if everyone in the world thought I snored, but telling my little brother that I was in love with him, even in jest, was rapidly pushing me over the edge.

"I am not in love with you, Jake Johnson, and I don't snore like a freight train. I didn't get one moment of sleep the entire time we were gone."

"Is that so," Jake continued despite the angry look I gave him. "I bet you didn't know that she drools too."

"No, she doesn't," Trevor stepped in to defend me. "She was sleeping in the den just a little while ago, and when she woke up there wasn't any slobber on her face at all."

"Thanks, little brother," I told him as I plunked the bowls down on the table a little too loudly. I was lucky one of them didn't shatter. "It's nice to know there is at least one person around here who will stand up for me."

"I will always stand up for you, Brylee. You're my sister."

"And you are more than just my little brother. You are my very best friend."

I smiled at him but ignored the man standing at the kitchen counter. I hoped Jake got the point that I wasn't interested in him, not now, not ever. This thing with Ben would be resolved soon, and I would be on my way back home to him. At least I certainly hoped that would happen. I had seen enough doom and gloom to last me a lifetime.

I watched Jake open the cans of chili and pour them into a pan to heat. It was so easy to hate him, especially now. He was everything Ben wasn't, but he was here doing everything he could to help. And where was Ben? Back home with Jennifer. He hadn't even made an effort to come to my father's funeral. It shouldn't matter that I had not ask him to come.

"You look way too serious," Jake said as we sat at the kitchen table after the dishes were done. I was relieved he hadn't mentioned my obvious bout of crying. My eyes were still puffy and red-rimmed. Trevor had run off to the barn with Copper following close behind to check on his animals one more time before going to bed.

"It has been a long few weeks," I told him. "I'm just tired. That's all."

He took a sip of his coffee. "You must be tired. I have never heard of you napping in the afternoon. Are you sure it's not more than that?"

I forced an unconvincing smile. There was no way I would ever tell him what Ben had written. It wasn't just heartbreaking. It was humiliating that the man who claimed to love me could actually believe I was capable of premeditated deception. I had never lied to him. I had only withheld an awful, embarrassing truth.

"It is nothing that would be of interest to you," I responded.

"Why don't you let me decide that? I do have a heart, even if you choose not to believe it."

I looked over at him and frowned.

"I know you have a heart, but this is something I can't talk about right now. It has nothing to do with you."

"I suppose that's good," he said. "I would never intentionally make you cry."

His comment was so preposterous it made me want to laugh, but I controlled the impulse by focusing on the worn tabletop. He had brought tears to my eyes dozens of times since I had returned to the outback but mostly, he just made me mad.

"Don't you sometimes wonder why things happen the way they do?" I asked, and then wondered why. I wasn't really in the mood for conversation, but figured one would happen anyway since we were alone together. I might as well pick the topic since I didn't want him probing into what was really bothering me again.

"Is that a trick question or a philosophical one?"

"It's just a question," I responded.

"But it had to come from somewhere. What's happened?"

The nausea I had been fighting since reading Ben's email was beginning again. I shouldn't have eaten anything, especially beans.

"Can't I just ask a simple question without it being turned into another natural disaster?" I snapped back. "I was just thinking about life in general and how some people seem to slide right through it, while others confront one problem after another. Doesn't it seem like we have had a little overkill in the tragedy department lately?"

"That depends on how you look at it," he said, putting his elbows on the table and leaning in towards me. "There is nothing we could have done about your father. He had been sick for a very long time. And the rain, it was only a matter of time for it. Other than some inconvenience and a little added expense, I would say we weathered that storm pretty well."

"And you sister? How could she just walk out on her son? Don't you see how devastated Trevor is? He thinks it is his fault that she's gone."

He took a long deliberate breath of air. "I don't know what to say about her. I called Emma this afternoon to see how she's doing."

"I hope she is well enough to come home soon because Trevor really needs her."

"It's hard to say just exactly how LeAnn is feeling. Emma said she hasn't seen my sister for almost two weeks. She left right after she found out we were okay."

The sudden pounding in my head was almost deafening. "You can't be serious! Where did she go?"

"To the coast. Emma's family has a cottage there."

I waited for my heart to quit pounding, but it didn't. "That is the most selfish and inhumane thing I have ever heard. How could she just leave like that? She has responsibilities here."

Jake gave me a hard look, but I didn't care. I was way past feeling anything but anger, mixed with a whole lot of guilt and remourse.

"Don't you think I know that, Brylee? Neither you nor I have the skills or the right to be Trevor's parents, but I don't see that we have much choice right now. You don't propose that we put him in foster care, do you?"

"That is the stupidest thing I have ever heard," I almost snarled. "We are his family and all he has right now."

"My point exactly. This might not be exactly what either one of us wants to be doing right now, but my dear sister seems to have left us with no other recourse. I thought we both agreed to put aside our differences so we could be there for Trevor. Are you sorry you promised him you would stay?"

"No!" I shot back at him. "I haven't changed my mind about anything."

"You could have fooled me. You have been mucking around here all evening like a piker that doesn't fit in. If I have noticed it, you can be sure that Trevor has too. Now, what gives? You've got your knickers in a knot over something, and I know it isn't me because we have spent very little time together the past few weeks."

It would have been so easy to unload my worries if he had been anyone other than who he was, but I could not allow him in. He would only complicate everything. I needed to talk to Ben, but right now it seemed more likely that I would find that proverbial needle in the haystack first.

"I apologize for being ill-tempered," I told him. "And I promise to try harder for Trevor's sake. And no, I am not mad at you right now. I'm just mad at life because Trevor deserves the chance to be a child."

Without another word of explanation, I stood up and pushed my chair away from the table. It's legs scraped across the floor making a sound not unlike fingernails scratching a chalkboard. It set my nerves to tingling, but if I didn't leave now I might say something I would only regret.

"Will you please tell Trevor that I will be waiting in my room to read him some bedtime stories when he comes in from the barn."

I didn't wait for his reply. I was afraid to. I simply hurried through the kitchen door and ran up the stairs as fast as my feet would carry me. I was caught up in a life I had not intentionally chosen—one that appeared to have no happy ending—and I was drowning.

I would try to stay positive for Trevor, but what about me? Didn't my wants and needs count for anything? If I didn't get some relief soon, I would go off the deep end just like LeAnn had done. I was beginning to see why she had decided to take the easy way out. Life was simply too hard at the ranch.

The next morning at our breakfast of oatmeal and eggs—Aunt Nora's chickens were beginning to produce again—Jake asked if we would like to go in to Edna the following day.

"For work or pleasure?" I questioned, not knowing which of the alternatives would be easier to endure. My heart was so heavily filled with guilt from hiding my past from Ben that I wasn't fit company for anyone, even my self-appointed enemy.

"How about a little of both?" he asked, giving me one of his challenging looks. "I thought it was time Trevor got to play with the kids he met at Macca's before the flood. You still think that is a good idea, don't you?"

"Of course," I replied, smiling at my little brother. "I will give Mary a call and see if she can meet us there. Would eleven be okay or is that too early?"

Trevor was literally bouncing up and down on his chair.

"We can do it, can't we, Uncle Jake?" he asked. "I have been working really hard."

"That you have," Jake told him. "So we will leave right after chores in the morning. I have to pick up a few things for Ned at Bowman's Electrical Supply. He had the foresight to shut down the breaker box before leaving the house, but the mud was pretty thick in some of the outlets. I can't blame him for wanting to rewire everything. They don't need a fire on top of the flood."

"They most certainly do not," I said, hoping he would think I was really listening when all my thoughts were about calling Ben—if I could get away from both of them long enough to do it. I had no idea what I was going to say. Doubt and confusion lay on my heart like a giant bolder, making it difficult to breath, but I had twenty-four hours to prepare. Surely, something would come to me by then.

"We'll have the house completely gutted this afternoon so we can start rebuilding," Jake was saying when my thoughts returned to the present. "People have been great about helping out. Old Eldridge loaned him a flatbed truck so we can haul the mess away, and Haroldsen's Lumber is delivering all the boards and sheet rock he needs some time tomorrow without charging a delivery fee. It's their way of helping people who have to rebuild."

"That's nice of them," I said, wishing there was someone who could help make things right between Ben and me. "Trevor and I can help today, if you would like."

"We can ride over together," Jake said. "I told Ned I would bring my truck in case the flatbed wasn't big enough."

"I'm sure he appreciates all you have done to help out," I responded, recalling the highly polished, dual-cab pickup truck Trevor and I had ridden in on our first adventure into Edna with him. He kept it locked away in a shed where it wouldn't get ruined. I hadn't even bothered to ask him if the flood had affected its tires.

"We help out any way we can, Brylee. It is called being neighborly. What's gotten into you? You are even more remote and spacey than usual."

I glanced at Trevor whose brow had furrowed into a frown. I couldn't ruin his day by being waspish.

"I guess my nap yesterday must have messed with my internal clock," I responded. "We will be ready whenever you want to go."

Jake decided not to challenge my evasiveness in front of my little brother, although I knew he wanted to. My attempt at keeping my problem to myself wasn't fooling him. He knew I was upset over more than anything I had admitted to thus far.

"Then be ready in fifteen minutes. We need to accomplish as much as possible if we plan on playing hooky tomorrow."

"We will be ready in ten," I said, rising to my feet and picking up our dirty bowls and plates. "I will even pull out the list of things we need from the market since there is nothing left around here to eat. Just let me know if you want something special added."

"I am sure whatever you write down will be fine," he said, carrying what remained on the table to the sink." And you don't need to hurry. Trevor and I will wash up the dishes and see that the chores are done. Won't we, sport?"

"Sure," Trevor replied, taking his cue from his uncle. "I'm getting really good at loading the dishwasher now that we can use it again."

I couldn't help but smile. No matter how bad things got in my personal life if I could stay focused on Trevor I would be okay. God had promised that he would never close a door without opening a window, and my little brother was certainly that opening of light in the darkest tunnel of my life.

I was ready before they they came back for me. It was going to be another long, arduous and hot day, but spirits at Uncle's ranch were still good and that was because of Aunt Nora. Even though she had lost the entire lower level of her home, she never played the "pity me" card. She was always positive and upbeat, and she helped Uncle Ned with everything.

When we arrived, she was throwing broken wallboard and insulation onto the flatbed truck. She removed her gloves and wiped her wet brow when we pulled to a stop in front of the house. Jake and Trevor bid her good morning before going inside to find Uncle Ned who was calling the lumber company about adding a few additional items to the order that would be delivered the following morning.

"It's gonna be another scorcher," she said. "I told Ned we would all have to be treated for heat exhaustion before this mess is cleaned up, but I am not complaining. At least we have water and some electricity. Ned wants to change out all the boxes before we cover up the wires again. I'm not sure it is necessary, but I always listen to him. He hasn't been wrong about anything yet. By the way, the kids are coming next week, and Molly and I are going shopping for new furniture, appliances and naturally new clothes for her. Why don't you come with us, Brylee? We need a girl's day out, and Jake and Ned can watch out for Trevor."

"I don't know," I said, not wanting to spoil their time together. It would be impossible to pretend like I was having fun when my whole life stunk. "There is so much to do, and Trevor is having a really hard time without his mother."

"Listen," she said, putting her arm around my shoulders. "I won't say that I know what you are going through because I don't. Losing your father was hard enough, but LeAnn had no right to run off the way she did leaving you responsible for your little brother."

Tears formed in my eyes, and I bit my bottom lip to keep them from falling. I needed someone to talk to—someone who would tell me that everything would be okay—that Ben would forgive me and we could go on with our wedding plans. But that was not something I could share with any member of my family. They would be outraged and even more upset with Ben because he had not come for my father's funeral. I would just have to keep them believing that the only real concern I had was about LeAnn and her relationship with Trevor.

"I'm sorry, Aunt Nora," I said. "I'm trying, but I just don't understand what is wrong with LeAnn."

She gave me a motherly smile. "Why don't we take a walk? The guys won't miss us until they have another pile of junk for us to load on the truck. It must be a male thing, but I simply cannot understand why they don't just load it as they tear it apart. It would only mean a few more steps for them and would definitely save my back. My bones just aren't as young as they used to be, though I would never admit that to your uncle. He tells me that I am as pretty as the day we met. I tell him he needs glasses, but it is still nice to hear."

She started off towards what was left of her fruit orchard, and I followed along. The leaves had been stripped from the branches of nearly all her fruit trees by the wind and the rain, but the trunks and the roots were still alive. With any luck, she would have a bumper crop of everything next summer. There would be no fruit of any kind this season.

"I am glad you have each other, Aunt Nora. You and Uncle Ned make a relationship look so easy."

"Land almighty, girl," she said, sitting down on the bench Uncle Ned had built around the trunk of one of her peach trees. "There is nothing easy about being with the same bloke for over thirty years. You have to work at it every day, even when you feel like strangling each other. Men can be as stubborn as mules and about as bright as some of those sheep out there." She nodded towards the wooded hills in the distance where just a touch of green could now be seen. "But you have to love them because they are just little boys at heart, and all they really want is for us accept them as they are."

"But what if love isn't enough?"

The tears were sliding freely down my cheeks now, and I looked up at the brilliant blue sky with the soft, billowy, white clouds. I wanted to be on one of them as I slowly drifted away into oblivion.

"What if you love someone with all your heart, but you made a mistake and don't know if they will ever be able to forgive you?"

I hadn't meant to say anything of a personal nature, but I couldn't seem to help it. I had been alone with no one to talk to about things that really mattered for far too long.

"Anyone who can't forgive the person they claim to love is not worth having around," she said. "Ned and I would not have survived the first week together if we hadn't been willing to overlook a whole lot of flaws, and a few indiscretions too. People are human. They make mistakes. But if two people really love each other they can get through the tough times because as hard as things get, they know they are better off together than they would ever be apart."

"But what if you should have told the person you love something, and you didn't because you were afraid he would not understand, and then he heard a lie from someone else and believed it? How can you ever make that right again?"

"I don't want to make light of anything, love, because I can see the pain you are in, but I have learned through many years of living that things are seldom as bad as we make them out to be. Sometimes people just have to sit down together and talk things out—even things that were not revealed when they should have been."

"But what if you can't sit down and talk about it?"

"Why don't you tell me what is really going on?" she asked. "I am a pretty good listener and never betray a confidence."

I knew I could trust her, but how could I tell her about my problems with Ben without sounding judgmental, a little bit immature and most certainly unworldly? She and Uncle Ned had been together for over thirty years and had never married, while Ben and I had committed to wait until after we were married to make love. And what would she say if I told her about being raped? There, I had admitted the ugly truth without calling it sexual assault. She would feel obliged to tell Uncle Ned, and he would go berserk since he had promised my father he would take care of me. No, I couldn't burden her with my problems. They would only take on a life of their own and make so many people miserable.

"I am just very confused and discouraged right now," I told her. "Nothing is turning out the way I planned. I was supposed to come home for two weeks, work things out with my father, and then go back to Ben. We were going to find an apartment, and I was going to live there until we got married, but now that might not happen because I made promises to both my father and Trevor."

"We all make promises we can't keep. I understand your father's desire to have you stay here and a build a new life with your family, but he didn't give you any wiggle room when it came to plans you had already made. I think it was asking a little too much of someone as young as you are. It would be very different if you wanted to make this your permanent home."

"I do want to stay here, but I want to be with Ben too. I love him so much, Aunt Nora."

"Then I suppose it is time you start thinking about what you really need to be happy. We would all hate it if you left, but we would understand. You have to follow your heart, and if that means breaking one promise to keep another, then so be it."

"But I don't want anything to happen to the ranch. I want it to be here for Trevor when he grows up. Maybe some of my own children will want to live here one day. But I did make a beautiful life for myself after I ran away. I can't condone what I did as a teenager, but I was just trying to escape all the pain."

Aunt Nora leaned back against the coarse tree bark while her brows knit. I was laying too much on her. Why couldn't I just let the past go? Rehashing it wasn't healthy for me, and it certainly wasn't winning me brownie points with anyone else.

"No one has ever blamed you for what you did. Your father and LeAnn were keeping an awful secret from both you and your mother. Do you really think you would have been prepared to deal with LeAnn and Trevor right after your mother's death, especially after how it happened?"

"Probably not," I admitted. "It was hard enough finding out about them when I came home as an adult, and I'd had five years to get over losing my mother."

"But you still handled it with forgiveness and understanding."

"Not exactly! I was very angry at first."

"So was I, Brylee." She took a deep breath and folded her arms against her chest. "I loved your father dearly, but what he did was wrong. He never should have been unfaithful to your mother, no matter how miss-matched they were in marriage. If you cannot trust each other, you do not have much of a foundation to build a relationship on."

"No, you don't," I thought as we both sat there looking up into the leafless branches of the tree. I thought I could see some new nodules of life forming, but it might just be the sunbeams dancing.

I had never meant to betray Ben's trust by not confessing my secret, but I had wanted him to see me as a virtuous woman, a woman above reproach, and a woman who would never put herself in a situation where her chastity could be stolen. He had kept himself pure from the sins of the world so he could serve God and marry a girl who had done likewise.

Unlike me, he had known long before we met what kind of wife he wanted and what qualities he was looking for in his children's mother—one who would help mold their lives by teaching them about Christ through righteous example. I knew so little about being the kind of person he expected me to be. No wonder he had been so willing to listen to someone else.

Still, regardless of my mistakes and inadequacies I was a daughter of God and he loved me—just as he loved all his rebellious and righteous children. I would call Ben when I got into town tomorrow. But tonight, when I knelt on my knees, I would pray to know my Eternal Father's will for me and give him the fear that kept me from moving forward. It was the only way I could exercise faith, and the only way I would know what was truly right for me.

Chapter 5

Mary Jenkins was happy to hear that we would be coming into town the next day. She suggested meeting at the city pool so the kids could play in the water before having lunch and asked if Jake would be joining us. I assured her that he would, but he had errands to run so I didn't know if he would be staying to visit. She sounded disappointed, but I wasn't in the mood to play matchmaker when my own love life was such a mess.

I charged my cell phone before going to bed. It had crossed my mind earlier in the day that I might soon be forced to accept that God had never intended for us to get married—that Ben had been sent into my life only in preparation for my mission within my own family. I couldn't do that if I was living our fairy tale life with him in L.A. But I had forced that possibility back because I wasn't ready to give up on us. That would only happen after I had explained myself and he had completely rejected me.

I thought Trevor might be up with the dawn he would be so excited to see his new friends again, but we had kept him so busy at Uncle Ned's hauling debris, picking up nails and taking care of the pigs and chickens that he was thoroughly exhausted when it was time for him to crawl into bed. That meant the house was quiet until six the next morning when I heard the back door slam shut and knew that Jake was in the kitchen below fixing his pot of morning coffee. It was just one of the habits I wished he didn't have. The others were smoking, drinking, swearing, sleeping with women and being generally unhappy with me. I doubted he would willing give up any one of them.

I hadn't seen Aunt Nora smoke since my father's death, but Uncle Ned and Jake hadn't even slowed down. They took smoking breaks every hour or so when we were working. It seemed like such a waste of time, in addition to killing their lungs and other vital organs. No wonder employers hired people without the habit whenever possible. They took much less time off for illness and needed far fewer breaks. But getting anyone to change was impossible if the desire wasn't there, and apparently watching a loved one die from a preventable cancer wasn't deterrent enough.

"You are very pensive today," Jake said after we had taken off from the small runway behind the barn. He had filed flight plans the night before, and I couldn't help but wonder if he had made plans to spend some time with Janet or Beth as well. "But then you haven't exactly been yourself since the power was restored. You aren't sad about returning to civilization are you? I figured you were more of an indoor plumbing kind of girl."

"I'm glad things are getting back to normal," I told him as I gazed out the plane's small window at the hills below. The only green visible was above the water line, and the brown silt that covered all the lowlands seemed to stretch for miles in every direction. No wonder he hadn't wanted to take Trevor up before. Seeing everything covered in one swirling mass of dirty brown would have given him nightmares for weeks. Even my nose was beginning to tickle as I pondered on everything that had been lost. If I looked at Jake now I would most certainly cry.

"Then what's up?" he asked, not seeming to understand that I didn't feel like talking. "There certainly can't be trouble in paradise because you haven't been able to keep in touch with that bloke of yours? He would be stupid not to understand that you have been without power if he has been following the news at all."

I threw him an angry look. "What's going on between us is none of your business, Jake."

"Ouch!" he replied. "It looks like I hit a nerve. Is lover-boy seeing someone else since you have been gone for over four months? I know we have had the 'man has needs' discussion before."

"And it is no less distasteful now than it was before. Our relationship is nothing like the ones you have had with many different women."

I clenched my teeth until my jaw hurt. If a parachute had been available, I might have considered jumping just to get away from his knowing expression.

"You don't mince words, do you?" he said. " But showing how much one cares comes in many forms and some of them are simply more intoxicating than others."

"This isn't the time or the place to be discussing what men and women do or do not do," I retorted, looking back at Trevor. He was staring at us with a confused look on his face.

"It's okay, Trevor," I told him. "Your Uncle Jake is just stating opinions that aren't shared by everyone."

"Why not?" he asked.

"I would like to hear the answer to that myself," Jake said as he looked at me with one of his most galling smiles.

I glanced at him from the corner of one eye. How satisfying it would be to wipe the smugness right off his chiseled face, but I couldn't do it when we were flying.

"I think we could make better use of our time by going over what we need to get at the market," I said while opening my purse and removing the small tablet I had been compiling a list of supplies on. It ranged from laundry soap to tuna fish and toothpaste.

"What about my cigarettes and beer?" Jake asked with a wicked smile. "A man can't get along without things like that, especially when his other needs are not being met."

"That is hardly my concern," I responded, willing my heart to quip pumping so hard. "I gave you a paycheck last week. Things like that should not be coming out of the household budget anyway."

"When will you quit smoking, Uncle Jake?" Trevor asked, saving me from another unpleasant tête-à-tête. "I don't want to lose you like I did father."

"You're not going to lose me, Trevor," he replied, gripping the wheel and looking away from both of us. "I am perfectly healthy and intend on staying that way."

"That was what father always said. But you can't know what is going on inside of your body."

I was amazed at his perception and willingness to state it, but then he had a much better relationship with his uncle than I did.

"Let's not worry about my health," Jake told him. "I really am thinking about quitting."

That ended conversation for the rest of the flight, and when we arrived at the airport in Edna I saw that Janet was not on duty. Jake didn't say much to either Trevor or me before dropping us off at the city pool in the car he borrowed. Apparently, they still kept a certain number of them available for the ranchers who frequently flew into town. It was a nice gesture and saved valuable time.

Mary and her children were waiting for us. She was wearing a bikini with a wrap around her waist. She came over to the car and bent over next to Jake's window so he would have to roll it down to talk to her if he didn't want to appear rude.

"Hey, handsome," she said as Trevor and I got out of the car. "I hope you brought your suit. We could have a lot of fun in that pool and then you could rub suntan oil on my back and I could return the favor."

I slammed the car door shut much more loudly than necessary. Did women have no shame? No wonder Jake had an inflated sense of his desirability. Mary was just like all the others who were only too willing to let him know they were available and willing.

"I am sorry, sweet Mary," he said, and I wondered if he was doing it for my benefit. "I would love to stay and chat, but I have a few errands to run while you and Brylee play with the young ones. Maybe next time."

"I will hold you to that," she said, giving him a coy smile and running the back of her hand down his cheek. "You are one delectable bloke, Jake Johnson."

I expected him to say something equally repulsive in return, but he surprised me.

"You could really tempt an unwary bloke with your abundant charms, but my heart belongs to someone else."

"That is too bad," she replied with a pouty frown. "I hope she understands just how lucky she is. You are a real gentleman, in addition to being one sexy hunk of male flesh."

"I am still trying to convince her of that," he said, tilting his head in my direction.

My heart jumped and I suddenly felt like I was living in an alternate reality where nothing about my life made any sense, but instead of a verbal reaction I pulled my top lip into my mouth and hurried around the back of the car where he could no longer see me.

Why would he joke about something like with a total stranger? He knew I was committed to Ben. Maybe it was just his way of telling her that he wasn't interested without hurting her feelings, and maybe he was just tormenting me like he always did.

"See you later, Uncle Jake," Trevor said as he ran off towards the pool with his friends. I followed so I could pay his way in.

I was wearing my suit underneath my Capri's and a light pink t-shirt so I wouldn't have to change when we got there. I wasn't much of a swimmer, but I loved the sun when there was water to cool off in. Reclining chairs and tables with stripped green and orange umbrella tops lined the enormous pool on three sides. The remaining side was reserved for the head lifeguard and changing stations. An additional lifeguard walked the parameter with a floatation board in his hands. The kids would be perfectly safe here.

I needed time to think about what I was going to say if Ben answered my call. So I selected a chair as far away from the screaming children as possible, but where I could still see Trevor. I didn't even make it halfway there before he was calling my name.

"Come join us, Brylee," he shouted, looking so happy I couldn't disappoint him, even   if my heart wasn't into splashing around in the water.

Mary was stretching out on a recliner without removing her sunglasses. I noticed that her children were not calling to her. Perhaps they had some unwritten rules when they were at the pool.

"Would you mind watching my purse and our towels?" I asked as I pulled my hair away from my face and put a scrunchy around it.

"Knock yourself out," she replied. "I never go into the pool. All the chlorine ruins my hair."

Apparently her perfect blonde hair came from a bottle, and she had no intention of having it turn green. I was glad I didn't have to worry about anything like that.

The moment I stepped into the pool, Trevor came up behind me and threw his arms around my neck. It was so uncharacteristic of him that it knocked me off balance, and I promptly slipped underneath the water and came up spitting.

"Oh, you are in for it now, little brother," I called out as I quit choking and tried to grab him, but he eluded me with childish glee. I had never seen him so animated and quickly decided it was worth a few dunks to give him a few minutes of fun.

Mary's children were soon climbing on me just as he was doing. I was splashed and pushed under from behind until I was too tired to play with them any longer.

"Time out," I finally shouted, making the traditional hand signal coaches used when they needed to say something important. "You guys are too hard on me. I have to take a little break."

I was surprised they didn't bombard me with protests, but when I looked back at them from the side of the pool where I had pulled myself out of the water to rest, they looked just about as tired as I felt. I had never really played with children before, and it was much harder than it looked to the casual observer.

Mary was still reclining in her chair, but a man was sitting next to her, and they appeared to be engaged in a lively flirtation. I almost envied her ability to go from one man to another with such ease, but that was not in my nature. I was what society called a one-man woman and when I loved it was with all my heart. That was how I felt about Ben, and there had to be some way of convincing him that I was still worthy of his love. I would do anything he asked of me.

When I looked up again, Jake was standing outside the chain link fence surrounding the pool and motioning for me to approach him.

"Listen," he said, when I had walked across the hot concrete in bare feet. "I just talked to Emma, and she hasn't heard from LeAnn since she left. She has called the cottage several times just to see how she is doing but never gets an answer. My sister shouldn't be alone like this."

"You don't think she would hurt herself, do you?" I asked.

"At this point, I don't know what I think. She has never disappeared like this before. She always stayed locked in her her to brood."

He was gripping the wire fence, and I could tell from the look in his eyes that he was scared. That frightened me even more than not knowing what LeAnn was doing. Jake was a man of action and was never at a loss as to what to do.

"What do you propose?" I asked as I felt the weight of the world collapse more forcefully on my shoulders. I should have gone back to Ben while I had the chance? I didn't have the strength left to go through one more tribulation without him.

"I want to fly out to the coast and bring her home. This pity-party of hers has gone on long enough. She is not the only person who has lost someone important. For God's sake, you and Trevor have lost your father! What makes her think she is the only one who needs to grieve?"

I forgave his reference to deity because of the circumstances. I might not be so forgiving the next time.

"She lost the man she loves," I said. It would serve no purpose if both of us were too angry to think clearly.

"And that gives her the right to destroy everyone else's lives? Hell, she has a stake in everything that goes on at the ranch. It's her son's future we are trying to protect."

"I'm sure she knows that. People mourn in their own way.'"

"Have you had a chance to mourn your loss? Hell no, you have been too busy taking care of her son."

His question and statement startled me, and I looked down at the concrete beneath my feet. There were tiny sugar ants crawling all over looking for food. I was surprised they hadn't started to make their way up my legs. I shifted my position anyway.

Jake was right. I hadn't grieved for my father, and that realization caused all sorts of unpleasant emotions to erupt. I had been too busy trying to run a household and take care of the people who lived there since the day after my father's funeral. I hadn't minded so much at first, but then the rain and the flooding came, and now it looked like I had lost the man I loved. LeAnn needed to be home to carry out her responsibilities so the rest of us could go on living.

I hadn't noticed that I was clutching the fence until Jake's fingers closed over mine.

"I am sorry for bringing up a painful subject. It was tactless of me to ask if you'd had time to grieve. I know the sacrifices you have made to stay here and honor your father's request when the life you want most is literally thousands of miles away."

My eyes moved upward to his face. Even wearing sunglasses, I could see compassion in his dark, brooding eyes.

"It's not just that," I told him, fully aware that his fingers were still closed over mine as we both clung tightly to the fence. It was almost as if we shared the same lifeline.

"Then what is it?' he asked.

"I want to be here too. I want to watch Trevor grow up and get to know my cousins again, and I want with all my heart to fully comply with the promise I made to my father."

"But you can't do that and still be with the man you want to marry. Poor Brylee . . . ." he said as he moved his hand ever so slightly and caught one of my tears on the tip of a finger. "Her heart is in two places at the same time, and she doesn't know what to do."

There was no malice or sarcasm in his voice this time, and I could think of no reason to move away from him, although I recognized that I needed to.

"I wish I could banish your pain, but maybe if we can get LeAnn to come home the three of us could sit down and hash a few things out," he continued. "You should be allowed to be with the bloke you love."

"We all deserve to be with the people we love, Jake, but sometimes that just isn't part of the plan."

"Well, it should be," he replied. "Beautiful women deserve to be happy."

Trevor came running up then, breaking the complexity of the moment and saving me from having to respond.

"Are you going to come swimming with us, Uncle Jake? We have been having so much fun. Brylee's been dunking us in the water."

"She has," Jake said. "I am sorry to have missed it. Maybe she can dunk me some other time."

I removed my hands from the fence. Our time for having a real exchange was over. We were back to snide remarks and game playing.

"I know she would, Uncle Jake. She just got out to rest for a few minutes."

"Well, it hasn't been nearly long enough, little brother," I said. "Besides, it's after twelve and time for us to get out of the pool. We don't want to overdo it in the heat and the sun."

"Your sister is right," Jake said. "I think we should grab a bite of lunch, and then I want to talk to both of you about something."

"Can my new mates come too?" Trevor asked. Mary's children had come up behind us and so had she.

"This is family business," he said. "Maybe another time."

"It wouldn't take long for lunch," Mary responded as she leaned seductively against the fence, obviously disregarding what he had just said. "I mean it wouldn't matter if some of us had wet hair or were wearing our bathing suits."

I could tell where their conversation was headed, and the children didn't need to be exposed to it.

"Come along, kids," I told all of them. "Let's rinse off and change out of our suits. We will meet both of you in the parking lot. We won't be long."

I fumed over Jake's odd behavior as the cold water of the shower slid over my body causing goose bumps even in the heat of the day. How could people act like they did? There was more to life than playing games of cat and mouse. I pitied the person who ended up with either Jake or Mary.

I replaced my wet suit with the clothes I had worn over it to the pool. Fortunately, I had anticipated getting wet and had brought a brush and some make-up with me. I didn't take time to apply anything more than a little mascara, but at least Mary wouldn't be able to say I was a complete tree-hugger.

Jake was leaning against the rental car from the airport with his arms crossed in front of him when we got to the parking lot. Mary was standing close enough that their bodies were touching. Apparently, she liked hard-to-get men.

"You ready to go?" he asked in a question that included both Trevor and me. "I told Mary we couldn't stop for lunch today because we had some place we needed to be."

Trevor looked disappointed. "But what about Macca's? We were going to play on the toys."

Jake ruffled his wet hair. "Sorry, sport, but we need to get moving."

I put my hand on my little brother's shoulder and led him around the car. "We will make arrangements for you and your friends to get together again soon, I promise. Maybe you could call them from home. We do have their phone number."

"Okay," he said with a sigh as he climbed inside the car and slammed his door shut. "But I am still hungry. When are we going to eat?"

"Right now," Jake said as he slid in behind the wheel, leaving Mary Jenkins standing in the hot sun with her children.

"I really am sorry for cutting your outing short, Trevor, but we are taking a trip to the coast in the plane."

My look of surprise was genuine. He had mentioned the idea of going while standing at the fence, but how could he instantly decide something that drastic without talking it over with me first? What would happen if we couldn't find LeAnn? And even if we did, what if she refused to come home or even talk to us? Trevor didn't need any more hurt right now, and I could not protect him if I didn't have all the facts.

"Why are we going there?" Trevor asked as I tried to slow my racing thoughts. "We have never done anything like that before."

"Then it is about time we did. I have already cleared our flight plans and we can be there in a little over an hour once we are in the air."

I wanted to voice my concerns but couldn't do it with Trevor present, and Jake's plans had left no room for discussion anyway. He was a man with a mission and wasn't about to let me interfere.

He stopped at Macca's drive through window and ordered burgers, fries and drinks. We ate what he got for us on the short drive to Edna's only airport. While Trevor sat in a chair near the main window to finish his lunch, I pulled Jake aside so we could speak in private.

"I'm not sure it is a good idea to take Trevor to see LeAnn. What if she isn't receptive? It would devastate him, and he has already suffered enough?"

He pushed his sunglasses to the top of his head, looking very much like he was trying to figure out what to say that would not make me more upset than I already was.

"Whether you believe it or not, Brylee, I have considered how this will affect Trevor but the longer LeAnn stays away, the less likely she is to come back. She knows she has hurt her son and disappointed a lot of other people who rely on her being around. That's why she left Emma's. She was tired of feeling guilty."

"If that's true, then how will she react when we show up unannounced? She has hurt Trevor most of all."

"I'll give you that," he admitted. "But she also loves Trevor more than anyone else. I am hoping that when she sees him all those motherly feelings will come back. Children can forgive anyone. Knowing that he doesn't hate her for running away should help convince her that it is okay to come home."

"That sounds like a pretty big gamble to me."

"Can you think of anything better? LeAnn is needed at home so the rest of us can get on with our lives, and Trevor needs to know that his mother still loves him. Those seem like good enough reasons to give it a shot. We can't live in limbo forever."

I was still hesitant about going along with his plan, but if it worked I might be on my way back to Ben in a few days where I could talk to him in person. If not, we wouldn't be all that much worse off than we already were, except for Trevor. I couldn't bring myself to think about how awful it would be if he even thought his mother was rejecting him again.

"Can we play in the ocean when we get there?" Trevor asked me once we were in the air and heading in an easterly direction.

"Haven't you had enough water for one day?" Jake asked him.

"Nope!" he replied. "Besides, a swimming pool isn't like the ocean. There aren't any waves."

"I used to do a little surfing when I was younger," Jake told him. "Maybe when you have grown a few inches I can teach you how it is done."

He looked at me as if to say that Ben wasn't the only guy in the world who knew how to ride a wave.

"Could Brylee learn too?" Trevor asked him.

"She probably already knows how. That bloke she is going to marry is a big California suffer dude. Isn't that right, Brylee."

I chose to ignore his sarcasm.

"Ben has won several trophies, but I have never been on a board. I would rather cheer from the sidelines."

"But you would go with us, wouldn't you?" Trevor prodded.

"That I would have to think about! You forget that I was born and raised in the outback just like you, Trevor."

"Well, I think it sounds like fun," he said. "When can we do it?"

"It's not that simple," Jake replied. "You have to be a really good swimmer first, and that is rather hard to do when you're not around a pool very often."

Trevor signed before lying down on the floor of the cargo hold and closing his eyes. I knew he was trying to think of a solution to his latest problem. He was a very smart little boy, but I hoped he would fall asleep before thinking of anything else he wanted to try. I hated telling him no.

I might have closed my eyes too, but I couldn't stop my mind from thinking about all the bad things that could happen when we saw LeAnn again. And then there was Ben. I hadn't called him before leaving Edna. I told myself there hadn't been time, but maybe I was just afraid. If he rejected me over the phone, I would have nothing else to live for. I would be in exactly the same place LeAnn was, only I wouldn't have the man of my dreams waiting for me in the next life if both she and my father accepted what I already

Chapter 6

It was nearly three in the afternoon when Jake radioed the tower for landing instructions. Trevor was awake and had his nose pressed to the window as the Pacific Ocean came into view.

"It's huge," he said in utter amazement.

I glanced out the window too. Being in a small plane instead of a huge airliner certainly gave a different perspective to the rocks, the gulls, the sand and the sea. The waves were crashing against the coastline and miniature people dotted the white sand beaches. There was an old lighthouse sitting on the highest outcropping of rocks and copper-roofed houses set so closely together that it was hard to determine where one began and the next one ended. I wondered where along the coast Emma's family vacation home was located and what LeAnn had been doing since her arrival.

What if we ended up staying the night? We didn't have reservations at a hotel or even a toothbrush between us. Men never thought about things like that. They could improvise through almost anything, but with girls it was different. We needed a few of the niceties just to survive.

A young girl with big blue eyes and wearing a black suit greeted us as we walked into the terminal. It was larger than the one in Edna, but not by much. She asked us pleasantly if we needed a rental car or a reservation at one of the resorts two larger hotels.

Jake told her that we wouldn't need accommodations because we wouldn't be in town that long.

She appeared disappointed. "That's too bad," she said as Trevor and I listened to their conversation without taking part in it. "We have some of the best beaches in the world for snorkeling and some of the best restaurants in all of Australia."

"Maybe another time," Jake told her, just as he had told Mary Jenkins and her children earlier. "We re here on business. How far away is 2918 Oceanside Drive?"

"Let's see," she said, picking up a brochure that included a map of the area from a stack on the counter. "I should know where all the streets are by now, but the truth is that I have only been here for six weeks. I grew up in Brisbane but wanted the experience of working in a tourist town instead of a big city. It is so much nicer when neighbors know each other."

"I couldn't agree with you more," Jake said. "I am a Brisbane boy myself, at least for the first few years of my life."

"Wow," she replied, "It really is a small world. What brought you out here?"

"Business," he said again. "I live about two hours outside the town of Edna in the outback."

"It must get awfully lonely living out there where the animals outnumber the people a thousand or more to one."

I could tell that Jake was becoming impatient. The girl at the counter was very pretty and very nice, and she appeared to be more than casually interested in him. But that wasn't unusual, everywhere we went, women flocked to him.

"I like the peace and quiet, but perhaps we will come back here on holiday sometime," he told her.

"I know you and your wife and son would really enjoy all that we have to offer."

Jake didn't correct her assumption, and that surprised me. Maybe he was just tired of explaining our rather unusual situation.

"I am sure we would, but right now we are on rather a tight schedule."

The girl immediately looked down at the pamphlet she had spread out on the counter.

"It's right here," she said, pointing with a ring-clad finger at a place on the map I couldn't see. "You take a left right outside the door, and it's about six blocks away. Not a bad walk if you don't mind a few hills."

"I'm sure we can find it," Jake replied, pulling up the edge of the pamphlet until the girl was forced to relinquish it so he could take it with us. "You have been very helpful. Thank you."

His near rudeness was disturbing, but I understood why he was acting that way. He was as worried as I was about what would happen when we found LeAnn.

I took Trevor's hand as we followed him through the tinted glass doors and onto the sidewalk. The cool breeze from the ocean was refreshing after the constant heat of the outback. No wonder so many Aussies traveled to the coast on the weekends. Besides being a wonderful place to play, the weather was much more agreeable.

Trevor didn't complain as our feet rapidly took us away from the small airport, past a number of independently owned businesses and towards a row of houses that lined the sandy beach we had seen from the air. I didn't know how Jake was going to explain our search for LeAnn to Trevor. If she was at the beach house as Emma had told him, a lengthy explanation might not be necessary. But if she wasn't there, it would be hard to explain why we had come to the coast if we were not planning to stay long enough to enjoy the ambience and the water.

Even knowing the potential disaster that lay ahead, I had trouble concentrating on our meeting with LeAnn because I was so worried about what was happening with Ben. I had not been able to write to him for nearly a month because of the damage brought by the rain and understood that I could not blame him for thinking my lack of communication was a sign of guilt, especially since I had been putting off the inevitable since the power had been restored at the ranch.

But his old girlfriend's presence was complicating everything. My absence gave her the perfect opportunity to rebuild what they had once shared. It wasn't just coincidence that had brought her back when I was no longer around to protect my relationship with Ben. As scared as I was, I had to call him before we returned home.

Jake stopped walking in front of a small, whitewashed frame house with a copper-colored roof like all the rest of the houses on the street. A white picket fence separated a pebble walkway from the street and flowers in multiple shades of rose and yellow lined the way up to a red front door.

"This is it," he said, although I wasn't sure he realized that he had uttered the words out loud.

Trevor gave me a curious look. "Who lives here?"

I shrugged my shoulders while Jake answered. "The house belongs to a friend of your mums."

That was all it took for him to voice the question Jake and I had been asking ourselves since the moment we started on this unexplainable journey. "Is she here?"

He looked around to see if there was any indication of her presence. Jake and I did the same. We had approached the house from the side furthest away from the carport.

"Oh, she is here," Trevor suddenly exclaimed, breaking free of my hand. "That's our car parked next to the house."

He was right! It was our Land Rover. LeAnn had to be inside or very close by.

"Not so fast!" Jake's hand shot out and grabbed his upper arm. "She doesn't know we were coming."

"That's okay, Uncle Jake," he said. "She will be ever so glad to see us. I dreamed about her on the plane."

Jake's brow furrowed as he looked from Trevor to me.

"Let him go," I said. "The situation is out of our hands now."

I wasn't sure if I felt relieved or just accepting of the inevitable, but in a few moments the answer as to whether or not LeAnn would come back with us would be known.

I felt a cold chill as I crossed the short distance to the front door behind my little brother. There were white eyelet curtains at every visible window. The flowerbeds were weed free and the grass recently cut, but that didn't surprise me. Everything about this house was picture postcard perfect.

I held my breath while Trevor knocked on the door a second time and then I heard footsteps from inside. My little brother turned his head and gave me one of those smiles that turned my knees to putty. Jake's look was nothing less than dubious.

"Oh, Father," I prayed. "Don't let him be hurt again."

And then it happened! The door opened, and LeAnn was standing in the shadows in front of her son.

"Oh, my God," she exclaimed, sinking to her knees and drawing Trevor into her arms. "Is it really you? I have been thinking about you all afternoon and wishing you were here with me. It has been a perfect day on the beach, and you are so much bigger than I remember."

It was a tender moment and tears began to slide down my cheeks. I brushed at them with the sides of my fingers, wondering if their reunion was affecting Jake the same way, but couldn't bering myself to look at his face.

"I missed you so much, mum," Trevor said as he put his arms around her neck and returned her embrace. "Why did you go away and leave me behind? I have been so scared and would have gone anywhere with you."

LeAnn sniffled back tears. "I know you would have, but I was being both selfish and stupid. I couldn't see what a wonderful gift I had in you."

"I miss father too," Trevor sobbed, clinging to her neck.

I felt like an intruder, so I stepped onto the grass and pretended to be looking at the flowers so they could have some privacy.

"Thank you," I silently uttered, looking heavenward. "I can handle anything now that I know my little brother is no longer in such great pain."

I didn't know how soon that resolve was going to be tested, but for that single moment, the world quit spinning and life seemed good.

"We dodged a bullet on that one, didn't we?" Jake said so close to my shoulder that I almost jumped.

My brow furrowed as I responded. "I guess we did, but you do know that you were taking a horrible chance that could have turned out very differently?"

"I prefer calling it a calculated risk. My sister loves her son no matter how poorly she behaves at times. She just needed to be reminded."

"We still don't know if she will come home with us?"

"She'll come," he said. "It may take a few days for her to get used to the idea, but where else would she go? We don't have any extended family and she has no other means of supporting Trevor. Unless she goes back to waitressing, and I doubt those long hours away from home would even be considered after what she has already put him through."

I bit my bottom lip and closed my eyes, more than grateful I was wearing sunglasses. I didn't know my new family very well, but the thought of not seeing Trevor every day was too unbearable to even entertain. We shared our father's blood. That was a tie stronger than any other.

"Mum wants you to come into the house for supper," Trevor said, separating me from my uncomfortable thoughts. "She says it won't be much because she wasn't expecting company."

He looked happy—almost radiant—and I hoped nothing would take that joy away.

Jake gave me a weary, but relieved smile, and then we followed Trevor into the house. It wasn't a large dwelling, but that wasn't necessary since it had been built as a vacation home rather than a place where a family lived year round. The small living area had two wing-backed, red velvet chairs and a multi-colored sofa, quite old-fashioned but in good condition.

LeAnn was sitting on it waiting for us. Jake took one chair and I took the other one, while Trevor sat down close to his mother. LeAnn put her arm around him, and he nestled in close to her. I hoped I would have children as loving and forgiving as my little brother some day.

My new stepmother cleared her throat while Jake and I waited somewhat impatiently to hear what she had to say.

"I am sorry for causing so much concern. I know I bailed at the worst possible time—especially for Trevor." She kissed the top of his head. "But I truly believe I had some kind of breakdown when Jack died. He was my life and had been sick for such a long time, and when he was gone I felt like nothing else mattered. Getting away from everything and everyone involved seemed like the only way to save what little sanity I had left. I knew Trevor would be okay because both of you love him so much."

"But he needed you more than anyone else, Lee. You can't deny that," Jake said.

I knew he loved his sister and hated being critical, but he also needed to understand why she had gone and if she was going to come back to stay.

"I know what I did was wrong, but I couldn't deal with being in the house and   bedroom Jack and I shared for so many years once he was gone. There were too many memories, and some of them not so good."

She wiped at the tears that were starting to slide down her cheeks. She had always maintained that their life had been pretty much perfect, but they'd had to deal with death, deception and betrayal—trials mostly of their own making. But who was I to judge anymore? Wasn't my own life much the same? I was on the verge of losing almost everything too.

"I know I could have talked to both of you about how I was feeling but was afraid you would persuade me to stay. I needed time alone to find myself again."

"And have you found yourself?" Jake asked. "You need to be home where we can take care of you."

"That's what I am afraid of."

Jake cleared his throat. "Why would you say that?"

She smiled at him like I had seen her do in the past. It was the way a mother would look at her grown child—with love and a certain amount of trepidation as to just how far she could push before he pushed back.

"I don't think any of us will completely find ourselves any time soon because life keeps changing, especially mine."

I frowned in confusion. She looked down at Trevor who seemed perfectly content just to be sitting beside her again.

"I saw a doctor here in town this morning. He gave me some very unexpected news."

I felt my head start to throb. We couldn't lose another member of our small but very misguided family.

LeAnn looked at me and laughed. "Don't look so scared. It's not bad news. In fact, it is quite the opposite. I am going to have a baby!"

I don't know who was more surprised—Jake or me. But while we sat suspended in shock, Trevor began bouncing up and down on the sofa. He was excited enough for all of us.

"You mean it, truly, mum?" he cried out, looking like he had just been given the best prezzie ever. "Am I going to have a little brother!"

"Well," LeAnn said, resting against the back of the sofa and running her hand across her abdomen. "I don't know if it will be a boy or a girl, but we will all know for sure in a little over seven months."

"I thought that wasn't possible," Jake said, looking at her skeptically. "Are you absolutely sure? Jack was too weak towards the end for that to happen."

"I think we have you and Brylee to thank for this blessing," she said as she started to cry again, but this time they were tears of joy. "If you hadn't planned such a romantic wedding night for us, Jack might not have found the strength to show me just how much he loved me. He wanted to give me a special night I would remember for always, and now I will."

I fought back my own tears. This was something I definitely had not expected, but then I hadn't expected much of what had happened since I had come home.

"I am sp happy for you," I said, moving across the room to give her a hug and a kiss. "I can't think of anything more perfect."

"It is perfect, Brylee, but I wasn't kidding when I said that I would need someone to take care of me when I come home. This is going to be a very difficult pregnancy. I am nearly forty-three, and the doctor told me I would pretty much have to stay in bed until the baby comes if I want to keep it."

"You know we will do whatever it takes, Lee," Jake told her.

"I know you will, Jake, but it is Brylee who will be making the biggest sacrifice if we want this baby to be a part of our family. I am going to need her for so many things and don't have the right to ask for anything more after the awful way I treated her. I really am sorry for my behavior."

I took a deep breath before giving my reply. I could forgive unkind words and less than mature actions, but what she was asking me to do would change my life completely. I wouldn't be able to go home and explain things to Ben, and our wedding might never take place. But who would help out if I wasn't willing to do it?

"You can count on me," I told her, trying to make the tone of my voice as light and steady as possible.

But with that one declaration of service and support, I felt all my hopes and dreams for the happy future I so much wanted being dashed to pieces like waves against a rugged shoreline. Still, I knew I would not be able to live with myself if I made a different choice. God was giving our entire family a very unexpected blessing. I might not understand why it was happening now, but I couldn't deny his hand in this miracle. Medically, there was no way my father could have given LeAnn another child.

"I knew you would be supportive," LeAnn told me, reaching the short distance between us and taking my hand. "But I had to ask. You have a right to your own life."

"Things always seem to work out the way they were meant to," I told her, fighting back tears of both apprehension and joy. "I would never want to miss seeing a little sibling come into this world."

We talked for a few minutes more, but there wasn't a whole lot left to say until the shock of her announcement sunk in. Jake offered to order a pizza for dinner while Trevor and I got LeAnn back into bed. For all her joy and bravado, she didn't look well. She was far too thin and pale. She would need healthy, nutritious meals and plenty of stress free relaxation if both she and the baby were going to make it. That meant I really would have to learn how to cook and care for a family. It just wasn't the family I had been anticipating.

LeAnn expressed her wishes to rest before dinner, so I took Trevor down to the beach to pass some time while Jake waited for the delivery person to arrive. From what I could tell, there was only one bedroom in the house, and some kind of a loft. It would make for an interesting night since it was too late to fly back to the ranch, especially with LeAnn in such a delicate condition.

"So what do you think about your mother's news?" I asked him as we sat on the white sand and looked at the waves as they rolled in. We were sitting far enough away from the water that it did nothing more than tickle the ends of our feet.

"I don't know," he said with a heavy sigh. "I have never been a big brother before. What if I don't know how?"

"You will do great," I replied as I watched him draw a line in the wet sand with a twig that had fallen from a nearby tree. "That new little arrival is going to be very lucky."

"Will it be like you and me?" he asked. "I didn't know how to have a big sister until you came."

"I imagine it will be pretty much the same, only a baby will be very small and won't be able to do much besides eat and sleep for a long time."

"Then how will it know who I am?"

"Because you will learn how to hold and take care of it, and it won't be long until he or she will be able to sit up, roll over and even talk gibberish."

"Aren't you scared?" he asked.

"A little since I have never been around a baby before."

Trevor gave me a confused look.

"But you are a grownup."

"I suppose I am, but that doesn't mean I have been around babies. I spent all of my childhood and youth alone on the ranch and at boarding school. Then I went to college and studied and worked. It will be as new for me as it is for you."

"I guess that's good," he admitted.

"Of course it is. We will be able to learn everything together."

"Pretty soon father will have three children. That makes us a pretty big family, doesn't it? Most families only have two kids."

I couldn't fault his logic. In all the families he knew there were only two children. Uncle Ned and Aunt Nora had Molly and NJ. Father had Trevor and me and then there were his new friends, Veronica and Jesse. Families were definitely shrinking in number as affluence gave people more time for recreation and less of a desire to raise children where sacrifices of both time and money would have to be made.

"It will be a big adventure for all of us and so much fun," I told him, but in my heart, I knew it would not be the adventure I wanted—my own family with the man I loved. How could I have told LeAnn I would stay in Australia when my real life was in California with Ben? At least I still hoped he was waiting for me.

We sat around LeAnn's bed a short time later eating pizza and making plans for the return trip to the ranch the following day. Jake decided that it would be best if LeAnn and Trevor flew home with him. That left me to drive the Land Rover back. Not that it would be such a huge task because it could easily be done in a day, but it would give me too much time alone to think, and I wasn't sure that was a good idea. In my present state of mind, I might drive straight to Sydney and take the first plane back to the United States. Staying here could mean giving up my own dream for a happily ever after.

Chapter 7

After we'd eaten, Trevor decided he was going to sleep with his mother so he would be there if she needed him. Jake would take the couch, and I would sleep in the loft. I didn't even know if it had a bed, but I was tired enough to sleep on the floor if necessary.

Jake put the trash in the garbage can by the Land Rover and then disappeared. Trevor and LeAnn had secluded themselves in her bedroom for the night. With nothing else to do and no one to talk to, I went outside to the back deck and stood looking over the wood railing at the ocean as its waves brushed up against the white sand of the beach and then receded again.

It was peaceful listening to the sounds of the ocean and the occasional cry of a seagull, but my mind was in turmoil. I couldn't put off calling Ben any longer, or he would be at work and unable to talk. So I took a deep breath and dialed his number. It took a few seconds for the connection to be made, but then I heard his voice, and my heart flew to my throat making it difficult to breath.

"This is a surprise, Brylee," was his greeting, and the tone of his voice betrayed all the disillusionment and anger he still felt against me. "I was beginning to wonder if I was ever going to hear from you again."

"I am sorry," I told him, fighting to hold back the tears. "But I haven't been able to get into town to call you until today."

"I sent three emails after I heard about the flooding. I was worried sick about you."

"We didn't have electricity and some of the roads were washed away."

"I understand that, but why didn't you answer my emails when you did get power. That couldn't have taken five weeks. We might not be in the best place right now as a couple, but I still care about you as a person."

He didn't say that he still loved me, I pondered as I began walking down the steps towards the beach below. It was almost dark, except for the lights coming from inside nearby cottages, and everything was so still I could hear my own heartbeat. Had he already made up his mind about walking away from me?

"I didn't know what to say, Ben."

"You could have defended yourself—told me it was all a lie. I would have believed you."

It was a few seconds before I had the courage to speak again. Secrets and lies—the deeper one got into them the easier it was to just leave them in place and disappear. That was what I wanted to do now. I was so tired of running and hiding, but there was no longer any place to go. I had exhausted both time and excuses.

"Would have?" I questioned. "But you wouldn't now?"

"Don't put words in my mouth, Bry. That was not what I meant. I just want to know the truth. What he said sucked the life right out of me."

"I can only imagine how awful that must have been, but everything he said was a lie. Jon and I never . . . ."

My breath caught in my throat and I had to clear it before I could continue speaking. How could I explain why I had remained silent if I couldn't even voice what had happened. I squinted my eyes against the beam coming from the lighthouse as it passed in front of me.

"He raped me after a date, Ben. It happened in the front seat of his car, only I was too humiliated to tell you. I know I should have, but I thought you would no longer love me the same if you knew."

"Do you really think that poorly of me?" he asked.

"I don't know what I was thinking, only that I couldn't bear to utter the words. You have to know that I would never voluntarily give myself to someone like that unless he was my husband. I am not that kind of a person, even if I wasn't raised the same way you were."

"But why would he go into such graphic detail about the kind of relationship you shared unless it was true?" he asked, and I could visualize the look of pain and confusion in his eyes as he shook his head in disbelief. "It doesn't make any sense, and you are too smart to get raped."

Smart! The word stung me beyond belief. Being smart wouldn't have stopped Jon from hurting me. He was much too convincing and strong. I had been naïve for trusting who he claimed to be until it was too late, but that had nothing to do with what had happened.

"I didn't do anything to cause it," I said as my knees began to tremble.

Suddenly I was freezing. I had made a conscious effort to quit reliving that night so I would have the courage to face each new day. But mostly my dreams still turned into nightmares, and I was never far from falling into state of depression because I had not been able to stand up for myself. I loved the fact that Ben never made any inappropriate advances and always let me know by both word and deed that he respected me as a daughter of God and wanted what we had to last forever.

But perhaps Ben's open display of love and acceptance was part of the problem. I had let him shelter me from every discomfort, leading me to believe that living in state of denial and ignoring what was always chipping away at my soul was okay. But at some point, I had to admit that Jon had done more than strip my virtue from me. He had taken away my belief and trust in men. I could be around Ben because I didn't feel threatened, but what would happen on our wedding night? Would I be able to respond to the experience of loving him openly, or would I pull away in shame and fear because I had yet to face up to what had been done to me?

I suddenly realized that trying to rebuild my relationship with my father was only part of my past that needed revisiting. Without mourning the loss of the gift that had been so cruelly stolen from me, I would never be whole enough to truly love anyone else because I was still having trouble loving myself. Maybe that was the reason I was still in Australia when I could easily have gone home to Ben.

"But you didn't report it," Ben was saying when my mind returned to the conversation and the awfulness of what was happening on a beach that should bring feelings of both peace and pleasure.

"I was afraid to. He came from a powerful family with connections in all the right places. I was alone with no money and no friends or family to turn me. How many women do you know who have been raped and believed, especially one who came from nothing?"

I wished he could hear my anguish? It had to be so obvious in my voice, but he didn't say anything for what seemed like forever. I could still hear him breathing and wanted to die all over again.

"I am incredibly sorry for what happened to you, Brylee. It is an unconscionable thing, and the man should be in prison, but do you know what hurts me the most? You didn't trust how much I loved you to tell me the truth before it came out in such a public and awful way. I would have understood."

"But you don't understand now?" I asked.

"How do you expect me to understand after having been humiliated so completely? What he said meant that everything we shared was built on a lie, or at least an omission of the truth?"

I was shaking so hard I had to sit down on the bottom step so my knees would not buckle. My ability to defend myself was rapidly draining. Trust meant everything to Ben and I had destroyed that.

"I wanted to tell you so many times," I whimpered, my eyes glassed over with tears. "But how could I when you told me so often how you had saved yourself for the woman you were going to marry? I felt dirty and ashamed because I knew you expected the mother of your children to be pure and clean, and I was nothing but damaged goods."

"If it happened the way you said, it wasn't your fault."

"No, it wasn't my fault! But those feelings don't go away just because a person wills them to. I suppose you have discussed this with your old girlfriend."

"It was rather hard not to since we were together when it happened. Who wouldn't need a listening ear when he learned that the girl he was going to marry had been intimately involved with some other guy who had no difficulty flaunting their relationship. She was very considerate and understanding."

"I'm sure she was," I responded.

"Don't lay this on Jennifer," he said. "I don't know what I would have done if she had not been there. It was literally the worst night of my life, even if it wasn't true."

"And you are not completely sure there wasn't a grain of truth in it even now, are you?"

"I have had nearly five weeks of believing it might true. That is a mighty long time."

"And I have only known what happened at that party for a few days."

I heard his sharp intake of breath. "You got my emails a few day ago and never bothered to contact me before now? What were you doing, trying to come up with a good story?"

I almost ended the call. Obviously, neither of us were in any condition to talk about what happened rationally, but if I did, I might never hear is voice again.

"I didn't have to make up a story. I just didn't know what to say."

"The truth would have been nice."

"You have heard the truth, and it wasn't something I could write in an email."

"Maybe not, but if you had been honest with me from the start none of this would have happened. What I don't understand is why he would risk telling me something like that if it wasn't true. He could still be prosecuted."

"He is studying to be lawyer like his father. No charges were filed, and there is no evidence left. I would say that gives him all the reason in the world to be cocky. He can say whatever he wants knowing he has gotten away with what he did. I wish I could take back what happened, or at least how I handled it, but I can only say I am sorry. And I know it is a little too late for that."

"It might not be if you would come home. Couples have worked through worse things together."

"Does your family know about it?"

"I couldn't exactly keep it from them when they saw how upset I was."

"They must think I am a horrible person, quite unlike your old flame."

"They have always been fond of Jennifer. Our families go way back."

"And she is the girl they wanted you to marry?"

I didn't know why I was saying that, but for some reason it seemed important. Family opinions mattered, and if his family had lost their faith in me, getting it back would be next to impossible. That fact alone could easily destroy what Ben and I might be able to salvage if we saw each other again.

"Why all this talk about Jennifer. What we had has been over for years."

"And yet you have been spending a lot of time together recently."

"She is a good listener, and I value her friendship."

"I think you value more than just her friendship, Ben," I said. "She is the kind of girl who would be worthy to be your wife and the mother of your children. Unlike me, who couldn't even be honest with you about the most horrible thing that ever happened to her."

It was a statement I wished he would refute, but he didn't.

"We have become close again—I won't deny that—but you and I are still engaged. If you would just come home, maybe we could work things out."

His words were not reassuring, and the only one that registered was "maybe". Maybe didn't mean anything.

"I can't come back right now, Ben," I heard myself saying. "LeAnn just told us she is pregnant and has to stay in bed if she wants to keep the baby."

"I don't see how that is your problem. If you really loved me, you would be on the first plane out of there so we could try to rebuild what we had. I'm sure there is someone else who could step in and help out."

I dragged some of the moist, night air into my lungs. How could I go back to him when it sounded like he had already made up his mind about us? I would be forfeiting two lives and would have no place else to go.

"There isn't anyone else who can help," I said. "What about you coming here?"

"Now?" he asked.

"As soon as you could. I know we need to talk this out in person."

"But why can't you just come back like planned? You already have a plane ticket, and my new job is very demanding."

It seemed as if we had reached a brick wall and there was no way of going around, through or over it, unless I was the one willing to make all the concessions. And even if I returned like he was suggesting, there was no guarantee that our lives could go back to the way they had once been. Too much had already happened, and Jennifer would be there to pick up the pieces if we couldn't make it work.

"I love you, Ben," I said. "And I want to be your wife more than anything else in the world. But so much has happened lately and it has left me so confused."

"Join the club," he retorted. "I have been somewhat confused myself the past four months. I need you, Brylee, but I won't wait forever. I want a wife and a family, and I want it soon."

"Then don't wait," I heard myself say as my heart fractured into a million tiny pieces. "Find out if Jennifer is the girl you were supposed to marry all along. The only thing I know is that I love you and want you to be happy."

I wanted him to fight for me, for us, but he didn't even try to change my mind.

"What about you?" he said. "How do I say goodbye to the girl I was going to marry?"

"The same way I will say goodbye to you. By thanking God for the time we had together. You'll never know how much I love you and how grateful I am that you and Becky shared the gospel with me."

"I still love you," he said, and his voice broke with a sob. "A part of me always will."

"Same here, but it seems that God has other plans for us right now. If he didn't . . . ." I nearly broke down but stopped myself in time. "I would be back in your arms right now."

"What about your things? You have to come back to get them."

"I don't need anything I left behind. Keep what you want and give the rest to charity. I will send your ring back as soon as I can."

"No, Brylee, don't," he said, but I wouldn't let him finish. I pushed the icon on my cell phone and the call ended. I was glad it was dark because there was nothing left I wanted to see.

I sat still as a mouse on the step for the longest time, staring out into the night without seeing anything except for the glimmer of house lights that reflected on the crests of water as they crashed against the rocks that lined the beach in several different places. The sound was cold, harsh and indifferent, and it suited me.

Now I understood how LeAnn felt about losing my father. No wonder she had run away. That was exactly what I wanted to do. But where would I go? The universe wasn't big enough to separate me from the loss and pain of losing Ben.

I replayed everything that had happened during the past few months while my toes dug into the damp sand, but I couldn't move. Both my body and soul seemed to be frozen in this one moment of pitiful agony. I thought about Christ in the Garden of Gethsemane and on the cross suffering for the sins of all mankind collectively and by choice? Even with his sacrifice, I wasn't sure I could make it through my first real heartbreak. After everything I had already lost, I just wanted to sink into the sand and be done with it.

But after a few moments of wishing I could cease to exist, the world fell into place and l put my cell phone down on the step beside me. Without Ben to talk to, I didn't need it any longer. And without him in my life all my hopes of having my own happy ending were gone. If God really was my eternal Father, and if he really loved me, he would put the pieces of my splintered heart back together so I could still have my dream.

"Where are you, God?" I challenged as I walked along the water's edge and listened to the sounds of the ocean. How vast and cold and deep it was. Just a few steps into the waves and I would be washed away. By the time someone knew I was missing, my body would be far beyond the tides that splashed ashore and would likely have been devoured by some hungry shark.

But suicide wasn't the answer if I wanted to be with my parents again. Maybe I should just take the car and disappear. I could easily get lost in Sydney or some other huge city on the continent. I could live on the streets if I had to and turn to the bottle or illegal drugs like so many homeless people did, but what would that solve? I couldn't run from my memories, and there was no one left to blame for how my life was turning out.

It had been my choice not to tell Ben the truth, and my choice not to go back to him. My father would have understood why I couldn't keep the promise he wanted me to make, but my heart had become divided. I hadn't been able to choose one life over the other so the choice had been made for me. Ben would marry Jennifer, and I would be left alone.

I walked long the beach in mindless turmoil not really seeing where my steps were taking me until I came to an outcropping of rocks that made it impossible to go any further unless I climbed over them or walked out into the ocean. Instead of getting wet, my feet soon took me to the top of the formation, and I sat down sat down high above the crashing waves, and well behind the bright beam of light that guided fishermen to safety. It was still warm on land, but the waves brought a definite coolness as they sprayed over me.

"Oh, Father," I prayed, resting my head on my knees and closing my eyes. "What am I going to do now?"

As I sat there with only the sounds of nature to keep me company, I must have fallen into a light sleep because warmth enveloped me much like the heat of a summer day in the outback.

I was a child again, wearing a white sundress with flowers in my hair and carrying a small wicker basket. It was Easter morning, and I was running through the grass barefoot searching for hard-boiled eggs. My mother was sitting on the back stoop of the house in a pink, flowered dress, her long hair braided and wrapped around her head like a halo. She was laughing and calling out, "You're getting closer, little bug. Just a few more steps to the right."

Following her voice was easy for me, and hidden next to a log that separated the lawn from our small vegetable garden was the perfect blue egg I had dyed and decorated the day before.

Father was snapping pictures as I danced amongst the grass and flowers.

"Give me a big smile," he said. "And show me what you found."

I smiled until my teeth showed and my jaw ached. I was happy. It was a perfect holiday.

"No, "I cried out as a noise forced the vision away. "I don't want you to leave. I want to go with you."

Great sobs of pent-up emotion were wracking my body with torment when I forced open my eyes and saw Jake looming over me. I hadn't even heard his approach.

"Go away!" I shouted at him.

He was wrapping his shirt around my shoulders. I tried to brush it away, but he wouldn't let me.

"I was worried about you. Why didn't you answer when I called your name?"

"I didn't hear you," I said, squeezing my eyes tightly shut to stop the tears from falling. "Please go away? I want to be alone."

"I am not leaving you here. It isn't safe on the beach after dark."

"I don't care if I'm safe," I said as I put my head back on my knees. "Why can't you just do as I asked?"

"Because you shouldn't be alone right now, and it is not just a matter of physical safety."

"What makes you such an expert on what I need or don't need? You don't know anything about me."

"I know a lot more than you give me credit for," he said, sitting down beside me on the rock. The strength and warmth of his body were strangely comforting.

"You don't care about me," I snapped. "You just want to gloat because I have to admit that you told me so."

"I didn't come here to gloat. I was worried about you when I saw your cell phone on the back steps." He held it out in my direction, but I didn't open my eyes or make a move to take it from him.

"You might as well toss it in the ocean. I won't be needing it again."

"That is a little mellow-dramatic, don't you think? I'm sure you will be able to work things out with your boyfriend."

"It's too late for that." I forced myself to look over at him with cold defiance in my eyes, even though it was so dark I doubted he could see them. Oh, how I hated him for always being right, and for knowing things about me I didn't even recognize myself. "I kept something from him that he had every right to know, and now he will never trust me again. It doesn't get much more final than that."

"We all have secrets," he said, resting his elbows on his knees and clasping his hands together. "And we always hurt the ones we love. That may be a line from some corny song, but it's still true. When we open our hearts, we forever run the risk of being burned. You are a warm, bright, compassionate and beautiful woman, and your Ben is a fool for not forgiving some minor indiscretion."

"It wasn't minor! I was raped the year before we met and didn't tell him about it," I cried out as another wave of pain and disillusionment swept over me. "The guy who did it told Ben we had been involved for months and he had weeks to believe that was true because I was stuck on the ranch and couldn't answer his email right after it was sent."

"Damn it all to bloody hell," Jake's voice boomed, and I knew he was ready to hit something until there was nothing left of it. "No man hurts you that way and gets away with it."

"Well, he did get away with it because I didn't press charges, and now Ben will never trust me again because we promised we would always be honest with each other and I blew it."

"What kind of man blames the woman he loves for not wanting to talk about being violated in the most heinous way imaginable?"

"He should blame me. I purposely kept the information from him because I was humiliated and afraid. I should have known it would not remain a secret forever."

"I hope he gave the bloody pervert a beating he would never forget. I would have killed him."

"Ben's not like that, but he was devastated because it came up at a party he was attending with his old girlfriend."

"Unbelievable," he replied, although his voice was still laced with anger. "You've had quite a night. No wonder you want to be by yourself."

"So you will leave me alone?"

"No! And that is not open to discussion. So please help me understand why he is so angry with you when he is doing things behind your back with his old flame. Doesn't he understand that you were the victim in all of this?

I took a deep breath before responding. Telling Jake the rest of the story might give him more fuel to use against me but it might also stop some of his tormenting. Besides, what did it matter now? I had already lost my happy ending.

"You really want to know the truth?" I asked

"Only if you want to tell me."

"Then this is it! Ben was saving himself for the girl he married, and I led him to believe that I was as innocent in that area as he was."

"But rape is different, Brylee."

"Maybe Ben would have understood that if I had come clean before we became engaged, but I waited too long and that made Jon's story believable because I wasn't there to defend myself."

"Damn!" he said. "I thought you were only protesting my unwanted advances so I would keep my distance."

"You don't have to mock because we are not like you, Jake. I know you don't believe in celibacy."

"I'm not ashamed of giving in to my natural desires, Brylee. God made us that way for a reason." He tilted my chin upwards and turned my face towards his. "Making love is the most beautiful and natural thing in the world, and I am so sorry some devilish bloke without a conscience stole that from you."

"It's not just that," I said.

But instead of responding, he reached out with his other hand and ran his fingers slowly and methodically down my cheek. I opened my mouth to protest because his touch was making my heart race and I needed someone to help me believe in living again.

"You are an amazing woman," he continued as the waves of the ocean made contact with the land again, spraying us with another gentle film.

"I can't do it." I whispered. But my body was working against me. Jake really was a master when it came to knowing what women both wanted and needed. No wonder they couldn't resist him.

"Maybe not now," he said. " But it is not wrong to want to feel close to someone else. I find you the most exciting, desirable woman I have ever met, Brylee Hawkins. A man is a bloody fool if he doesn't want to make you his."

His face was so near mine—another inch and we would be kissing. I knew I should pull away, but Jake had wanted me for a very long time and I had resisted every advance because he wasn't Ben. I had told myself that his tattoos and pierced ear were gross and I hated his arrogance and the way women fell all over him. But sitting beside him in the moonlight, I found him exhilarating, attractive and most definitely dangerous. His slightest touch sent electrical shocks that radiated to my very core.

I wanted to touch him, to run my hands through his hair and over his broad shoulders and chest. I wanted to kiss his lips and feel our breath mingle. I wanted him to make me forget about Ben, about being raped, about losing everything that had ever mattered to me.

"Let me help you forget," Jake whispered against my cheek as his lips touched my ear and began working their way along my jawbone. "You are absolutely amazing—a woman to be loved, adored and cherished."

My hands moved towards him, regardless of the fact that I was willing them not to. The stubble of beard on his cheeks was not unpleasant but supple and comforting. And his eyes— those dark, brooding eyes that were always so filled with anger and contempt now gleamed with desire for me. It would have taken another act of nature to pull me away because pain and desire are heady emotions when mingled together.

And then his lips touched mine teasing me with the pleasure they could bring if I would just let them. Oh, how I wanted to forget every moment of pain, loss, hurt and betrayal.

Was it so wrong to want to be held the way Jake was holding me and scorching me with each touch?

My heart was pounding as I felt the muscles in his arms tighten. Who would ever know if I crossed the line just once? Ben was out of my life because I hadn't trusted him enough to share my past and would have Jennifer for always if that was what they both wanted. Didn't I deserve just one night of feeling alive before the pain of an unfulfilled life settled on me again?

When his lips found mine more deeply, I was actually quivering. Did I love God enough to turn away when every part of my body was screaming out with the desire to be loved? Ben might be lost to me, but that didn't mean there would never be anyone else.

"No, Jake," I found myself whispering as my breaths came in great gasps. I managed to put my hands on his bare chest and push him ever so slightly away. "I am not thinking clearly right now."

"Maybe not," he countered, reaching for me again. "I know what you went through must have seemed like hell, but with the right man it isn't the least bit like that. I want to show you how wonderful it can be."

"And I know you could," I responded.

"Then what is stopping you? I am not the guy who raped you, and you just said that you and Ben broke up. It's not like I would be stepping on anyone's toes, unless you just don't want me."

"It's not that simple," I said above the noise of the blood pounding in my ears. "I promised God that I would only make love to my husband."

I was feeling a little stronger now that our bodies were no longer touching. Satan was a crafty devil. He would use anything to stop me from keeping the covenants I had already made and I was attracted to Jake. I had been all along but didn't want to admit it because of his reputation with women and the fact that he could never give me what I really wanted.

"I applaud your dedication to this God you believe in so strongly, but he wouldn't have given us such strong desires if he didn't expect us to use them to show people how much we care. I like you a lot, Brylee, and I don't think you are as indifferent to me as you claim to be, but I am a very patient man. I can wait until you are ready. It's not like we were going to do anything tonight. I just wanted to give you comfort."

I leaned back against the smooth surface of the rock behind me and tried to steady my breathing.

"I'm not indifferent to you, Jake, but I am not myself tonight, and it wouldn't take all that much to push me over the edge."

"We all need to be held and comforted. There is no shame in that."

"There is if you are only using it to escape horrible memories or the loss of someone you loved with all your heart. I know myself quite well by now, and I would regret it the moment it happened."

He sighed. "You are a funny girl, Brylee Hawkins, and since it wouldn't do my ego much good to get caught up in a rebound relationship, I will respect your wishes. Just remember that I really do care about you and would never do anything to hurt you, unlike so many of the other men in your life."

"I believe you," I said, sitting up beside him again. I knew that he was paying me the highest compliment possible by shutting down his own desires to honor my wishes. "And I really care about you as well."

I couldn't tell him that nothing would ever happen between us no matter how great the attraction was. He was a good man according to the world's standards, but he couldn't give me what I needed because he didn't believe as I did.

"Listen, Brylee, " he said. "I might not know much about this new religion of yours that frowns on nearly every aspect of my life, but I respect your right to believe what you want to. I also admire your dedication, but life isn't always black and white and people aren't bad just because they can't accept what you have."

"I would never force what I believe on anyone," I told him.

"But you do, all the time. I am not saying that having high standards is wrong, but you make the rest of us feel like we are less than adequate humans."

I frowned. Was I really such an opinionated shrew?

"I don't feel like I am better than anyone else, Jake. I respect all religions."

"But that is part of the problem. Not everyone is religious. I am just waiting for the day you tell Ned and Nora they are living in sin because they aren't married."

"I would never do that! I love my family regardless of what they believe or do."

"And I am just playing the devil's advocate, Brylee. But if you really believe in. All that tolerancet, you would never have taught Trevor that little song that reflects your religious beliefs without asking permission first?"

"LeAnn wasn't around, and Trevor was confused and hurt. I thought knowing that he had an eternal Father who loved him would help. We talked about this before."

He shook his head and laughed.

"So we did! In ways, I feel sorry for you. It must be difficult trying to live a life that is diametrically opposed to most everything the world has to offer. I heard what your father said when you told him you had joined a new church. People, in general, aren't accepting of religious beliefs that condemn the behavior of others."

"I don't condemn others. I have just chosen something different for myself."

He took my hand, and I didn't try to pull it away.

"You have set yourself up for a great deal of heartache because few humans will ever live up to what you expect of them. How many people do you know, other than Ben, who don't have a few vices? I would say you are part of less then one percent of the world's population. How do you plan on finding another bloke who can be anywhere near what you want him to be?"

I looked out at the wide expanse of ocean in front of me. If God could create both heaven and earth, he could certainly bring another worthy man into my life. If not, I would simply have to be content alone because it didn't look like I would ever be leaving Australia again.

"I don't know if there will ever be anyone else in my life, Jake, but I can't walk away from everything I know in my heart is right?"

He lifted my hand and pressed it against his chest.

"Feel that?" he asked. "That is my heart beating. I may not be anywhere as good a man as you claim Ben is, but I am here right by your side, going through all of these hard experiences with you. I would never leave you to suffer anything alone. I would be with you every step of the way, if you would just let me."

I wanted to counter what he was saying but couldn't. I had been in Australia for over four months, and Ben had not come to see me even when he knew I was in incredible pain. It shouldn't matter than I had not specifically asked him to. But Jake, even with all his vices and ties to the world that I didn't exactly approve of—along with our constant bickering—always pulled through when I needed him.

"Jake, I do care about you, more than I should," I reiterated.

He was still holding my hand but had removed it from his chest. It offered a feeling of belonging and securing that scared me.

"Why more? The only reason I gave you such a hard time was because you belonged to someone else when I wished you didn't."

"And I gave you a hard time because I didn't want to like you."

"Because I wasn't your ideal man."

"Because I was engaged to Ben until tonight."

"But you are still going to run away from me, aren't you?"

"Only because I know what I need to be happy."

I didn't want to hurt him any more than I already had, but how could I explain eternal marriage and all the requirements necessary to enter the temple after what had just happened between us. I had felt myself responding to the pressure of his kiss and was more than certain he had noticed. But even with Ben gone, those things still mattered, even though I might never have them.

"When you fall in love, Jake," I said without further hesitation. "I mean really fall in love, wouldn't you want to be with that woman forever, not just for the remainder of this life?"

"I've never thought about it. Keeping a relationship going for a few months or even a year or two is about as good as it gets for me."

"But that's not the way it is supposed to be."

"Maybe not," he admitted. "But marriage and I don't seem to mix, and nothing lasts forever."

"But it can, Jake. That's what I am trying to tell you. Families will continue after we die. If they didn't, what would be the purpose of having them in the first place?"

"Hell if I know," he said, dropping my hand and rising to his feet. "But this conversation is getting us nowhere."

"It might if you would just try to understand that my beliefs govern me in both this life and the next. I want to be with the man I love forever. That can't happen if the marriage union is broken when one spouse dies."

He looked down at me, and I knew everything had changed between us again.

"Brylee, I applaud the fact that you have dedicated your life to something you believe in, but you cannot expect the rest of us to change every part of our existence just because it would make things easier for you. Hell, I can't make sense of what goes on in this life most of time. And yet you want me to accept that there is some rosy future after death where we will all be blissfully happy with our families when we can't even get along most of the time in this one. It just doesn't compute in my book."

He started climbing down the rocks as I sat in stunned amazement. "Was I going to alienate everyone before this night was over?

"Are you coming?" he asked, without turning around. "It's not a good idea to be alone on the beach after dark."

I didn't want to go anywhere with him, especially now that he had made me feel like a fool because I could not explain what was in my heart. Besides, how many bad people actually roamed Australia's beaches after dark looking for someone to hurt? If it wouldn't just give him another reason to be angry with me, I would stay on these rocks all night no matter how cold or uncomfortable it got.

But when I stood up to follow him, my cell phone dropped from my lap onto the rocks. I had forgotten it had been returned to me.

"Just a minute," I said. "I dropped my phone."

I bent over and began running my hands through the crevices in the rocks around me. It couldn't have fallen far.

I heard Jake's irritated breathing as he climbed back up to where I was. "You won't be able to find it until morning. Let's just head back to the house and look for it when it's light outside."

"But it's got to be right here," I said as he directed the beam from a flashlight I hadn't known he had with him towards my feet.

"You are the most stubborn female in the world," he said, with a light nudge of his elbow that was meant to let me know that he would take over now and I needed to step out of his way. "I will look for the damned thing myself. I thought you didn't even want it anymore."

But I was already standing somewhat precariously on the mist-covered rocks and that slight movement caused me to lose my balance. I cried out with surprise as I slipped backwards into the darkness.

"What the hell," Jake shouted as he reached out towards me, but I had already fallen beyond his grasp.

Chapter 8

It was the strangest feeling, free-floating through the air as I listened to the waves slapping against the rocks, but the feeling didn't last long. My left foot caught in a crevice, jerking me slightly upwards, and then the back of my head hit something hard. I saw a spattering of brilliant tiny stars as my eyes closed and the throbbing began.

"Are you okay?" I heard Jake shout.

I wanted to answer, but when I tried to move more bright flashes of light floated in front of my eyes, and the pain in my left ankle was almost unbearable. I fell back against the rocks moaning softly.

He reached me only seconds later. "Don't try to move," he said, his hands searching the darkness that encircled both of us. "I'm going to have to twist your foot to get it out. Just hang on to me."

I couldn't even shift positions without causing more strain on my injured limb, but still gripped his shoulder as another onslaught of pain and nausea swept over me. He maneuvered me into a sitting position against his chest so he could support my back while he tried to dislodge the foot that was wedged between two large boulders. His heart was hammering as loudly as mine, and I bit down on my bottom lip to stifle the need to scream.

"That's got it," he finally said, and I moved my legs into a more comfortable position. "I can't see anything in these damned shadows. I dropped the flashlight somewhere above us, but I don't feel any blood or broken bones. Do you think you can move?"

He was running his hand up and down my leg trying to access the damage.

"I'm okay, I think," I said, reaching my hand around to the back of my head where a big lump was already forming.

"Don't touch it," he instructed, following my hand with his own. "We need to get you to the hospital."

"I don't need a hospital. Catching my foot kept me from falling very far."

I would have one killer headache in the morning, along with a throbbing ankle, but I didn't want anyone fussing over me. This whole night had been one disaster after another.

He bent over and kissed my forehead.

"You could have a concussion and a badly sprained ankle, and it is my fault for acting like a bloody jerk."

"It was an accident, Jake. I should not have insisted on finding my cell phone in the dark. I was being childish."

"You were hurting and I was pushing buttons like I always do. We likely won't find it even in the daylight. The fissures between rocks can be very deep. But I rather enjoyed being gallant at the end of one of our disagreements for a change."

"And I had to ruin even that with my senseless chatter," I responded.

"We are two very different people whose only common ground seems to be family, but at least we can agree about that."

I tried to move myself into a more comfortable position, but it seemed as if every part of my body hurt. "I really am sorry I can't be the kind of person you want me to be, Jake".

"I'm not!" he said, surprising me. "You have convictions and are willing to stand by them. I would say that is pretty rare in today's world. And I really don't want you to change, even if you do think I'm not good enough for you. A woman would be wise not to count on me too much anyway."

"I don't believe that. You could have bailed on us any time you wanted to but didn't."

He pushed the hair away from my forehead and I almost forgot the pain I was in and the fact that he was not a man who could make my dreams come true. I wanted to feel his lips on mine again and get lost in his caresses, but it would be best if everything about tonight were forgotten. Forbidden paths were much too tempting, and I was far too weak not to get lost somewhere along the way.

Suddenly the muscles in his arms tighten. "I need to get you back to the house. You could have injuries we don't know about."

"Other than one massive headache and a sore ankle, I think I will survive," I told him.

He contemplated our situation thoughtfully for a moment. "Do you think you can walk?" he finally asked, sliding away from me before standing. When upright, he extended his hand and I took it.

"Ouch," I said, when trying to put weight on my left foot.

He squatted down and ran his fingers around the ankle I was holding helpless in the air. I reluctantly put my hands on his shoulders for support. The rocks were definitely slippery. No wonder I had fallen.

"I still don't feel any broken bones, but it's swollen and you really should keep it elevated until it heals."

"I will be fine," I told him again. "I can slide down the rest of the rocks. It isn't that far, and I used to be very good at it."

His snort of laughter startled me.

"You think I'm making that up, don't you? But there was this giant slide that went straight down the hill behind the house when I was a little girl. My parents always told me to stay away unless one of them was with me because it was dangerous. It was made from wood and scrap metal, and I had to be very careful not to get my clothes snagged on some of the rough edges, but it was so much fun climbing as far up its surface as I could and then sliding down. I haven't thought about it for years."

"You never cease to amaze me," he said, stepping over boulders while I slid down them, more than grateful he hadn't volunteered to try to carry me. We would both have injuries if he did.

"What makes you say that?" I asked, trying to keep from thinking about the throbbing in my head, the sting in my ankle and the tender kisses I was trying to forget.

"Because you are the strongest woman I have ever met, and you are willing to forgive others too. My know-it-all attitude just now could have gotten you killed instead of just maimed, and I feel awful about it."

"The rocks were slippery and you were only trying to help. Please don't mention it to anyone. We were both at fault and I really don't want to repeat what I told you to anyone else."

"My lips are sealed, Brylee. I just wish I could redo the past hour. I don't know why I am so prickly at times, especially around you."

"Because we are human and tend to let our emotions get out of hand when we are upset. I wasn't seriously hurt so it's best to forget it ever happened."

"I'm not sure I can do that, but if it's what you want I will try."

"It is," I responded. "My emotions were all over the place tonight, and I am equally responsible for anything that happened."

"Wow!" he said. "You do have an inner strength that seems to get you through anything."

I wanted to tell him that any strength I had came directly from God but that would only set the stage for another disagreement. So I decided to take a less preachy route.

"If you think that, you should have seen me right after my call to Ben ended. I had pretty much decided that walking into the ocean was the only thing that would make the pain go away."

He stopped moving downward and turned to look at me. The beam of light from the lighthouse passed over us again. We were nearly to the bottom of the rocks. The only thing separating us from Emma's beach house now was a long strip of sand.

"What brought you away from the water?" he asked. "People take the easy way out all the time."

I took that moment to catch my breath and let my ankle rest. "Because I realized I was just feeling sorry for myself. It's not easy ending a relationship with the love of a lifetime. I can't imagine my life without Ben in it."

"You feel that way because the pain is still raw, but it will pass eventually. Personally, I think there are many people we could be happy with. It's all about allowing oneself to fall in love with someone new and then giving him or her a fighting chance."

"Maybe you are right," I said "But that seems very unlikely right now. Do you really think you will fall in love again? I thought your fiancé was the love of your life."

"All these questions and no real answers!" he retorted with a shake of his head.

He was avoiding my questions just like I avoided so many of his. But there really was no way of knowing what would happen to either of us in the future, or just how long it would take to get over past torments.

"Come on," he said when I didn't respond. "Slide yourself down the rest of those rocks before I have to come up and get you. Trevor would never forgive me if I left his sister stranded."

"I'm not really stranded," I said, scooting myself one rock closer to the sand. "It might take me a little longer to make it back to the house, but I can still do it on my own."

"I do believe you could, but what's the fun in that?" he asked.

When I reached the bottom rock and had my bare feet rather precariously planted on the cool, white sand, he reached out his hand to help me. "I'll race you back to the house. I will even give you a head-start."

"Funny," I said. "I couldn't beat you even if I was given every advantage. You are taller and have longer legs."

"So you noticed," he said, taking another step away from me. He was giving me the space I desired, but I wasn't ready to let go of the feeling of tender belonging that being in love brought. If only he could be the right man, but he wasn't.

My next step was taken to prove that I didn't need anyone to take care of me, but even the slightest amount of pressure on my injured ankle made me wince.

"That's it," he said. "You can go back to your irritating independence tomorrow, but I'll be damned if I am going to leave you to make it back to the house on your own in the dark. LeAnn and Trevor would never forgive me."

He bent down and scooped me up in his arms. I wanted to protest but that would be foolish. So I put my arms around his neck and snuggled against him. I needed his strength right now even if he never knew it. That was what I missed most about Ben—his ability to make me feel safe.

But safety meant different things to different people. Ben cared about my eternal welfare, and with that promise of forever gone, I was vulnerable to any attractive man who let me know that he was interested in more than just friendship.

Mary Jenkins and the other women were right. Jake was definitely hot in a very manly, sensual way, and I would do best never to forget that.

I tried not to think about his strong arms that made carrying me seem almost effortless or the powerful beating of his heart as he made his way through the soft sand on the way to the beach house. I didn't even protest as he climbed the stairs with me still in his arms. When we got inside, he carried me into the living room and lay me down on the sofa. Then he sat down beside me to get a better look at my ankle that had already turned a nasty purple and black.

"I'll get some ice for that," he said. "And I will see if there is something in the bathroom to help kill the pain. Too bad you're not a drinker. A good shot of whiskey and you wouldn't feel anything until morning. I really would like to take you to the hospital. You could have a concussion."

"We have already discussed that," I said, folding my arms defiantly across my chest. "I'll be okay. I just need a little rest."

"But you're not supposed to sleep after a head injury. Why won't you allow anyone to help you?"

"Because there is nothing wrong with me except for a sore ankle that you said yourself wasn't broken. All a doctor would do is tell me to stay off it for a day or two and watch for signs of a concussion like acute headache, blurry vision and loss of consciousness. I can do that just fine right here."

There was no reason to tell him I no longer had health insurance. That had dried up when I left my job for more than the allotted time I had asked for and likely wouldn't be accepted in Australia anyway.

"Okay," he conceded. "I don't happen to agree, but you are an adult and can make your own decisions."

"Thank you," I told him with a firmness I didn't really feel. "I appreciate what you have already done, but there really was no reason for you to come looking for me in the first place. I would have made it back once I quit feeling sorry for myself. I just needed time to think."

"Maybe I was feeling protective," he countered. "Besides, what else was I supposed to do when I saw your cell phone and sandals on the step? LeAnn and Trevor haven't been out of the bedroom since dinner. I think he was very glad to have his mum back, even with her unexpected news."

My smile was genuine. "I'm glad LeAnn is coming home with us, and I am excited about the baby. It is definitely a miracle."

"A miracle, maybe, but it means you will be needed at the ranch for a very long time."

"It's not like I have any other place to be right now," I responded, sinking back into the folds of the sofa as sorrow descended over me again. "In fact, it is kind of nice knowing someone needs me."

"You will always be needed," he replied. "But at some point you will have to decide if being needed is more important that being loved for the right reasons and by the right man. You can't live in someone else's shadow forever."

He didn't give me time for a comeback. He simply went to the kitchen, filled a plastic baggie with the promised ice and returned with it and a hand towel that would keep the cold from freezing my skin. Then he sat in a wing-back chair in silence giving me the space I needed to think.

I must have fallen asleep, and he must have allowed it, because my headache had subsided considerably when I opened my eyes again and found that it was morning. Jake had tucked a blanket around me at some point during the night, and there was another one folded on the chair next to the window that hadn't been there when he had turned out the lights. I wondered if he had watched me while I slept.

It was amazing that I had been able to relax enough to even close my eyes. Giving Ben his freedom was the right thing to do, but my heart was still broken. I would concentrate on the idea that if we were meant to be together, we would find our way back to each other some day. In the meantime, I had to remain true to the covenants I had already made with God. If that meant keeping Jake Johnson at arms-length, then that wass how it would have to be.

Everyone was seated at the small table in the kitchen when I hobbled into the room. All of us, except LeAnn, were wearing the clothes we had arrived in. I had run the brush I had used at the pool the day before through my hair but my mouth felt gross, and I hoped my shirt didn't smell. I was definitely a person who liked a daily shower and toothpaste.

"Are you hurt bad?" Trevor asked as I slid into an empty chair.

"I am feeling much better," I told him with a forced smile.

LeAnn frowned at me. "Jake told us you fell on the rocks last night. It was foolish for you to be out there alone in the dark, but I am not going to make a federal case about it after the stunts I have pulled the past few weeks. I am just glad you appear to be doing better this morning."

I prayed that my falling was the only thing he had told them. A promise could easily be broken and I would be mortified if anyone knew we had shared even the briefest of kisses. And I would die if they knew what had happened to me at the university and how Ben had reacted.

"I will be more careful in the future," I promised. "But it really was an accident that could have happened to anyone. It was dark, and the rocks were slippery."

"None of that matters now. There could still be repercussions from such a fall," she continued, assuming her most motherly tone. "And the fact remains that you can't drive with an injured ankle and a knot on the back of your head. It just isn't safe. You will have to fly back with Jake in the plane, and I will bring Trevor in the Land Rover with me."

"What about the baby?' I asked. "You can't take any chances, especially if it is a high risk pregnancy."

"There are risks with every pregnancy," she replied as her hand moved protectively to her stomach. "But I don't see that we have much of a choice."

I looked to Jake for help, but apparently he'd already had this conversation with his sister because he simply shrugged his shoulders and shook his head. But I wasn't about to be told what I could or could not do when it came to the safety of an unborn child. LeAnn could be back at the ranch in less than two hours if she flew back with Jake. If she went by car, it would take well over eight.

Besides, there was nothing to eat at the ranch. We had intended to stop at the grocers when we flew into Edna the day before, but Jake had changed those plans by insisting we fly to coast. I wasn't angry with him about anything any longer. Life happened and people had to adjust, but after releasing Ben from his promise of a life with me, I wasn't about to lose another member of my family—even an unborn one.

"I hate to disagree, but I will not be babied," I said. "And I will not risk the life of my little brother or sister. Someone has to do some shopping if we're going to survive. That hasn't been done since before the rain came."

I looked at my stepmother who seemed surprised that I was taking a stand on anything. I had been much too passive with her since coming home, and that was going to change. It might not be pleasant, but I could make the drive to the ranch. My left ankle had been injured, not my right one.

"You are not supposed to be on your feet, LeAnn, and Jake can't go shopping because he is the only one who can fly the plane," I continued. "If Trevor was older, he could drive the Land Rover but since he isn't, that leaves me. I only need my right foot to use the gas pedal, and I am sure there will be plenty of young men at the grocers to carry things if I can't do it myself."

"Bravo," Jake said, clapping his hands while LeAnn shot him an angry look. "A few minutes more, and we would have ourselves a regular catfight. But Brylee is right, Lee. There is more than just pride involved here. A new life to be considered so here is what I propose. LeAnn, you will come back with me. I am sure we can scrounge up enough to keep body and soul together for a day or two. As for you, Brylee Hawkins, you need to stay here and keep your foot elevated and iced for at least another twenty-four hours. You can head back in the morning if you are up to it, and I expect you to be back home before dark so no one has to worry about you."

"What about me," Trevor asked his uncle, as if he didn't want to be the only one without something special to do.

"You will come back with us. Your animals need to be fed and watered since we missed doing that last night, and I am sure your mum will have plenty of errands for you to run."

Jake looked across the table at me. "Besides, I think your sister could use a few hours to herself. She hasn't had much of that the past few weeks taking care of you and me."

I felt like kissing him, but after what had happened the night before I didn't want to cause any more misunderstandings. I hated that I was beginning to see why women found him so irresistible, but he could be the most amazingly thoughtful man when he wanted to be.

"A few hours alone sounds surprisingly good right now," I said. "There have been a lot of changes in our lives lately."

No one, except Jake, knew that I was talking about the ending of my relationship with Ben, and it appeared he had been kind enough not to mention it to his sister. But somehow, I ha known he would be that way. He would let me tell LeAnn in my own way when I was ready.

"Well, I hope you enjoy the house," LeAnn said. "I will call Emma and let her know what is happening. Maybe you could drop the key off at her place when you get back to Edna. I know she would like to meet you."

"Can I have more pancakes, mum?" Trevor asked. "I finished everything on my plate."

"You will have to ask your Uncle Jake about that. He's the cook this morning, not me."

"Can I, Uncle Jake?"

"Why not," Jake said, handing the serving platter with tiny blue flowers around its rim to him. "I can always make more. It's not that hard adding a little water to some flapjack mix. How about you, Brylee?"

His tone almost dared me to keep from flinching as his eyes sought mine. I steeled myself not to look away before he did. "Would you like some of my pancakes?"

"Most certainly," I said with a smile. "I think the pizza from last night has completely worn off."

He stood up and handed the platter across the table to me. Our fingertips touched, and the brief contact brought a flush to my cheeks. How could I ever explain my behavior last night? I hadn't meant to react as I had. Ben was still the only man I wanted, but I had given him his freedom because it was the right thing to do.

"By the way," Jake said as I was pouring maple syrup on my pancakes. "Your sandals are sitting on the deck. They were a little damp so I left them outside to dry."

"Thank you," I said, grateful that no one at the table asked why he knew where they were and I didn't. It would serve no purpose to ask him about the cell phone. He would have told me if he had found it anyway.

"I guess I should get packed so we can leave," LeAnn said, taking a sip of coffee from her cup, and then pushing her chair away from the table. "I'm not sure how I will handle being confined to bed until the baby is born, but I do know that I wouldn't be able to do it without all of you."

"You haven't seen how much we charge for our services yet," Jake said. "You might change your mind when you get our bill."

LeAnn gave him one of her brightest smiles. "You can charge me anything you like, and I will find a way to pay it.

The only thing that matters is bringing this baby safely into the world. I still can't believe I am not dreaming. The doctor said I should see him every two weeks. Since distance alone prohibits that, I will have to go back to the doctor in Edna that delivered Trevor. Won't he be surprised? And then I will have to prevail on you, little brother, to chauffeur me around in your plane."

"I can do that," Jake said, looking down at the watch on his arm. "But we really need to be leaving. I filed flight plans first thing this morning, and take-off is in a little over an hour."

"I won't be long," LeAnn told him. "Why don't you come and help me, Trevor. I need someone strong to carry my suitcase."

"She is still in a very fragile state," Jake said after they left the room. He was clearing the table while I finished the last bite of a surprisingly good breakfast. I quite enjoyed watching him work. "As happy as I am about her big news, I can't help wondering what will happen if this baby doesn't make it, or if it has any special needs. LeAnn is in those danger years, or so I have heard, and if things don't go the way they should . . . ."

"You don't have to finish that thought, Jake." I said, limping to the sink with the rest of the tableware. "She is going to be okay and so is the baby. We have to believe that as much for her sake as for Trevor's. I don't think I have ever seen him happier than he is this morning."

"He is pretty stoked about being a big brother. That was all he could talk about while we were fixing breakfast."

"I can't believe I didn't hear you rattling pans around. I must have been dead to the world."

"You were pretty tired," he said. "I'm just sorry things didn't work out with Ben. I know how much you loved him."

I took a jolted breath. Would I ever come to a point when hearing his name didn't cause me to react with anguish? He had been my everything for such a long time.

"Sometimes we have to let the people we love go."

"I can identify with that," he responded. "Talk about bad karma. All three of us have lost the people we thought we would be growing old with."

I clutched the edge of the gray Formica countertop as I looked out the window above the sink at the ocean. The sky was overcast. The coast might be in for some rain. "Karma or not, at least we will be able to comfort each other. And thank you for being there last night. I'm sure it wasn't much fun listening to me cry over something that can't be fixed."

"I have big shoulders and you can cry on them any time you want."

I knew he was being sincere, but there wouldn't be a next time. I could never afford to get that close to him again.

"Are we okay after last night?" I asked as my brow furrowed.

"We're fine," he replied, but I could still detect the hurt in is eyes.

After all, he was a man who had offered me comfort, and my rebuke had been anything but gentle. "You're absolutely sure! I wasn't at all myself."

"I understand losing someone you love, but what if it was the real you last night wanting to break free? We all change, Brylee, and life does go on even after losing the love of a lifetime. LeAnn is proof of that."

He was right, just as he had been right about so many things, but I wasn't ready to   accept his counsel. When I opened the back door to get my sandals, my cell phone was sitting beside them on the deck. I opened it on a prayer, but Ben hadn't called. That pained me almost as much as our conversation the night before. It really was over, and it was my own fault for not trying hard enough to get him to understand.

Jake drove us to the airport in the Land Rover. My job was to drive it back to the house and wait until morning before heading back to Edna, and then on home once some shopping was done. I was to stop at Emma's to return the key LeAnn had borrowed and pick up all the things she had left. It sounded like a simple plan, and one that I could easily follow once I had given my ankle a few more hours to heal. I wasn't so sure about all the alone time, but I did need to figure out what I was going to do now that the life I had planned on living was gone.

LeAnn hugged me goodbye before heading towards the concrete slab where the plane was waiting. "Thanks for being so good to my son, and to Jake, while I was gone. Trevor told me all about your adventures after the flood. You did some amazing things, and I will be forever in your debt for taking care of my family when I couldn't."

I assured her that it had been my pleasure.

"I love you, Brylee," Trevor told me when he put his arms around my waist and gave me a kiss. "But I want you to do something for me," he continued, as he tugged on my hand and led me away from where LeAnn and Jake were making the final arrangements so the plane could take off.

"What is it?" I asked.

"It's something I thought about all night," he replied with a conspirator's smile. "I want you to buy something special for the new baby when you go to town. I want to be the first one to give him a prezzie."

Tears formed in my eyes when he opened his hand so I could see what was inside.

It was the twenty-dollar bill our father had given him the day he and LeAnn were married.

How well I remembered him wanting to pay for our breakfast with the only money he had, and now he wanted to use it to buy a gift for an unborn child. My love for others paled in comparison to his.

"Why don't you hold on to that money, and I will take you into town to go shopping when we need groceries again. The baby won't be here for a long time."

But he wouldn't be deterred from what he wanted.

"That will be too late," he said. "I want to be the first one. As soon as everyone else finds out they will be buying prezzies too."

"Okay," I relented, not wanting to force the look of complete joy from his face. "What do you want me to get?"

"A teddy bear. One he can play with when he is older."

"What are the two of you whispering about?" LeAnn asked as she reversed her steps and came back to take Trevor's hand. I hoped she wouldn't notice my tears and ask for an explanation.

"Just a surprise, mum, but I am not going to tell you what it is."

"Then I will have two things to look forward to—a surprise from my handsome son and a new baby for all of us to love."

"We're up next," Jake said as he came over to get LeAnn and Trevor. "Make sure to stay off that foot today and be safe driving home tomorrow."

He squeezed my arm and walked away before I had time to respond.

I felt a sudden wave of loneliness as they disappeared behind the guard who was checking identification, but it was a different kind of loneliness than I had ever felt before. They were the only family I had now, and I didn't want to be a spinster because my standards were too high for the people around me. But I couldn't discard them either. It was very unenviable place to be.

I spent the rest of the day with my ankle elevated and iced while I contemplated all the things that had gone wrong in my life. I wasn't feeling sorry for myself this time. I was simply trying to understand the changes that had occurred since I had sat on that plane wondering what would happen when I saw my father again.

Now, four months later, my father was gone and so was Ben. But in their place I had found a little brother, and God-willing, there would soon be another addition to our rather unusual family. Apparently, I was meant to stay in Australia and share the gospel with people who were not even willing to listen yet, except for Trevor. Everyone else thought I had lost my mind and needed to come to my senses so I could be saved.

It would be so much easier to let what I had learned about our Savior, our Heavenly Father and the amazing plan for our salvation just fade away. With LeAnn confined to bed for the next seven plus months, it would be impossible to attend church on a regular basis. Could my fledgling testimony survive that long? And there was still Ben? Maybe after he had really thought about our conversation, he would decide that I was still the girl he wanted to marry.

Conflicting ideas swarmed through my mind as I tried to relax and let sleep overtake my disturbing thoughts. Truth or lies? Right or wrong? Happiness or sorrow? Life was filled with little daily decisions that determined where a person would spend eternity. Was I willing to quit fighting for what I wanted now that Ben was gone? Or did I trust in God's plan for me, even though I had no idea what it might be?

The last thing I remembered was the ticking of the grandfather clock in the living room as sleep brought some much needed relief.

It seemed as if my eyes had barely closed when I heard a knock on the door. I contemplated not answering, but when I looked through the keyhole, I saw a pizza deliveryman in a red shirt and baseball cap standing on the front porch with a box in his hands.

"I'm sorry," I told him when I cracked the door open, leaving the safety chain in place. "This must be a mistake. I didn't order anything."

"It's no mistake," he said. "The guy who came in to get a pizza yesterday called this morning to have cannelloni delivered here tonight."

"Oh," I replied, quite overcome with Jake's thoughtfulness. "How much do I owe you?"

"Nothing! It's all been taken care of." He handed me the box and then began to whistle as he walked back down the sidewalk towards the street.

The minute the front door was closed and locked again, the phone range. I hobbled to the kitchen as rapidly as my injured ankle would allow and managed to reach the phone before the ringing stopped.

"Hello," I cautiously answered, wondering how I would explain my presence in the house when I didn't even know the owner.

"You must be Brylee," a kind voice said. "LeAnn called this afternoon to give me the news about the baby, and to let me know that you would be staying in the house overnight because of a nasty fall. I hope you're okay."

"I'm doing much better," I told her, hoping she wasn't upset because LeAnn had allowed a stranger to stay in her home. "And thank you for letting me stay. It's very kind of you."

"My pleasure," she replied. "I'm just sorry you got hurt. Those rocks can be treacherous at night. I have fallen on them a few times myself. I am sorry to interrupt your convalescence, but when I got back from the diner I had the strongest feeling that I needed to call. I don't get those impressions often so I tend to act on them when I do. LeAnn has told me a lot about you the past few weeks."

"I hope it wasn't all bad," I said, feeling more than a little confused. Jake had arranged for dinner to be delivered, and now a complete stranger had called to see how I was doing. Was God trying to tell me something? I wished I knew.

"LeAnn has nothing but praise for your kindness and acceptance. I hope you don't mind that she shared a little of what has gone on since you came home with me. We have been friends for many years. We worked together at the diner before Trevor was born."

"So you knew my father."

"Everyone in town knew Jack Hawkins. He and Ned spent a lot of time in Edna when they were young. I even met your grandparents a time or two—lovely people. I have a few pictures of them and their two boys. I even have a picture of their sister. She was so beautiful and young when she died."

"I have an aunt?" That news shocked me every bit as much as the news about LeAnn's pregnancy, and I felt cold chills return even though it was warm in the house. "Are you absolutely sure? No one in the family ever mentioned her before."

"That's not surprising," she responded. "Most people don't like talking about painful things."

I thought about my situation with Ben, but this was different! I had an aunt and no one had ever mentioned her existence—not even my father when he was dying. What could she possibly have done that was so wrong?

"I guess there is still a lot about my family I don't know."

"Families are funny like that, especially when it comes to the sad times. Why don't we sit down and have a nice chat when you come to get LeAnn's things. I will tell you everything I know? I'm just glad she has finally gone home. That's where she needs to be, especially now. I am so happy about the baby. The rest of you must be over the moon with excitement."

I was excited, but it meant that my life with Ben really was over. Unless he came looking for me, I would never see him again. How could I pretend that was okay with me?

Chapter 9

When I got up the next morning, the swelling in my ankle was almost gone. There were still a number of ugly bruises, and it hurt to put much weight on it, but I would be able to drive back to the ranch with little difficulty.

Before leaving the house, I made sure the kitchen and bathroom were clean, and anything that might spoil was removed from the refrigerator and taken to the trash receptacle outside. I wanted to spend more time there now that my ankle was feeling better and I could get down to the beach, but I had other responsibilities now. Maybe Emma would let me come back once LeAnn's baby was safely here.

My mind kept drifting back to Ben as I passed one landmark after another on the six hour drive back to Edna. What if I had been too hasty giving him his freedom? What if him finding out about my past was just a test to see how much we would be willing to forgive and forget to be with each other? Maybe it wasn't too late. Maybe all we needed was look in each other's eyes again to see that the love we shared was still there.

But as much as my head told me to turn the Land Rover in the direction of Sydney and go back to him, my heart wouldn't let me. LeAnn and Trevor needed me, and I couldn't desert them no matter how much I hated the way they had come into my life. If there was a reason for everything, certainly God would let me know what it was when the time was right.

And what about Emma? She seemed like a compassionate and caring woman who had not only taken care of LeAnn for the past few weeks but had given me information about my own family that no one else had ever mentioned. Could she be part of the plan? It was definitely something to consider. After all, she said she'd had a prompting to call me. I had heard about things like that happening since joining the church but had never experienced one myself.

I arrived at her home a little after one. She had lunch ready for me, but her hospitality wasn't what peaked my interest when I walked inside. On a wall in her entry way was a picture of President Russel M. Nelson.

"That picture," I said. "It's the prophet of the church I belong to."

"It is," she replied, with a great deal of surprise. "Most people think it's a picture of my late husband. He has been gone for many years now. How long have you been a member?"

"Not long," I told her as a feeling of warmth and acceptance washed over me. "I joined ten months and sixteen days ago. I was supposed to be getting married in the Los Angeles temple as soon as I had been a member a year."

"You sound like that might not happen now."

I tried to blink back the tears that were forming.

"Do come in and sit down," she said, leading me into her small living room. There were pictures of many different people and a beautiful seascape on the walls. A hymnbook lay open on the piano.

"LeAnn told me you had been having a hard time adjusting to all the changes since coming home, but that must have been at least partially expected after being away for five years."

She looked so kind, almost benevolent, like a woman who had seen a lot of life but still cherished living. Her hair was almost white, but it was hard to judge her age because her face was mostly unlined.

"Changes yes, but finding out about LeAnn and Trevor was a real shock," I admitted.

Emma began pushing herself back and forth in a wooden rocker that must have been at least a hundred years old. The strips of curved wood that propelled it back and forth had been reinforced, and there were bands of black tape holding the spindles on the back of the chair in place.

"Being a member of the church changes just about everything—or at least it should. I never really understood repentance or forgiveness until I joined myself."

"How long have you been a member?" I asked.

"Let's see," she said with a smile. "Robert and I had been married for about five years when two wonderful young men came to our door and told us the 'good news'. We threw away our cigarettes and alcohol and joined a month later."

"That was fast," I said.

"How could we not join when the chance of having an eternal family was presented to us? Robert and I had been trying to have a child, but in those days doctors didn't know how to help women who couldn't conceive."

"But you eventually had your family," I said as I looked around the room to see if there were any pictures of children.

"No, dear, we didn't," she said. "But I still have hope that someday Robert and I will have the children we were denied in this life."

"I'm hoping that too," I replied with a great deal of heaviness in my own heart.

"What about that young man in the United States? You are still so young. You will have plenty of time for a family."

"But I'm not engaged any longer. We broke up two nights ago over the phone."

She leaned forward and reached for my hand. Her gesture spoke volumes about her character—warm, compassionate and understanding. "I'm so sorry."

"it was just one of those things that couldn't be helped," I responded, trying to keep my emotions in check.

"You have had your share of troubles lately, haven't you, my dear." She softly pinched the flesh on the back of my hand. "I wish I could tell you that everything was going to be okay, but that would be foolish because we are not guaranteed anything except that someday we will say this mortal experience was worth anything we had to suffer while being here."

"Sometimes I hate all this testing," I said as my face contorted in bewilderment. "I understand logically that we can't expect to be saved just because we say we accept Christ, but sometimes I don't know if it's worth the fight."

"You're questioning your testimony, aren't you?"

"Yes," I admitted, letting go of her hand and leaning back in the green brocade chair I was sitting in. "I don't know if I have the strength to go on fighting for something no one in my family even wants to talk about. They all think I'm going to be damned for leaving the Catholic faith. Maybe I only joined the church so Ben would marry me."

"My, my," she said with a thoughtful sigh. "You really have been doing some soul searching. I can't tell you how to find what you are looking for, but I can tell you that walking away from the church isn't the answer."

"Why not? It would solve so many problems."

"And create so many more! I learned that the hard way. I thought that joining the church would show God that I deserved having a child. When that didn't happen, I quit going for over ten years. It was easier to stay away and nurse my broken heart than to be around other sisters who had children and were always telling me that my time was coming."

"But your time never came. How could you be so strong when the thing you wanted most was withheld?"

"I did a lot of crying and pleading with the Lord, but by the time Robert and I considered adoption we were too old to be given an infant. They wanted to place an older child with us and we wanted a baby, so we pulled our papers. I wish now that we hadn't. It would be nice having more young people in my life. Maybe that was why I formed such an attachment to LeAnn and Trevor. She seems more like a daughter than a friend, and Trevor is like the grandson I never had."

There were tears in her eyes, and she wiped them away with a tissue she took from her apron pocket. She had been baking bread. The house was filled with the wonderful aroma. Why hadn't I noticed it before?

"Maybe I shouldn't be so ready to give up on my dreams," I told her, hoping it would help restore her former positive attitude. I hadn't meant to make her cry.

"Never give up on your dreams, Brylee, but they do have a way of changing. All I can tell you is that God has something wonderful in store if you will just pay attention."

"I'm trying, but it's hard when I keep losing the people I love, but then you know all about that."

"I certainly do," she responded. "I may be old enough to be your grandmother, but I haven't forgotten what it's like to want things. There's an old saying that *it is hard to stumble when you are on your knees*. I've lived by that for years."

She took me into the kitchen shortly after that where we shared a delicious meal of homemade soup and bread, with a fresh blueberry pie for dessert. It was wonderful eating something that actually tasted good after all the bad meals I had prepared at the ranch. And there was no smell of coffee and tobacco. It was almost like I was back home with Ben and his family.

That's what I missed most—the environment active LDS families created where language was soft and the spirit could be felt from morning until night. It wasn't like that at the ranch, even though I knew Jake and LeAnn were trying to be considerate of my feelings. They simply lived a different lifestyle than the one I had chosen.

But then it struck me that LeAnn had known Emma for years, and yet she had said nothing about her when I told my father the name of the church I had joined.

"Does LeAnn know you are a member of the church?" I asked. "I know that may sound insensitive, but she has never mentioned having any friends who believe what we do. Everyone in the outback seems to be Catholic or atheist. Jake even got mad at me when I taught Trevor a verse of *I Am A Child of God*."

"That's not surprising," she said. "LeAnn used to balk at my beliefs so much I simply quit talking about them. I figured she would come around when the time was right, and my responsibility was to set a good example and accept her for who she is."

"And there wasn't any conflict when she was staying with you?"

"Hardly! She barely came out of her room and when she did, she didn't feel much like talking. But why don't we talk about that later since you are short on time. I pulled out the pictures I wanted to show you."

She refused when I offered to help with dishes and took me directly to the dining room where an old leather-bound photo album sat waiting for us on the table. There were pictures of my parents, Uncle Ned, my paternal grandparents and LeAnn and Trevor. When she offered them to me, I graciously accepted. I wanted to know about all my family but was most interested in the aunt I had never heard about, so I asked Emma to tell me what she knew.

She sat back in her chair and folded her hands in her lap. "I only saw her a few times because she was a sickly child and seldom allowed out of the house."

"What was wrong with her?" I asked.

"A bad heart. Your grandparents said she was born with a hole in it, and they didn't know how to fix things like that in those days. She was such a beautiful child with dark hair and eyes. You look very much like her."

I felt my heart race. I looked so little like either of my parents or even Uncle Ned that I had often fantasized about having been adopted from one of the tribes in the outback.

"I think I have a picture of her in a drawer in my bedroom," Emma said. "I put it away after she died. It was just such a tragedy and made me feel even worse because I had never even had a child to love."

So my aunt was dead. No wonder my father had ever mentioned her, but people should not be forgotten just because they were no longer among the living.

Emma excused herself and went in search of the picture while I thumbed through the ones she had already given me. My parents looked so happy standing in front of the fountain outside the courthouse with their arms wrapped around each other. It must have been their wedding day. My mother told me they had eloped when she was seventeen.

My paternal grandparents looked stern but kind. Their picture reminded me of ones I had seen in magazines and on television where the farmer was wearing coveralls and holding a pitchfork, and the wife was wearing a gingham dress with her hair severely pulled back from her face in a bun. I barely remembered my grandfather, and suddenly wished I had known my grandmother. What stories she would have been able to tell.

Emma came back carrying a small brass frame.

"Here it is," she said, dusting the glass with her apron. "Such a lovely little thing. She was only ten when she died."

I looked at the picture she placed in my hands. The resemblance between us was uncanny. She could have been me when I was her age, or at least my sister—the same dark eyes and olive skin. She even had a dimple in her right cheek that was as visible as mine when I smiled. I studied it for the longest time.

"Can you tell me anything more about her?" I asked.

"Well," she said, resuming her place at the table. "She loved pretty things. I think she was holding her favorite porcelain doll in that picture."

I automatically glanced down at the image in my hands. She was definitely cradling a doll in her arms. It looked very old and fragile.

"And she liked books. She always had her nose in one even when her parents brought her into the diner. And she was the most polite child ever. She never left the diner without thanking me for whatever she had eaten. She was an amazing little girl."

"What was her name?"

"Oh, my," she said. "If that doesn't beat all! Her name was Brylee. I think she told me she had been named after a great-grandmother somewhere along the line. That must be how you got your name. You could have passed for twins when you were babies. I saw you once when you were small but never got to hold you. You mother was reluctant to let you out of her sight."

"My mother was afraid of a lot of things, but I loved her dearly and still do. I just wish we'd had more time together. Do you know where my aunt was buried?"

"In the Hawkins' family plot," she replied. "I'm surprised you haven't stumbled on her headstone. There can't be that many of them there."

"No, there aren't," I told her. "But maybe it was covered with something. I will look for it when I get home. I still can't believe I have an aunt, and I was named after her."

"Secrets," she said. "I have never had much use for them, even if they are well-intentioned. You can take that picture with you. I always wondered why I didn't just get rid of it when looking at her reflection just made me sad. Now I know I was saving it for you."

"Thank you for everything," I told her before leaving. "You have helped me understand that I still have a purpose for being here, even if it is not what I expected."

"Life is full of twists and turns, but one thing is always constant—our Heavenly Father's love and his plan for our happiness," she said. "Would you like me to call Nora and see if she can sit with LeAnn for a few hours next Sunday? You need to get back to church. It's important to be around people who believe the same things we do."

"I can call her," I responded as I gave her a hug and a kiss on the cheek. "Is it okay if I think of you as my grandmother? I never knew either of mine, and I am beginning to understand that we are all family anyway. It would mean a lot to me."

Emma was crying again when I broke our embrace.

"You see what I was saying, Brylee? God does bring people into our lives when we need them most. I was feeling rather blue when I found out LeAnn was going home, and now I have a beautiful granddaughter who can sit by me at church. I can't think of a more perfect blessing."

My own eyes were swimming with tears. Ben might no longer be part of my life, but Emma had given me a larger sense of family, and that was the most important part of living anyway.

"Then I guess I will see you on Sunday," I said.

"And I will be waiting on the second row of chairs in our makeshift chapel. I would say that I don't want to miss anything but that is rather hard to do when there are so few of us present. You are going to love President Downing."

"I already do," I told her. "I met him my first week here and he gave me a beautiful blessing. He also came to the mortuary to pay his respects to my father."

"My, what a small world we live in, my dear. Drive safe and never forget how many people—both here and on the other side—love you."

I left her standing on her front stoop waving. I felt lighter in spirit than I had since returning to the outback. I needed the gospel! I needed the fellowship of my brothers and sisters who shared my faith. And maybe, after the baby was born, I would be able to drive to Sydney for a weekend to attend a single's activity. The idea was terrifying, but I didn't need to think seriously about it now. My heart still had a whole lot of healing to do.

Although my ankle was still sore, I managed to do what shopping was necessary at the market so we could survive for another week or two. I even went to the mall to look for a present Trevor could give our new little sibling. It was indeed a miracle that LeAnn had been able to conceive under the circumstances. I just hoped nothing would happen to the baby. It would break my little brother's heart.

Trevor came running out to greet me when I pulled to a stop in front of the ranch house right before dusk that evening. My visit with Emma had made me later than planned, but I was so grateful God had brought her into my life. She had shown me that there was more to living than hanging onto moments of unhappiness. I had an entire family I knew relatively little about to concentrate on.

He threw his arms around my neck and wrapped his feet around my waist almost propelling both of us to the ground. My ankle was feeling better, but it would be a few days before it was completely healed, and I grimaced in pain.

"I'm sorry," Trevor said, immediately dropping himself to the ground. "I forgot about your foot, but I was so excited to see if you got it."

"I did. It's in the big bag on the passenger seat. I hope it is what you wanted."

He raced around the Land Rover, opened the door and took out the plastic bag. I couldn't help but notice how big his eyes got when he pulled out the 24-inch black and white Koala bear I had purchased at the toy store in the mall.

"It's perfect," he said, hugging the bear to him. "I am going to put it in the crib so he can look at it every day."

"Since you had some extra money, I got something to go along with it. They were having this big sale, and I couldn't resist it. Check out the other bag on the seat."

I would not tell him until he was much older that I had kept the $20 dollar bill our father had given him. I couldn't bear the thought of handing it to someone else. It would be returned to him someday along with a letter expressing my gratitude for all the lessons about love, service and sacrifice he had taught me. I hoped our little sibling would be half as amazing as he was.

Trevor opened the remaining bag and was thrilled with the mobile inside. It had a dozen Australian animals dangling from it and played "Hush-A-Bye-Baby" when turned on. It was a song I remembered my mother humming when I was small.

"Can we get the crib out of the attic tonight?" he asked. "I want to see how it looks all set up. Mum said I slept in it when we first came to the ranch."

"That's something we will have to discuss with your mother and your Uncle Jake," I told him as I lifted the back door of the Range Rover so we could get the groceries and other supplies into the house. I had spent over $400.00 and that bothered me, but we had been out of almost everything and stocking up again was both necessary and expensive.

Trevor passed Jake as he ran into the house with his gifts for the new baby.

"I'm glad you are back," he said. "I was beginning to worry."

"I had lunch with Emma, and we spent some time talking. Did you know she knew both my parents and grandparents?"

"That doesn't surprise me," Jake replied. "She's over eighty, and it would be hard to miss what goes on in a place as small as Edna, especially when you are the proprietor of the best diner in town."

My brow knit in confusion. Emma hadn't said anything about owning the diner. She had merely said that she met LeAnn while working there.

"What diner was that?" I asked him.

"The one we ate at the day we went into town to get the things for the wedding. LeAnn was working for Emma when she met your father. I guess you could say she had front row seating for all that went on between them. She was even at the hospital with LeAnn when Trevor was born. LeAnn wanted her to be his Godmother, but she wouldn't agree to it. She said she was too old and just wanted to pretend he was her grandson."

"That explains a lot," I told him without offering an explanation.

He didn't seem to mind.

"They went through some pretty rough times together. LeAnn had just started working at the diner when Emma's husband, Robert, died. I think my sister was all of fifteen. I don't know all the details, but they have been friends ever since."

"I can see Emma being that kind of a friend. She told me I could call her grandma, if I wanted."

"Are you going to?"

"I think so! After all, we are all part of God's family, even if we aren't related by blood. And you won't believe this! She told me I had an aunt who died as a child? We look enough alike to be twins, and I was named after her."

I'm not sure why I was telling him about my aunt after what had happened between us on the beach. On the drive back to the ranch, I had vowed to stay as far away from him as possible. It was the only thing that would keep me from making another colossal mistake.

"I didn't know your father had a sister," Jake said. "You sound just like a little girl when you talk about her."

"It's because I am excited," I told him as I picked up the first grocery bag. "I have never known anything about my relatives, except for Uncle Ned."

"And now you are carrying on a family name."

"It isn't just any name. It belonged to a great-grandmother before her. Don't you ever wonder about your ancestors?"

"Not often," he replied as he took the grocery bag away from me and reached inside for more. "The early ones were convicts, and the ones who came after them weren't much better. I would prefer it if no one knew who any of them were."

I refused to let his negative attitude affect my desire to learn more about my family. I was more convinced than ever that God had a special work for me to do in Australia now that I had received the blessing of the restored gospel and lost the man I loved.

"Well," I said with a smile I didn't quite feel. "I intend to find out everything I can about mine because I wouldn't be here without them."

"Then, good luck," he said, shaking his head at me a second time. "But be advised that you might find out more than you bargained for. Sometimes it is best to leave the past alone."

Chapter 10

After fixing breakfast for everyone the next morning and cleaning up the kitchen, I went to the attic to see if I could find anything that would help in my genealogy fact-finding mission. I wanted to learn everything I possibly could about my ancestors, even if it was unpleasant. Trevor and Copper followed me up the stairs.

"Are we going to get the baby's bed?" he asked. He had put the packages containing his presents on a chair in his room after showing them to his mother. His thoughtfulness had made her cry, just as it had me.

"We can look for it, but I think it would be a good idea to keep it in the attic for a couple of months. That way, it won't seem like such a long time until the baby comes."

I didn't want him knowing the difficulties this pregnancy could bring. It was best to take things one day at a time until LeAnn was much further along.

The air in the attic was already sweat-producing since A.C. had not been vented to that part of the house. I had even brought a hand towel with me this time to keep the moisture from running into my eyes as we worked, but Trevor didn't seem the least bit bothered by the heavy, musty air. He immediately went to the trunk he knew contained the remainder of our father's toys. The soldiers I had allowed him to take before the funeral were still lined up on a shelf in his bedroom. There had been so much sadness and loss the past few months. We needed this baby to help restore some life and laughter.

I had looked through the old family Bible in the den the night before. It listed marriages and christening dates back ten generations to the late-seventeen hundreds. And sure enough, among those names was Brylee Hawkins, not once or twice, but four times. It went clear back to the first grandmother recorded who never left her homeland of Scotland and ended with me. Even if I couldn't find more pictures, I felt certain that with Emma's help I could construct a family tree for my father's ancestry. It would be much more difficult with my mother's family since I knew nothing more than her parent's names and the date of her marriage to my father.

Sorrow welled up inside when I saw her cedar chest sitting underneath one of the two small windows that brought outside light into the attic. I would never be able to open it with her again and listen to the stories she told about her childhood with her governess on a huge estate in Perth clear on the other side of the continent before moving with them to Edna. I wondered why they had left their family home to move to a town as uncultured as the one closest to my home. It offered no intellectual or financial advantages, and with the exception of the construction of the short strip mall it was much like it had always been. People still went to the corner drug and dime for many of their more personal needs and the grocery store had been in the same place for generations since it was family-owned and run. I needed to write down the experiences she had shared before they were completely lost to memory.

The chest had been collecting dust since her death, and I brushed the top clean before sliding the metal fastener and lifting the lid. The inside smelled of cedar. The first object I pulled out had been wrapped in white tissue paper that had turned a shade of   yellow with age. It was my christening dress. The note pinned to it read:

"You were the most beautiful baby in the world, Brylee, and this is the dress I wore for my christening, and the one I dressed you in for your special day. It was one of the few things I took with me when I married your father. My mother and grandmother wore it before me. Father Frederick performed the ceremony and afterwards we had a celebration dinner at Emma's Diner. I wish it could have been the happy time I had always envisioned with lots of family and friends, but Uncle Ned, Aunt Nora and Grandpa Hawkins were the only family members who came. Maybe someday my parent's hearts will soften, and they will want to be part of their granddaughter's life. They are missing out on the most incredible blessing by letting anger and pride keep them from the important things in life. I hope you never have to know such pain."

Such a strange custom I thought. It didn't matter if the baby was a boy or a girl, it wore the same dress while a priest sprinkled water on its head and repeated a prayer—as if an infant needed to be saved. Still, the dress was an heirloom I would cherish. Maybe someday I would have a daughter who could wear it when she was blessed and given a name.

There were a few other items in the trunk, but not what one might expect to find in a place of memories. It must have hurt her dreadfully to be disowned by her family for following her heart and having a baby with a man they didn't approve of. There was a gold-edged miniature tea set, a few dolls and some pictures she must have painted as a child. They were the only reminders of her childhood she had to pass on, but someone in her family must have forgiven her because there were a few embroidered linens and the baby quilt made by her grandmother before I was born.

I cried as I held the green satin fabric to my heart because I remembered carrying it around until one day it simply disappeared. Some of the edges were frayed and soiled where I had rubbed it between my thumb and finger so often. It truly had been my security blanket as a toddler and I had sobbed and thrown one of my few childhood tantrums when she told me she didn't know what had happened to it. Now, I realized she had simply put it away so I could have it when I was old enough to know its value. I would take it back to my room as a reminder that I could be part of an eternal family—if I just did my part while I was still here.

Trevor was busy playing with iron models of a gray bailer, a thresher, a tractor, and several other models of farm implements I couldn't name. So I decided to continue rummaging through the trunk to see if I could find anything that might tell me more about my mother's family. I was so intent on finding something important that I almost missed the few sheets of paper slipped between the pages of *David Copperfield*, her favorite childhood book.

The writing was her own—probably a school assignment. It told about the day her brother, John William Olsen, was christened and listed the names of both sets of grandparents who had been at the ceremony. Chills ran up and down my arms as I read his name.

"I had just turned six when mother had a baby. She had been confined to her room for months. Father had told us girls that she was ill and needed her rest. I believed him, not knowing where baby's came from, but my sisters knew different. They were teenagers and seemed to like every bloke they met. They were always laughing and whispering when I came into their room. It made me feel bad when they told me I was too young to understand anything.

"I might not have understood much, but that was only because no one in the family ever talked to me. I was very lonely, especially since I wasn't allowed to talk to the hired help either. I didn't understand anything about social classes,

and how we were supposed to be better than other people because father was a banker and we had plenty of money.

"But I learned that we really weren't all that different from the poor people with vile manners and horrid tempers who lived in shacks on the other side of town the night my brother was christened. Both sets of grandparents went to the church with us while Father Peter sprinkled water on John William's head to save him from the clutches of Satan. It didn't seem right that a tiny baby was capable of the sins Father Peter was denouncing in him, but mother had cried so I knew it must be the right thing to do.

"Later that night, after I was supposed to be asleep in my bed, I heard my older sisters, Edith and Maude, sneak out of their bedroom window. They were whispering about meeting some blokes whose names I had not heard before. When I got up the next morning, they were both seated at the kitchen table crying. Father was standing over them with a big belt that I later learned was called a razor strap. He was snapping it in his hands, and each time it popped, they cried louder.

"I was so scared! I just stood outside the door listening as father told them they had disgraced the family name by being caught in the company of blokes were not worthy to even glance in their direction, and they must be punished. They would both receive 20 lashes across the back and be confined to their bedroom for a week with nothing but bread and water. After the first sound of leather hitting flesh, I ran to the dark place underneath the stairs and plugged my ears with my hands. But it didn't help. Their screaming and crying went on and on. I decided right then that I would never like a boy if it meant getting beaten by my father."

What a sad, frightened child she must have been with no one to explain how a father could beat his daughters because they had embarrassed him. No wonder she had married my father while still a schoolgirl. It was her way of escaping a man who sounded like a tyrant to me. But I had names! Names I could use to uncover the secrets of my mother's family. She had sisters and a little brother! Maybe I even had cousins somewhere.

I closed my eyes and prayed for the hurt little child that had always resided somewhere inside of my mother, making her timid even with me and my father. Had she been afraid that he would become violent like the man who had raised her? I would never know that in this life, but I had to believe that both of my parents were at peace now and were learning to love each other again. I certainly hoped so.

Aside from discovering what I could about my family, one of my goals in coming to the attic was to see if I could find the doll my Aunt Brylee was holding in the picture Emma had given me. Surely it had to be somewhere, but Trevor was becoming bored and wanted to visit his animals. I had enough to think about anyway. I had the names of my mother's brother and sisters. That would go a long way in trying to find them, and I understood even more about the woman who had given me life. I put the items I had been looking at back in the trunk and closed the clasp but took the sheet of paper back to my room so I could study it.

With LeAnn in bed and needing constant attention, I didn't make it over to Uncle Ned's to help with the spackling and painting inside the house like I had promised. Jake still went and occasionally took Trevor with him. It was during one of those first mornings of reprieve that I went into the den and turned the computer on. With the names of so many ancestors listed on a sheet of paper in front of me, I searched for the genealogical link on the church's web site.

I had no idea what issues I might encounter as I created a user name and password for the database called Family Search, but the instructions were so clear that within an hour I had found that the birthplace of both my maternal grandparents was Perth. As soon as the baby arrived, I would go there armed with the information I had gathered and look for any living relatives. It was what my mother would want, despite her frightening childhood. And finding a way for her family to be together again was the only gift I could really give her now.

Emma and I talked about my discoveries during our nearly daily phone conversations. She was the only person I knew outside the family, and our shared religious beliefs made me feel like I could discuss most anything with her. She was a born conversationalist, always cheerful, and always filled with golden words of wisdom. I had attended church with her the first weekend after bringing LeAnn home, but then Aunt Nora got sick, and I didn't feel like I could ask Jake to look after her. So, I stayed home the next week to do it myself. Now, we were heading towards the third Sabbath, and since Aunt Nora was feeling better I had every intention of spending the day in Edna.

But attending church again left me with an unexpected problem. Trevor wanted to go with me. I told him it was something I needed to discuss with his mother first. It would not be an easy exchange since I had never met a Catholic who wouldn't be upset at the thought of one of their family members crossing the threshold of another church's door, but I couldn't deny his request. He needed a religious background and wasn't getting it at home.

My feet took me towards the master bedroom where I gingerly knocked on the door. In the weeks that LeAnn had been home, I had become almost as confined to the house as she was. I was afraid to be out of hearing distance for more than a few minutes at a time for fear she might need me.

"Come on in," my stepmother said. She had propped a couple of pillows behind her back so it was easier for her to read. She had been doing that every day since coming home. Jake had asked her if she wanted the television moved to her room so she could watch something more entertaining, but she had refused saying that books were better for the baby. She looked both relaxed and content.

"I'm sorry to bother you while you are resting, but Trevor asked me something that I need to discuss with you."

She closed her book and placed it on the bed beside her. During the brief time since learning about the baby, she was already looking so much healthier and almost happy.

"Come sit by me," she said, motioning towards the chair that had been placed close to the bed so people could visit without shouting. "I'm getting bloody tired of loungng in bed while you do all the work, but I am determined to do this for the baby."

She put her hands on the mattress and pushed herself into a more upright position.

"It will all be worth it when you hold the baby in your arms for the first time," I told her, sitting down with a sigh. Despite everything that had happened, she was a very lucky woman to have been given something so miraculous and unexpected.

I wished I could say the same about me, but Ben hadn't emailed since we had talked on the phone, and my hopes for him changing his mind were pretty much gone. I knew in my heart that he was moving on with Jennifer, and even though I had released him from his promise to me, it still hurt. I tried not to think about him and managed quite well during the day when I was busy, but nights were still painful and I wasn't sleeping well.

"I'm worried about you, Brylee," she said. "You haven't been happy since the day I came home. Are you sorry I am back?"

"Most certainly not," I responded with surprise since I had been trying my hardest to remain upbeat. "This is where you should be."

"But you want to be someplace else, and my pregnancy is stopping you from doing that. You haven't mentioned a single word about Ben. Is everything okay with him?"

Her sincerity and concern touched my heart. But the problems between Ben and me had started long before I even came to Australia. Still, she deserved an explanation for my less than genial behavior. She might not know about eternal marriage, but she did know what it was like to lose the man she loved.

"Ben and I aren't together anymore. It happened the night we found you on the coast."

Her look was filled with compassion, and there were tears in her eyes when she spoke. "I knew something awful happened that night, other than just slipping on some bloody rocks but you didn't seem ready to talk, and I didn't want to pry."

"I wasn't in a very good place."

"I know about being in a bad place," she said. "I have spent most of the past three months there, but thanks to you, Jake and Trevor, I still have some fight left in me."

"That's good," I told her. "You have a lot of people here who love and need you and before long, you will have another beautiful baby to cherish."

"Oh, I cherish this baby already. It's a gift I never dreamed possible, but you are the one I am worried about now. Maybe you should have gone home to Ben like planned instead of staying here because it was what your father wanted. I love Jack Hawkins with all my heart, but he was stubborn as they come when it came to this ranch."

"It has been in our family for generations."

"And it will stay that way, but you have to think about your own happiness. Having a family is the most important thing a woman can do."

I swallowed back the lump in my throat as a bittersweet longing filled my soul. I wanted my own family with all my heart, but maybe that simply wasn't in the cards for me.

"Staying or going won't make much difference now," I told her. "I didn't tell him something I should have and he no longer trusts me, so I gave him his freedom."

"Oh, my dear, Brylee," she said. "I had no idea! But maybe all you need is to sit down face to face and talk things out."

"He has his old girlfriend to talk to and doesn't seem to need me anymore. I thought he might try to contact me since we talked, but he hasn't."

"And you don't feel like you can make the next move?"

"How can I? I am the one who released him from his proposal."

"That doesn't mean you both have to live with a decision that was made in hast and probably under a whole lot of duress. Your father and I would not have lasted a month if we hadn't been willing to compromise."

"I'm afraid this isn't a matter of compromise. I purposely kept something from him because I was afraid, and he found out about it from someone else. Only what that person related wasn't the truth."

"It sounds like a mighty tangled web, but I know you will talk about it when you are ready. Is there anything I can do to help?"

I leaned back in the fabric-covered chair and sighed. In some ways, it would be an enormous relief to tell her all that had happened, but I couldn't lay that kind of burden on her right now. She needed to remain calm so my little half-sibling would make it.

"The only thing that might have changed what happened was my being honest with him in the first place. But I am not even sure that would have changed the eventual outcome."

"Why not? You don't really believe he has moved on with his old girlfriend?"

"I don't know what to believe anymore, and she isn't just his old girlfriend. She was his high school sweetheart—the girl his entire family wanted him to marry. Maybe they were meant to be together anyway."

"Well, I think he is an absolute fool if he believes he can find anyone better than you. But something tells me that you may have broken things off with him in words, but your heart is not doing so well."

"My heart is so shattered I am surprised it's still beating," I responded, trying not to let all the bitterness show. "All I know is that I still love him and probably always will, but he is the one who needs to decide who and what he really wants. If it isn't me or what I can give him—regardless of my many faults—I will just have to live with it. Despite everything, I want him to be happy."

"You are a brave woman," she said. "And you have given up everything so Trevor could have a future here on the ranch. I can only say that your sacrifices will not go unrewarded forever."

"I hope you are right," I told her. "But as it stands now, this ranch is as much my future as it is Trevor's since I am not sure I will ever leave Australia again."

I looked down at my rough, red hands. Ben would no longer even want to hold them. I fought back more tears of disillusionment and sorrow. Why were some dreams allowed to come true while so many others weren't? It was something I would never understand.

LeAnn reached out and touched my arm. "I know this won't make up for what you have lost, but we all love you and are so grateful you are part of our lives. And I can promise that you will not be alone forever. You are young and beautiful and I will make sure you have a chance to meet eligible young men as soon as the baby comes. I hate that my condition is confining you to the ranch, but I don't want some stranger in my home looking after my son. I want him to learn what is right, and if I am not able to teach him that then I know you will."

I looked at her with understanding. Trevor was an impressionable child who picked up on even the slightest nuances around him, and he desperately needed to know his elder brother, Jesus Christ, and his eternal Father.

"That is sort of the reason I came to talk to you, LeAnn," I said as my head began to pound. "I am going to church again on Sunday, and Trevor has asked if he could go with me."

She leaned back on her pillows and bit the inside of her lower lip as her brows knit together. I knew my request went against everything she believed. Not one of my family members attended church services, but they still clung tightly to the faith of their fathers and mothers.

"I don't know," she finally said. "I see the kind of person you are, and I want Trevor to grow up to be like you. I don't want him smoking or drinking excessively or breaking one girl's heart after another. I get what you stand for, but Father Frederick would never approve. He would say I am sending my son straight to hell."

"I would never ask permission for something like this if I thought it would negatively affect Trevor."

"Then tell me what you do there."

"We have Sacrament meeting where we listen to talks on anything from the Atonement of Jesus Christ to being better prepared for whatever happens in our lives. We also take bread and water in remembrance of our Savior's sacrifice for each of us. After that, I go to a Sunday School class or a meeting with the other women called Relief Society. The children attend Primary."

"I have never heard that term before."

"Primary is where children sing songs, have lessons and do activities that help strengthen family values and teach them more about Jesus."

"They won't pressure him to be baptized?"

I knew where she was heading, and I didn't want her to think that anything would be done behind her back. That wasn't the way we did things anyway. Baptism was a personal choice and people had the right to decide for themselves if they wanted to join a church. That couldn't be done until they were old enough to understand personal choice and know right from wrong.

"No! He will only be taught to know and love his Heavenly Father and Jesus more than he already does. He couldn't be baptized without your permission until he is eighteen anyway, and that's a long time in the future."

She was silent for so many seconds—with her brow furrowed in anxiety over the decision she was making—that I was almost certain she would refuse my request.

"This is a tough decision," she finally said. "My head tells me no, but my heart tells me yes. I honestly don't know what to do."

"Then pray about it," I said.

The words slipped out without conscious thought, and I wished I hadn't been quite so bold.

"I have been remiss in that endeavor since I was a very small child," she replied. "Praying wasn't a top priority unless something awful was happening, like when your father got sick. I wanted him to get well so much I prayed night and day, but when he didn't I sort of gave up asking for divine help. Your father was a wonderful man who loved his family, and now he will never even get to see his youngest child."

Her tears returned and I almost wished I had not mentioned anything about Trevor's request.

"We wouldn't learn much in this life if we didn't have challenges," I told her, simply because I could think of nothing else to say. "That is how we become stronger people."

"I don't want to be any stronger," she retorted, "I want your father back so he can watch this baby grow up."

"But you know that can't happen."

"Of course I know that can't happen, but it doesn't stop me from wishing things were different. A child should not have to grow up without one of his or her parents."

"He still has a mother, a brother, an uncle and a sister who love him dearly. I hope that will count for something."

There was a long moment of silence before she looked at me through narrowed eyes. "I am sorry for acting ungrateful again. I know God didn't have to give me this baby."

I watched as tears slid down her cheeks. She looked like a frightened, lost child. It was my turn to offer comfort, so I rose to my feet and put my arms around her trembling shoulders.

"It would be nice to understand why bad things happen, LeAnn. I would certainly like to know why Ben couldn't still be a part of my life, but having you and Trevor in it means everything, and there is going to be a beautiful new baby in our family soon. I can't be totally miserable when I think about that."

I wanted to be fully focused on her problems. I had forgiven her for being cross with me and for leaving her son behind while she nursed her grief, but I wanted my own baby with Ben. It was horrid having to accept the consequences that came from making the wrong decisions, but my secret had destroyed my one chance at happiness.

"We seem to have gotten a little off-topic," she said. "You didn't come in here to rehash what cannot be changed."

"Not exactly, but if it helps, Emma will be at church with me."

"My Emma?" she asked with complete surprise, and I nodded my head. "We haven't discussed religion for ages, but she is the most amazing woman I have ever known. If both of you will be there, I guess it won't hurt Trevor to go just this once. He should be learning about Jesus. That is one thing your father and I rarely talked to him about."

"Children seem to know intuitively that there is more to life than just the physical world they life in. They might not understand what they are feeling, but they are very open to the truth when they hear it."

"Is that how you felt when you first heard about this new church you joined? I can't believe I never put two and two together until now."

"Emma said she never tried to force religion on you."

"She didn't and was always the perfect example of Christian charity. But what made you decide to break away from your roots. I didn't say anything about it when you told us because I knew how hard it was on your father."

"Father understood, at least after we were able to discuss the issue a little more rationally. But in answer to your question, once I read the *Book of Mormon* and prayed to know if it was true, there was no doubt left."

"I want to believe you, Brylee, but you have to understand that this is very difficult for me. The thought of someone in my family even visiting a different church never crossed my mind until I met you. If I let him go, you have to promise that you will protect him, keep him safe and not fill his head with anything than would cause me even the least amount of concern."

"I will protect him with my life. I want my family together forever."

She took a deep breath. "Then take him with you, but don't tell Jake. He finds religion stifling and would only be upset with both of us"

When I left LeAnn, I went straight to my room and knelt down on my knees to thank God for softening her heart so Trevor could attend church with me. The windows of opportunity were opening so rapidly I could no longer doubt that he was preparing those I loved to hear the truth. If losing Ben meant gaining eternal life with my family, then maybe everything I was going through would be worth it one day, but it didn't take away the throbbing of loss in my heart.

After the night on the beach when Jake had tried to kiss me, he quit coming into the house for breakfast. He fixed his coffee and whatever else he was eating in the bunkhouse before leaving for Uncle Ned's to continue the work of restoring the lower level of their house. He came home right before dark and went in to talk to LeAnn for a few minutes before grabbing something from the kitchen and heading to bed.

I rarely saw him except from a distance, but I made sure there were enough leftovers from our evening meal that he would not starve. It hurt that he was avoiding me on purpose because I had refused his advances. I missed his company, his ready laugh and sparkling eyes. I experienced vivid dreams of us together at night that scared me with their intensity, but something inside of me had changed when my own visions for a happy future ended.

I no longer viewed Jake with disgust or contempt for his self-absorption, arrogance and combative behavior. I had caught a glimpse into his heart as he tried to comfort me and liked what I saw behind the often gruff and irritating facade. But that sudden realization made me more afraid of him than ever. Not that he would ever intentionally hurt me, but he could never give me the kind of eternal relationship I wanted. That meant no relationship at all, especially since I now knew he desired me.

My first few weeks back at the ranch as an unengaged woman were spent in a kind of stupefied daze. I wanted to email Ben but knew it would only mean breaking each other's hearts again because nothing had changed. I put my engagement ring away in a small box I found in the attic fully intending to send it back to him, even though he had told me to keep it. But it was nearly impossible to get into town during the week with LeAnn practically bedridden, and the post office was always closed on Sunday.

Aunt Nora kept me updated every evening on what was happening with her home. The walls were up, and she was putting spackling compound in the holes left in the wallboard by gripper screws once the men were finished for the day and the dust had settled. Still, I continued to feel guilty for not being there to help, and she continued to be gracious when we talked—always reminding me that I was doing something more important than rebuilding a house by helping to ensure the safe arrival of a new family member.

LeAnn's mood continued to lighten. Instead of crying because she was confined to the room she and my father had shared, she was making plans to turn the wall opposite the fireplace into a sort of nursery until the baby was old enough to be moved into one of the smaller rooms on the second floor. She ordered several magazines and books to help her solidify ideas.

Once Trevor understood that the baby's arrival was not going to happen any time soon, he began getting restless at having to sit with his mother for long periods of time. But she soon insisted that he resume school lessons—activities that had been sadly overlooked during her absence. He was none too excited about that, but liked learning new things so it made part of each day pass a little more quickly.

To alleviate more of his boredom since he was used to spending an inordinate amount of time outdoors, I began taking him to the attic nearly afternoon while LeAnn was resting. I didn't want to leave her alone in the house, and going through boxes and finding "treasures" as he called them helped pass the time for both of us.

And many of the items we found were in truth treasures because they brought us closer to our ancestors. The day I found my Grandmother Hawkins' wedding dress was the epitome of a treasure hunt for me. It had been wrapped in brown paper that was supposed to keep it from yellowing and packed away in a trunk with a lock whose key appeared to be permanently lost.

I soon became so tired of hunting for it that I went to the barn and brought back the wire cutters that were used for building or repairing barbed wire fences. I could have asked Jake for help, but he had been the one to set the new boundaries on our relationship, and if I was truthful I didn't want to see him any more than he wanted to see me. It was just too complicated, but I was beginning to wonder when Trevor would notice that we never spent time together any more and would want to know why.

After watching me struggle with the cutters for a short time, without making much more than a dent in the metal lock he finally had enough.

"Why don't we just ask Uncle Jake to help? I have seen him cut through things thicker than that with one chop." He brought his hands together until they made a popping sound to drive his point home.

I looked over at him and frowned. "Your uncle is busy helping Uncle Ned and Aunt Nora with the house and is really tired when he gets home. I don't want to bother him with something as silly as this. If we can't cut through it in a day or so we will ask for his help, but right now I want to show him that we are okay on our own. We don't want him to worry about us, do we?"

Trevor rolled his eyes, but after a moment or two of thought, he took the cutters from me and tried to do it himself.

I watched in amusement as his small hands pushed the handles together with all the strength they possessed. It appeared that even little boys liked to fix things without asking for help. After taking turns for over an hour, the old lock finally gave way.

"What's that?" he asked once the trunk was open and I could get at its contents.

The dress I help up was made from the finest cream gauze I had ever seen. It had a fitted empire bodice with row after row of fine lace. The sleeves were gathered at the shoulders and had a cuff that was nearly six inches wide. It was sheer elegance and easily the most beautiful wedding dress I had ever seen. The piece of paper pinned to the sleeve said that Hawkins's brides had worn it for three generations. Perhaps my mother would have been allowed to wear it if she'd had a wedding instead of an elopement.

"Are you going to wear that when you marry Ben?" Trevor asked. "It's really pretty."

His question made my stomach lurch. I had never considered telling him that we were no longer a couple, even though I was fully aware that he missed little when it came to what was going on around him.

"I don't think so," I told him as tears formed in my eyes. I hated crying. It never solved anything. "We broke up."

"It will be all right," he said as his arms found their way around my neck, and I let the dress slip to the attic floor. "You will always have me and mum and Uncle Jake and the new baby. We will make sure you aren't sad any more."

"How can I be sad when I have all of you in my life," I responded as I hugged him back. But reality was rarely as simple as fantasy, and owning up to my mistakes was not a pleasant task. "Ben doesn't know what he is missing by not having you in his life. You are the best little brother in the whole wide world."

He hugged me for a moment more and then went back to play with the iron farm implements he had found in our father's box of toys.

I bent over and scooped the wedding dress my grandmother's had worn from off the floor. How I wished I had known the great ladies who worked side by side with their husbands to carve out a livelihood in one of the most beautiful, but harshest environments on the planet. It was almost a tragedy that I would never get to wear the dress—even if it fit. On my wedding day, I would be dressed in the purest white because I intended on making sure that my dream of having an eternal marriage came true—even if it didn't happen until I was as old and white-haired as Emma.

Chapter 11

The next few weeks slipped by without major incident. Jake flew LeAnn into Edna every other week to see the doctor who had delivered Trevor. He concurred with the doctor who had examined her on the coast. Her blood pressure was elevated and her cervix was weak. He was afraid they might have to sew it shut as she got closer to the delivery date, but for now he felt that bed rest would keep both her and the baby safe. The visits did not assure her that everything would be okay, but at least she was reassured that nothing had gone wrong yet.

The traditional Thanksgiving of America slipped by without conscious thought. Australians held their day of thanks in May, and then it was almost time for Christmas.

I had tried not to think about its approach, even though I was very grateful for my Savior and all he had done for mankind. Perhaps I was simply trying not to fall apart because Ben and I had planned on being married during the holidays. I had read somewhere that people could die from a broken heart, and sometimes I wondered if that would be my fate. Never before had I known pain and loneliness so intense that it brought me to my knees several times each day because there were so many moments when I thought I might not be able to hold it together any longer, but with God's help I always did.

It might have helped if I had been able to attend church regularly but I hadn't been back since asking permission for Trevor to accompany me. Aunt Nora was consumed with problems of her own and adding something more to her plate was something I couldn't bring myself to do.

With LeAnn was confined to bed for the duration of her pregnancy and Jake avoiding me so completely I could no longer remember when we had spoken last, I was left with the responsibility of pulling off a holiday celebration for Trevor—whether I wanted to or not. I suspected that all the adults in the family wished it could just be forgotten, but that wasn't fair to a child who had lost his father only days after his birthday—not to mention the trauma of surviving a flood and having his mother disappear.

But when I added my broken engagement and LeAnn's pregnancy to the mix, I was more depressed than ever. Not only would there be no husband for me, there would be no children either. Those were two things I wanted more than ever now that the possibility of having them was gone—at least for the foreseeable future.

Ten days before we were to celebrate the birth of our Savior, LeAnn called me into her bedroom to talk about it.

"I know it's not fair to ask," she began. "But Trevor needs to celebrate the holidays. If it wasn't for him, I would forget about the entire season."

"Me too," I admitted, since it seemed pointless to pretend to be happy when I wasn't. "There hasn't been a whole lot to celebrate this past year, except for the new baby."

"I am so sorry about your broken engagement, Brylee. It makes me want I cry every time I see you. I hope you know I would do anything I could to fix it."

My forced smile was anything but reassuring.

"Some things just weren't meant to be, I guess."

"Maybe, but you still needed a chance to see if you could work things out. Not knowing for sure has to be almost unbearable."

"There isn't much else I could have done. I told Ben how sorry I was, but I think he was halfway out of the relationship anyway and just needed an excuse to call it quits."

"You really loved him with all your heart, didn't you?"

"I still do! I'm not sure I will ever fall in love again. It's just too hard and it hurts so much."

"I can identify with that," she said with a sad and weary smile. "Even with the blessing of this baby coming, I can't forget that I will never see Jack again, and he will never get to hold his new son or daughter. I don't know if I am even capable of being a single mother with two children. I can't even take care of myself."

"There seems to be a lot of that going around lately," I told her, wishing I had the luxury of giving in to my own insecurities and grief. But with her out-of-commission for the next few months, I was the only one who could hold things together.

"You are doing a wonderful job around here, Brylee, and Trevor absolutely adores you. I know I don't tell you that enough."

"You shouldn't have to tell me that at all. We are family and need be there for each other."

"But it seems so one-sided. You should have been allowed your own happy ending."

"I selfishly concur," I replied, wishing I could act truly happy for even one day. LeAnn might not know the specifics of what had happened between Ben and me, but she understood loss and sorrow. In many ways, we had become closer because of the similarities in our lives.

"I wish we could do something more than pretend," she responded.

"So do I, but Trevor needs a Christmas. I suppose we all do, but I have been dragging my feet. So tell me what you want me to do, and I will see that it's done."

"Thank you," she said, reached for the pen and pad of paper that was sitting on the nightstand. "I have been making a list."

I sat down on the chair next to the bed. Was there ever a family more messed up than ours? Father was gone. LeAnn was confined to bed, and Jake and I weren't speaking because of that night on the beach. Trevor was the only one interested in finding something good about the holiday season, and I suddenly realized I had changed the subject every time he mentioned it. That had to change. Even if I couldn't find happiness in my own life, I would make sure he had at least some measure of it in his.

"There is an artificial tree in the attic," LeAnn was saying. "We haven't used it for the past couple of years since your father wanted Trevor to pick out a real one, but it will do in a pinch. There are also a few boxes of ornaments and decorations somewhere in the clutter. I have been meaning to get up there and do some cleaning but never got around to it."

I had seen the artificial tree when I was rummaging around. It wasn't much to look at—more like a Charlie Brown tree than anything else—but maybe it would look okay with enough lights and ornaments on it. At least it would make Trevor happy.

"We usually put up stockings for everyone, but maybe this year it would be best to only put Trevor's on the mantel. It might be too hard for him to see his father's hanging next to his."

"I will ask him about it," I said. "He might be more upset if he thinks we are trying to forget."

LeAnn thrust the list in my direction. I knew I had hurt her feelings but didn't have the energy to formulate an excuse.

She sighed and slumped back onto her pillows. "I don't want you to think I am losing it again by saying this, but do whatever you think is best since I can't do anything more than lay in this damned bed. Your Father and I had so many plans for the future and now he won't even get to see his own baby."

I wanted to tell her that I believed father was with that baby right now, and even if he wasn't, he knew what was happening with the people he had left behind. But in her present frame of mind, LeAnn would not be receptive. I prayed all the time that the baby would make it with all of its faculties intact. We needed this miracle because I was afraid of what might happen if it didn't materialize.

Surprisingly, Jake joined us for dinner that evening, and after we had cleared the table I talked to both him and Trevor about celebrating Christmas. Jake let his eyes roll, but Trevor was more than enthusiastic when I told him we were going on another adventure into the attic to find the artificial tree and any decorations we could uncover.

"Come with us, Uncle Jake," Trevor insisted, grabbing his hand and pulling on his arm. "You will love the attic. It has so many cool things in it, doesn't it, Brylee?"

I wriggled my nose to keep the tears at bay. I hadn't been home for Christmas since before my mother's death, and I wasn't sure I wanted to go down memory lane any more than Jake did, but we had to do this for Trevor.

"There is a lot to look at," I said as I followed them up two flights of stairs to the door that was now left unlocked.

"Isn't this the neatest place ever?" Trevor asked his uncle when we stepped into the room that was still filled with boxes and an assortment of memorabilia and useless castoffs, despite my effort to organize and de-junk.

Maybe Jake knew where we could take the things we would never use that were still in good condition. I wasn't sure about some of the older items yet. I needed to learn the stories behind them before making a permanent decision. But perhaps in the long run, all my worry over what to do with trinkets and castoff clothing, linens and appliances would be wasted because the house and most everything in it now belonged to LeAnn, not me.

"I'm sorry you had to come up here tonight," Jake said as we watched Trevor attack a small mountain of boxes that had been labeled Christmas. "It must bring back a lot of sad memories."

"I'm trying not to think about that," I told him, forcing the acidity from my voice and wishing I had the courage to tell him that I had spent an inordinate amount of time in the attic already trying to come to terms with certain parts of my past. "I haven't been around since the Christmas before my mother died, and I wasn't planning on being here this year, but life has a way of throwing curve balls we are not prepared for."

I was afraid he might say something about Ben, but he didn't.

"My parents died when I was so young I really don't remember them, but LeAnn tried to make the holidays special. She has been both sister and parent to me for over twenty years. It breaks my heart to see her in so much pain—even with a new baby growing inside of her."

He sat down on a box of old magazines and put his head in his hands. I had never seen him so emotionally vulnerable, and it tore at my heart. Jake was a good man, and he had lost every bit as much as I had. I placed my hand on his shoulder and looked down at his bowed head. There was no arrogance in the man sitting in front of me.

"I am sorry for all your losses," I told him. "I have never understood why some families seem to have it so easy while others are plagued with challenges from day one."

He looked up at me with a half-hearted smile. "I'm glad you didn't say that whatever doesn't kill us will make us stronger. I have always hated that analogy."

"Even if it is true?" I asked.

"Especially if it's true. I don't like seeing the people I love in pain. It seems like God—if there really is one—could do a little bit better in spreading the good times around."

"If there was only good in our lives, we wouldn't appreciate it very much."

"I would," he said. "I would like to see both you and LeAnn happy and smiling again. There has been so much darkness here the past few months."

"That's why it is important we make Christmas as much fun as possible."

"And how do you propose doing that? We can't bring your father back or make LeAnn get out of bed without risking the life of her baby."

"Maybe not, but we have a house to live in, enough food to eat, and someone around to help if needed. There are people all over the world who have much less than that, but they are still trying to be happy."

"I am not really up to one of those speeches about all the starving children in Africa, if that's what you are getting at. We wouldn't make a dent in their suffering if we gave them everything we have."

"You're right," I said, taking a step away from him. If I started thinking about all the negatives in my life again, I would never be able to celebrate Christmas. There had to be something in our lives worth celebrating.

"Here it is!" Trevor shouted, as he opened a large cardboard box.

I crossed the cluttered room to his side. "What's here?" I asked as he pushed away some plastic bubble wrap.

"Baby Jesus, of course!" he exclaimed, pulling a wooden manger and a ceramic baby Jesus from the box.

I looked down at the figurine in his hands. It was over a hundred and twenty years old and very fragile. It had been in the Hawkins' family for generations. My mother had let me hold it when I was a child, but playing with it was strictly forbidden. It appeared that LeAnn had been more generous with a family treasure, but I reminded myself that it was only an object. What really mattered was people like my little brother.

"I remember that," I told him. "It belonged to our great, great, great grandmother. She brought it to Australia from England when she was a little girl."

He held the figurine out to me, and I took it lovingly in my hands. "Do you know the story behind this?"

His head moved back and forth. "All I know is that father wouldn't let me play with it. He said it was some big word I don't remember."

"An heirloom," I prompted him.

"That's it," he replied. "Father also said that it belonged to you when you came home. I guess that means it is yours now, just like Thunder is mine."

I kissed his upturned face and tried to keep the tears that were tickling my nose from flowing.

"Well, I am more than happy to share. Great, great, great grandmother's family decided to come to Australia to join her father who had been sent here as a convict."

"Convicts are bad," he said. "Like the one's father told us about."

I looked over at Jake. I wasn't sure I could handle this discussion right now, but once again, he came to my rescue.

"Not every convict is a bad person. Sometimes people break laws because they don't have any other options."

Trevor eyed him curiously. "Because they are hungry?"

"That's what it was like back in the old country," Jake told him. "Most people who break the law today do it for very different reasons, but my ancestor—and I guess that means yours too—was accused of stealing a sheep from the squire he worked for and was sentenced to life in prison. His father was dead and his family was hungry. He wasn't guilty, but even the thought of him doing something so evil broke his mother's heart, and she died a few weeks after he was incarcerated. By the time the man who really stole it was found, my great grandfather was already on a ship headed for Australia and the penal colony here."

"But that isn't fair, Uncle Jake. Why didn't he just go back home?"

"Because it took nearly five years before he learned what had really happened, and by then his sisters were married and gone. It didn't seem like there was much to go back to, so he decided to stay here. Eventually, he married and had a family of his own."

"But it's still not right," Trevor lamented. "People shouldn't be punished for something they didn't do."

"True enough, but the law doesn't always work as swiftly as it should, and in those days people were guilty until proven innocent. It doesn't work like that any more, I am more than happy to say."

Trevor was thoughtful for a moment. "Maybe when I grow up I will help people who can't help themselves."

"I thought you were going to live on the ranch forever."

"I am going to do that too, Uncle Jake," he defended his latest ambition. "Father said I could do anything I wanted to when I grew up."

I had been watching the fading sunlight dance across the small object in my hands. It was crudely made by today's standards, with a face that looked much older than that of an infant, but it had belonged to someone whose blood ran through my veins. And knowing that my father had left it to me made it more than priceless.

"Tell me about the little girl." Trevor's voice brought me back to the reality I was living in where it didn't appear that anyone was going to get a happy ending, except maybe Trevor when he grew up. He crossed the short distance to where I was standing in the fading pink light.

"I think father said her name was Mary Catherine, and she was the youngest child in the family. When they left England to sail to Australia to be with her father, she was told she could bring one toy with her on the ship. Her sister took a doll with long golden hair, and she took this porcelain baby Jesus. When they arrived here, her father was out of prison, and he made this little wooden manger for baby Jesus to sleep in. I don't know how the other pieces of the nativity set were acquired, but this piece and the manger he sleeps in are more valuable to me than anything money can buy."

"That's quite a story," Jake said, looking at me as if he didn't quite believe what I had said, but I refused to let him upset the moment.

"It's what my father told me, and I have no reason to doubt its authenticity."

"I wasn't questioning that," he said with a frown. "I was just wishing there were stories like that in my family. LeAnn and I know very little about our ancestors, except for the story I just told. We don't even know if we have any living relatives. Our parents never told us anything about where we came from, except for being the descendants of convicts. That is not much of a heritage to pass on."

I thought back to the day I had told him about my Aunt Brylee. He hadn't seemed the least bit impressed. "And you have never thought about trying to find out more about your family?"

"There are thousands of Johnson's in this part of the country. We could be related to all of them or none of them. I guess I have never been interested enough to even attempt making connections."

"Maybe you will someday," I said as I watched him pick up the artificial tree and head towards the door of the attic. "Everyone should know where they come from."

I trailed along behind him, wondering how LeAnn must have felt the first time they decorated a Christmas tree as a family at the ranch. She must have brought some of her own things with her, but she still had to know that many of the decorations in the house had belonged to my mother. Had I been her, I am not sure I could have used them knowing the part I had played their previous owner's death.

Jake assembled the tree next to the big window in the living room while Trevor and I hauled boxes down from the attic. His radiant face took away the unpleasant thought of repacking everything and hauling it back up the stairs once the holiday season was over.

Jake strung the lights and tested them while Trevor decided where each ornament would be placed. It should have been a joyous time, but all I could think about was the diamond ring I had put in a little box but hadn't shipped back to Ben yet. I should be getting married to him instead of mourning the loss of my father and trying to make life easier for a family I hadn't even known existed until I came home.

Trevor decided to decorate his mother's room since the tree was too big to be set up there, and she wouldn't be able to join us in the living room for any longer than the amount of time it would take to unwrap presents on Christmas morning. So we hung lights along the bedroom mantel and set up a wooden Santa and reindeers in one corner. She pretended to be thrilled with the gesture for her son's sake, but the sad look in her eyes told me that she was every bit as miserable as I was.

My little brother was thrilled with the tree that looked less than impressive to me and insisted that the lights were on every moment he was awake. He would sit in front of it almost mesmerized for what seemed like hours. One evening, I sat down beside him and asked what he was thinking about.

"I just keep wondering what it is going to look like with prezzies under it. We have always had them before."

That spawned another conversation with LeAnn, and the daunting task of asking Jake if he would be willing to fly us into Edna to do some shopping. I would have driven, but I didn't like leaving LeAnn for a long period of time even when Aunt Nora offered to sit with her. It would be touch-and-go with the baby until it was delivered, and I wanted to make sure we were doing everything humanly possible for both of them.

Jake was not thrilled over the prospect of spending an afternoon of shopping with us, but LeAnn had given me a list of all the gifts she wanted to buy—a bike for Trevor, new work boots for Jake because he never went shopping for himself, and a Hickory Farms basket for Ned and Nora, so it had to be done. She also wanted me to get enough stocking stuffers for everyone just in case, a game we could play as a family, a basketball and hoop Jake could nail to the outside of the barn so Trevor could learn how to play, a few books and whatever else Trevor seemed interested in when we went to the toy store to look around.

It was a mammoth undertaking for a single afternoon, but it wouldn't be the first time since coming home that we'd had to pull off a celebration in a few hours. Still, this was infinitely harder than the surprise wedding. How could any of us feel happy on Christmas morning when father wasn't there to share the joy of the season with us?

I had been avoiding holiday music because all it did was make me cry. Too much of my life appeared to be over, and I couldn't see past the moments of hurt and betrayal to enjoy a season of hope and gratitude. But the minute we reached the outdoor mall, Christmas music was blaring over the speakers, and I could see that a Santa was sitting on a high-back chair in the middle of the small park around which the mall had been constructed. Children and parents stretched from one end of the courtyard to the other waiting to talk to him. I asked Trevor if he wanted to sit on Santa's lap like the other children were doing, but he said he just wanted to go to the toy store. That made it easier for all of us.

Jake and I divided the list of gifts that needed to be purchased for Trevor, including the things he would find under the tree on Christmas morning. That left time for doing some shopping of our own. It wouldn't be easy keeping all the packages hidden from my little brother because even a somewhat timid boy had mountains of curiosity, and despite all the sadness around us he was very excited about the prospect of opening presents.

I took him shopping for his mother and uncle while Jake put a cherry red bike on layaway at the toy store. He would have to come back another day to get it, but that was okay because someone would have to buy groceries if we were going to have a Christmas dinner for the family.

Trevor had trouble deciding what he was going to buy. We looked at everything from jewelry to pots and pans for his mother. I had decided to buy her some pajama bottoms and maternity tops she could wear in bed. It wasn't original, but under the circumstances, it seemed the most logical choice of gifts. Trevor finally decided on a silver charm bracelet with add-on charms for both him and the baby. We got some fancy lotions and some slippers to go with it.

Buying something for Jake was decidedly harder. I had never bought presents for any men other than my father and Ben, but Trevor knew exactly what he wanted to get him—a new utility knife since his had disappeared during the flood. I asked him what he thought I should get for Jake. It couldn't be something personal like men's cologne since I didn't want to encourage something that could never be, but it also couldn't be something as impersonal as socks, although I knew he likely needed them.

We decided on a new leather wallet. Trevor said he needed one, and I thanked him for the suggestion. We got gift certificates for both NJ and Molly, and picked up the basket LeAnn wanted from Hickory Farms.

Jake was waiting for us at a small table in the food court drinking a soda when we finished. The open space with fewer than half a dozen food booths was both crowded and noisy. I had to lean towards him to hear what he was saying, but I could not miss the dubiously look when he saw at all the packages we were carrying.

"Didn't you leave anything in the stores?" he asked in a mocking tone that wasn't lost on me but fortunately went right past my little brother.

"We can't tell you what we bought, Uncle Jake," Trevor told him with a smile that symbolized the expectancy the season should bring. "You have to wait until Christmas, or it won't be a surprise."

"Then I guess I can't show you what I bought either, but I can tell you that I spoke to Santa."

Trevor's eyes began to dance as he put his hands together on top of the small table and sat down. "What did he say, Uncle Jake?" he pleaded.

"He said he was bringing you something extra special this year."

"He really said that?"

"Cross my heart."

"But how will he know what I want most?"

"Santa knows everything," Jake told him. "I think his elves must do a lot of traveling during the off-season."

"No, they don't. They are at the North Pole making toys."

Trevor looked from his uncle to me. "Can we go to the toy store now, Brylee? I have bought presents for everyone and haven't decided what I really want most this year."

"Right after we eat something," I promised. "You didn't finish your breakfast, and we won't be home for several hours."

It took a little persuasion—and the assurance that everything at the toy store would not be gone before we got there—to get him to eat a chicken wrap and drink a carton of chocolate milk.

By the time we left the mall a couple of hours later, we couldn't have packed anything more into the cargo hold of the plane if we tried. I was grateful there was wrapping paper in the attic so we didn't have to buy that too. I had purchased a Play Station and a few games I thought would be appropriate for Trevor while he was looking at more toys with Jake. He needed to be introduced to more technology, but I wanted to make sure he wasn't exposed to some of the games I had seen kids in L.A. playing. They were violent and destructive. I wanted to help him remain innocent to the influences of the world for as long as possible.

I tried to stay optimistic and cheerful for Trevor's sake during the final days leading to Christmas. Although I knew he was beginning to heal from the traumas of the past few months, he deserved to have as many happy experiences as possible after everything he had been through, so I helped him wrap his gifts and put them under the tree. He went back several times each day to see if any new packages had been added. I forced myself to put only one present at a time under the tree so he would have something to look forward to.

I had never been given much candy as a child, but one of the traditions I remembered from my own childhood was a five-pound box of chocolates that Santa delivered on Christmas Eve. I loved opening that package, and since I was only allowed to eat two pieces each day, the box lasted until Valentine's Day. I wanted to share that with Trevor. The other tradition was opening a new nightgown I could wear on

Christmas morning. I just hoped Trevor wouldn't be disappointed at unwrapping something to sleep in on Christmas Eve instead of a toy. LeAnn seemed to be okay with my suggestions.

Since I hadn't taken the time to put the scrapbook of father and LeAnn's wedding together, I decided to do it for Christmas. I scoured the house looking for pictures of Trevor so I could make a book for him too, but I had come up almost empty-handed until LeAnn told me about the box of photos she stored underneath her bed. I asked if it would be okay if I used some of them in a project I was planning. She agreed, saying that she wasn't an arts and crafts kind of person, and the pictures would be lucky to find themselves in an album of any sort someday.

I let Trevor help me with the wedding book. He wasn't very skilled at putting the pages together since his small motor skills had not yet fully developed, but he loved looking at the pictures, especially when they were of him and our father. I worked on his scrapbook after he was in bed at night. Aunt Nora brought over a shoebox that was filled with pictures I had never seen before the morning after I called to ask if she had anything I could use and stayed long enough to see what I was up to.

"I can't believe all the work you are doing," she said as I showed her a few of the pages I had already created. Trevor was in the barn with Copper and Newton.

"I love doing things like this," I told her. "As strange as it might sound, looking at pictures of father actually makes me feel closer to him."

"I get that," she said as tears formed in the corners of her eyes. Aunt Nora was not a demonstrative person by nature, but I had seen much of her tender side since coming home, and family was at the center of everything she did. "I love looking at pictures of my parents. They have been gone for a long time, but when I see their faces, it is almost like time has stood still. I remember everything about my mother, even the way she smelled. It was always of lavender. That's why I grow it I my garden. I hope I will get to see them again someday."

"You will," I promised. "God made families for a reason."

"It's funny you would say that."

I frowned without realizing it.

"Why?" I asked.

"Because I like to believe that they are with us, especially during the holidays. My father died two days before Christmas, and they have been a challenge for me ever since. He loved spending time with his family. Did I ever tell you that he appeared to me a few years after he died?"

A jolt of spontaneous excitement traveled the length of my body, and I inadvertently shivered. "No," I responded. "What was it like?"

"I thought it would be scary, but it was more troubling than anything else because I couldn't understand why it happened."

"Did he just appear, or did he actually say something?"

"He said he had a message for me! I was expecting the twins and feeling very sad because they would never know their grandparents. I had grown up living close to both sets of mine and had spent every moment I could with them. It just didn't seem right that my babies would not know any of theirs. Ned's parents were gone by then too, but you already know that since Grandpa Hawkins died when you must have been two or three."

"I don't remember much about him, but I am sorry for everyone you have lost." I said, feeling an ache in my own heart because my children would never know their grandparents either, unless I married a man whose parents were still living—a man like Ben.

"There is nothing to be sorry about," she said. "It's funny, but I haven't thought about that experience for a long time. I have never even told anyone about it, except for Ned, not even the kids. I must be in a sentimental mood because it only seems right that I share it with you."

I didn't know what to say. She was extending an honor I hadn't expected, a once-in-a-life-time sacred experience.

"Anyway," she continued before I had a chance to respond. "My father came to tell me that he and mother were very happy and had learned something that would allow our family to be together again. He said it was something he hadn't known while he was here, but that I would understand what he was talking about when the time came."

The chills I had been experiencing rushed to every nerve in my body, and I had to wrap my arms around myself for warmth. Aunt Nora's father was talking about the gospel, and he wanted his daughter to know what he now did. Never before had I felt such complete assurance as to why I needed to remain in Australia. My family was too important to lose and I had been given the responsibility of sharing what I had learned while I was gone with them. I would love Ben forever for giving me such a valuable gift, even if I never saw him again.

"You look a little shaken," Aunt Nora said, giving me a worried look. "I hope what I said doesn't make you think I am going a little loony."

I took a deep breath and then let the air slowly out of my lungs giving me more time to think. "Not at all, Aunt Nora. I know exactly what your father was talking about."

"How could you? You were only a child when he died."

"Because I learned the same thing he did—the only way our families can be together forever."

She looked at me and shook her head. "You are talking about this new church you found in America, aren't you?"

My heart was pounding so hard I thought I might be having a heart attack or a stroke. How did I explain what I had both learned and accepted? Aunt Nora was one of the best women I had ever known—honest, hard-working, patient, loving and kind—but she had lived her life with habits and behaviors that would be incredibly hard to break. Still, if God was not in charge, she would never have told me about her vision. Surely, she would be receptive to what I had to tell her once she had time to really think about it.

"Yes!" I told her as the chills I had been experiencing began to subside and my heart quit racing. "I had a similar experience with my mother where she let me know that what I found was right."

"Your mother came to you in a vision?"

"Not exactly. It was more like a strong feeling of her being right next to me. I honestly believed that if I could peel away whatever was separating us I would have been able to see her face."

"She told you that you needed to join this new church?"

"I had already joined, but she confirmed that what I had learned was the only way we could be together as a family again one day."

"That doesn't sound like something a good Catholic girl would suggest, especially one who had already been saved. Father Frederick took care of that with her last rights."

"And you don't think God would require any more of us than receiving last rights if we want to be with him again?"

"I won't pretend to understand God's mysteries, but I trust that Father Frederick knows what he is talking about."

"But what about the marriage vows people take?" I hadn't meant to bring it up since she and Uncle Ned were still co-habituating, but some things have a way of just slipping out. "It says until death do you part. Doesn't that seem a little strange for a religion that is all about families?"

"I suppose it does, but I happen to believe that if two people really love each other they will be together after they are dead, even if they aren't legally married."

I had been rightfully chastised for speaking my mind and should have left it at that, but this might be my only chance to talk about something that meant everything to me.

"I know how much you and Uncle Ned love each other, but death is the end to most relationships unless certain steps are taken."

Her eyebrows furrowed into two vertical lines. "And you believe all this stuff, even though you are no longer with the man you love? I suppose it was Ben who introduced you to this new way of thinking."

"It was, and my heart still aches because we aren't together, but I understand why our breakup happened. We have different missions in life."

"And your mission is to convert all your heathen relatives to some new church so they can be together after they are gone, regardless of the fact that they already believe that is going to happen? It sounds like a mighty big undertaking since there might be people in our family who don't want to be together. I can't exactly see your mother and LeAnn as bosom buddies."

"Maybe not the way things are right now, Aunt Nora, but people change and it only makes sense that the truths lost from the Bible had to be restored if we want to understand everything Christ taught. You do believe there are errors in the Bible, don't you? It couldn't be any other way after all the hand translation over the centuries. I have to believe that God would never leave us in the dark forever about certain things, especially the reason for being born into families."

"That is quite a mouthful," she said. "And even though I have no intention of ever leaving the Catholic faith, I have to admit that I have been curious about your new religion. The Brylee I knew when she was growing up would never have been able to forgive her father for betraying her mother, and she would absolutely never have accepted LeAnn and Trevor as part of her family."

Her comment made me wonder just what kind of a child I had really been. Overly protective of my mother, certainly, but I had never thought of myself as being judgmental, but perhaps running away when things got tough was more telling than I had ever imagined.

"I loved my mother with all my heart, and I won't pretend that seeing another woman in her home using her things wasn't incredibly hard. And it was even harder finding out that I had a little half-brother who was born while she was still alive, but I am not the judge! I want God to forgive me for all the things I have done that are wrong, and I can't expect that if I am not willing to forgive others."

"You really mean that, don't you?"

"Absolutely!" I told her. "I love my family, even if we are one of the most dysfunctional ones in the universe."

"Well, if anyone can bring some very unlikely people together, you can," she said, rising from the kitchen chair she was sitting on. "And I do want to continue our conversation at some point. You have given me a lot to think about, but I have a little soul searching of my own to do before I commit to learning something new. My family has been Catholic for as long as recorded history. We might not do everything right, but our beliefs are strong. That has to count for something too."

I hadn't seen much of Jake since our trip to town, but I knew we were both busy with holiday projects and the never-ending work around the house and ranch. He had flown back into town two days before Christmas to get the things we needed for dinner. I was learning that advanced planning for everything from meals to ranch supplies was necessary since extended outings had to be organized days in advance. They were both costly and time-consuming.

Trevor and I spent many hours in the kitchen trying out new recipes. Some of them met with more success than others.

We made fudge and divinity and even dipped pretzels in white chocolate so we would have a few plates of homemade goodies when family arrived for Christmas dinner. That only included Uncle Ned, Aunt Nora and the twins, but it was good enough for me since they were the only extended family I knew about.

Still, no matter how full I packed each day, I couldn't stop myself from thinking about all recent changes in my life. Losing my father and Ben still kept me awake at night crying, and my conversation with Aunt Nora haunted me. I knew she loved her parents and wanted to be with them again, but I wasn't sure she could accept the gospel the way I had. It defied so much of what the world accepted as being okay. All the rules had been hard for me at first too, but I couldn't dismiss the fact that living them was the only way I could be with my mother again. Now my father was counting on me too.

When we talked on the phone about Christmas day, Aunt Nora was kind and polite, but I sensed hesitancy in our communication that made me wonder if I had overstepped my bounds as a niece. I understood that conversion was an individual experience that couldn't be rushed, and that I might only be the one to plant a seed, but I wanted everyone around me to know that we would indeed see the people we had lost again, and we could be together as a family if we were willing to make certain concessions.

Aside from worrying about that, I often found myself thinking about my mother's family. Perhaps I had relatives who would accept me now that she was no longer around to condemn, but I had no idea how to find them. It seemed such a travesty—parents turning their backs on their children over something as ridiculous as falling in love with the wrong man. I would never do that to mine—if I was ever lucky enough to have them—no matter what they did or how much they hurt me.

Still, it pained me deeply that I had been the kind of daughter who could desert her own father when times got rough. At least God had given me the chance to see him again, and Ben had been instrumental in that too. He had forced me to come home and face my demons, not understanding any more than I did that it would be the end of us.

I still missed him with every fiber of my being and often found myself standing in front of the computer and wanting to send him an email. I endlessly wondered what he and Jennifer were doing, and if his family was happy that they were together again. They had been the golden couple as teenagers and even though they had drifted apart, they could still be happy for always if that was what they chose to do.

And what fate did that leave for me? Becoming a bitter old woman with no one to love in a husbandly way? It was too tragic to even contemplate, but sometimes I just couldn't help myself.

On Christmas Eve, we assembled in LeAnn's bedroom to read the story of Christ's birth from the book of Luke. LeAnn cried as I read, her hand on her slightly swollen stomach where a new little Hawkins was clinging to life.

I had Trevor unwrap his pajamas—short bottoms and a t-shirt—before going to bed. If he was disappointed that his gift wasn't a toy he didn't let it show, especially since I had explained about it being a family tradition when I was a child, and that I planned on taking lots of pictures on Christmas morning.

But with the anticipation of the coming day, it took over an hour of reading before he was able to unwind and fall asleep. I knew he would be up early. He always was. When one lived in the outback, the hours before the sun rose too far in the sky were the most pleasant of the day. I thanked Heavenly Father each night for the invention of air conditioning, and that my father had decided to have it installed in the house. Life was almost unbearable during the summer months without it, and we were smack in the middle of them.

When I left his room, I went directly to the den where my scrapbooking supplies were kept. It would take a couple of hours to finish Trevor's surprise. I hadn't found as many pictures of him as a child as I had hoped even with LeAnn's help, but from now on my phone would be ready to capture every event I could. I might not be using it for calling anyone or texting, but I had taken pictures at the wedding and even a few of my father before his death.

I cherished every moment we had spent together even the bad ones—like when he told me about LeAnn and Trevor, having inoperable cancer and his belief that turning my back on the family religion was wrong. It helped knowing that he now had the option of changing his mind about one of those things. Maybe he already had.

I had been working on a card table so Trevor wouldn't see what I was doing. It wasn't as convenient as spreading everything out on the dining room table like I had done with LeAnn's scrapbook, but I wanted my little brother to be surprised, and he wouldn't be if he saw any of the pages before he opened his gift.

As I put the finishing touches on the last page, I began having doubts about the timing. Christmas was a time for joy. Would looking at pictures of my father doing things he loved take what little joy we were able to find from the day? It would be hard enough celebrating without him.

Jake knocked on the door when I was cleaning up.

"So this is where you have been hiding the past few evenings. I saw the light from outside."

He looked over my shoulder at the binders on the card table. I had brought the one for LeAnn into the den so I could keep them together.

"Have you been looking for me?" I asked.

"Not exactly! I figured you were working on Christmas stuff just like I was."

I scooped a bunch of paper fragments into my hands. "Did you get the bike assembled? I could have helped you with it."

"It was a one-man job, and it's finished. I just wheeled it into the living room."

I thought he would leave after telling me that, but he didn't. He walked over to the card table and began thumbing through some of the pages in one of the binders.

"This is good," he said.

"You don't think it will make them feel bad? After all, tomorrow is supposed to be a celebration."

"Why should it? It is not like any of us will forget that your father isn't here."

I dumped the contents of my hands into the wastebasket near the desk, and turned to watch him. He had never appeared so discouraged before. But how could I help him when I was barely keeping it together myself?

If all the trauma of the past few months had happened before I had joined the church, it would have been very easy to open the locked cabinet where my father kept the hard liquor —brandy, whiskey, bourbon and vodka. That was what so many people used to forget, but alcohol would not bring anyone back. It might dull the pain for a moment or two, but only the Savior could restore the soul.

"I know what you are thinking," Jake said, looking over at me. "If anyone had the right to go on a bender it would be you. I don't know how you have managed these past few months without a few stiff drinks. I certainly couldn't have done it."

"Drinking won't solve anything," I replied, moving away from the desk and unwanted temptation.

"Maybe not, but it sure is nice not having to think for a while. I was about to pour myself a shot or two. Are you sure you won't join me?"

So that was why he had come to my father's den. He wasn't looking for me. He was looking for something to drink that was stronger than beer.

"No, thank you," I said as I walked back to the card table and picked up the binders so I could take them upstairs to wrap.

I needed to get out of the room, and not because I was afraid of being tempted. Liquor had cost my mother her life. I would have liked nothing better than pouring every bottle of the vile stuff down the drain, but that wasn't my call. The house belonged to LeAnn, and Jake was part of her family.

He got a bottle of amber liquid and a shot glass from the cabinet. I watched him from the corner of my eyes.

"You hate me because I drink, don't you?" he said, filling his glass.

"I don't hate you, Jake," I said, not daring to look at him. "You have every right to do whatever you want to with your life."

"But you should hate me," he said, swallowing the contents in one swift movement. "I have done nothing but make your life miserable ever since you got here. It didn't have to be that way, you know."

"Actions run both ways," I told him. "I didn't give you much of a chance either."

"I'm tough," he said, pouring another drink. "But I think you are even stronger than me, especially when it comes to convictions. You live what you believe. I admire you for that. Most women say one thing and do the exact opposite."

He was standing next to my father's desk where he had put the open bottle of whiskey but took a step towards me. He had his drink in one hand, and I felt a moment of panic. Just how many drinks had he already had before coming to the den? He was acting very strangely.

"I need to get these wrapped," I told him, stepping backwards in the direction of the door. I knew he wouldn't hurt me physically, but he could definitely say something that would only make matters between us worse. Unfortunately, so could I.

He swallowed the shot in one gulp again. "You don't have to run off. I am through here. But before I go, I would like to know why you are still so afraid of me."

"I am not afraid of you," I said as my eyes widened and the muscles in my stomach became tense. "It's just a very emotional time, and I don't want to do or say something I might regret."

"Like returning my kiss when we were on the beach? You can't pretend you didn't because I could feel your entire body responding. That kind of sensitivity can't be faked. Do you really regret it that much?"

I looked up at him from over the two binders I held tightly in my arms. "What I regret is falling apart in front of you."

I was putting him down again without meaning to, but that was one of the reasons we needed to keep a safe distance between us.

"It's okay to need other people," he said, touching my arm and sending shivers down my spine. He was more than seductive. He defied everything I believed in. "I have already told you that I am a patient man. I would never force you into doing something against your will, but there is nothing wrong with a simple hug or kiss. We all need to feel connected that way. Whether you believe it or not, you don't have to be alone. That is a choice you consciously made."

"Maybe it was," I admitted as he inched even closer. I could smell the alcohol on his breath. "But I am not very trusting after what happened with Jon."

"You can trust me," he said, leaning his head towards mine. I knew he was going to kiss me, and every nerve in my body began to sizzle. "I won't ever let anyone hurt you again."

His kiss was gentle and warm even though I could taste the whiskey on his lips. But before I could respond, he pulled away.

"I will see you in a few hours, Brylee, and Merry Christmas."

"Merry Christmas," I mumbled as he left the room. I had been tempted to melt into his arms so I could feel alive again, but he was protecting me from myself.

Chapter 12

I heard Trevor get up long before the sun made its appearance. Christmas morning had arrived, and for his sake, I had to pretend to be happy. But it wasn't going to be easy. If I hadn't come home, and if my father hadn't died, I would have been married and spending my first holiday as Ben's wife.

Jake carried LeAnn from the bedroom and put her down on the sofa in the living room so she could watch Trevor enjoy Santa's gifts, and the ones we had wrapped for each other.

Trevor was thrilled with the new bike and other presents that had been left for him underneath the Christmas tree. There were puzzles and books and a small laptop computer with educational games he could play that would help him do better in school. I knew Jake had purchased it and the thought made me sad because, regardless of his faults he would make an amazing father one day.

LeAnn cried when she saw the scrapbook of the wedding I had made for her, and Trevor could not believe all the pictures I had found of him and our father. But my presents were not the only ones to bring tears. Unknown to anyone, except Jake, father had made sure there was a gift for each person he loved underneath the tree.

I thought LeAnn might go into shock her face was so white and her hands shaking so uncontrollably as she opened a diamond pendant, but it was the message inside the box that reduced her to another blitz of tears. She didn't share what he had written, but she was still crying when she asked me to fasten it around her neck. It sparkled in the multi-colored light coming from the Christmas tree.

Trevor ran to her side and gave her a hug and a kiss. It was a simple gesture of both adoration and affection, but it brought unwanted feelings of both sorrow and joy to me. If the people I was growing to love so much would just listen to the message I had to share, they would know that father was still part of our lives, and we could all be part of the same forever family. I trusted that God knew how to do that, even if I didn't.

I don't know where father found it, but Trevor got a large model horse that looked just like Thunder—the horse he had raised from a colt that now belonged to my little brother. LeAnn read the message out loud. I hated listening to a letter that had been written for someone else, but Trevor was too young to read it himself.

"Dear Trevor," father had written. *"I don't know how to say goodbye to the son who means everything to me. I wish I could be there to watch you grow up and have sons of your own that will keep the Hawkins' family name alive, but I will be watching you from heaven. Take good care of your mum and sister for me, and ride Thunder often when you are old enough to do it by yourself. He likes you. I could tell that the first time your mum put you in the saddle with me. Those were some of the best days of my life. Listen to what your mum has to say, even if you don't like it. She will help you grow into an honorable and responsible man. I love you. I just wish I could hold you in my arms again and never let you go. My love forever and always, Father."*

I couldn't look at anyone in the room. Tears of remorse were falling so rapidly I could barely see my hands in front of my face. When Jake touched my shoulder and then handed me a small box, I thought I might actually faint.

"You don't have to open it now," he said. "These gifts and messages are private. I was just the messenger."

I could feel his eyes on me, even though I didn't look up. Why did he have to be so nice when I was still trying so hard to loathe him?

"But I want to see what father gave Brylee," Trevor said, crossing the short distance between us with his new horse in his hands.

"It's okay, Jake," I said as my fingers began lifting the edges of the scotch tape that kept the wrapping paper in place. The ring inside literally took my breath away. It was a large, perfectly cut emerald, surrounded by diamonds and must have cost a small fortune. Its beauty-defied explanation, and I immediately knew where I had seen it before—on the hand of my great, great grandmother in the picture I had seen in the attic.

The note he had written was short, yet poignant.

"Dear Brylee," it began. *"The thing I regret most in dying before my time is not getting to know my beautiful, compassionate daughter. I never understood about family when you were growing up, and I neglected you terribly. My heart is filled with gratitude that you came home when you did. Nothing would make me happier than giving you away at your wedding. You will be an incredible mother. I know this because of the way you treat Trevor. Never doubt my love for you. You will always be my little girl, and I wish I could be there to protect you from all hurt and pain. Let your new family into your heart. They will be there for you when I can't. I love you with all my heart, Father."*

I took the ring from the box and placed it on the third finger of my right hand. It was a perfect fit.

"It is beautiful," LeAnn said, figuring the diamond around her neck. "Your father must have kept it in the safety deposit box at the bank. I have never seen it before."

"It belonged to my great, great grandmother Hawkins. She was wearing it in a painting in the attic," I told her as tears sprung from my eyes and ran down my cheeks. I couldn't help but wonder if she was mentally calculating the cost between our two gifts. Father had purchased hers because it was new, but mine was nothing short of priceless. I tried not to read anything more into it than that.

"Then it is something you will always cherish."

"I will," I told her. "I never realized how important family was until I came home."

"And I hope you will always stay here with Trevor, me and the new baby, and of course, Jake, unless he finds some sweet young thing and decides to leave us."

"That is not going to happen," he responded, giving me a look that made my face turn a shade redder. "I promised Jack I would stay here to see my nephew grow into a man. Besides, I like it out here. I am not sure I could live in town again. Edna is too confining and I have already seen the rest of the continent, even if it was just from the air."

"You will change your mind when the right girl comes along," LeAnn told him. "But for now, I am just glad that we are all here together. It's what Jack wanted. Why don't you open what he left for you? There is still one gift under the tree, and the rest of us have already received ours."

Jake suddenly looked more uncomfortable than I did. "It's not something I am sure I should keep."

"Why not?" LeAnn asked. "You haven't even opened it."

"I don't have to. I already know what is inside."

"How could you possibly know that, unless he told you?"

Jake picked up the gift and tore off the paper. Inside another small box lay the pocket watch that had belonged to my paternal grandfather. Father always kept it in his pocket and looked at it many times each day.

"See," he said, holding it up so we could all get a good look at it again. He didn't seem to notice that a slip of paper had fallen to the floor in the process. "This belongs to Ned or Trevor, not me. I am not even a legitimate member of this family."

"Don't say that, Jake," LeAnn told him, looking a little shaken herself. "He gave it to you because he wanted you to have it. Just read what the note said."

Trevor picked it up and tried to hand it to him. "That is something I cannot do. Give it to your mum."

Trevor obediently handed the note to his mother. I couldn't look at anyone when she started to read.

"I know exactly what you are going to say when you open this, Jake. You will claim that I shouldn't be giving it to you because you are not a real member of the family, but that couldn't be further from the truth. You took care of LeAnn and Trevor when I couldn't, and you will continue taking care of them when I am gone. I have relied on your generosity and selfless service more times than I can count these past few years, and you have never asked for a single thing in return. If that doesn't define family, I don't know what does. I want you to wear this pocket watch like I did, and let its built-in compass show you the way if you should ever get lost. It happens to the best of us at times, but there is always a way back if you want something badly enough. Love, Jack"

Jake cleared his throat most loudly.

"Put it in your pocket," Trevor told him, rushing to his side. "Now we all have something special from father."

Jake looked over his head at his sister. "Are you really sure it's okay, LeAnn?" he asked.

"I think you have just received your answer. There are no selfish people in this family, and it was Jack's wanted to give. Wear it with pride the way he wanted you to."

Jake turned it over in his hand and then slid it into one of the front pockets of the jeans he was wearing. "I am still going to talk to Ned about it," he said.

"Do what you feel is right," she responded. "But I am not sure I would want to meet Jack in heaven if I didn't value something he had left to me."

I wasn't sure what she was getting at, but it didn't really matter. My father had selected something of significance for each one of us. What we did with it was up to us.

I began gathering up torn wrapping paper while Jake carried LeAnn back to the bedroom, and Trevor carried his presents up the stairs to his room where he could put them with the rest of his toys. I had promised to teach him how to play the games on the Game Boy I had given him as soon as everyone had gone home after Christmas dinner. Jake would take care of the educational games on the computer.

I was stuffing the last of the paper in a large, black garbage bag when Jake walked towards me and smiled.

"I just wanted to thank you again for the wallet. You didn't have to get me anything."

"I wanted to. You have done so much for all of us."

"I do have something for you," he continued. "Though after seeing the ring your father gave you, I am a little embarrassed to hand it over."

I looked down at the ring on my finger. It wasn't something I would wear very often, and it would be much safer back in the bank, but I loved the fact that my father had given me something of great sentimental worth.

"I love his gift and will cherish it always because of who it belonged to and who gave it to me but I never knew my grandparents, let alone my great, great grandparents. I wish I had."

"Sometimes life really sucks," he said, handing me a small wrapped box. "I found the rock the second night we spent in the outback together."

But it wasn't just a rock he gave me. He had polished it until it literally glowed and then mounted it on a chain I could wear around my neck.

"It's beautiful," I exclaimed, turning it over in my hand. "It looks like half of it is gold."

"It is," he said. "I took it to a jeweler in town before polishing it."

"Does that mean there is gold on our property?"

The thought excited me. Maybe our worrying days about finances were over.

"Could be, but that stone could have come from anywhere," he clarified. "It could have been dropped by an old prospector, or it could have been carried here from miles away by one of the floods we've had."

"I guess it doesn't really matter where it came from. It only matters that you gave it to me, and I love it." I stood on my toes and kissed his cheek. "You are an amazing man, Jake Johnson."

"I am a simple man," he said. "And when I love someone, it is with all my heart."

"I loved with all my heart too," I replied. "But love doesn't always last and broken hearts take time to mend."

"I know you are still hurting, Brylee. Hell, it took me years to get over Wendy, and sometimes I wonder if I am over her yet. But there does come a time when the past has to be buried, or one will never have a future."

He picked up the garbage bag and left me alone in the living room. If it weren't for the gospel, I would run after him and let him know that my feelings for him had changed. But if I did that, there would be no turning back, and the thought of all the women he had been with over the years and the ones he was seeing now terrified me. I wasn't sure I could handle it if he found someone else after he was through with me.

Uncle Ned and his family came for dinner around four. It was pleasant having the house filled with people and laughter again. NJ and Molly talked about college life and all the girls and guys who were part of their lives. I thought I might be jealous as they went on and on about the parties they had been to and the dates they had been on, but I wasn't. I had moved past that part of my life because of Ben, and the thought of going back to it made my stomach churn.

It was hard believing I had ever been their age, even though they were only four years younger than me. Losing both of my parents and the man that I loved had put me years beyond my calendar age emotionally, but I did feel one moment of jealousy before they left.

Molly had given Jake an expensive sweater that he was instructed to wear when he went to Sydney to take her out to dinner. That might not have been so bad if she hadn't climbed onto his lap as he sat in a chair by the window, and planted a long, hard kiss on his lips. It left me so emotionally shaken I had to leave the room. NJ followed me.

"Don't let Molly upset you, cuz. She is like that with every attractive bloke she meets, and it doesn't help that she's had a little too much bubbly to drink."

"I am not so sure about that," I told him, trying to disguise my feelings as nothing more than cousinly concern. "I have watched the way she acts around him. She is interested in him as more than just a friend."

"So she wants things to get physical. It really is no big deal. That is so 20th century."

"Not to me," I said. "I believe in the sanctity of marriage and what that means."

"Then it might be a long, lonely winter for you because there are not that many really good mates available—married or otherwise—between here and the coast. I really am sorry it didn't work out with that bloke in the states. Why don't you come to Sydney for New Year's Eve? There will be some great parties, and I could introduce you around. I know Molly is going to try to convince Jake to come. You really need to get away from this dreary ranch. It will suck the life right out of you if you don't."

I was glad when they left. It was hard pretending to be happy when I wasn't. As soon as all the tableware had been loaded in the dishwasher, I went up to my room and closed the door. I needed time to feel sorry for myself, and then regroup so I could handle what came next.

Trevor needed me right now because his mother couldn't get out of bed, but once the baby was safely here and LeAnn was on her feet again, I might just take a trip to Sydney to see if there was anything left in the world for me.

Chapter 13

Bright and early the next morning, I asked Trevor if he wanted to take a ride with me. I couldn't get past the idea that there might be gold on the ranch. It was the only distraction I had. But my little brother said he would rather stay home and play with his new toys, so I asked Jake if he would be around for a few hours so I could go by myself.

He objected to my riding alone, especially since I couldn't tell him where I was going. But how could I explain that I wanted to see if I could find more rocks like the one he had made my necklace from? He would think I had lost my mind. Besides, it was highly unlikely that I would be able to find the place where we had spent our second night while herding sheep to Uncle Ned's for shearing. All the hills on the ranch looked the same unless one were familiar with the landmarks, and the flood had destroyed many of those. But even if I couldn't find the place where we had camped, I needed time alone to think.

There was a slight breeze blowing when I left the house about 7:30 that morning. I had a canteen of water and a few granola bars with me. I told Jake I would be back around noon, but not to worry unless I didn't show up before dark. I was preparing for a good cry. I had been stuffing my feeling away for months, and if I didn't release them, I feared my own sanity would soon be part of my past like so many other things.

But once I was a mile or so from the house, some of the heaviness inside my heart lifted, and I could actually hear birds singing. This was my time—something I had missed since coming home—and I needed to make a few decisions. I had gone from being an engaged woman planning her fairy tale wedding to a member of a family I had known nothing about before my arrival. Since then, I had been forced to accept my father's affair, a half-brother, my responsibility for the ranch's financial success, a marriage, my father's death, LeAnn's disappearance and pregnancy, my confusion over my feelings for Jake, surviving a flood, the task of raising Trevor when his mother couldn't and losing Ben. When I thought about all the changes in my life, I was overcome with a weariness that had nothing to do with age.

My horse, Rupert, was glad to be out of the pasture, and I gave him the lead as we raced away from the ranch down the long driveway. My hat, that was supposed to shield my face from the burning rays of the sun, blew off, but I didn't stop to retrieve it. I loved the feeling of freedom and motion that came as I turned my horse in the direction of the closest hills.

I was riding farther away from the ranch than I had ever done by myself before, but it was exhilarating. Rupert's hoofs stirred up little clouds of dust as we galloped along. I knew better than to take him into the tall grass and undergrowth during the coolest part of the day. Snakes liked the damp and would not hesitate striking a horse if it got too close. There was a stream further back in the hills fed by the Darling River where he could drink and eat fresh grass.

I'm not sure what I expected to happen as I lost sight of the ranch house and all that was familiar. Perhaps an epiphany that would let me know where my life was headed, and what I needed to do to earn the blessings I most desired. But nothing unusual happened, except a feeling of peace as I began reciting in my mind the blessings I still had after all the loss and confusion during my months back in Australia. I had rediscovered my family, accepted a new one and made peace with my father. I still had the gospel and a few good friends like Emma, Margaret Mitchell and the branch president in Edna. I had inherited half of a ranch, along with the responsibility of making sure it remained in the family long after I was gone. I even had a place to live and all the necessities of life as long as I chose to take advantage of them.

So what if I felt overwhelmed at times? It was better than having too much time to think about things that could not be changed. What was happening half a world away was out of my hands, most likely forever now.

I could have spent the rest of the day riding and thinking and looking for fool's gold, but it all seemed rather pointless once I recalled that this life wasn't meant for pleasure and easy living. I was here to be tested to see if I would do all that Heavenly Father required without constant complaint or simply giving up. If I truly believed he had a plan for my life, I would accept this rough patch as necessary refinement. There really was no time for a pity-party when life was viewed that way, especially when there was so much work to do.

So after eating a granola bar and taking a long drink of water as I watched a few sheared sheep climb slowly up an incline towards better pasture, I turned Rupert around and headed back home. I would take Trevor up the hill behind the house to see if we could find the remnants of the slide I remembered from childhood. Maybe Jake could help us repair it. That would give me something constructive to do besides worrying about LeAnn, the baby and why my life hadn't turned out the way I expected it to.

I made it home a little after twelve, rubbed Rupert down and made sure he had plenty to eat and drink. He was a great horse and an even better friend because he accepted me just the way I was. I loved the feel of his soft nose and the way his black eyes seemed to bore into mine when we looked at each other. He was steady, reliable and affectionate. I wanted him to know that I loved him every bit as much as Trevor loved Thunder.

My little brother and Jake were sitting at the kitchen table eating sandwiches when I walked into the kitchen, hot and dirty from my ride. They both looked up when the screen door slammed shut.

"You're back early," Jake said, taking in my disheveled appearance.

I walked to the sink to get a cool drink of water.

"I thought I was right on time. I said I would be back around noon."

"I guess I just figured you would be gone longer. You looked pretty upset this morning."

When I didn't answer, he continued. "Ned wants me to come over and help with some fencing. I told him I couldn't come until you got back."

"So I guess that means you can go now. Thanks for being here with LeAnn."

"My pleasure," he responded through narrowed eyes. "It shouldn't take long. Nora went back to Sydney with the twins for a few days."

I pulled my top lip into my mouth and opened the cupboard to get a plate so I could fix myself something to eat too. I wished my own mother had missed me enough to come for a visit when I was away at boarding school, but she always had an excuse when an invitation was extended. It was my father who made sure I had what I needed, including transportation to and from the ranch.

Why hadn't I recognized his love and concern before running away? I had always thought my mother was the better parent because she spent more time with me when I was little, but there was more than one way to show devotion.

"I will be back in a few hours if there is something you need me to do," Jake said as he put his plate and glass in the sink. "If not, I guess I will see you at dinner."

I sent Trevor to LeAnn's room to get her dishes while I ate. The bread seemed to stick in my throat as the heaviness in my heart returned. So much for counting my blessings! I wasn't a new person. I was still a very confused and hurting one who had no idea how to move forward again.

"How about doing something a little different this afternoon?" I asked Trevor when he returned to the kitchen.

"Like what?" he responded in anything but an enthusiastic tone. Something was really bothering him.

"I thought we could take a hike up the hill behind the house. Did you know there used to be a big slide that went from the top clear down to the back yard?"

His frown deepened. "Did you slide on it?"

"A few times," I said. "My mother didn't like me to get dirty, but father and Uncle Ned used to take me up there. I had to be really careful because the slide was narrow, and I couldn't hold onto the sides or I could get splinters or burns."

"Doesn't sound like any fun to me."

It was time for my own brow to pucker. Apparently, I should have started with the more positive aspects first. "But it was fun, Trevor! I would sit between a grownup's legs and let the wind whip through my hair all the way down. I also screamed out in a joyous kind of fear because I had never moved so fast. It was better than any other ride I have ever been on."

"Even the big ones at the fair? Father took me there once, but I only got to ride on baby ones. I wasn't tall enough for anything else."

I forced myself not to fall into another bout of sorrow because our father had never taken me to the fair.

"Then this could be much better than that because we could slide down it more than just once a year and it wouldn't cost us anything."

"I guess if it was that much fun, it wouldn't hurt to find it. Could I ride between your legs?"

"Most definitely! Maybe we can even talk your Uncle Jake into going with us, but I am almost positive it will need some repairs first."

"Oh," he said with a shrug of his shoulders. "I thought we could go down it today."

"We have to find it first. I used to be able to see it from the kitchen window, but brush must be covering it now."

"Do I need to put on my heavy boots? I don't want to run into another snake."

"Neither do I! They are pretty disgusting."

"You were really scared when we saw it, weren't you?" he asked, and I knew he was remembering his own fear when the Eastern Brown had moved slowly in front of him.

"Yes, I was scared," I admitted. "I am not overly fond of snakes or anything else that crawls around where it shouldn't."

"I thought grownups weren't supposed to be afraid of anything."

"Grownups are afraid lots of things. They just don't like to admit it."

"Mum's scared. I can see it in her eyes when I ask about the baby."

So that was his concern. He was worried about his mother and the baby that wouldn't be born for a few months yet.

I put my hands on his shoulders and made him look up at me.

"Both your mother and the baby will be fine as long as she stays in bed like the doctor told her to."

"What if she doesn't? She might run away again if something happens to the baby. It is the best gift father ever gave her, even better than the diamond necklace. She said so."

I felt my heart plummet. It was so easy for adults to say things in the wrong way, and so easy for children to misunderstand.

"Your mother is not going to leave again," I told him, hoping it was true. "She knows her life is right here in the ranch with you."

He didn't say anything else as we left the house, but he followed closely behind as I climbed slowly up the hill through tall, dry grass and a constant swarm of insects that buzzed around our faces and found their way into every crevice of our exposed bodies.

"How you doing, little brother?" I called out as I stopped to catch my breath. I wished I had called Uncle Ned to ask where it was before starting out. It had been nearly fifteen years since I had slid down it with my father. Maybe it had even been dismantled. But one thing was certain. This wasn't the activity I had planned on sharing with Trevor. It was miserable on the hillside, and we might not even find what we were looking for.

I waited for him to catch up. He was panting, and his face was covered with dust, sweat and a few red spots where insects had bitten him. All signs of moisture from the flood had been gone for weeks now.

"I think this was a bad idea," I told him as he swatted at more bugs that had flown out of the brush. "I don't remember it being like this when I was your age."

"We can still look for it if you want to," he said.

I looked down at him with more than adoration and compassion. He was just a little boy who wanted to please everyone, and I shouldn't have forced him to come with me. I felt terrible inside.

"Let's go home," I responded. "We can look for the slide another day."

"Will you show me how to play the Game Boy?" he asked as we started back down. "You were going to do it last night, but Uncle Jake told me not to bother you because you were tired."

So that was another reason he was unhappy. I had broken my promise to him because I was upset and had hidden away in my room after everyone left. I wouldn't do that again. Nothing was more important right now than my little brother.

I hoped no one would have to know about our ill-fated trip up the hillside. I put calamine lotion on Trevor's face and arms as soon as he got out of the shower, but the insect bites were still visible, so I went to apologize to LeAnn for taking him with me.

"I could have told you about the slide if you had asked me," she said. "It was still there a couple of years ago. Your father wanted to fix it up for Trevor, but I told him it was too dangerous. Little boys have no fear, and I didn't want him going up there by himself."

"I would never let him do that."

"You can't watch him 24-7, Brylee, and I don't blame you for wanting to share something from your childhood with him. I might feel differently if I could see for myself that it is really safe." She looked down at her hands. "I just feel so helpless. You shouldn't be left with the responsibility of raising my son."

"I love being with him."

"And I appreciate that more than you will ever know, but he is still my child. I'm not sure I will ever forgive myself for not being there for him after your father died."

"You were in survival mode."

"I used to criticize your behavior all the time before you came back, did you know that?"

Her statement caught my attention.

"No, but that was to be expected. You didn't know me."

"I didn't have to know you. I loved your father and he was devastated when you left. I couldn't understand why you would run away when you had to know how much he needed you. I even blamed you because he walked out on me."

"Really," I said. I had done everything in my power to make her life easier, yet she almost sounded like she hated me. Something was definitely going on in this house. We should be celebrating the season instead of lashing out at each other.

She must have noticed the stunned look on my face.

"I don't blame you for running away anymore, Brylee, and I have only myself to blame for what happened in my own life, but no one likes to admit sins or failures." She looked over at the magazine about having babies she had been reading. "And I don't know why I brought it up now. I just get so angry sometimes. My children should not have to grow up without their father, and I shouldn't have to be a widow when I am still young."

"You're right," I said. It was the first time she had mentioned the new baby as being a viable child. At least she must be feeling more confident about its birth.

"It's just so unfair. Why do other people get all the good luck?'

"I can't answer that," I said with a shake of my head. Her life might seem like a train wreck, but at least she'd had some happy years with my father and was going to have another child that was his. I had lost my chance at marriage and might never know the blessing of motherhood.

Still, I thought about what she had said as I walked back to my room later that night. We were all going through a bitter time of adjustment, but as adults it was easier to talk about what we were feeling. Trevor didn't know how to do that yet. His thoughts and feelings came out in third person as if he was talking about one of his animals. I decided it was important to help him understand what was happening inside so he would never want to run away like both his mother and I had done.

"Do you want to go for a walk?" I asked him three days after Christmas.

He sighed. "Is it up the hill again?"

"No. We have seen plenty of that place for a while. I was thinking about going to the cemetery to talk to father."

"You can't talk to him. He isn't there."

"I know that, but I really miss him and feel closer to him when I am there. I want to tell him that I love him."

He looked at me with the expression of an injured animal and ran from the room crying. I was so shaken by his reaction that it took a moment or two before I was able to follow him.

The door to his bedroom was shut, and I asked him if I could come in.

"I don't want you to," he said.

"Why not, Trevor? I didn't mean to make you cry."

"You didn't make me cry. I am busy talking to Copper."

I felt worse than ever. For the second time in three days I had made a huge blunder when it came to my little brother. Maybe everyone would be better off if I just left again. LeAnn blamed me for hurting my father by running away. Jake was angry with me because I couldn't return his feelings, even though I was beginning to think I might want to. And I had violated Trevor's trust by not playing with him on Christmas day.

If making everyone around me miserable was part of Satan's plan to keep me from sharing the gospel, he was certainly doing a bang-up job of it. If things kept going the way they were, I would alienate everyone in the town of Edna by New Year's Eve.

I went back to my own room and flung myself across the bed. If I could just talk to Ben, he would know what to do. But that wasn't an option now. I had made certain of that by breaking our engagement.

My own tears were harsh and bitter. LeAnn didn't have the corner on disappointment. I was a young woman in the prime of her life. I shouldn't be stuck on a desolate ranch in the middle of nowhere with people who would never understand where I was coming from. I deserved to have a life of my own. I wasn't responsible for my parent's mistakes.

But as the tears dried, I knew not everyone got a happy ending in this life. God had given me a sacred responsibility I couldn't neglect if I didn't want to end up in the belly of a whale like Jonah. He had been trying to neglect his responsibilities too.

I must have fallen asleep because when I opened my eyes, Trevor was sitting on the bed beside me. He was holding Copper in his arms.

"I'm sorry, Brylee," he said, as fresh tears started to fall. "I didn't mean to be mad at you. I miss father too."

I sat up and pulled him into my arms. "I know you do, Trevor. Bad things just happen sometimes."

We sat there for the longest time as I kissed his soft, rather messed-up hair. I would have given anything to take away his pain, but the best I could do was share it. Maybe someday, we would both understand.

Fortunately, no one at the ranch seemed interested in celebrating the arrival of a new year. Uncle Ned was meeting Aunt Nora in Edna after her trip to attend a party, and the twins were in Sydney with their friends. I almost asked Jake what he was going to do but thought better of it. My feelings for him seemed to be changing a little more each day, especially after he had given me the necklace for Christmas. I wore it underneath my clothing where no one would see. It helped me believe that I had not made such a huge mistake by staying where I was. He left in his plane in the early afternoon and didn't come back until late the next morning. I didn't ask where he had gone and he didn't give me an explanation.

Chapter 14

The next two weeks were routine. I got up each morning hoping that my life would have changed miraculously while I slept. I had never felt so alone. Trevor was my one spot of joy during the day, but even he was becoming restless with his mother still in bed. I tried to do something special with him each afternoon, but there was only so much food we could cook and after the near disaster in trying to find the slide, I didn't want to take him anywhere on foot again.

LeAnn kept him with her several hours each morning so his schooling could continue. It was my job to make sure she had everything she needed the night before so she could review the lessons before she gave them to him.

I suggested that I take over some of the responsibility of helping Trevor with his math and reading, but she refused. It was the only thing she could do right now to help him adjust to a new kind of normal that none of us really wanted. I understood her need to be part of his daily life, but it left me with two or three hours each day when I had nothing concrete to do.

There had been no additions to the ranch's financial accounts since the sheep had been sheared and some of them sold. It reaffirmed my belief that the job my father had asked me to do could be done from anywhere in the world. Jake had to be paid each month, as did the utilities and other assorted bills, but other than that, my father's accounts looked almost identical to what they had been when he had trained me.

I still hadn't taken any money for myself, although there were a few things I really needed. I had left all my earthly possessions with Ben and the cost of shipping them back would be far greater than their worth, but I was still living out of a suitcase in my own home. Even the few things I had found in the attic were becoming threadbare. Uniforms had been required at boarding school and I had taken most all the regular clothes in my closet when running away. That was nearly six years ago now, and I had purchased little for myself since then that wasn't absolutely necessary.

Perhaps that was part of the reason for my sporadic despondency. I still felt like my life was in Los Angeles with Ben, and even knowing how unhealthy it was to live in the past, I couldn't seem to stop myself from doing it.

But all that changed one Friday morning three weeks after Christmas. I needed a change of scenery to clear my head, so I took one of the motorbikes out for a ride while Trevor was having his lessons. I told LeAnn what I was doing so she wouldn't worry and Jake was in the bunkhouse if she needed anything. Trevor pleaded to go with me, but his mother was firm when it came to his studies.

I had long since given up trying to keep a hat on to save my complexion, but Jake was adamant that we wear a helmet and protective clothing when we were on the motorbikes.

At the end of the driveway, I shifted into first and turned my bike in the direction of the outback's interior. I could have ridden into Edna but it was too far and I didn't feel like talking to anyone, not even Emma who called every day to see how we were doing. It was the second time in less than a month that I had felt it necessary to be away from the house to try to sort out my feelings and figure out how to accomplish what God intended for me to do. Presenting the gospel to my family was not going as smoothly as hoped. Aunt Nora hadn't broached the subject with me again, and I hadn't been able to take Trevor to church. Something always came up that prevented it.

For the first few miles, I did nothing but let the anxiety about my future slip from my body until I felt a sort of peace enter my soul. I wasn't a typical Latter-day Saint girl—raised in the church, without major blemish, and deserving the husband and family she had spent her life preparing for. In a nutshell, I wasn't a girl like Jennifer.

I had too much baggage, and as long as I let it control me, I would never be really happy again. But how could I build a new life when the past and the present had collided with such force that I felt incapable of moving beyond where I stood? I wanted to get over Ben and share the gospel with my new family, but could never get past a rather lame introduction. Life would definitely be easier if I returned to Catholicism where nothing was demanded except confession and a few Hail Mary's if I did something wrong.

I found a secluded spot near enough a bog to sit down without being scraped by dry brush and grasses but far enough away not to have to worry about the insects and animals that might come to water. People had so many misconceptions about Australia. Kangaroos and Koala bears did run free, as did feral animals like camels, brumbies, pigs, foxes, wildcats, dingos and rabbits—most of which the government spent millions a year trying to eradicate because they destroyed the environment. That meant few people were likely to see them, unless they knew where to look.

I had never seen a camel except at the zoo, and I hadn't seen a kangaroo since my father had shown me a family of them when I was a child. Like the people who inhabited the outback, the animals were solitary creatures that stayed out of sight and preferred being alone.

In some ways, I felt a great deal like them. Relationships were difficult, but they were also what separated humans from God's other creatures. I watched a flock of cockatoos fly into the branches of a nearby Mulga tree whose blue-gray color helped keep the heat from soaking in. They were strikingly beautiful birds with vibrant colors of red, green, gold and blue and incredibly cheerful cries. They seemed to be in stark contrast to everything else around me including the tumbleweeds.

I was so tired of living in a sunburned realm and seeing little but shades of brown, tan and red. I wanted to see the waterfalls, the small oasis, the lush greenery, the sugar cane fields, the diamond mines, the brilliant ocean and interesting animals that existed in other parts of the country. Even the ants, lizards, spiders and snakes on the ranch lacked color, unless they were of the poisonous variety.

I wanted to feel alive again, but that meant finding a way to reconnect with Ben or give in to my escalating feelings for Jake. That was something I simply could not do. His overnight trip to town on New year's Eve told me that there was a still a whole lot I didn't even want to know about him.

I was gone for less time than anticipated. Facing my fears and disappointments in solitude was no easer than facing them in the house, so I decided to see what I could come up with that might taste palatable for dinner. I was learning my way around a kitchen, but most of my offerings were still far less edible than what LeAnn or Aunt Nora fixed.

Trevor came running out to the shed when he heard me return to the ranch.

"The Postie's been here!" he exclaimed. "And he brought four huge boxes for you."

My stomach tightened to the point of nausea.

"Where did they come from?" I asked.

"The United States. Can I open them, Brylee? We have never gotten boxes like that before."

I forced an apprehensive smile. I knew what the boxes contained—all of my earthly belongings. If I hadn't known before that Ben and I were through, I knew it now. He was making our break complete. He didn't even want my things around to remind him that I had ever been a part of his life. In the almost debilitating pain Trevor's news brought, it never crossed my mind that at least he still cared enough to return them at great personal expense, rather than just give them away.

I slammed the door to the shed more forcefully than necessary after putting my hemet away. My emotions were all over the place, and I wanted to be alone when I opened them, but I didn't know how to tell Trevor when he was so excited by such an unexpected occurrence. My hands were literally trembling when he led me into the house where the boxes were neatly stacked against one wall in the entry.

"It's just my clothing and stuff," I told him, feeling more irritable and despondent than ever.

His disappointment was evident. "I thought there would be something fun inside."

"Nothing fun," I assured him. "How did your lessons go today?"

His shoulders moved up and down while he frowned. "Okay, I guess, but I would much rather go riding with you."

"We will go again soon, I promise. But it is important to learn everything you can. Do you know how many years I spent in school once I left the ranch?"

"No," he mumbled.

"Eight and counting. We should love to learn because we will be doing it all our lives."

I took him outside to shoot a few baskets although I was very bad at it. I needed time to prepare mentally before opening the boxes. Ben had been my first love. I wondered if he would be my last.

When Jake got home from Uncle Ned's, I asked him to help me carry the boxes up to my room.

"I am sorry," he said as he climbed the stairs with the biggest one in his arms. I was following with one of the smallest.

"This isn't your fault," I told him. "I am the one who messed up."

"I wish you would quit talking like that. You did nothing wrong, except falling in love with some bloody awful bloke who was never worthy of you."

"Ben is a good man and will make a wonderful husband and father."

"So you keep reminding me," he said, dumping the box on my bedroom floor. "I will bring the rest of them up for you."

He was upset with me and had every right to be. Once again, I had spoken my mind and offended him. I couldn't keep running back to Ben—even in my mind. It wasn't fair to anyone, and it was keeping me from moving ahead even when I had no place to go.

Ben had labeled the boxes 1, 2, 3 and 4. I wondered why. It didn't seem like it should matter which one I opened first. The experience was going to be excruciating anyway. After cutting through the packing tape with a pair of scissors and folding the flaps of the first box back, I saw an envelope with my name on it.

I wanted to throw it away unopened, but I couldn't.

"Dear Bry," it began. *"It has taken me a long time to get to the point where I could send your things back. I have done little besides think about you and all we shared before you went home. I kept thinking you would call back and say that you had changed your mind—that you were willing to give us another chance."*

"Another chance," I thought as I rubbed the tears from my cheeks and tried not to cry out in angst. Did he really want me to come back to him?

"For the first few weeks after we talked, I was in so much pain I could barely go to work. I kept thinking about why you hadn't trusted me enough to share something so personal, although I still believe I had a right to know. You had been violated in the most inhumane way imaginable, and it must have completely destroyed your faith in men—me included since we hadn't been together long enough for you to feel completely safe again. I should have waited for you to explain instead of nursing my wounded ego. I wish I had beat that guy to a pulp while I had the chance. Now, all I want is to see him put behind bars for the rest of his life, but that can't happen unless you press charges and I would never ask you to come back for that.

"You never did anything wrong! You were a victim of a violent crime, and I never should have blamed you for anything. I hate myself for doing that, and I don't blame you for not wanting to see me again. I wasn't being the supportive, loving fiancé you deserved. I should never have listened to anyone but you.

"After much soul-searching, I now realize that we can't change the past no matter how much we might want to. Perhaps we both had different missions in life all along, and that is why you couldn't come home. You have so much missionary work to do amongst your own family, and you can't do that if you are living back here with me. That doesn't mean I will ever forget you because I won't.

"I still hear your laughter and see your smile when I close my eyes, but I respect your wishes in wanting to do what your father asked. I wish I could be there to help you but know that my mission is here. I will always love you. It's different from how I feel about Jennifer. She and I have been friends forever and we get along great, but you will always be the girl of my dreams—he one just out of reach. You are always in my thoughts and prayers. Be happy! Stay safe!

And let the Holy Spirit guide you. Love forever and always, Ben"

So that was it! The numbness in my body descended to all my extremities, rendering me unable to move. He was going on with his life with Jennifer.

"P.S. The little box contains a Christmas present. It's just one of the things I wanted to give you."

I pulled Capri's and shorts, t-shirts and skirts from the largest box until I found the small gift that had been wrapped in Christmas paper. I set it on my bed not having the emotional strength to see what it contained. It would be my last tie with Ben.

I opened the next box. Ben had sent my pictures, jewelry, shoes, school projects, CDs, and a few of the small nick knacks I had been collecting for our home. I had so few personal belongings and had always lived in furnished apartments because it had taken every penny I earned just to pay tuition and buy books. I had lived on instant oatmeal, Ramen noodles and macaroni and cheese and had often wondered how my body could be healthy existing on a diet of carbs, but I was the epitome of a poor college student until I met Becky and Ben.

I was hanging the last of my meager assortment of clothing in the closet when I heard Trevor's knock.

"Can I come in now?" he asked.

I opened the door, and he walked straight past me to the items that were still laying on the bed.

There we so many things I needed, but I had used a huge chunk of the money in my account to pay for Christmas and still couldn't justify giving myself a salary when Jake did most of the hardest work. I spent ninety percent of my time taking care of LeAnn and Trevor and the housework that never seemed to be done.

But once the baby arrived and LeAnn was back on her feet, I would spend more time in the outback. I had no idea where the animals were allowed to roam or where to find sufficient food and water for them. I was literally at Jake's mercy. He held the keys to the ranch's success or failure. For all I knew animals could be dying every day, and I would never know about it unless he decided to tell me.

"Are these your pictures?" Trevor asked, and I looked over at him sitting cross-legged on my bed with a small photo album in his hands.

"You can look at them if you want to," I said. "But you won't know anyone."

I had no desire to see the smiling faces of anyone from L.A. Ben and I had been so happy together, and looking into his eyes—even in a photograph—would only make my loneliness more acute. And then there was his letter. I wasn't sure which of the things he had written affected me most—the fact that he would always love me or that he and Jennifer would likely spend eternity together when he should have been spending it with me.

My future had been so bright and perfect before I came home. Now I was wallowing in a quagmire of doubt and uncertainty. I had no money, no friends, no place to go, and a man I could barely talk to controlling the livelihood of the people I had grown to love. My life couldn't be more complex if my worst enemy had planned it.

"Is this Ben?" Trevor asked, holding out the small album to me. "He looks nice."

"He is nice," I said, not even glancing towards him.

"Did he send you all the boxes?"

I wanted to tell him to go away and quit asking me questions, but I couldn't blame him for what I had done to jumble up my own life. He was an innocent child, and I had already hurt him twice in the past few days.

So I walked over to the bed, pushed everything to the center and motioned for him to sit beside me while I told him about the places I had seen and the people I'd met while I was thousands of miles away from Australia.

Looking at the images of Ben and me together made me want to crawl away somewhere and die, but I pushed those reactions aside. There would be plenty of time for tears. Right now, I needed to mend fences with my little brother.

On Sunday morning, Trevor and I both got up early. Every previous week something had come up making it impossible for us to attend church, but Aunt Nora had volunteered to sit with LeAnn for a few hours quite unexpectedly. She called right before we were ready to leave saying she would be a few minutes late because she was making cottage cheese, and it was taking longer for the milk to turn than anticipated, but she would be there in plenty of time for us to make the trip. I hadn't explained where we were going, only that we wanted to go into town. She didn't know that the service began promptly at nine.

LeAnn assured us that she would be okay until Aunt Nora got there. Jake was in the bunkhouse if she needed anything sooner. Earlier, I might have been anxious leaving her alone with Jake when they might have more time for a leisurely talk, but there had never been any indication that he had revealed to anyone what had happened that night on the beach.

Trevor came down to the kitchen at six-thirty that morning dressed in the white shirt and black pants he had worn to our father's wedding and funeral. I would have to get him something else to wear—something that could be associated with pleasant memories.

"Will Jesse and Veronica be there?" he asked me, referring to the friends he had gone swimming with before Christmas.

"I don't think so," I replied, hoping he wouldn't be too disappointed. "But there should be other children so you can make more friends."

"I'm scared," he admitted, putting his hands in his pockets and rocking back on the heels of his shoes. "I have never been to church before. What if nobody likes me?"

I crossed the room and knelt down in front of him. He looked so little and frightened. Maybe I was expecting too much of him, but he needed to spend more time away from the ranch. His life was weighted down with too many adult worries he could do nothing about.

"You will love it there, and the people will love you," I told him with a hug and a kiss on his cheek. What I was asking him to do was far different than any of the experiences I had exposed him to over the past few weeks. "You will get to learn more about Jesus and sing songs like the one I taught you."

"Will you stay with me?" he asked, fingering a tendril of my hair that had fallen over my shoulder.

"I will be with you as long as you want me to. And Trevor," I said, standing upright and picking up a book I had placed on the table earlier. "I have something special you can take with you."

It was the quad of scriptures I had purchased before coming home just in case my father was willing to learn about the church. That hadn't happened, but since LeAnn was allowing Trevor to go to church with me, I had to take the chance that my little brother might be the key in getting to share the gospel with the rest of my family.

"I brought this for father, but since he isn't here, I want you to have it. It is something that means a great deal to me. You can take it with you today. Maybe it will help you feel closer to both father and me."

He took the book from me and opened its pages.

"I can't read this! It's too hard," he said, looking up at me.

"Your teachers at church will help you and so will I."

He sighed, closed the book and gave me a hug. "I will take good care of it, Brylee, because it was going to be fathers."

"I know you will, and I promise that you will learn so much about Jesus and how much he loves each one of us."

He gave me an odd little smile and put the book back on the table before getting a bowl so he could have some cereal for breakfast.

It wasn't a gift a child raised outside the church would appreciate, but I knew the other children in Primary would have their own scriptures, and I didn't want him to feel even more out-of-place than he already would. I just hoped the people at church would understand his ignorance when it came to religion and be kind.

Jake came out of the bunkhouse with a cigarette in his right hand while Trevor and I were getting into the Land Rover. I didn't stop the car, even though he waved as we drove past him. He was the last person I wanted to talk to, especially today. He would just say something cryptic that would make Trevor uncomfortable, and I wanted my little brother exposed to the gospel in the most positive way possible.

Emma was waiting for us when we got to the makeshift meeting house in a store front. She put her arms around Trevor and gave him a hug.

"You probably don't remember me, but I am a friend of your parents. They used to leave you with me when you were little so they could go to a movie or out to dinner. You look just like your father."

"It's nice to meet you," Trevor told her, reaching for my hand and then clinging tightly to it. This was a monumental day for him. I wondered if my parents had ever left me with someone so they could do something fun together. I couldn't remember being any place but home until I was sent away to boarding school.

"I have something for you, Trevor," she said, removing a small box from her handbag.

Trevor knit his brow in confusion. Two prezzies in one day when it wasn't his birthday or Christmas must have been bewildering to him, but he took the box from her anyway and opened it.

"It's a ring," he said.

"It's not just any ring," Emma told him. "It's a CTR ring. It's to help you remember to make the right choices. Why don't we see if it fits?"

She took the little ring out of its box and slipped it on the third finger of his right hand.

"Do you know what CTR stands for?" I asked my little brother as he looked suspiciously at the ring on his finger. It was obvious he had never worn one before.

He shrugged his shoulders.

"It stands for 'Choose the Right'."

"Do you have one?" he asked me.

"I do," I told him. "Ben gave it to me right before I joined the church. It was in one of the boxes he sent."

"Then why aren't you wearing it? Shouldn't big people make the right choices too?"

"They should," I admitted, wishing I'd had to foresight and courage to wear it. "I'll get it out when we get home and we can both wear them to church next week."

I didn't tell him that I had purposely put it away, along with everything else Ben had given me. It was too painful to wear, but I couldn't hide from the realities of life forever. I had made so many wrong choices, but my biggest regret was not telling the man I loved something important when I should have.

Trevor sat between Emma and me during Sacrament meeting. He took the bread and water when it was passed to the congregation, although he had no idea why we were doing it. There was just so much I wanted to teach him, but trying to help him feel comfortable in a new environment was my greatest concern for the day. Having Emma with us made it easier. I liked having a grandmother-figure in my life and had no expectations as to how our relationship might develop. I just hoped Trevor would soon come to love her as much as I did.

I took Trevor to the Primary room after Sacrament meeting. He clutched my hand tightly, but the Primary president who greeted us at the door put all my fears to rest.

There were three other children in the room, but she squatted down in front of him so their eyes would be level and shook his hand. "I am so happy you are here today," she said.

Trevor ducked his head behind my arm.

"This is my little brother, Trevor Hawkins," I told her. "It's his first time at church."

"Well, that's even better," she said with understanding. "We have another child about your age in our Primary. Would you like to meet him?"

Trevor nodded his head as he peered at her from behind the safety of my arm. She reached for his hand so she could lead him to where the other children were already sitting quietly on small chairs listening to music.

"We are going to learn some new songs today," she told him as he obediently went with her. I had no choice but to let him go, but this was going to be as hard on me as it was on him.

"He's in good hands," Emma told me as we walked away. "Mandy is wonderful with children. I had her when I was teaching Primary years ago. She has three little ones of her own now."

I was glad she felt confident because I certainly didn't. I worried about him all during my own class, but no one brought him to me. I hoped that meant he was fitting in with the other children and having fun.

"Look what I made," Trevor said as he ran up to where I was waiting for him outside the primary room door. "It's a picture of Jesus holding the children."

He had colored it almost perfectly.

"It's beautiful," I told him.

"I'm giving it to mum when we get home. Did you know that Jesus loves everyone, especially children?"

Tears welled in my eyes. It was such a simple concept, yet so many children around the world had never been given the opportunity to hear it.

"I did, Trevor," I told him. "And he is especially happy today because you have been able to learn more about him."

Emma cleared her throat and I knew she was feeling almost as emotional as I was because she had been waiting much longer than me to introduce the gospel to LeAnn and her family.

"I have prepared lunch for all of us," she said. "So I hope you are getting really hungry, Trevor."

He looked up at her and smiled. "Is it okay if we eat fast? I want to give this to mum and tell her what I learned."

"Absolutely," Emma replied. "Would you like to ride to the house with me? I baked cookies yesterday. Maybe I could sneak one to you while we wait to eat lunch. I think your sister would like to talk to the branch president for a minute or two."

I didn't know how she had discerned my need for that, but I was awfully glad she had.

"Do you?" he asked me.

"Yes, I do," I replied, trying to keep the tears from forming. Brother Downing was my spiritual adviser, and I needed his help desperately. "Maybe Emma has a few pictures you could look at while you are eating your cookie. I promise I promise not to be long."

He returned my hug and walked out of the front door with Emma. So far, the Sabbath had been a very special day.

"So good to see you again," President Downing said as he escorted me into the room he used as an office. "I have often wondered what was going on in your life after seeing you at the mortuary."

His words were kind, making it easier to express what was on my mind. "That's what I wanted to talk to you about, if you have a few minutes."

"I always have time," he replied. "My wife knows what my Sunday's are like."

I sat down on one of the chairs that had been placed in front of a small wooden desk that could be used as podium for lessons or a table for more creative activities. I loved the picture of Christ praying in the Garden of Gethsemane that hung on the wall behind it. I had certainly found my own garden of pain and misfortune the past few months.

"How have things been going?" he asked me as I placed my scriptures and purse on the empty chair beside me and clenched my hands together in my lap. I hated being wimpy but if I didn't talk to someone about how I was feeling, I might drive myself crazy.

"Not good!" I told him. "I feel like my entire life is over."

"You are still in the grieving process and that takes time."

"I have more time than needed right now, and I am drowning in it."

"I take it you haven't seen your fiancé yet."

"Ben is not my fiancé anymore," I told him as my eyes filled with tears. "We broke up after he found out that I had been raped from the man who did it. Only he made it sound like we had been physically involved for months."

He leaned back in his chair and gave me a look filled with compassion and understanding—not shock or censure. "That is most unfortunate since you were not there to defend yourself. How did it happen? If you feel like sharing, that is?"

The words just seemed to come rolling out as I told him about Jennifer, the party they had attended together, how they had met Jon and all the lies he had told. I reiterated the part he already knew about keeping the whole sordid experience from Ben and how he no longer trusted me. I explained that it happened during the flood when we were without power for five weeks and how our phone conversation ended. I didn't tell him about Jake and the beach. That would come another time, after I had fully processed everything else.

"I'm so sorry, Brylee. I wish there was something I could say that would help. Maybe it is time for you to think about going back to the states so you can face Ben in person and explain your side of the story."

"I wish that was even a possibility, but I gave him his freedom and he has already moved on. He sent all of my things back, even the small items I bought for our apartment. Besides, it's impossible for me to go anywhere right now. LeAnn is pregnant."

His eyes widened in surprise.

"It's my father's baby," I assured him. "But she is on bed rest, and I have to be there to take care of her and Trevor."

"Rather a mixed blessing, isn't it?"

I nodded. "I'm sad and excited at the same time."

"Understandable, but you do understand that your Heavenly Father loves you and you are never truly alone."

"I get that logically, but my heart is lagging behind."

Until that moment, I had been relatively calm but the floodgates suddenly opened, and he handed me a box of tissue. I took several sheets and began wiping at my eyes and nose. "I don't want my life to be over."

He looked at me with what seemed to be complete understanding. "Even if you don't get back together with Ben, your life is far from being over. You are a beautiful, loving, righteous young woman, and I know without a doubt that God has a very special mission in store for you. Look at what you have already accomplished! You survived possibly the worst thing that could happen to a woman, joined the church and learned what it was like to be loved by a good man. You found your way back to your family and are introducing them to the gospel. You even made it through a heart wrenching breakup and were able to bring your little brother to church today. How amazing is that?"

"I am grateful he is here, and I won't quit trying to share what I believe with anyone who will listen, but sometimes I wonder if I what I want most in life will ever be mine. Being a member of the church has changed my entire focus. I just want to be worthy of having a righteous husband and an eternal family someday."

"God will not withhold those blessings from you, Brylee, whether they are answered in this life or the next. That is one promise you can be sure of."

"But I'm afraid," I responded, suddenly realizing that I would not get the help I needed by withholding pertinent information. That was how most of this mess had started in the first place. "Something happened the night Ben and I broke up. I went for a walk on the beach so I could clear my head and Jake, LeAnn's brother, came to find me. He was trying to comfort me and when he kissed me, I let him."

"There is nothing wrong with a simple kiss, if that's what it was. You've had some very rough months."

"I have also set some very firm boundaries, but when he touched me, I realized that I cared about him. I just hadn't accepted it because I had Ben, and because I was always so busy picking away at his faults."

"Does he feel the same way you do?"

"He was very clear about his feelings and his desires, but I was able to push him away."

"That's a good thing."

"I only did it because I knew he was the worst possible man in the world for me. He knows how I feel and what I believe, but that only makes him think I am always judging him because he drinks, smokes, swears and does whatever feels good to him without any guilt. The problem is that he can be really kind and sweet when he wants to be, and I need someone in my life who really cares."

President Downing took a deep breath and there was a short pause where I could hear my heart beating before he said anything more.

"It sounds like you are facing another crisis and don't know what to do."

I nodded my head and blew my nose on another tissue I had taken from the box. I had a whole pile of soiled ones sitting in my lap already.

"I just want to run away and never come back, but that just isn't possible. I have to be strong enough to be around him so I can take care of LeAnn and Trevor like I promised my father, and now there is going to be a new little half-sibling."

I bit my bottom lip to stop its trembling.

"I think your father would excuse you from that promise if he knew that your eternal salvation might be at risk."

"But I can't excuse myself. If I leave, the chance of introducing the gospel to my family goes with me. I have a responsibility to my ancestors too."

"Is there any chance Jake would be interested in hearing about the gospel."

"Not likely," I said with a dismal laugh as I sniffled and wiped at my eyes again. "I know God doesn't ask anything of us that we can't make it through with his help, but sometimes I get so scared I just want to stay in bed with the covers over my head."

"You were strong that night on the beach, and you can be strong in the future if the need arises. It sounds like Jake knows and accepts where you stand, even if he doesn't like it. Most men are honorable, not like the man who raped you."

"Why can't life just go back to the way it was before I came home? It was so simple then. I had a wonderful man to marry. We were going to have a family and spend forever together. Now he will still get that life, and I am left with nothing."

"We were never promised life would be fair, or even enjoyable much of the time, Brylee. Overcoming challenges is how we grow, and we can't expect to return home our Heavenly Father if we aren't willing to pay the price of true discipleship. It's not pleasant, but sometimes that price includes a whole lot of loss."

I put my face in my hands and thought about all the things that had been lost to me—my parents, the man I loved, the family I wanted to have, and the joy that came from being around people who believed the same things I did. The road ahead seemed very dark and endless, and regardless of what he had said about me being strong, I wasn't sure I could keep resisting Jake's advances.

He just sat quietly and let me think and grieve until my tears were spent and my thoughts had become more centered.

"I'm sorry," I finally said, grabbing another handful of tissues and blowing my nose again. "I didn't mean to break down. I have been trying so hard to be strong for everyone who needs me."

"But you have needs too. Maybe that is part of the problem. You have been so busy taking care of everyone else that you haven't taken time to figure out how all this change is affecting you. It's not selfish to take a few deep breaths and decide what you need to be happy. You can't give strength to anyone else if it's depleted in you."

"But there isn't time to take a vacation. I couldn't afford one even if there was."

"Are things that bad financially? Emma told me your home wasn't affected by the flood and that most of your animals were safe."

"It isn't that," I told him. "I just don't feel right about using my father's money for myself when I have done nothing to deserve it? I can't even pay tithing because I have no income, and I want to go to the temple someday."

"Certainly your father made provisions for you to live if you stayed here."

"He did, but how can I spend money when LeAnn, Trevor and the new baby are going to need it?"

"But you are part of his family too, and it doesn't matter what happened in the past. You will discover that one day when you have children of your own. Nothing they do or say will stop our love for them, or our wanting to make sure they are happy and being cared for."

I looked down at my hands that were still clutching so many soiled Kleenex. I was so weary of trying to find answers to questions I didn't understand.

"What should I do, President Downing? I don't know which way to turn any more."

"I can't tell you what to do, but I do know how you can find the answers you need."

"How?" I asked. "I will do anything."

"Just get down on your knees or open your scriptures and you will find direction. It might not come like a bolt of lightening, but if you are humble and willing to hear, you will know what to do."

"But what about Jake? The ranch is his home too?"

"That is a tough one, but I suspect that many of the feelings you had that night on the beach were a direct result of breaking up with Ben. You were alone and hurt and needed comfort. Try to step back and see if you care about Jake as a person and not just someone who was there when you needed him. Not everyone we are attracted to becomes spouse-material. Some people are meant to bring joy into our lives through friendship alone. That is a huge blessing too."

We finished our talk, and he gave me another blessing before I left his office. I couldn't say that my spirits were lifted significantly on my drive to Emma's house, but our wonderful branch president had given me plenty to think about.

People did come into our lives for special reasons, and they came when we needed them. Emma was a very unexpected friend who was bringing peace into all of our lives because she cared. Maybe the same thing could happen with Jake if I put what had happened between us on the beach aside and concentrated on rebuilding the more harmonious relationship we had shared the few weeks after the flood when there was a common goal to work for.

I dried my eyes again as I pulled up in front of her home. The trim needed painting. Maybe Trevor and I could do that for her once LeAnn was able to be left alone again.

Trevor opened the door to let me in.

"Emma's putting lunch on the table," he said. Then he looked at my red, swollen eyes. "It will be okay, Brylee. Mum and the baby are going to be fine, and I am going to help out with everything. You will see."

I put my arms around his shoulders and gave him a kiss. "How did I get so lucky to have you for a little brother?"

It was a rhetorical question, but he returned my hug anyway.

"It would be okay someday," I told myself as we stood together in the small entry to Emma's home where a picture of President Nelson had been hung. My life wasn't over. It had just taken an unexpected and disheartening turn. Maybe if I told myself that often enough, I might actually come to believe it.

When we got back to the ranch, Trevor immediately ran inside the house to tell his mother about his experience at church. I had quizzed him most of the way home about what he had learned, fearful that he might say something that would upset LeAnn so she wouldn't let him go with me again. But there wasn't anything negative about his adventure. When he talked about Jesus, his face literally glowed with love and acceptance.

Besides, how could anyone find fault with a religion whose soul purpose was to bring people closer to Christ? Trevor had made more friends with more children, and he was being exposed to concepts that could only bring peace and acceptance into his life.

I was locking the door to the Land Rover when Jake descended on me. When I looked up at him, he threw his cigarette on the ground and rubbed the flame out with the toe of his boot.

"I don't know how you did it, but you certainly got my sister to do something I never dreamed possible," he said. "I still can't believe she allowed her son to attend a church that claims our religion is wrong."

"I never said anything about Catholicism being wrong."

He looked at me much the same way he had when I had first arrived home. It was a look that said, "I don't trust your motives for being here, and I certainly don't trust anything you say."

"You don't have to bad-mouth what others believe openly," he continued. "If your church is right, then ours is wrong. It can't be both ways."

"Religion is undebatable because it changes most everything inside of you, Jake."

"Not just inside," he countered. "Your life isn't the least bit like ours, and you make us feel like we're not good enough simply because we have habits you don't approve of."

"We talked about this before," I said, taking a deep breath and a step away from him. How had our relationship regressed so far when just a few weeks earlier we had shared a brief kiss? "I don't condemn you or anyone else for what you do. How can I when my own life is a total disaster?"

"So you are going to play the 'poor me' card. I thought you were better than that."

I looked over at the few marigolds that fought daily to survive the ever-present sun and lack of moisture. Their bright golden petals should have made me happy, but they only made the tears well up in my eyes again. It had certainly been a day for crying, and Brother Downing knew what he was talking about when he said that I hadn't finished grieving over anything yet.

"I can't talk about this again right now," I said, glancing up at him with all the courage I possessed. "Why can't you just be happy that Trevor had a good time today and made some new friends? Do you really want to know what he learned?"

He opened his mouth to reply, but I didn't let him.

"He learned that Jesus loves everyone. It doesn't matter who they are, what church they belong to or what they have done. I think that is a pretty basic Christian belief. Maybe if you spent some time reading the Bible for yourself we would have something to talk about."

I stuck my chin boldly in the air and walked right past him up the steps and into the house. I was shaking uncontrollably when the door closed behind me. I couldn't believe how quickly I had broken my resolution to try to become actual friends, but he knew just how to push my buttons. He was arrogant and chauvinistic and thought he knew everything. Detesting him was certainly easier than trying to get along. Maybe Brother Downing was right. The change in my feelings for him had been purely circumstantial because we were almost back to where we had started.

He didn't come into the house for dinner. Trevor took an extra tray into the bedroom so he could eat spaghetti and salad with his mother. I was too upset to think about food for myself, so I cleaned up the kitchen and told Trevor I would be in my room if he needed me. When he didn't come for over an hour, I got ready for bed and climbed in between the sheets, praying that sleep would come before my mind exploded.

Chapter 15

It was still pitch black outside when I heard someone call my name. Not the soft, plaintive whisperings of someone who had awakened with a bad dream, but the fearful lamentation of someone who was in a great deal of pain. It frightened me so badly I bolted upright up in bed. The clock on the nightstand said it was one-thirty in the morning.

"Brylee, come quickly," it said again. "I need you now."

My heart was pounding furiously when I realized it was LeAnn. It could only mean one thing. Something was wrong with the baby.

I jumped out of bed and ran towards the door, stubbing my left big toe on the casing. "Damn," I said before I could stop myself from swearing. Could life possibly get any worse? But I immediately knew that I would have to stop asking that question because obviously it could.

The light was on in the foyer, and LeAnn was standing at the bottom of the stairs. One hand was clutching her stomach and the other was clinging tightly to the railing.

"What's wrong," I asked, running down the stairs in my bare feet. Her eyes were large and filled with terror.

"I don't know what happened! I have done everything the doctor told me, but when I got up to go to the bathroom just now . . . . I'm spotting and don't know what to do. I can't lose this baby."

"Let's not jump to any conclusions," I told her as I took her arm and propelled her back towards the bedroom. "The doctor said this could happen and not to panic if it did."

"But it's not supposed to! I still have over two months to go."

"That is why you are going to crawl back in bed while I get Jake. He can get you to the hospital faster than I can."

I pulled the sheet up over her shoulders and then ran through the front door and across the hard-packed earthen driveway to the bunkhouse. I pounded loudly when I got there.

"Jake, wake up," I shouted. "LeAnn needs to get to the hospital."

I heard a thump as his feet hit the floor. "What the hell is going on now?" he shouted in a very irritated tone as he crossed the small room and cracked open the door. He squinted into the harsh light that was coming from a pole in the driveway. He was only wearing boxers, so I looked up at his face hoping he would think I hadn't noticed.

"LeAnn's spotting. It might not be anything serious, but we need to get her to the hospital anyway." I was shaking in my own scant clothing and bare feet. We were heading into the winter season, but my appearance didn't seem to bother him.

"Bloody hell," he mumbled as he hurried back inside to get dressed. "Why do emergencies always have to happen at night when people are supposed to be sleeping?"

But I didn't wait around to hear anything else. My mind was already busy planning how I could make a bed for her in the plane. She was in no condition to sit up on the short flight there.

LeAnn was still lying in the bed where I had left her, sobbing silently into the sheet that covered her body.

"It's going to be okay," I told her again, wishing I truly believed it. "Jake is filing flight plans and will have the plane ready to take off by the time we get there."

I ripped the bedspread off and grabbed a couple of pillows. Then I told her to sit up while I slid her slippers onto her feet. She was too frightened to protest.

"Where is your robe?" I asked once that was done.

"I can't remember," she said, sitting so still on the edge of the bed that I thought she might be going into shock.

I grabbed a sweater that had been thrown across the back of the chair I usually sat in when visiting with her. I didn't know much about pregnancy, except that a little spotting was considered normal. But in LeAnn's case, it could mean so much more.

Suddenly, this pregnancy became more important than anything else that was going on in my life, including my personal misery. It was no longer just another trial or inconvenience. LeAnn was carrying my little brother or sister, and I couldn't let anything happen to either of them.

"Please God," I prayed as I put the sweater around her thin shoulders and then helped her to her feet. "Don't take this baby away from us."

I wished I had the physical strength to carry her—anything that would help protect the precious life she was carrying—but I needn't have worried. Jake whisked into the room and picked her up in his arms as if she weighed no more than a feather.

"Grab the stuff on the bed. I wish you could come with us, but we can't leave Trevor alone, and he doesn't need to be part of this."

I stripped the rest of the blankets from the bed and followed him. He was so strong and dependable, especially when the situations demanded it. He ran straight down the steps and across the driveway with me trailing behind while trying to keep the bedding from dragging in the dust.

"Get inside and make her a bed," he instructed as I stood on my tiptoes so I could reach the handle on the passenger door of the plane. I threw the bedding inside and then grabbed the bottom of the seat for the help I needed to get inside.It was impossible to see where I was going, but I managed to slipped through the narrow gap between the seats in the cockpit and spread the blankets out so LeAnn could lay down on them. She would have to keep her knees bent, but at least her body would be flat. Then I opened the door to the cargo hold.

"Help me with her," Jake shouted as I stepped into the opening. He held LeAnn as high in the air as he could, and I pulled while he guided. The weight of her body forced me to the floor of the aircraft, but in less than two minutes LeAnn was where she needed to be.

I squeezed her hand. "Hang in there. You will be seeing the doctor before you know it."

When I stuck my head out the door into the cool night air, Jake stretched out his arms and lifted me to the ground.

"Call the hospital and have an ambulance at the airport when we land. We should be setting down in about twenty minutes. I will call as soon as I know anything."

"Be safe," I told him as he hoisted himself up and into the plane through the opening I had just vacated. I backed away before the propellers began swirling through the air.

It would be another long night. I was just grateful Trevor had not been awakened by all the commotion. That would give me time to think about how I was going to tell him that the baby he had bought a prezzie for might not be born alive?

After the plane disappeared into the darkness, I hurried into the house and called the hospital. The attendant on duty assured me that an ambulance would be waiting when they arrived. There was nothing else I could do, so I went into the den and curled up in the chair next to the window. There would be no more sleep tonight, and I could answer the phone from the extension on my father's desk when Jake called. I just hoped it wouldn't be too long until I heard his voice again, and when I did, I prayed it would be good news.

Oh, how slowly the minutes pass when people are waiting for something to happen. A million thoughts flittered through my mind as I sat in the dark and listened to the occasional hoot of an owl or cry of an animal I could not identify without seeing it. We needed this baby to survive, but what if it didn't? I pulled a worn afghan around my shoulders as chills continued to invade my body. I couldn't give up hope. It was all any of us had left.

I closed my eyes and tried to count backwards, but even the ticking of the clock kept me distracted. I wasn't going to be worth anything in the morning, but even the thought of no sleep at all until I knew what was going on would not stop my mind from churning with unpleasant possibilities. I literally jumped to my feet when the phone rang a couple of hours later.

"Hi, Brylee," Jake said when I answered. "They have LeAnn stabilized and the bleeding has stopped. The doctor even took an ultrasound and everything looks good with the baby. He wants to keep her here for a day or two. I didn't understand all the stuff he was talking about, but apparently her cervix has weakened considerably and she has pre something. I was a little too rattled to take everything in."

I was no surer of what the doctor was talking about than he was, but I still heaved a sigh of relief. "So they will both be okay?"

"For now, but we can't rule anything out," he responded. "The doctor hopes the situation can still be managed with rest, proper attention and possible medication."

"I don't understand," I told him.

"Neither do I, but I guess we have to trust the experts for now."

"Have you talked to LeAnn?"

"Only briefly. She was in pretty bad shape by the time we landed. All she did was cry and say that God couldn't be so cruel as to take her baby away after he had already taken her husband. So much for this God of mercy you are always talking about."

I was tempted to say something biting but thought better of it. Jake was upset and rightly so. He didn't need any platitudes about God's love when we could so easily experience another devastating loss.

"Will she be up for visitors in a few hours?" I asked him instead. "Trevor will want to see for himself that she is okay once he wakes up."

"The doctor didn't say she couldn't have visitors. Do you want me to fly back and bring both of you here in the plane?"

"That's not necessary," I told him. "I can bring him in the Land Rover. You haven't had any sleep. So why don't you come back and get some rest while Trevor and I keep her company."

"That's not a bad idea, but what about you?" he inquired. "And don't try to tell me you will be fine like you always do. This isn't some contest about which one of us can survive for the longest with no sleep."

"I plan on closing my eyes until Trevor gets up. Tell LeAnn I will bring a few things she might need later this morning. If there is anything specific, have her give me a call or you could just tell me when you get back."

"Thanks for caring so much," he said. "You have certainly been at the heart of a lot Johnson-Hawkins drama these past few months, but I want you to know that we wouldn't have made it without you."

"She is my family too," I responded, once again surprised at how kind he could be when the right spirit moved him. "I don't want anything to happen to her or the baby."

His sigh was heavy. "Neither do I. This family could really use a little good luck."

"Trevor and I will take care of the chores before we drive into town. That way, all you will have to do is crawl into bed when you get here."

"You could warm up that bed for me," he teased. "I could use a little TLC after the bloody, awful night I've had."

"I will keep that in mind," I said, as my face grew hot with embarrassment. I would never in a million years do what he asked—even if I thought he was serious—but I could do something special to show that I appreciated everything he had done for all of us. Men needed to know they were appreciated every bit as much as women did, perhaps even more because they rarely said anything about their personal needs, even in jest.

"Then I guess I will see you later, and don't worry about the chores. You have enough to do with Trevor."

"My little brother is a joy to be around, and he loves taking care of the animals because he considers them part of his family."

"Then do what you think is best," he said, dismissing me. "I think I will sit with LeAnn for a while before I come home anyway. She's had a pretty rough night, and I don't think any of us understand just how important this baby is to her. She told the nurse that it was her wedding present from her husband. I'm not sure she can survive another blow."

The way Jake's moods changed was infuriating, but I was too tired to force another argument. "Then we will just have to keep praying that God will watch over all of us since we are in this together."

"I hope you don't live to regret all the confidence you place in someone who can't be seen. I think I will stick with what the doctor tells me. At least I know he is doing everything he can."

"I'll talk to you later," I said, ending our call. Jake was a complex man. I accepted that, but if he would just allow himself to believe—even like the proverbial mustard seed—he might actually discover that the world wasn't such a dismal place after all.

I lay down on the sofa and pulled the afghan back up to my neck. Perhaps it was best to give up even trying to understand the man who was consuming so many of my thoughts. President Downing was right when he intimated that Jake could easily break my heart in more ways than one if I allowed him to.

"Brylee," I heard Trevor calling my name a couple of hours later. He sounded anxious and even a little afraid. "I looked in mum's room and she isn't there."

"In here," I called back. "And don't worry. Your mother is fine."

The door to the den burst open. "But she's gone, Brylee. I looked in the bathroom and everywhere."

"It's okay. I can explain," I said as I slid my feet to the floor and patted the sofa beside me. He hurried to my side and sat down. My head was still in a fog, and all I wanted to do was sleep now that this latest ordeal was somewhat under control, but I had my little brother to think about.

"Your Uncle Jake took her into town a few hours ago, but you don't have to worry, both she and the baby are fine."

"Then why did they go to town?" he asked.

I questioned just how much an eight-year-old needed to know in order to understand what had happened during the night before giving my answer.

"She wasn't feeling well, so we decided it was best if she saw the doctor right away. Sometimes, people just need to be reassured."

He gave me a funny look. I knew what I was trying to tell him made little sense, so I put my arm around his shoulder hoping to calm at least some of his fears.

"Why don't we get dressed and do the chores, then we can drive into town and you can see for yourself that everything is okay."

He was ready for the day and had bowls and cold cereal on the table so we could eat by the time I had taken a shower and slipped into my own clothes for the day.

"You're quick," I said.

"I fed and watered my animals too. What took you so long? You were in the shower forever. I heard the water running."

His question brought a smile to my face. I loved the lack of pretense in children. They told it like they saw it—nothing more, nothing less.

"I didn't get a whole lot of sleep last night, and needed a long shower to wake me up. Thanks for fixing breakfast."

"Do you want Corn Flakes or Trix?" he asked as he held up a box in each hand.

"Corn Flakes," I told him, and he filled my bowl with cereal. I got the milk from the refrigerator and put it on the table before we sat down to eat.

"How is Newton this morning?" I asked him between mouthfuls.

"He is almost taller than me. Uncle Jake says when he gets that big we have to put him out with the other cattle so they will accept him, but I don't want to let him go. He is my best friend."

"What about Copper? I thought she was your best friend."

I looked around for the little puppy that followed him everywhere, unless she was in her kennel. He had obviously left her there since he knew we were going into town for a couple of hours.

"She is my best friend too. It's okay to have more than one best friend, isn't it?"

"More than fine," I told him, ruffling his hair with my hand. We needed to comb it before seeing his mother. "You are taking excellent care of all your animals, and I am very proud of you. You are going to make an awesome big brother."

I wished I hadn't said that the moment the words slipped out. LeAnn wasn't out of danger and neither was the baby.

After eating, Trevor and I watered the horses and put them in the pasture behind the barn for the day. Some of the fence boards were getting loose. I made a mental note to fix them the first chance I got. The fence could use a coat of paint too.

Then I packed a few things in a bag for LeAnn while Trevor made a roast beef sandwich and covered a piece of pie with Saran wrap for Jake to eat when he got home. It wasn't the most original thing to let him know that we cared, but under the circumstances, it was the best I could come up with. I also wrote a brief note saying where the food was and telling him to get some rest before tackling anything else. I had Trevor sign it before taping it to the bunkhouse door. I didn't want to give him any false hope. I was committed to my dream of a marriage that would last forever, and one kiss on a beach wasn't going to change that.

It was another long drive into town with nothing much to talk about except LeAnn and the baby. I almost wished I had taken Jake up in his offer of taking us in the plane. Thirty minutes versus two hours was a huge difference when it came to keeping a conversation going with an eight-year old who was worried about his mother and a baby that had yet to be born. There was nothing I could say to assuage his fears because I was as worried about them as he was.

Around fifty from Edna, we saw a school heading towards us.

"Do you ever wish you could ride a bus to school like other kids your age?" I asked as we watched it pass by. I was surprised to see it so far out of town. Most of the children in the outback were homeschooled using the School of the Air Satellite System or radio for curriculum guidelines.

"Why would I want to do that?" he asked. "I go to school with mum at home and she is the best teacher ever."

"And she is doing a wonderful job,' I responded. "I did the same thing with my mother when I was your age, but it can be very lonely. The only other kids I knew were NJ and Molly until I was sent to St. Mary's Catholic Boarding School in Sydney."

"I never want to be that far away from home. Weren't you scared?"

"Sometimes, but I am glad I went now. I needed to learn how to make friends outside of the family."

I hoped he wouldn't ask me anything about them other than their names because the only real friends I had made at boarding school were Torrie and Betsy, and I had no idea what had happened to either of them. We lost contact the day I found out my mother was dead.

Even the girls I roomed with while going to college had been nothing more than acquaintances. We had never done anything together, except share the same roof and an occasional meal. Becky and Ben were the only true friends I ever had until coming home and being reunited with my family. Now, I was beginning to understand that family members, no matter how mixed up they might be, could end up being the best friends of all.

Still, I didn't want Trevor growing up the way I had. He deserved to know that the world was a wonderful place, filled with people and experiences that could enhance his life. Perhaps if I had been exposed to more than the ranch before turning twelve, I would have learned how to stand up for myself. I blinked back tears as I looked out the window so Trevor would not see how emotional I had become. He didn't need to think I was keeping something important from him.

"What's your favorite subject?" I asked him as a way of deflecting my inner thoughts. There would be plenty of time to figure out his schooling since he was only in the second grade.

"I like to read and draw and learn stuff about science."

"What kind of stuff?'

"Mostly about the oceans and the animals that live around here."

"Even snakes like the one we saw?"

That adventure seemed like it had happened a million years ago now, but it was as vivid in my memory as the day it had occurred.

"I hate snakes. You know that. I only like animals with fur on them," he said, turning his gaze towards the side window and not looking back at me.

My feeble attempt at trying to start a conversation was over, and we rode most of the rest of the way into Edna in silence.

Jake had told me what room LeAnn was in when he called back with a list of the items she wanted, and no one had stopped us on our way there as they would have done in L.A. But it was a small town and a small hospital—less than 30,000 residents and fifty hospital beds. Jake was no longer there.

Her room was like every other one we passed on our way down the hall, sterile and unimaginative in design with pale blue walls and the smell of antiseptics so strong it made me want to turn and escape. But Trevor didn't seem to notice as he ran straight to his mother and buried his face in her shoulder. She was hooked up to an IV and a fetal monitor I knew would frighten him once he noticed they were there, but for now he was content just being in her arms.

"I missed you, mum," he told her. "I was so scared about the baby, but he is going to be okay, isn't he?"

LeAnn ruffled his hair and then kissed it as she pulled him even closer.

"We are both doing just fine, but I am afraid we have a few more decisions to make," she told him as she looked at me from over the top of his head. It was easy to see the anguish in her eyes. Things were not as good as Jake had led me to believe.

"The doctor wants me to be closer to the hospital until the baby comes. It takes too long to get here from the ranch."

I gulped in some of the stale air and fought back the desire to break into tears. The baby couldn't be born healthy for another two months. What would happen in the meantime? Trevor couldn't be separated from his mother again. He needed the security of seeing her every day, but it appeared she had been doing some major planning during the few hours she had been away from the ranch because Jake and Emma joined us a few minutes later with a great reveal.

He looked dreadful, and my heart went out to him because I suddenly realized that he was sacrificing his own life—just as I was—for the larger good. Emma stepped right into the role of doting and practical grandmother.

"Have there been any updates?" she asked LeAnn after greeting both Trevor and me. I returned her warm embrace, but Trevor refused to leave his mother's side.

"The doctor will be here in a few minutes to explain things better than I can. I told him you would all be here by noon so we could decide what needs to be done together. This baby is an obstinate one. He is determined to let us know exactly what he wants."

LeAnn was trying to be brave and doing a pretty good job of it for Trevor's sake, but it was impossible not to feel the fear behind her words. There was no way anyone could predict what would happen, not even medical experts.

"All I can tell you right now is that he wants me to stay here for a few days until he decides if I need more than just bed rest."

I looked over at Emma, but she smiled reassuringly at me.

"I wanted everyone here so we could listen to what he has to say and there wouldn't be any misunderstandings. This isn't just my decision because it involves all of us, and the additional sacrifices that might have to be made. I wanted Emma here because she has known Jake and me since we were little more than children and is the closest thing to extended family we have."

"We will do whatever it takes," Jake said. "I think we all agree about that, don't we?" He looked at me, and I looked over at Emma.

"We most certainly will," she said without hesitation. "You can all stay with me for as long as you like. It gets mighty lonesome in that old house."

"I'm hoping that won't be necessary, and that is not why I wanted you here, Emma. I value your wisdom and judgment, and heaven knows we could all use some of that right now."

"Now, look here, missy," Emma said, squaring her shoulders. "You just said you value my wisdom, but it doesn't take a genius to know that traveling back and forth between here and the ranch is no longer possible. I have a home just waiting for a family, so let me use it for that purpose."

I swallowed back the lump that had found its way to my throat but could do nothing about the tears that were sliding down my cheeks, except wipe them away. Emma was the most remarkable woman I had ever met, but she couldn't be saddled with an entire family at her age. So, I added my own take on what could be done to help remedy the situation.

"I can take care of the house and help Trevor with his lessons," I volunteered. "That way, Emma won't be left with all the responsibility and I can bring him into town as often as possible. I want to meet the newest member of the Hawkins' family just as much as the rest of you."

LeAnn forced a tentative smiled. "I wish I didn't have to ask any of you for more help, but it appears that my body refuses to cooperate like it should."

"A true Johnson," Jake said, looking gravely at her. "You just take care of yourself and that stubborn baby, and leave everything else to us."

The doctor had no further information to share, but he let us know that he was cautiously optimistic since the bleeding had stopped and the condition of the pregnancy had stabilized. He assured us that they were doing everything medically possible, but time, the condition of the cervix and LeAnn's blood pressure were the deciding factors. They would continue to monitor both mother and baby over the next few days at the hospital, and if nothing changed, she would be released at the end of the week. He didn't tell us that a safe delivery was guaranteed, even if she did exactly as he instructed.

"Why don't you keep your mum company?" Jake told Trevor after the doctor left the room. "We adults have a few things to talk about."

"Work out all the details was more like it," I thought as I sat down on a sofa in the waiting room next to Emma. The sun was intense and searing outside but thanks to the tinted windows it didn't add any undo heat to the interior of the building. Jake pulled a chair up in front of us. Then he sat down and ran his hands through his hair.

"This is tough," he finally said. "LeAnn's condition is critical regardless of what the doctor said. It was no small miracle that the baby survived the night. I'm just afraid that all the sacrifices in the world won't make any difference in whether this baby lives or dies."

"That is no way to talk," Emma scolded him. "This baby was a miracle from the very beginning, and I fully believe it would not have made it this far if it wasn't meant to be born. We need to trust God and have faith."

"You know I don't believe in all that stuff, Emma," Jake told her. "Either the baby is meant to survive or it isn't. What you call faith has nothing to do with it except to make you feel better."

I was shocked at his rudeness and about to tell him so when Emma advocated for herself.

"Someday, Jake Johnson, you will have to admit that God exists and has a plan for each one of us."

Jake leaned over, took her hand and kissed it.

"If that day ever comes, Emma, I will be the first bloody bloke to admit it, but right now I choose to put my trust in logic and modern medicine."

She shook her head and smiled fondly at him. "I'm going to hold you to that. You know that, don't you?"

"Wouldn't have it any other way." He kissed her hand again, and then let go of it.

"No wonder all the single women in Edna are captivated by you," she chided. "You are quite a charmer when you want to be."

"I think Brylee would disagree."

"That's not fair," I muttered, looking down at the floor. He might know exactly what women needed, but I would never become one of his conquests. It was too dangerous. "You know I care about you."

"If you do, you certainly have a strange way of showing it most of the time."

Emma shook her head at both of us. "Do I need to send the two of you to time-out? We have some rather important issues to discuss, and it's not whether the two of you can get along for more than two minutes at a time without a referee."

Jake turned away from me immediately. "You always did know how to put me in my place," he told her.

"This isn't about you sneaking cookies at the diner when you thought I wasn't looking, Jake. There will be plenty of time for nonsense once that baby is safely here."

I frowned at her assessment of the situation. Jake and I were not two silly teenagers flirting. There were serious problems between us, but maybe it was her way of disarming a potentially explosive situation. This really wasn't the time to worry about a kiss that never should have happened or confidences that had been shared under duress.

"What do you think, Brylee?" Jake asked, giving me a look of distain that let me know he was aware of the fact that my mind was wandering again.

"I'm sorry," I said, trying to refocus my thoughts on the present where they belonged.

"Emma was wondering what would be better for Trevor—staying at the ranch with us or staying in town with her where he can go to a real school."

"I don't know," I said, not really wanting Trevor to be any place except with me. We had become more than just siblings during the past few months, but it wasn't my call since I was only his sister. "Do we have to decide that right now?"

"We have to decide something since it is quite obvious that LeAnn can't come back to the ranch until the baby is born, and Trevor needs an education," Jake said.

"I can teach him. I already said I would."

"But is that the best thing for him or for you? You have already taken over all the household responsibilities. Do you really think you can handle anything else?"

I threw him a challenging look. "I can handle anything I need to."

"I'm not just talking about physically," he said.

I was about to throw him another barb when Emma cleared her throat.

"Well, I might have an answer to your dilemma, if you will both agree," she said. "Why couldn't he stay in town with his mum and me during the week and go to the ranch for the weekends? That way, he could be a part of both worlds. Once the baby comes, you can all go back on the ranch. It would be fun having him around the house more often, and it would be good for LeAnn."

"But we haven't decided where LeAnn will stay once she is out of the hospital," Jake protested. He definitely didn't like people making decisions for him any more than I did.

"Nonsense! We all know it is the perfect solution. She can't go back out there, and she can't stay here in town alone."

"But it's too much to ask. You may still have your bark, Emma, but let's face it, you are not exactly a spring chicken and you definitely don't need all the drama."

"I could still whoop your arse, Jake Johnson, and don't you ever forget it," she retorted, surprising me with both her candor and her language. She had always seemed so mellow and ladylike to me.

He only laughed, but some of the fire in her eyes dissipated anyway.

"We have no idea where any of this might lead, Emma. LeAnn should never have gotten you involved in the first place."

"And why not?" she asked. "I may not be as spry as I used to be, but I am healthy as a horse for a woman my age and would like to be doing something useful with my life. The diner practically runs itself."

"You should have sold that place years ago."

"Why? I still make the best pies in the country, and I am not senile. People don't have to be young to be productive, Jake Johnson. The good Lord has kept me here for a reason, and maybe this is it."

"I suppose it could work," he relented after a few moments of silent meditation during which time I was smart enough to remain quiet. "You are as stubborn as you are beautiful, Emma. If you were forty years younger, I would go after you myself."

"Make it fifty, and I would let you," she responded. "But do we have a deal? I know it can work if we all stick together."

I had been watching the proceedings with amazement and a certain amount of amusement. There was a lot I could learn from Emma about putting Jake in his place without making him mad or causing a scene.

"I don't mind flying into town a couple of times a week, but Iam not the one who has to make the most concessions. What do you think, Brylee?"

His question caught me off guard. I was chewing on the end of my thumb. It was a great idea, except for one thing. It would mean that Jake and I would be left alone at the ranch during the work week. What if something unexpected happened? I felt stronger now that I had talked to the branch president, but there were never any guarantees that a compromising situation might not arise again.

"It's workable, but I have to agree with Jake," I finally said. "You shouldn't have to take on all our problems, Emma. It is asking way too much."

"You are not asking. I'm volunteering, and I like having young people around me. That's why I haven't sold the diner. It helps with the loneliness since Robert passed."

"But if we do this, and I am not saying we will," I told her. "I want you to be compensated for food and all the work you will be doing by having two extra people to take care of."

"Rubbish," she scolded me. "You are my family! I've had a rich, full life except for having children. That's why, in my heart, I have adopted all of you. I couldn't love you more if you had been born to me."

Her honesty and generosity touched my heart, and I started to cry.

"You are an amazing woman, Emma. When I told you I wanted to think of you as my grandmother, I never thought we would ever be needing you as much as we do."

"Land, child," she said, handing me a Kleenex from the seemingly endless supply she kept in her pockets. "You are going to make all of us blubber if you don't stop. This is a joyous occasion. We should be thanking God for the blessing of having another child in the family instead of being upset because it is going to be a little challenging to get him or her here."

Jake had been leaning back in his chair observing us. There was no way to tell what he was thinking. His face was set like a mask, and a very tired one at that.

"Maybe we are being a little premature with all this talk and planning," he said. "We don't even know if the baby will make it to the end of the week so LeAnn can be released."

"I choose to believe that God is in charge," Emma said, looking around the room with the light blue walls and speckled tile floors. There were very few people waiting. That made it easier to discuss our situation in more than whispers. "And even if the baby decides to come in the next few days, there is every reason to believe that little one will make it."

"Not without a whole lot of medical problems," Jake responded. "I'm not sure any of us are ready to deal with something like that."

"We will deal with what we have to. But for now, my mind is made up. LeAnn and Trevor are coming home with me—end of discussion."

"It is the best solution, at least for the time being," I reluctantly admitted.

Jake only made a scoffing sound. "I think you are both rather delusional, but I learned long ago never to argue with a gaggle of women when their minds are made up over something. I just hope this whole damned thing doesn't blow up in our faces."

Chapter 16

It took little convincing to get LeAnn to agree to stay in town with Emma. It truly was the only alternative, unless I moved into town and we were able to find place to rent for a couple of months. And that seemed like a huge waste of resources when LeAnn and Trevor already had a place to stay. Besides, Jake couldn't do all the work on the ranch by himself, even though I knew it would be a challenge for us to work together without letting our negative feelings or unwanted desires get in the way.

The issue of Trevor's schooling wasn't so easily resolved. LeAnn asked Jake to take him to the cafeteria for a snack while we women-folk discussed our options. She wanted her son with her, but enrolling him in public school presented a few problems, like what would happen after the baby was born and everyone returned to the ranch? Was it fair to ask him to leave friends and a more formal setting to be tutored at home again by his mother? Even his animals and a new baby would not compensate for the loss of being with children his own age everyday.

My teaching abilities even came into question. I knew I could do it if someone showed me how, but daily telephone conversations with LeAnn and working directly with teachers from the School of the Air wouldn't guarantee Trevor's ability to learn from me. Besides, I liked being his sister and friend and was afraid our relationship would change into something less desirable if I had to be in charge of his education too. And there was the fact that he needed the security of being around his mother after her lengthy disappearance. He had forgiven her the moment he saw her again, but I knew from experience that forgetting would not come nearly as easily.

We even talked about LeAnn continuing his instructions while they lived with Emma, but Trevor was a boy who was used to wide-open spaces and being with his animals. Staying inside a small house with two women all day with nothing to do but study or watch television seemed a fate too cruel to ask, even if it was only for a couple of months. And if LeAnn ended up in the hospital again . . . . Well, it would only mean more disruptions to an already uncertain life.

"I still don't know what to do," LeAnn said after we had discussed every aspect of the situation until there was nothing left to say. "Am I just being selfish wanting this baby so much?"

"No," Emma and I said in unison.

I looked over at the woman who had stepped in to help when she didn't have to. What made her sacrifice time, health, resources and freedom to take care of people who had only lived on the outskirts of her life until now? The only answer seemed to be that she was truly one of the Savior's most compassionate and loving disciples. Maybe we all needed the lessons only she could teach us.

"This baby deserves the right to be born, LeAnn," she was saying when my mind drifted back to the conversation in the room. "Not one of us would ever forgive ourselves if we made decisions based on convenience or even the fear of future fallout. God won't let us go too far off track as long as we seek his guidance and then do as he directs."

"I wish I had your faith," LeAnn said, blinking back tears. She looked so helpless lying in the hospital bed with her protruding belly clearly visible beneath the light blanket that was supposed to keep her warm. "I want this baby more than anything, but I don't want Trevor getting hurt again. He is such a good little boy and has been through so much the past few months. My running away was inexcusable. I was being selfish and cruel and never want to be like that again."

Emma crossed the small room to LeAnn's bed and put one hand on her arm. "Do you want to know how I really feel about all of this?" she asked.

"Of course," LeAnn replied. "I trust you more than anyone."

Emma brushed her hair away from her face, like she would have done if LeAnn had been a child—her child.

"God is giving you a most marvelous gift. There is nothing more sacred or precious than bringing one of his sweet spirits into this world, even if certain sacrifices have to be made. I never had the chance for babies of my own, but I am being given the opportunity to help one of his children be born right now. I want to be there when this little one arrives."

I listened as she talked. God certainly did work in mysterious ways. LeAnn's problems had rippled out to encompass all of us, but instead of looking at them as a hardship that was putting me in a more precarious situation with Jake, I should be looking at them as a way to increase my own faith. He hadn't made any physical overtures since the night on the beach. Naturally, he made comments occasionally and had even sneaked a kiss on Christmas Eve, but he couldn't run the ranch without assistance. Besides, he wasn't a predator, and he would never harm me the way Jon had done. This wasn't about me anyway, at least not directly.

"What do you think, Brylee?" LeAnn asked.

"I think only you know what is right for Trevor. As for the rest of us, we are just glad to be here to help. This baby is family and that means everything."

"Even if it is not the kind of family you were hoping for?"

"I will always love Ben for many reasons, but I know God has something else in mind for me right now than being his wife and the mother of his children. This is my home, and I intend on staying for as long as you will have me."

LeAnn's smile was warm. "Then you will be here forever. I just wish you could find someone else. You deserve to be happy."

"One can't force something that was never meant to be."

"Maybe not, but you are much too young to give up hope. You need to be out meeting people your own age instead of being exiled to some forsaken spot of land in the middle of the outback with only the animals and my brother to keep you company. I love him dearly, but he can be a bloody trial at times."

"It's not such a bad fate, at least for now."

She eyed me curiously. "Does that mean the two of you have settled some of your differences? Jake has been acting very strangely since that night on the beach when you broke up with Ben and come to think of it, so have you."

Although she knew nothing about what had happened back then, I looked to Emma for help. I didn't need anyone speculating on the dynamics of our relationship, especially since it looked as if we would be spending more time alone together on the ranch. I was committed to making sure nothing else happened between us and needed people to respect where I stood, even if they did not understand.

"Brylee has been through a rough time. That is a truth that cannot be denied, but it isn't the issue right now," Emma said as her way of easing me out of a potentially disagreeable confrontation. "We need to concentrate our efforts on making sure this baby is okay and figuring out what to do about Trevor's education."

"But I don't want to go to school!" Trevor exclaimed as he walked into the room with Jake. "I want to stay here with mum. She can teach me like she did at home, and I can help her with the baby."

"Come here," LeAnn told him while Emma stepped out of the way. "You need to go to school, and I am not going to be a very good teacher for the next couple of months."

"But you did it before. I will be really good and do everything you tell me."

He was close to tears and every adult in the room knew it, but this was something he would have to endure on his own.

"I know you would, and I love you for it, but I can't go home right now. I need to stay in town until the baby comes. Emma said I could stay with her."

"What about me?"

He started to cry, and I could do nothing but stand helplessly in one corner of the room and watch.

"Oh, honey," LeAnn said, turning his face to hers and wiping his tears away with the back of her hand. "You can stay with us too. The baby and I need your help, but there is still school to think about. I suppose I could teach you like we have been doing, but it would be the perfect chance for you to attend public school. It might be fun meeting other kids and having a real teacher."

"But what about Copper and Newton?"

"Listen, sport," Jake said, stepping up behind his nephew and putting his hands on the little boy's shoulders. "Here is what we were thinking. Your sister and I can take care of your animals during the week, and you can take care of them on the weekends. I can fly in on Friday afternoon to take you to the ranch and then bring you back on Sunday evening. How does that sound?"

His little brow furrowed. "But I didn't bring any clothes with me."

"That is the beauty of it," I chimed in, hoping to dissipate the mood of hopelessness and despair that hung so heavily in the room. "We could go to the mall and buy some new clothes and any school supplies you might need."

"You know," Emma said. "Sister Benchly at church teaches fifth grade. I am sure she could help us with all the details."

"So what do you think, Trevor?" LeAnn asked. "It could be fun, and just think about all the new adventures you will have."

"I guess it would be okay," he said without conviction. "When would I have to go?"

"How about a week from today? That would give you plenty of time to go shopping with your sister and spend some time with your animals. Uncle Jake can fly you back into town whenever you are ready to come."

"But who will take care of you if I'm not here?"

"I will," Emma said. "And I want you to know that I am very excited you have decided to stay with us. How would you like to help clean out the attic and have that for your very own room?"

"Could I bring father's toy soldiers?"

"You can bring anything you want," LeAnn smiled lovingly at him. "This baby is going to be so lucky having you for a big brother."

So the issue of Trevor's education was resolved. Jake flew back to the ranch. Emma went to her house, and I took my little brother shopping while LeAnn tried to rest. It had been an emotionally and physically draining few hours, but at least the adults involved had been able to put aside differences and work together when it came to making the most important decisions. Everything else had to be left in God's capable hands.

Like most little boys, Trevor was not excited about shopping for clothes but the sale's clerks in the stores were more than helpful. In a couple of hours we had purchased socks, underwear, a pair of tennis shoes for gym, five shirts, a pair of long pants and three khaki-colored shorts. I even purchased church pants and some dress shoes, although I doubted he would be needing them. With the few items of clothing he had at home, he would have enough to wear without Emma having to wash every few days.

By the time we dropped the things we had purchased at Emma's house, she had talked to Sister Benchly about the supplies he needed for class. I felt better knowing that there would be an adult from church to help him at school, but I was more grateful that a few of the kids from Primary would be there too.

Sister Benchly was going to make arrangements for either Jake or me to register him as long as we had the proper documentation. That meant the logistics had been taken care of since LeAnn knew exactly where the records we needed were kept, but I wasn't sure I could handle the emotional loss of not seeing my little brother every day. He was the most important person in my life now that Ben was no longer a part of it.

After putting our packages on the kitchen table, Emma led us up the narrow stairway to the attic where she had already started moving things around to make room for Trevor.

"I hope this will be okay," she said as we watched Trevor survey his new surroundings. The room was smaller and even more cluttered than the attic at the ranch, but I tried to see possibilities.

"It will be perfect," I told her, all the while wondering how we would ever fit a bed and some place to keep clothes in a room where one had to push boxes out of the way just to get inside it.

"I have been going to clean up here for years but never seemed to get around to it. Disposing of things, even things I will never use, is like saying goodbye to the people I love all over again."

I knew exactly how she felt. Nearly every box I opened in the attic at home brought feelings of sorrow or remembrance. I had missed out on so much by not knowing the members of my family who had come before me.

"I went through some of the smaller boxes while you were shopping," she continued as I tried to order my thoughts. "Maybe you could help me get them down the stairs. I am not as steady on my feet as I used to be and would hate to take a tumble."

"We can't have that happen," I told her. "And we will be forever indebted for all you have done to help us. How does it feel to have an instant family forced on you?"

She sat down on an old steamer trunk and smiled. "I have been thanking God every minute since I got home that he has finally given me the chance to use the maternal instincts I was born with for more than just counseling the girls at work. It's hard to believe that at my age I am finally part of a real family."

"I'm not sure we are a real family quite yet," I told her as I looked over at Trevor who had disappeared around a stack of boxes. I didn't want him to overhear something out of context. "But we are trying to get along."

"I can't begin to imagine how difficult it has been with all the adjustments you've had to make since coming home, and I am sorry I wasn't more help at the hospital when LeAnn brought up the subject of her brother. It's easy for even an old war-horse like me to see that the two of you have some issues to work through. Jake is great guy by the world's standards, but I know you don't want to get involved with him because he can't give you what you most want."

"That's just one part of the problem," I reluctantly admitted. "I am starting to get past some of his faults—obvious and otherwise—and it scares me."

"Jake would never hurt you," she said. "He has a very soft heart, despite his rough exterior, and he would fight to the death for any member of his family."

"I have seen that side of him occasionally, but I'm not exactly family, and we fight all the time."

"That's called sexual tension."

My eyes opened wide in disbelief. Emma was over eighty. Women her age didn't say things like that.

"Don't look so shocked, Brylee. I may be old, but I have been running a diner for over 50 years, and have done my share of listening to the brokenhearted and those who actually found love. I know few things, and one of them is that Jake Johnson is in love with you, and he is fighting it with everything he's got."

"No, he isn't," I fiercely whispered, looking over my shoulder to make sure Trevor was still occupied. "He just wants to make me one of his conquests."

She clasped her hands together and pulled her eyebrows into a frown. "If he only wanted you as a conquest, you would be one by now," she whispered. "I have seen the way he looks at you. He is trying to pretend he doesn't care because he knows you are different from any woman he has ever met and he likes what he sees, even if he doesn't understand it. He is not like that with the other girls in town. Believe me, when I tell you that I know all about Jake Johnson's love life. Beth is head-over-heels in love with him right now, and so is Janet at the airport."

"How do you know that?" I asked.

"Because they both talk to me. Being old does have a few perks. People know you are no threat to their love life so they tell you things."

"And they have both told you they are in love with Jake."

"On more than one occasion."

"They came to my father's funeral together."

"That's because they have been friends for years and know that eventually Jake has to make a decision on which one them he wants to be with the most."

"That's awful! How can they share his attention and affection? The very thought turns my stomach."

"You would be surprised at what a woman in love will put up with. I would have been at the funeral myself, but I got the wog and wasn't able to get out of bed for a few days."

"I'm sorry you were ill. Are you sure this isn't going to be too much for you?"

"Quit worrying! I have never been sick for more than a day or two in my life. Everything is going to work out. Even this situation with Jake will resolve itself in time."

The room was suddenly so hot and oppressive I thought I might faint, so I stepped into the landing with pictures of cats on the wall and leaned against the doorframe to make sure I remained upright.

I knew she was right. Women in love did crazy, stupid, irrational things and the thought that I might actually fall into that category was as repulsive as it was terrifying. Somewhere along the way, my feelings for Jake had changed. I couldn't say it was love like Beth and Janet did, but it was definitely something powerful. Maybe that was why I hadn't pressed harder to straighten things out with Ben. He made me feel safe and secure, but Jake made me feel alive.

"It's not wrong to care about someone, even if it is painful," Emma said as she followed me to the doorway and stood blocking my entrance back into the attic.

Tears and sorrow had been my constant companions for so long I could no longer imagine what life had been like without them, and I hated it. I wanted to be happy, to smile and see the sun as something more than a continuous source of life-giving energy. I wanted it to warm my heart so I could believe there was something in life worth fighting for again, other than the happiness of everyone else.

I looked at my new friend who seemed to understand so much more about life and living than I did. "But it is wrong to become involved with someone when you know in your heart that it will never last. Jake can't give me what I need to be happy. You said that yourself."

"I was simply making a comment based on what I have observed, but are you happy now?"

Her rhetorical question made me frown before looking down at the scuffed wooden floor on the landing that needed refinishing.

"We don't know why things turn out the way they do, Brylee, and I am not saying that you shouldn't be cautious around Jake, but why not give him a chance? If he knew that you had genuine feelings for him, he might take an entirely different approach to life. Love has changed many a man."

"Can you really see Jake in church or without a flock of adoring women following him everywhere he goes?" I asked.

"Robert was the catch of the town when we met, and neither of us believed in God. We had seen too much of the harsher side of life, but when a better way of living was presented to us in the right way and at the right time, we embraced it. Jake might do the same thing. He wants love and acceptance, but he's scared."

"Jake scared!" The idea was preposterous! He wasn't afraid of anything.

"Yes!" Emma said, wrinkling her brow at me again. "He might claim he is not the marrying kind, but that is just to cover a broken heart. He was devastated when he found out his fiancé had been unfaithful to him. That's why he pretends nothing matters and why he can be so abrasive at times."

"But he has more than just two women fawning over his every word. He seems to get along well with everyone else. I am the only one he treats with contempt."

"Women will always go after a handsome, available man, even if he is unattainable. But have you ever seen Jake chasing anyone?"

"I have seen him flirting, and he is very good at it."

"He does it because men have needs."

"That's just an excuse for reprehensible behavior. No man has the right to hurt a woman." I was thinking about Jon and all he had stolen from me. I would never let that happen again.

"People in the world don't look at sex as hurting anyone as long as it is consensual, Brylee, but you should know that by now."

"I do know that. I just don't happen to agree with it."

"Neither do I, but men have no reason for not giving in to their lust unless a woman gives it to them. Jake may get involved with certain women, but he hasn't given his heart to anyone for over ten years. You are the first woman he has been more than casually interested in since his engagement fell apart."

"But what about all the girls in town, like Janet and Beth and Mary Jenkins? They are all attractive, available and willing."

"Mere distractions."

"That doesn't speak too highly of him or his motives."

"Jake is a virile, passionate man, but it would only take the love of one good woman to turn him around. That was how it happened with Robert and we were deliriously happy together for over 45 years."

"You never told me that before."

"Oh, honey," she said with a slightly wicked smile. "Robert could have had any girl in Australia. He was the most handsome bloke I had ever seen, and women of all ages were crazy about him, but I had something he couldn't refuse."

"What was that?"

"Pure, undefiled love! I refused to give in to him until our wedding night, and then I made sure it was a night he would never forget."

"Emma," I said, with a smile I couldn't repress.

"I was young once, but I always knew that I wanted to be the kind of girl a man would sacrifice anything to protect and cherish for his whole life, not just a few days or months. I was also smart enough to know I couldn't do that by sleeping around. Men may claim they can't live without women, but very few of them actually marry the ones they have been intimately involved with. They want someone every bit as special as we do."

"But it is such a double standard."

"It's still a man's world, but even at that we women can make a big difference in the lives of the men we love if we will just give them a chance."

"Suppose you are right, and Jake really is looking for that kind of love. It still doesn't mean that he would be willing to give up the only kind of life he has ever known."

"Nothing can be forced, Brylee, but I do think you need to give him some options. He might just surprise you."

I put my arm around her shoulders. She was a small woman, barely five-feet tall, but she had a mighty spirit, and the biggest heart in the world.

"I will give it some serious thought," I told her as I moved away from the doorframe and back into the small, cluttered attic. "But right now we need to get things ready so Trevor and LeAnn can stay here."

I had just bent over a stack of ancient magazines when Trevor approached us with a box containing an old, brightly-colored train set.

"I haven't seen that for years," Emma said as she removed the red engine and held it tenderly in her hands. "That was Robert's when he was little bloke. Would you like to set it up and see if we can get it to run? I know he would want someone else to have fun with it."

"Sure," Trevor said. "I have never played with a train before."

"Then it's about time you did. There should be some adjustable tracks and a few buildings in another box around here somewhere."

I looked over her head at the disorder in the attic. It might take hours to find what she was looking for, and we needed to get back to the ranch before dark. Maybe I could look for the rest of the train set while she decided which things she could live without. When I made the suggestion, she agreed.

It didn't take long for Trevor and me to find the box labeled *train set parts.* But even with her resolve to clean out enough space for a bed and dresser, Emma had difficulty deciding what could be discarded. Each box she opened brought a different flood of emotions. Some of the items she looked at made her cry and some made her laugh, but each one came with a story. Trevor and I took turns carrying the boxes of things she felt she could get rid of down the narrow staircase and stacking them in the hallway next to the door. I would take them to the nearest donation center once we were finished, if she had not suggested an alternative way to have them removed by then.

By the time we finished for the afternoon, we had cleared the needed space and had even put a piece of plywood over some of the stacked boxes so Trevor could play with the train. There was literally no room for it on the floor. I determined that getting him an oscillating fan was necessary, regardless of the fact that Emma lived closer to the ocean and it was recognizably cooler than at home.

"That should do it!" Emma exclaimed, looking tired, but happy and well-satisfied with what had been accomplished. "I don't know why I hung onto all those old clothes, magazines and everything else. No one has used them since they were put up here. When you have more time to help, I would like to go through the rest of the boxes. You are more than welcome to anything you might find useful."

"Thank you, but right now I don't have a place to put anything of my own except in the guest room I'm using."

She took my hand and patted it. "It won't be like that forever. You will find the right bloke, and you will have that home and family you want so much. Just look at me, I prayed all my life for a family, and now at eighty-plus years, I have one. I couldn't ask for anything more."

Before driving back to the ranch, we decided that both Trevor and I would stay with her on Sunday night so I could take him to school on his first day. He would be afraid and I would be worried, but with LeAnn confined to bed I wanted to be the one to do it.

I talked to Rhonda Benchly about school supplies before we left Emma's, and then took Trevor to get everything on the list. His excitement grew as each new item was put in the shopping cart. It took so little to please him. We stopped at Macca's for dinner after spending a short time at the hospital with LeAnn where Trevor told her all about his day.

More change was definitely in the air, and I wasn't ready for any of them.

Chapter 17

The moment Trevor stepped out of the car at the ranch, he excitedly gathered up everything he could carry and made a beeline for the front door. He had most everything lined up on the dining room table where he could look at it by the time I made it inside with everything else.

"What's all this?" Jake asked when he came into the house to see how the rest of our day had gone. He looked so tired I wondered if he had gotten any sleep while we were away.

"It's all the stuff I need to go to school with other kids," Trevor proudly told him. "And look at the new rucksack I get to carry it in." He handed the camouflage backpack to Jake for his approval.

"See all the zippers. There isn't anything I won't be able to carry in it." He reached across the table to grab the lunch box we had purchased. "Brylee says I can fix my own lunch and take it to school everyday if I want to."

"Wow!" Jake exclaimed. "I don't think I have ever seen so much school stuff outside a store before. All I needed when I was your age was a notebook and a couple of number 2 pencils."

"Mrs. Benchly says we get to use computers too."

"Is she your new teacher?"

"No," he pouted. "She's Emma's friend from church, but she will be at the same school and so will my new friends."

"And what new blokes would that be?" he asked.

"The new ones I made at church last week," Trevor replied.

My hand flew to my mouth to suppress my laughter, and I noticed that Jake had swallowed hard to contain his. Trevor would adjust to life away from the ranch. He already was.

"You are awfully quiet," Jake said a few moments later. We had gone into the kitchen to see about fixing a light snack before bed while Trevor put all of his school supplies in his backpack to make sure everything fit.

"It's been a long day, and I am tired," I admitted. "Were you able to get any rest while we were gone?"

"Rest," he said, rolling his eyes like a misunderstood child. "What's that? Ned needed some help installing the kitchen cupboards. I just got back a few minutes ago. Nora invited us to come for supper on Friday night. I hope you don't mind that I accepted. I also told them about what happened with LeAnn and the arrangements we made with Emma until the baby is born."

"I'm glad you did, on both accounts. They are family and have helped us out a lot lately?"

"They're good people, like Emma," he said. "I just hope it won't be too much for her having LeAnn and Trevor under foot all the time. She is not exactly young, and we are not her responsibility."

"To her, we are family, just like Aunt Nora and Uncle Ned," I replied while leaning against the wall. Jake's presence seemed to fill the room as he walked over to the kitchen sink to wash his hands.

"We cleaned out a space in the attic for Trevor," I continued while watching him. "She is getting a new twin mattress and box springs from Good Will. They will be delivered when they pick up the stuff we moved to the entry today. I was going to do it, but it would have taken me half a dozen trips in the Land Rover."

"So that was what took you so long. I figured you woud be home hours before me and was about to call the police when I saw you drive up."

I forced a weary smile. Suddenly, I felt like the day had dragged on forever, and I was ready for sleep, although I doubted it would come easily. There was far too much to think about. "I am glad you didn't feel it a necessity to call for help again. I may be whiney at times, but I really am old enough to take care of myself."

"I know that," he said, looking down at the floor instead of across the room at me. "But I still worry about you. There isn't much traffic on the road between here and town, and even if there was, not many people are willing to stop and help anyone in need."

"I think you underestimate the goodness of people, especially when you consider all the blessing we have been given lately."

"You sound like Emma."

"I thought that was a good thing. I know you like her and amazingly enough, she likes you."

He looked surprised. "She said that?"

"Without even hesitating," I responded. "She even thinks you will be a great catch for the right woman."

I wished I could tell him that I liked him too, but the time wasn't right. Maybe it never would be.

"No, kidding! That is a surprise since she seems to take so much pleasure in needling me just the way you do."

"Maybe great minds really do think alike," I said, trying to make the tone of my voice casual. "Besides, what's not to like? You are strong, reasonably handsome and always dependable. You can even be sensitive when you want to be."

"Wow," he said for a second time since Trevor and I had returned, looking at me with more than a few questions in his eyes. "You ought to hang out with Emma more often. I don't think you have ever given me a direct compliment before."

I tried to smile, but the muscles around my lips were flinching. "Well, I should have. You have been nothing but good to all of us, and we rely on you more than we should."

"You can always count on me, Brylee—day or night."

"I know that, and I thank you for always being there when we need you."

My heart was beginning to pound unmercifully. He was definitely a man of contradictions. Maybe Emma was right. It might be worth taking the time and the risk to get to know the real Jake Johnson better than I already did.

I spent as much time as possible with Trevor during his last few days at home. I hated the idea of not having him at the ranch where I could take care of him, but I had to respect LeAnn's right to make arrangements for his education. It was a time of great adjustment in an already difficult life, but I knew we would make it with a little divine intervention. We always did.

On Wednesday morning, we saddled our horses and rode over to Uncle Ned's to see how the reconstruction was going. Aunt Nora came running out of the house to greet us as we slid to the ground and tied our horse's reins to the wooden fence outside the front door that had been replaced and freshly painted. Oh, how Ben's eyes would light up with laughter if I could tell him about it. People in California used carports and garages. Nobody rode horses, unless they went to a dude ranch.

"It is so good to see you," she said, pulling both of us into her arms for a hug that was a little too firm but comforting and friendly as well. "How is LeAnn today? We have been so worried about her and the baby. I keep telling Ned we need to get into town to see her, but there is just so bloody much work to be done out here. It seems like I find another mess left over from the flood every day."

"Well, everything looks wonderful to me, and LeAnn and the baby are hanging in there. In fact, she is being released from the hospital on Friday. That was one of the reasons we rode over. Trevor has something he wants to tell you and Uncle Ned."

I looked down at my little brother whose face shown with excitement and pride.

"I'm going to school in town!" he exclaimed. "Brylee and I bought all kinds of new clothes and school supplies. I will have my very own teacher."

"My goodness," Aunt Nora said, looking him up and down. "That sounds like a mighty big adventure, and I do believe you have grown a few inches taller since the last time I saw you. I hope you will be home as often as possible to see us."

"Every weekend! I need to take care of my animals. I wanted to take Copper and Newton with me, but mum said no."

"I can understand that," Aunt Nora said as she guided us up the steps and into the house. Everything smelled new.

"It's beautiful," I told her as we passed from room to room. The walls had been painted, and new carpet and hardwood had been put on the floors. Even her new furniture had arrived.

"I'm sorry I didn't get to help as much as I wanted to," I told her.

"You were where you needed to be. I just wish you had been able to go shopping with Molly and me. We ended up driving clear into Sydney since there was so little available locally. You wouldn't believe all the stuff in the furniture stores."

She was smiling like a child who had just received everything she had ever wanted for Christmas, but who could blame her? Ben and I had spent countless hours walking through furniture stores trying to decide what we were going to buy once we were in our own home, and it had been wonderful. Now he and Jennifer would be doing that while I spent the rest of my days living as a guest in LeAnn's house. It was a tragedy I didn't want to accept, but for Aunt Nora's sake, I had to be pleasant.

"Well, you and Molly did an amazing job."

"But you haven't seen the best part yet. I love my new kitchen more than any room in the house. Ned says I'm crazy, but you will see that he is not complaining about all the meals I am cooking again."

I followed her through the new family area that had been created in what had been the formal dining room.

"I like this," I told her as I looked at the new sofa and high definition television.

"So do I," she admitted. "I don't know why Ned and I ever thought we needed a fancy place for people to devour their food. No one in this family eats any place except in the kitchen."

I knew exactly what she meant. The only time the dining room at home had been used was for the wedding and funerals, and of course as a place to store supplies when the flood came. I was surprised I could think even about those hard times without crying. I still missed my father every day but was learning that life had to go on even if I wasn't ready for it.

Aunt Nora put some fresh oatmeal cookies on a plate and poured three glasses of milk straight from one of their cows. While I still hated the taste and the texture, I didn't have the heart to do anything but drink it and pretend to enjoy the experience. Trevor was used to it, but I had to wonder if his taste would change like mine had once he had been in Edna for a while.

Uncle Ned joined us at the kitchen table when he came in for lunch.

"My goodness," he said. "It seems like forever since you've been here. I hope Nora has been telling you about our dinner plans for Friday night. They have changed a little since I talked to Jake. The kids are coming home for the weekend."

His face was literally beaming with pride, and I couldn't help but rejoice over the fact that something so awful as the flood had turned out so well for them.

"That's wonderful, and we wouldn't miss it," I told him. "You have done an incredible job with the house. No one would ever know what you have been through."

"It's an experience I hope never to repeat, but we have been blessed. I was over at Mac Gilberts yesterday, and they have barely begun the work of rebuilding. His wife was so traumatized by the experience that she moved into town to live with their daughter. Says she won't come back until her house is fixed. Old Mac is lost without her."

"Is there anything I can do to help?" I asked. "It looks like I will have some free time now that Trevor will be spending his weeks in town."

"I heard about that," Uncle Ned said, giving Trevor one of his broad smiles. "That is something I always wanted to do, go to school with other mates every day."

"I would like it more if Brylee was coming with me," Trevor told him as a touch of anxiety surfaced.

Not wanting to make matters worse by acknowledging his fears, I forced a tentative smile. "You will do great without me, Trevor. Besides, someone needs to spend time with your animals until you come home for the weekends. Your Uncle Jake is way too busy for that."

How I wished I could stop thinking about him. It made me restless and frustrated living on the fringes of everyone else's lives with nothing to keep me grounded. I missed Ben so much, and it was hard not to be bitter over the experiences he was now sharing with Jennifer. My ever-changing feelings for Jake didn't help matters either. Despite what Emma and I had discussed, I still felt it was best to keep him an arm's length away. I was much too vulnerable and needy to risk anything else.

On Friday morning, Trevor and I visited our father's grave to tell him about the changes that were coming. I had been hesitant even making the suggestion after his violent reaction the first time I mentioned doing it, but I wanted him to know there wasn't anything scary about the family cemetery. It was a good place to think and even talk to the people who were no longer with us. I told him to bring Copper so father could see how much she had grown.

We went right after breakfast, before the heat of the day made us want to stay indoors. It was peaceful and calm as we sat side by side on the sparse, burned grass at the head of our father's grave where a tombstone would be set once things got back to a semblance of normalcy. I had always planned on getting a joint headstone for my parents, but that had been taken out of my hands when LeAnn became my father's second wife.

Copper sniffed the ground and darted back and forth as white butterflies landed close to her before flying away. I watched her play while I decided what to say.

"I like it here," I finally told Trevor as I pulled a blade of tan grass and began rolling it into a ball. "I feel so much closer to my parents when I am sitting here talking to them."

He frowned. "What do you talk about?"

"Anything I feel like sharing. I want them to know that Ben and I broke up, but I am okay with staying here because I have you. It is going to be really hard when I can't be with you every day." I wiped at the tears that were forming in my eyes before they began to fall.

"Don't cry, Brylee," he said, snuggling into my arm. "I will be home every weekend, and you will have Copper and Newton to keep you company. Uncle Jake said we could keep Newton in the barn longer so I can see him when I come home."

I covered his small hand with my own and brought it to my lips. "And I promise I will visit your animals every day and tell them what you are learning at school."

"And I will call you every night," he said. "Is it okay that I'm scared to go to school in town?"

"But it is a good kind of scared, isn't it?"

"I guess so." He left my arms and stretched out on the grass. "Should we tell father about the baby?"

"Absolutely!" I told him. "Why don't you do it right now?"

Trevor gave me a funny look.

"Are you sure he can hear me? He is all covered with dirt."

"Only his body was tired and sick. His spirit is back in heaven, and someday we will join him."

"Is it true, Brylee, really true that we will get to see him again? I miss him so much."

"Cross my heart. We'll see father again and every member of our Hawkins' family who came before us, but we have a lot to do before then."

My thoughts about bringing our extended family together were beyond him, and maybe that was a good thing. For now, he just needed to accept the fact that our father would always be part of our lives, even though we were unable to see him.

Over the next few minutes, Trevor told him about the baby and school and his animals. I was so proud of him for accepting so many losses and changes without giving in to tantrums or withdrawing from the people who loved him. He was teaching me so much about acceptance and forgiveness—concepts I very much needed to make a more permanent part of my life.

Still, it was nearly impossible to comprehend why our lives had been turned topsy-turvy so many times during the past few months. I understood the concept of trials being for our growth and refinement, but I was tired of feeling edgy and sorrowful all the time. I wanted to let go of the past and accept the present, but I didn't like what it had to offer me.

Perhaps God was helping me become a better mother by giving me time with my little brother, but where in the world was I going to find a worthy husband if I never left the ranch for more than a few hours at a time?

Trevor and I didn't remain long after he'd told our father all of his news, and maybe that was for the best. It was too hot to spend much time outside anyway, and I could feel the moisture pooling between my shoulder blades. Even winter in the outback was too warm for me.

Jake was drinking a cup of coffee in the kitchen when we got back to the house. He looked surprised when Trevor told him where we had been.

"I am glad you're here," I said after my little brother had taken Copper to the barn to see Newton and his other animals. "We haven't talked about the ranch all week, and I am sure there are things I should be doing."

He filled his cup again with the hot, dark mixture that was perking away on the counter. He had been brewing his coffee in the bunkhouse since we returned from the beach. I wondered what had changed, other than the fact that Trevor would be leaving us to start a new life in the next couple days.

"What do you want to know?" he asked, leaning back against the kitchen counter with his cup in his hands. "There is not a whole lot for anyone to do right now, except check on the animals every few days. Ned and I have been running the herds together. Every animal has been branded so it will be easy to tell them apart once the sheep are sheared again and the cattle rounded up. Other than that, it is pretty much just keeping things repaired."

"Is that how you and father did it?"

"Not exactly. Jack and Ned liked to keep the animals separate. A little sibling rivalry, I think."

"But I want to keep things the way father was doing them. That's important to me."

"Things change, Brylee. Since the flood and with LeAnn's pregnancy we aren't exactly as flexible as we were when your father was here. It just makes more sense to run the herds together because we have limited manpower right now."

"But I can help out more once Trevor is in town for the week."

I hated the way that sounded. Having him around was a blessing, not a burden for me.

"It really doesn't matter whose land the animals are grazing on. We want to keep all of them alive. It actually makes more sense to do it this way because it gives the grass longer to grow before it is mowed down again."

"I suppose that's logical," I replied.

"It certainly is! We are not leaving anything to chance, Brylee. You have to trust me on that. I can take you up in the plane any time you like so you can see for yourself that everything is working out better this way."

I bit the inside of my bottom lip and frowned. Trusting Jake wasn't easy, especially since we had butted heads so often in the past. I would talk to Uncle Ned about the new arrangements when I saw him at the barbecue. I wasn't about to risk my father's legacy just because Jake told me everything was okay. He could leave any time he wanted to. The rest of us had to stay.

Molly and NJ were sitting on the front porch with bottles of liquid refreshment in their hands when we arrived at Uncle Ned's in Jake's truck a short time later. I was going to tell him I could take Trevor with me in the Land Rover but knew that was being both silly and impractical. If I couldn't trust myself to be around him when Trevor was sitting between us, how would I ever manage when he was gone?

Molly put her drink on a small iron table and came running down the steps when we pulled into the yard, but her disappointment was evident when I opened the passenger door and climbed out before she had time to corner Jake. They hadn't seen each other since Christmas, but the image of her sitting on his lap had been irrevocably imprinted on my mind.

"It's good to see you," she said, giving me a quick hug. "Mum told me about Aunt LeAnn being in the hospital. I can't imagine having a baby sibling when I am old enough to have one myself."

I chose to ignore her comments. Explaining how I felt would hurt too much.

"There have been a lot of changes recently, but we are all very happy about the prospect of adding a new member to our family," I told her. "I just wish she didn't have to stay in town until the baby comes. It won't be the same without Trevor and her at the ranch."

"Are you crazy," she said, pulling me away from the truck as Jake got out and walked towards the house. I was surprised by her behavior. She was usually all over him.

"I would give anything in the world to be alone on the ranch with him. I have heard stories about him from older girls that literally make my toes curl."

My face flushed scarlet. I didn't want to hear about Jake's love life, especially from my younger cousin. And I certainly didn't want her thinking I was the kind of woman who would allow myself to become one his conquests.

"It's not like that with us," I told her, almost too abruptly. "We are family, and we work together. That's all."

"If you say so," she retorted with a shrug of her pretty shoulders. She was wearing Daisy Duke shorts and a top that had fallen off one shoulder. I was worried about her. She was way too flirty with men, and I didn't want her to go through the agony I had with Jon. It only took one deranged man to destroy everything—even for a girl who enjoyed sleeping around.

"Then why don't you come to Sydney for a visit if you are not interested in Jake?" she asked, linking arms with me and dragging me towards the front porch where Uncle Ned had joined NJ and Jake. They were all enjoying their favorite brand of neck oil—more commonly known as beer.

"I could introduce you to a lot of different blokes. You really need to meet someone who interests you. You can't do that when all you do is hang around family. Mum told me about your fiancé. I am awfully sorry things didn't work out. I know how hard it is having even the simplest of plans loused up."

Suddenly, I understood what she was trying to do. She knew I was now free, and that threatened her childish dreams. She wanted to make sure Jake and I didn't get together, and the best way of doing that was to hook me up with someone else.

"There isn't time for that," I told her.

"Nonsense, there is always time for fun. Listen everyone, Brylee has agreed to come to Sydney for a vacation," she said as she picked up her own drink and smiled broadly at Jake who was still wearing his sunglasses.

I grimaced. I had never given any indication that I was willing to go anywhere. She needed to learn that I wasn't a menace to her now, or ever. No man she was ever drawn to could give me what I both needed and wanted, regardless of how attractive and alluring he might be.

"She needs to get away for a while and meet some new people—blokes in particular since that awful breakup. She is only around family out here."

The movement of Jake's jaw told me he wasn't pleased with my cousin's comments. I knew he liked Molly, but she was a little too ostentatious and young for him.

"I haven't said I would come," I defended myself. "Molly just suggested it."

"Well, I hardly agree with my sister. You do need to get away, and I could introduce you to some of my most interesting mates." NJ gave me a hug and a cousinly kiss on the cheek. "I have been telling everyone at the frat house that I have this really hot cousin. Of course, they won't believe me until they actually see you."

"I appreciate the offers, but I am not ready for that yet."

Jake was looking at the drink in his hands, and I didn't want to make matters worse between us by pretending I was interested in what my cousins were proposing. We still hadn't come to terms with what had happened on the beach and I knew it bothered him, though likely not as much as it did me. Besides, all NJ and Molly could introduce me to were more men like the ones I had already known before meeting Ben.

"Then just come for a break and some good conversation," NJ interjected. "There really is life beyond the ranch, even if our fathers' refuse to believe it."

He gave Uncle Ned a manly hug. "Isn't that right, old man?"

"Someday, I hope you will understand what this life is all about," Uncle Ned told him. "Despite the tough times, this land has been good to us. I can't imagine having to account to someone else for everything I do. Out here, I am my own boss. If I have a good year, I can be proud of that. If I don't, I can figure out ways to make things better."

"I know you love it out here," NJ said. "I was just mucking around to get a reaction, but Molly and I might have other plans for our lives. There is a whole world outside the boundaries of this ranch."

"Those steaks won't cook themselves, Ned Hawkins," Aunt Nora said as she opened the front door to the house and stuck her head out. "Trevor and I have everything else set out on the table ready to be eaten."

"I'm coming." Uncle Ned gave her a kiss on the forehead. "You young bucks need to find a good woman like I did and settle down. There is nothing better than having someone to share your life with, even if she is full of spit and fire."

"I could get used to a woman like Nora," Jake said after they had gone. "She is hardworking and sensible and lets a man know where he stands. There are no games with the Nora's of the world."

"You would get bored with a predictable woman in not time at all," NJ told him. "I know I would."

Molly stuck her lower lip out before speaking. "You are both bloody impossible. Women are not commodities to be bought or sold like sheep at an auction. Most of our assets can't be measured."

"Well put, sis," NJ encouraged her. "I like the excitement of not knowing where I stand. There is nothing better for keeping a man on his toes than seeing other blokes as interested in the same lass as he is."

Jake looked at me with a crooked smile and shook his head.

"That is because the two of you are still young and haven't had your hearts broken. When that happens, knowing where you stand with someone actually means something, doesn't it, Brylee?"

I wasn't sure what he was getting at. The fact that I'd had my heart broken, or the fact that he still believed I was playing some kind of a game and using what I said were my religious beliefs as an excuse not to get close to him.

"It is never easy losing someone you love," I said, grateful that Aunt Nora had come back to invite all of us inside. It was going to be a very long evening, and I was right.

Chapter 18

Saturday went by far too rapidly. Trevor and I took the horses out for another ride, visited with his animals while he showed me how to take care of them, and then we went to the barn's loft to swing. Our time together was going by so fast. Tomorrow, he would be in town with Emma and his mother, and I wouldn't see him again for an entire week. I couldn't imagine being without him anymore than I could imagine being alone with Jake. Both prospects made me uncomfortable and sad.

I looked around the loft at the sparse number of hay bails, the unfinished board walls, the creaking hinges, the small openings in the floor where loose fragments of hay fell into the barn below and felt like crying. Everything on our homestead needed repair, and we didn't have the time or the resources to take care of even half of them. Why was it that Uncle Ned was able to take care of everything so quickly after the flood? One would never know there had been any damage on his homestead. Had my father really been that bad of a rancher, or had he just given his younger brother the best of everything so he would have no choice but to succeed?

Whatever the reason, I was determined not to let our part of the ranch fail. If that meant listening more to what Jake had to say, then I would do it. He was the key to our success or failure. Both my father and Uncle Ned trusted him, but even after all he had done for me, I was still having trouble believing that he wouldn't give in to his darker side again and do something to really hurt me.

"You're not pushing," Trevor shouted. And when I looked up at him, I saw that the swing was barely moving. I couldn't disappoint, so I pressed harder and faster and watched him move through the air until the muscles in my arms were screaming with pain.

The vibrations of his laughter seemed to fill the barn. It was a joyful sound, but I couldn't help wondering what it would be like when he returned after a week spent with children his own age. Would he still find pleasure in the simple things, or would he wish he was back in town?

Before long, I was too tired to push him any longer.

"I have to rest for a minute," I panted, sinking down on the nearest bail of hay. He remained suspended until the swing slowed enough that he could jump to the floor without spraining or breaking something.

"But we can't stop now," he said with a tortured look on his upturned face. "I haven't pushed you yet."

My smile was immediate. "Are you sure you want to do that? I am much larger and heavier than you."

"I'm big enough to do it. See my muscles?"

I pushed down on the small knot in his upper arm.

"You are right," I told him. "Your muscles are growing as fast as you are."

I had a severe case of the doldrums, but there was so little time left that I sat down on the swing and began pumping with my legs as hard as I could to help build the momentum while he pushed me from behind. Trevor was so willing to please, but he was still just a little boy.

I hated the knot in my stomach that formed every time I thought about him going to school in Edna. I loved spending time with him each day and being important in his world. Once he had made new friends our relationship would change, and I wasn't ready for that.

Jake must have felt the same way about him leaving because he joined us in the loft after feeding and watering the horses—something Trevor and I planned to do once we were finished playing.

"I was wondering what had happened to the two of you," he said without chastisement as he climbed through the hole in the floor that led to the upper level of the barn. "How can you stand the heat up here? It is hot as Hades."

"Not when you're swinging, Uncle Jake," Trevor told him, sighing heavily and wiping the moisture from his face with his arm. "Only when you are pushing."

"Really," Jake replied, lifting his eyebrow when he looked at me still moving slightly through the air on the board swing. "And just how high can you push your sister?"

"Not very high because she is bigger than me."

"Now that is a shame. Perhaps I should see if that could be remedied."

It all happened so quickly I didn't have time to jump down. Trevor stepped aside, and Jake had his hands around the ropes and was stepping backwards before I could even protest.

"You don't have to do this," I almost pleaded as my body began to move and my heart began to pound even more noisily in my chest.

"On the contrary. You deserve having someone do something for you as a change of pace. Wouldn't you agree, Trevor?"

My little brother didn't come to my defense. He just stood to the side clapping. "Push her higher, Uncle Jake. Make her feet go right out the window."

It was impossible not to smile. I loved the rush of flying through the air. So I just leaned back as Jake's hearty pushes sent my entire body through the opening in the front wall of the loft. I could see the family cemetery and way beyond. Little patches of green had sprung up everywhere, and there were bursts of yellow and lavender flowers in the pastures. The rain, destructive as it had been, had given renewed life to everything around us. I wondered how many small, furry animals had returned. Trevor and I would have to go looking for bunnies and foxes. But then I remembered that he wouldn't be here come Monday, and my momentary bubble of happiness burst. How would I ever manage without him?

Back and forth I went until my head started to throb, but the sensation of bliss that had been my first reaction to moving so rapidly through the air did not return. So I called out for Jake to stop pushing. He collapsed into the hay next to Trevor and waited until I had come to a stop and jumped off.

"I must be getting old and out-of-shape," he said as I sank down next to them. "I used to be able to work from sunup until midnight without breaking a sweat."

"I am afraid that level of bodily exertion is in the past for most of us, but you didn't have to push me for so long."

"You looked like you were having fun, so I didn't want to stop."

"I was," I admitted knowing that my face was flushed, and I was smiling. But it was impossible to disguise the sadness in my eyes. It permeated every part of me.

Trevor was back on his feet in an instant. "Push me, Uncle Jake," he pleaded. "I want to go as high as Brylee did."

"Thanks, little brother," I said with mock display of disappointment, but grateful Jake's eyes were no longer on me. "I was pushing you as hard as I could."

He bent down and kissed my cheek. "You do real good, but Uncle Jake is bigger and stronger. I just want to go as high as you did."

I couldn't afford to indulge in even a moment of self-pity with Trevor still around, but a smidgen of anxiety suddenly hit me upside the head. What if Jake wasn't careful enough, and my little brother fell off the swing and got hurt? He would automatically go higher than I did because he was so much smaller.

"You will be careful, won't you, Jake?" I asked.

He looked at me and laughed in that irritating way that helped keep me grounded.

"Don't worry, Mother Hen, I studied physics in high school and know what I am doing."

I scowled. Jake always had an answer for everything. The thing that bothered me most was that his assumptions and observations were usually right.

"I have an idea," he said as he walked across the floor to where Trevor was already sitting on the swing waiting for him. "Why don't we make this a short one and see if we can talk Brylee into letting us have some big bowls of ice cream?"

Trevor's eyes widened at the suggestion. "Could we?" he asked. "I love ice cream."

I leaned back and looked at them. Trevor's smile was genuine, and Jake looked relaxed and content. It was one of those extraordinary moments when time appears to stand still and all anxiety and fear pauses. I didn't want to be the one breaking the spell, but someone had to.

"I think that is a great idea, but you have to go to bed without any ruckus when the time comes. We have to leave the house by seven in the morning."

I didn't wait for his reply. A moment of cold dread had washed over me as I internalized the fact this would be our last night together when he might be totally content at home. Once he started school on Monday, everything in his world would change. That meant mine would change again too, and I wasn't ready for that.

"What's going on with you?" Jake asked me a short time later, after we had finished our ice cream and Trevor was tucked away safe in bed. I had gone outside to sit on the porch swing and try to fight off the desire to return to his room and watch him sleep.

"I am just being a female," I said as he stood there looking down at me. "I don't want Trevor to go to school in town."

"I've been feeling a little like I have been knocked off a teacup myself," he replied. "I have been with Trevor nearly every day since he was born, but this decision isn't up to us. Trevor is LeAnn's son, and she has the right to decide what happens to him with or without our input. But then she is full of surprises, I still can't believe she allowed him to go to church with you."

I pulled my knees under my chin and looked up at the blanket of stars in the sky. The heavens always seemed so massive and clear in the outback. How could anyone not believe in God? Everything about our lives reflected his love, even the bad times for that was when we needed him most.

"He was just learning about Jesus and how to become more like him," I said. "That can only make his life better."

"He could learn those same things in Catholic school. I don't understand all this fuss about religion anyway. If you want to believe in God, that's fine, but no one should be forced into compliance just because it is what someone else wants."

"Your analogy of the situation is anything but accurate, and I am much too tired to squabble over religion with you tonight. Either you believe something or you don't. It is all about faith and trust."

"So we are back to that same old, tired discussion," he said, leaning against the house and looking down at me. It made me feel small and insignificant. "It's not that I don't want to believe in something, but life has proven to me over and over again that the only person I can trust is myself. Other people always let me down—one way another."

"It doesn't have to be like that, Jake. Look at all the people who have helped us the past few months. I, for one, know I would not have survived without their kindness and God's constant love. If you can't believe in other people, you should at least give him a chance."

Jake laughed. "You are so passionate about the things you believe in, but you don't give people a chance any more than I do."

"That's not true," I defended myself. "I try to give everyone the benefit of the doubt."

"Is that so! All you do is push me away whenever I try to get closer to you, and I am not just talking about in a physical way."

"I don't mean to. I just don't want to be hurt again."

"And you think I am out to hurt you?"

"Not intentionally, but there are a lot of women who are crazy about you, and you can't end up with all of them."

"And you are still hung up on that bloody toe rack back in the United States."

I was starting to get angry. He knew how much Ben had meant to me. Why did he always insist on rehashing our failed relationship in the most infuriating way possible?

"We shouldn't be talking about this, Jake. All it does is cause a squabble."

"Maybe so, but we will practically be living together for the next couple of months. It might be the perfect time to discover just what could happen between us when we are not fighting. Your resistance is as intriguing as it is baffling to me."

"Just listen to yourself? You sound like you actually believe that women should lie prone at your feet just begging for crumbs and favors. Well, I am not one of your besotted groupies."

"I have never pretended you were, but you can't deny that there is something going on between us."

"And what if we found there is nothing between us but a rather distorted kind of chemistry? Can't you see how awkward and uncomfortable that would be? When I love someone, it is with all my heart. I don't know how to be any different."

"I'm not sure how to take that," he responded. "I guess I should be grateful that you see me as more than just an object, like a rock or a log in the middle of the road. You are going to change your mind about me someday, Brylee Hawkins, but maybe I will just let you stew in your own fabricated juices for a while longer."

I was glad it was mostly dark on the front porch so he couldn't see the pain in my eyes. It radiated outward from the hole in my heart. I was still grieving for the man I had lost, along with the one that was starting to mean far more to me than he should since he could never provide the kind of life I wanted.

"It is over between Ben and me," I said, without looking up at him. "I have accepted that, but I can't just jump into bed with someone I hardly know because I am lonely. I respect myself too much for that."

"And you think I don't respect you?"

His question caught me off guard, and I looked up to see him still leaning against the side of the house in his shirt that was open at the neck and blue jeans that were just a little too tight for me. He looked genuinely shaken and oddly sincere.

"Haven't my actions towards you been above reproach?" he continued. "I haven't mentioned what happened on the beach to anyone, even though I think about it constantly. That bloke who hurt you was a pig, and I would strangle him with my bare hands if I had the chance, but I am not a violent or abusive man. I just wish you could accept the fact that I care about you and would never intentionally do anything to cause you pain."

The conflict in my heart was reaching its breaking point. If I had never heard about the gospel, I would race directly into his arms. He had protected me so many times in the past few months, and I had shared with him the most intimate parts of my life, but I couldn't have an affair with him now that I knew the truth. He lived in an entirely different world than I did—a world I could never return to no matter how much I might want to right now.

When I didn't say anything, he pushed himself away from the house.

"Maybe it would be best for all of us if I found work elsewhere. LeAnn and Trevor won't be back for months. You could get Ned to help you out around here until you can find a suitable hired hand."

I heard his words but had trouble comprehending them. The sudden change in his approach made cold chills slithered down my arms, despite the heat left over from a warm afternoon. I didn't want him to leave. LeAnn and Trevor would never forgive me for driving him away. There had to be some way we could get past our feelings and learn how to be friends.

"I don't want you to go," I softly said as he took a step towards the stairs leading the driveway.

"And why not?" he asked, pivoting on his heels so I could see his face in the dim porch light. He looked incredibly tired and miserable. "I can't keep doing this, Brylee. Somewhere along the way in all our bickering I discovered that I don't dislike you at all. In fact, I want you in my life as more than a friend or a shirt-tail relative."

His honesty both frightened and excited me. My whole body wanted to be touched and held tightly. It was like a sickness needing relief, but I had made a covenant to serve and honor God no matter what it cost me personally. Nonetheless, the thought of him leaving with no intention of coming back was too terrible to even consider. I waited in stupefied silence hoping an answer I could live with would come, but my mind remained a swirling masses of confusion.

He put his foot on the top step. It was now or never.

"I'm scared of not making the right choices," I choked out, daring myself to look in his direction. He wasn't the fiend I wanted him to be so I could reject him and feel good about it. He was a man, a good man, an honest man, and a man who really cared about me.

"Who isn't, Brylee?" he said. "I have made a mess out of every part of my life, but there still has to be more than just getting by. I may not be as good as that saintly bloke you were going to marry, but I am not some monster who wants to use or abuse you like that coward who should be behind bars."

"I know that," I said, wishing I knew how to explain the conflict I was fighting so he could finally understand.

"Then talk to me," he said, crossing the short distance between us and sitting down beside me on the swing. I could feel the heat of his body, even though we weren't touching. "I want to understand."

"So do I, Jake. I care about you, I really do, but we are so different in everything except our love for LeAnn, Trevor and this ranch."

"Personal differences make us unique," he said. "We both value family, friends and home, and we work and play well together when we want to. That sounds like a pretty good foundation for a relationship to me."

When he put it that way, it sounded so simple and logical, but I couldn't live without the gospel. Maybe he would be willing to change, but if he didn't . . . .

"I'm getting tired of beating my head against the same bloody brick wall, love," he said after another long silence. "You won't give me a chance because I don't believe the same things you do. That is the truth behind everything, isn't it? You do know I haven't seriously considered any other relationship since you came home. Sure, I might do a little more than flirt with some of the girls in town, but it doesn't mean anything. You are the only woman I want to be with."

I wasn't sure I could accept his explanation about his dalliances with the girls in town quite so readily, but that wasn't our greatest impasse right now.

"What if the real truth is that I don't know how to be with any man?" I queried, knowing I might be opening an entirely different can of worms, but also knowing there were many misgivings I had never told anyone about until now. "Jon killed something inside of me, and I don't know if it will ever come back."

But even as the words came out, I knew they weren't true. Jake could give me what I needed tonight—the feeling of desirability and belonging to someone who cared. When I looked over at him there were tears in my eyes. He wiped them away with his fingertips while I continued speaking.

"I want to forget everything except for this very moment, Jake, but so much has happened the past few years, and I can't go back to the way I used to be."

"I would never ask you to do that. I would support whatever it is you need or want to be happy."

"But you wouldn't do it with me."

"I would give you my heart. Why should it matter what church I belong to as long as I am trying to be a good person? There are no perfect people. We are all just doing the best we can and hoping the people we love will accept us the way we are."

"I do love and accept you, Jake," I said, not realizing what I had done until the words were uttered and couldn't be retracted. He looked at me with an astounded expression.

"Did I hear you correctly?" he asked.

I willed myself not to look away. His eyes told me volumes more than his words ever could. He loved and desired me and wanted me to be his in the most intimate of ways. But most of all, he respected me enough not to push for something I wasn't ready for."

"You did, but I am not certain it changes anything," I whispered. "We are still the same people we were five seconds ago."

"I'm not," he said, turning his entire body so we were facing each other and then lifting my hands to his lips and kissing them. "I am a very patient man, Brylee. I know we have a lot to work through if we are ever going to be together permanently, and maybe we will find out that we don't belong together somewhere along the way, but at least that decision can be made after we have given it a shot."

I was just about to say something when Trevor opened the screen door and walked outside. I pulled my hands away from Jake and folded them tightly in my lap. My little brother didn't need to know what had just happened between us.

"I can't sleep," he announced. "I have never been away from home for over one night, and I'm scared."

I looked up at Jake and smiled. Our time for expressing how we really felt was over, but maybe it was better that way. Too many stars on an early winter night had been the downfall of many a girl.

"Now that is just plain silly," Jake said, standing up and putting his arm around Trevor's shoulders. "You might not be sleeping in your own bed at Emma's, but you will be with your mum. And from what I understand, you have a mighty fine room in the attic."

"I know," he said, looking younger than his eight years. "But what about you and Brylee and Copper and Newton? I don't want any of you to forget about me."

"Like that would ever happen," I said, springing from the swing so I could take his face in my hands. "I could never forget you, Trevor."

I gazed into his eyes that were swimming in unshed tears. He was trying so hard to be the man he had promised our father he would be.

"You are my little brother, and I will never love anyone more than I love you."

"What about Ben? You were going to marry him."

"I loved Ben very much, but he wasn't family. You and I share some of the same blood and genes. You can't get much closer than that."

Trevor threw his arms around my neck—almost choking me in his zeal to let me know that he felt the same way about me. I looked up at Jake who was smiling down at both of us. So this was the way family was meant to be.

"Promise, Brylee," Trevor spoke into my neck. "Promise that you will never leave."

"I'm not going anywhere," I assured him. "Your Uncle Jake and I will take care of your animals while you are gone, and you will be here every weekend. And during the week, you will be so busy with school and helping Emma take care of your mother that you won't even have time to miss us."

"I miss you already," he said. "What if the kids at school don't like me?"

"That's not going to happen," Jake told him, squatting down beside us. "In a few days, you will have so many new mates you won't be able to remember all their names."

"Why can't you and Brylee just come with me?"

Jake looked at me and smiled. He had such an amazing smile. Why hadn't I noticed it before? Things could be really good between us when we were trying to get along instead of fighting because we were both so afraid of compromise.

"For two really big reasons," Jake said. "Emma's house isn't big enough for all of us, and even if it was, the ranch won't run by itself. Your sister and I have a lot of work to do out here."

"But I could stay here and help. Brylee could teach me like mum did."

"I could probably do that," I told him. "But what about your mother? She can't get out of bed for a long time and needs your help. Besides, it would break her heart if you decided to stay out here instead of being with her in town."

I thought he was going to cry, but he didn't. He simply bit his lip and looked over at us.

"Okay," he said with a colossal sigh. "But we will talk every day, won't we, Brylee?"

"As soon as you get home from school. Just think how much smarter you will be every weekend. Your Uncle Jake and I will have to do some studying of our own so we can keep up with you."

Oh, how I hoped we were not making a terrible mistake forcing him to go to school in town. Children could be exceptionally cruel to someone they didn't know, and Trevor was a shy and sensitive child who had never learned how to defend himself. But I wasn't his mother, and I didn't have the right to make any decisions about his life while she was around. I gave him one final hug before Jake put his hand on Trevor's shoulder.

"Why don't we head upstairs to bed," I said. "I know I am tired even if you aren't."

"Will you read me another story?"

"I think that could be arranged," I said, taking his hand, but reaching out and touching Jake's arm with the other. It was my way of saying I was sorry we had been interrupted, but maybe it was just another blessing to save me from myself. I'm not sure what I might have done if we had been alone together in the moonlight any longer. It had certainly done its magic with my heart.

"But only one, Trevor," I said, taking a step away from the man I really wanted to kiss. "It is going to be light in a few hours, and we have another huge day waiting for us."

"Good night, Uncle Jake," Trevor said, hugging him around the waist. "Will you be up in the morning to see me go?"

"I wouldn't miss it, but your sister is right. I think all three of us could use a good night's sleep. I will see both of you in the morning."

He turned around and walked away, and with his departure I felt an unmistakable loss. Could it possibly be that a certain part of my past was already beginning to heal?

Chapter 19

Trevor was knocking on my door before the alarm went off the next morning.

"Breakie's on the table," he said. "Uncle Jake made bacon and everything."

I opened my eyes and stretched. The sun was already streaming in through my open window. It would be another day of new beginnings, and it was just a few minutes after five in the morning.

"Good morning, Jake," I said, when I walked into the kitchen a few moments later, still feeling a little rummy after having been awakened so unexpectedly. There hadn't been time for a shower, but Jake had seen me in far worse conditions. "Everything smells wonderful, but you didn't have to fix breakfast. We could have eaten cold cereal."

"You could have, but it is a long time until lunch," he replied. "I didn't want you to get hungry."

Trevor was already sitting at the table, eagerly devouring a plate filled with bacon, hash browns and eggs.

I sat down at the table with him while Jake fixed a plate for me. A glass of orange juice was already waiting beside the silverware.

"I didn't know how you liked your eggs so I scrambled them," he said, putting a plate of hot food in front of me. It was more than I ever ate for breakfast, but I didn't want to hurt his feelings by being picky.

"Aren't you eating with us?" I asked as he walked back towards the stove. I liked this new Jake. Or maybe it was just the old Jake I had never allowed myself to see before now. Either way, he was impressing me.

"Of course, I am," he said, filling a plate for himself and then joining us at the table. The chair at the head of the table where father always sat was still empty. I wondered if it would always be that way. It was impossible not to feel his presence in the house, even though he had been gone for seven months. It seemed especially strong today, or maybe it just seemed that way because most everything had changed.

"Can I have more hash browns?" Trevor asked before Jake had gotten a forkful of food into his mouth.

"I'll get it for him," I said, springing to my feet. "You shouldn't have to do all the work after fixing such an incredible meal."

Breakfast was good. In fact, it was probably the best morning meal I had eaten in months—even better than the pancakes he had prepared at Emma's house on the coast. If he ever got tired of working on the ranch, he could easily get a job as a chef. Beth would love having him at the diner with her, but that would only make Janet at the airport jealous.

Reminding myself that there were other women in his life helped keep me focused, especially after what had happened between us the night before. I had wanted to go the bunkhouse more than once after Trevor was asleep but managed to keep from leaving the house. What we were feeling was very new, and one false move would ruin everything.

"It was my pleasure to cook for both of you," he was saying as I watched the muscles in his arms ripple beneath the lightweight shirt he was wearing. "Besides, it's our last meal together until next weekend."

I frowned, not knowing if he meant that he would be fixing his own meals in the bunkhouse until Trevor came home, or if he just stating the fact that my little brother would not be eating with us again until then. Certainly sharing a few meals like we had always done had to be safe enough.

But what if sharing meals wasn't safe, I worried on the long drive into town. I did care about Jake more than I should and definitely more than I wanted to, but I hadn't forgotten about Ben. A part of me would always love him, but it was over between us. I tried to wipe thoughts of what might be happening between him and Jennifer from my mind. I hated feeling jealous, but she was going to get the life I had thought would be mine. And there was no one in Australia who could possibly replace him.

"Are you sad?" Trevor asked as we pulled into a parking space at the store front where church was held. "You hardly talked to me all the way into town."

I shut off the Land Rover's engine and removed the key from the ignition. In truth, he had been dozing most of the way, but I really hadn't felt much like talking when he was awake and our conversations had been somewhat strained.

"I am sorry for not being very good company," I told him as I leaned back in the driver's seat and closed my eyes, hoping the sudden rush of emotion I was feeling would go away before it exploded. Trevor was so trusting and vulnerable, and I should have made better use of the last few hours we would have together for nearly a week. But I hated change and my life had been filled with it lately.

"On't worry, Brylee, It's going to be okay," he said, touching my arm with his warm and comforting hand. "I will talk to you every day on the phone. That way you won't miss me so much."

I leaned over and gave him a hug. "How did you get so smart, Trevor Hawkins?"

He smiled sheepishly at me. "Because Jesus loves me. I learned that when I went to church the first time. He doesn't want me to be sad."

"You are absolutely right," I replied as fresh tears started to form. I couldn't let the adversary steal away any more of my happiness. I knew what I wanted and what I must do to get it. "We do set the course for our own lives, Trevor, with a little help from people who love us. We have been given so many blessings there is no reason for any of us to be unhappy."

I retrieved both my handbag and my scriptures from the back seat while he climbed out and closed the door behind him. He was attending church with me for the second time without complaint. That was a blessing I had never expected, but the spiritual high I got from the experience wouldn't last long unless my attitude about so many other things changed—especially what I was going to do about the man who had stirred so many feelings and promises I wasn't certain I could handle on my own.

I listened to a talk about letting go of the past so it would not consume the future, and then worried about Trevor attending Primary alone while I went to my own class. Emma had not come. She had picked up LeAnn at the hospital and taken her directly home to the guest room she had used after my father's death. For the next two months she would be as confined to the house as I had been during the first two trimesters of LeAnn's pregnancy.

It was a pleasant afternoon and evening visiting with both LeAnn and Emma and making additional plans. But when my little brother's bedtime arrived, I knew I had made the right decision about spending the night in Edna so I could take him to school the next morning. After completing his enrollment with the office staff, I wanted to meet his teacher and make sure she was aware of the special circumstances in his life that made going to public school necessary.

"Can you sleep in the attic with me, Brylee?" he asked after he had said goodnight to Emma and his mother. "I am afraid to be up there alone. It's not at all like my room at home."

"But it is a great room! You have the train set and father's soldiers to keep you company, and I will be sleeping on the sofa right at the foot of the stairs. I will hear if you make even the slightest peep."

"But I want you in the room with me. What if there are monsters hiding in the boxes? There are so many of them."

"There aren't any monsters," I responded, but that didn't stop him from clinging to my arm and staring to cry.

I wished I could ask Emma for help, but she had disappeared into her own bedroom and shut the door. I couldn't blame her. This was a very delicate situation that would set the tone for the rest of the time he spent in town, and I wasn't about to compel him to sleep in the attic before he was ready.

"Maybe I could lie down beside you and tell you a story until you fall asleep. Then if you wake up, all you have to do is call my name, and I will be here in a flash. I don't think your bed is big enough for us to share the entire night."

"I love you, Brylee, forever and ever," he said.

"And I love you forever and always."

He gingerly followed me up the stairs, and I told him one of his favorite stories about the rainbow serpent and how the earth had been formed. It didn't matter that it was only make-believe, it helped calm him and in a few minutes I was able to slide my arm out from underneath his neck and retrace my steps back down the staircase. I left the light outside the attic door on so he would be able to see his way if he happened to wake up.

I had been trying to dismiss thoughts of Jake all day. The fervor in his eyes and the curve of his lips were a heady experience, especially when I put them with the words of longing and desire he had expressed the night before. And then there was the matter of what I had said. That *I love you* could never be erased, and there was more to it than just trying to keep him from leaving the ranch. Perhaps that was one of the reasons I had decided to stay in town for the night. I didn't quite trust myself to be alone with him, even though I knew he would let me be the one controlling how fast or slow things between us went.

But I had promised to let him know how our day had gone, and if I didn't call, he would look on it as a retraction of what I had said about caring for him. No, about loving him. I wasn't quite sure what that meant because love had many forms. I only knew that I didn't want to lose him any more than Trevor and LeAnn did.

The phone rang once, then twice, and I breathed a sigh of relief. It would be so much easier leaving a message than talking to him, but just when I thought the answering machine would pick up, he said *hello* in a voice that immediately set my heart to racing.

"Hi," I responded, hoping my intonation didn't betray what I was trying to suppress. "I'm sorry I didn't call earlier."

"That's okay," he said. "I figured you had gotten busy. Things have been rather buggered up lately."

He was giving me a chance to bring up the conversation we'd had the night before, but I didn't take it. Instead, I twisted a strand of hair absentmindedly in my fingers.

"We played Monopoly with LeAnn and Emma. That game can take hours."

"You don't owe me any explanations, Brylee," he said. "You are a grown woman, and I am not your keeper."

The tenor of his voice made me scowl, but how could I expect him to be anything but miffed when I couldn't even make up my mind about something as simple as giving us a chance. He wasn't asking for a life-long commitment. He wasn't even asking for a physical relationship. He just wanted me to be honest with him about how I really felt.

"I know that, but I promised to check in," I said.

"Is that the only reason you called?"

"No!" I admitted with a heavy intake of air. Like it or not, I had fallen for Jake Johnson, tattoos, earrings, bad disposition and all. Denying it would be the biggest pretense of all. "I wanted to hear your voice and see how your day had gone."

"My day was damned lonely and boring, but I am glad you missed me."

"I did miss you."

"Then you should have come home and let Emma take Trevor to school in the morning. I could have prepared a special dinner for us."

I sat down on the sofa bed with a thud. "I suppose we could have done that, but it is going to be a very big change for Trevor. Besides, I promised."

"And you don't think I wanted to take him to school myself? I am going to miss that little bloke too."

"Then why didn't you say something before we left? We could have done it together."

"And have even more people think we are a couple? I know how you feel about that."

I could see his brow wrinkle, even though we were miles apart. I had been sending mixed signals for weeks. No wonder he was prepared to think the worst when it came to my behaviors and motives.

"I am sorry I don't always make sense, but I really am trying to figure things out," I responded. "Everything is just so complicated."

"It doesn't have to be complicated, Brylee. You said last night that you cared about me, and then you put off calling me all day. It only proves that you still have no idea what you want, other than what ia no longer available."

His insight put me to shame. I didn't like hurting him so often after all he had done to help us, but I couldn't just turn my feelings on and off like a light switch. I was afraid of losing everything else I valued, just like I had lost Ben.

He continued speaking while I was still lost in the dark recesses of my own thoughts. "I wish I could make you see that life doesn't stop just because one relationship ends. I have been thinking a lot about what happened last night, even if you haven't, and have come to a decision."

I held my breath, suddenly very aware of what he was saying. With all my indecision, he had decided to take a stand.

"I think it was far too soon for you to be thinking about another relationship since you aren't over the old one yet. And I don't want to be part of a rebound anything. Been there, done that, and it is pretty much a living hell."

"Just what are you saying, Jake?"

"I'm not really sure. It is damned near impossible keeping our distance since we live at the same address and are supposed to be working together."

The air held captive in my lungs came rushing out. Was this his way of suggesting I stay in town and not come home? Or worse, was he planning on leaving the ranch so he would never have to see me again like he had threatened to do the night before? We could not survive without him. Anyone with even half a brain knew that.

"Then what do we do?" I asked in little more than a whisper, wishing I had never accepted his kiss on the beach or admitted to how I really felt about him. "The ranch can't get along without you, and I have no place else to go."

He was thoughtful for a moment, giving me even more time to regret what had happened between us.

"Then I suppose we are left with little choice besides putting our personal feelings aside and trying to get along until we are both prepared for something else. The ranch is your home, Brylee, and like you, I promised your father I would help you take care of it."

I breathed a sigh of relief. He wasn't going to leave, at least not yet. That gave us time to make an informed decision, not just react to the poor choices made in the past.

"I am more than willing to try. I know father wanted us to get along."

"This isn't just about what your father wanted. It's about our lives, Brylee, and what we want to do with them. I can't keep on pretending that I don't care about you. Hell, I have been doing that for months. So I guess you will just have to understand that if I get in your face or act like a common toady it is only because I want to kiss you."

His honesty made me smile in the best way possible. If I thought, even for a moment, that he would come to believe in something greater than he already did, I would drive back to the ranch right now and throw myself into his arms. I would even admit that I had been attracted to him the first moment we met. He was handsome, dangerous and exciting, and if I was completely honest with myself, he was at least partially the reason I had not gone back to Ben.

"I can accept that," I told him. "If you can accept that I might act like a shrew occasionally because I am still trying to figure things out. I need you in my life. That is all I know for sure right now."

"I like it when you need me, Brylee, even if all you are doing is telling me to bugger off. I just wish your church wasn't keeping us apart."

The cold water of reality washed over me again in an instant. Jake might never understand why religion meant so much to me, and I could never walk away from it. Maybe there really wasn't all that much to work towards because love couldn't grow if it wasn't given the chance.

"I can't just forget about what I believe in, Jake. I want a forever family."

"I know, and it takes a man who believes as you do for that to happen. See, I do listen when you talk, but what if you never find that man? Are you prepared to be alone for the rest of your life?"

I looked at the picture of Emma and Robert that hung above the mantel. She had wanted a family so much, but God had not answered that prayer. Would the same thing happen to me? Would I be left without a husband or family because I had walked away from Ben? He was the only man I knew who could give me what I desired most.

"I hope that won't happen," I told him. "But if that is part of God's plan for me then I will just have to accept it."

The bitterness in his laugh stung deeply.

"That is utter nonsense! You're a beautiful, warm and compassionate woman. You need to pass those genes on to at least a million or two kids."

"Like that is going to happen! I would settle for two or three."

My comment surprised me, but it was so much easier to be my true self over the phone. When we were together, all I wanted to do was kiss him.

"A perfect number," he replied. "You will make an incredible mother someday."

"And you will make an amazing father. I watch the way you are with Trevor. I can see you with a couple of little boys of your own. They would follow you everywhere."

"Don't forget about my daughter," he said. "No bloody bloke would ever be good enough for her."

"I suppose you will be one of those fathers who gets out the shotgun to keep all the guys away?"

"Hell, yes! I wouldn't actually shoot them, but I would definitely make them dance."

"Then your daughter would be wretchedly miserable because she would have no one to date."

"That is just another plus for home schooling. Blokes wouldn't even know she existed until she was at least twenty-five."

Thoughts concerning my own childhood suddenly surfaced. I hadn't known any boys, except NJ, until I had been sent away to boarding school. Girls had to know how to take care of themselves long before that. Had I known what to look for, I might not have put myself in the situation where Jon could steal the most special gift I had.

"It's just too bad life doesn't always work out the way we planned," I told him with a sad smile that hurt clear down to the tips of my toes. Jon was a monster for what he had done, and I wished I could make sure he never assaulted another girl, but I had lost that chance by not reporting him when I had the chance.

"It can turn out any way we want it to, Brylee. We just have to be willing to risk the change that comes with trying something new. That is all I am asking of you."

"Then I will give it everything I have because I think you are worth it, Jake Johnson." I said before hanging up.

But the moment the line went dead, unwanted fears resurfaced. Life was complicated—regardless of what he said—and every decision made came with a consequence that could be good, bad or indifferent. And I was very afraid I might not be able to follow through with what I had just promised him I would do.

Emma fixed breakfast and packed Trevor's mid-day meal in the new lunch box we had purchased while I got dressed in my Sunday clothes so I could take him to school. I hadn't slept a lot, but that was becoming a habit. Since the kiss on the beach, my dreams were always about Jake—dreams that confused me almost as much as reality did.

Trevor clung to my hand as we walked up the sidewalk to the elementary school and passed through red double doors that appeared to have been freshly painted. Children were milling about everywhere, and Trevor watched them with trepidation. I said a quick prayer that his fears would be calmed and he would enjoy the time he spent here.

"Brylee," he said, tugging on my hand. "Can't we just go home? I am not going to like it here. Everyone keeps staring at me."

I knelt down in front of him and straightened the collar on his fresh, blue shirt. "That is only because so few people here have seen you before. The same thing happened when I went away to boarding school."

"What did you do?"

"I just smiled back and pretended that I belonged, and in a little while I did."

He looked up at the next group of children, but he didn't smile. It would take more than a few words of encouragement to assuage his fears.

"There you are, Trevor," a little girl's voice said from somewhere in the hall behind us. "I have been waiting all morning for you to get here. Mrs. Wilson said you would be in my class."

We turned around to see Nancy Wells, a little girl from his Primary class. Her brown hair was pulled back in pigtails, and her blue eyes sparkled.

"Are you sure?" Trevor asked.

"Cross my heart. You can come to class with me, if you want to."

Trevor looked up at me. His face was silhouetted in the overhead lighting. He looked strained and uncertain.

"Would that be okay?" he asked.

"Absolutely!" I told him with a half-hearted smile that I hoped was convincing. Trevor would not be the same little boy when I saw him again. "I will just go to the office and get you registered."

He released his grip on my hand and followed Nancy down the hall. It was lined with lockers, and teachers were standing outside their doors greeting each child who entered their classroom. Certainly Trevor would be okay. Millions of children went to public school every day.

I watched until he disappeared and the bell rang. The halls immediately emptied, and I was left standing alone and realizing just how empty my life was going to be without him. Leaving him in town and driving back to the ranch seemed more than impossible.

But I couldn't stay where I was forever, I so headed towards the office. LeAnn had told me where to find everything I would need. The principal, Mrs. Dearing, assured me that Trevoe was in good hands.

"There is nothing to worry about, Miss Hawkins," she said after the paperwork was complete. "There are few kids any more who haven't gone through rough experiences. Over half the children here come from single-parent homes. I wish there was something we could do to stop the epidemic of divorce, but people don't seem to value marriage much anymore. Excuse me for asking, but you and Trevor don't look much alike, and there is a big difference in your ages."

"We have different mothers," I told her, trying not to feel intimidated by her hawk like nose and narrow reading gasses that hung from her neck on a silver chain. "Trevor's mother is expecting and has to stay in bed until the baby comes. That's why I am the one enrolling him in school."

"I hope both she and the baby will be okay, but there is really no reason for anyone to worry about Trevor. He may have a few days of adjustment, but we have excellent teachers and some of the best students in the country."

"You will let me know if he needs anything. I will be at the ranch but can get here in a couple of hours."

"That won't be a problem. I saw where you listed Emma Donaldson as your secondary contact. She is a remarkable woman. I had my first job waiting tables at her diner. In fact, she is the one who encouraged me to go into education."

"Really," I said to be polite. "Trevor's mother is staying with her until the baby arrives. The ranch is too far away from the doctor."

"It certainly is a small world," she responded, extending her hand in my direction. "I have a parent meeting I must attend, but it was a pleasure meeting you."

"Likewise," I told her as I left the office and made my way to the parking lot. Trevor did have a great many good people looking out for him, but that didn't stop me from sitting in the car for the next half hour staring at the front doors and wondering if he might just come running out to find me. He was so young and inexperienced and had never been away from his family before. I had spent the first month in tears after being sent to boarding school. I didn't want Trevor to experience anything like that.

Emma was waiting when I got back to her house.

"How did it go?" she asked as she led me into the kitchen for a cold glass of lemonade and some of her ever-present, homemade cookies. "I figured it would take some time for you to feel comfortable about leaving him, but I hope the people there made an effort to reassure you that he would be fine."

I took a sip of the cool beverage. "I didn't see his teacher, but Nancy Wells from church is in his class, and the principal seems nice."

"Afton was the best waitress I ever had, but I am glad she decided to do more with her life than she first intended. She was voted *Administrator of the Year* last spring. She will take good care of Trevor, and I have the school's number on speed dial. LeAnn showed me how to do it."

I took a cookie from the flower-lined plate she handed me. "I'm being silly, right?"

"Not at all. I would be disappointed if it was easy for you to leave him. That would mean you hadn't grown to love him."

"Oh, I do love him," I said as tears filled my eyes. "And I worry about him all the time. He seems too little to be left in a building filled with strangers. All I wanted to do was take him back to the ranch with me."

"Well, you can't do that. LeAnn needs him here with her, and you need a chance to figure out what you are going to do about Jake. Like I said before, that guy is in love with you, and I have a feeling things have changed a little since we last talked. You seem more distracted than usual, and I can't help but wonder if something I said pushed you in a direction you really didn't want to go."

I shook my head as looked towards the white shuttered window with flowers in the box beneath it. Emma may have been the one who planted the seed about giving Jake another chance, but I was the one who mentioned the word love. The circumstances surrounding that disclosure really didn't matter.

"I'm still trying to figure out what I want, but it always comes back to an eternal marriage, and Jake can never give me that."

"Are you sure? Men will do just about anything when they are in love."

"I don't want him joining the church because he thinks that will convince me to give us a chance. He knows where I stand on the topic of religion, and I am not going to change my mind. He won't budge on the issue either."

"So you have talked about it?"

"We've tried, but he thinks religion is the only thing keeping us apart."

"So you really have moved beyond the dislike you once shared."

"We are way past that now, Emma. I let my guard down last night and told him that I more than just liked him."

"Oh, my," she said. "That does change things."

"You think?" I sarcastically responded.

"I certainly do," she replied without skipping a beat. "And I am sorry if my big mouth put you in another compromising situation. Jake is more than a little rough around around the edges, and just because I think he is worth taking a risk on, I have no right to encourage anyone to look past his most obvious issues because most of them are unlikely to change."

"I fear most of us are a little set in our ways, Emma. But Jake has the warmest heart at times, and you should see him with Trevor. One would think he was his son, not his nephew."

Emma put her hand over mine. "I take it he is not the only one who has been bitten by the love-bug, so to speak."

"It's so much more complicated than that," I responded. He was walking away, and I couldn't let him go."

"And now you are having second thoughts about going back to the ranch because you are not sure that is how you really feel?"

"Oh, it is how I feel. All I do is think about him, even when I'm trying to sleep."

"That is a sticky situation," she admitted. "Especially knowing how he feels about you. My offer still goes that you can stay in town with us for as long as you want."

"You don't know how tempted I am to take you up on it, but I can't run away from him forever. He wanted me to come back to the ranch last night, and then he told me that he thought our getting involved was a mistake. He doesn't want to be caught in some rebound relationship any more than I do."

"That sounds very wise, but good intentions don't always work out. The heart wants what it wants."

"We are both determined to make things work for Trevor, LeAnn and the new baby. They need a home where they will all feel safe, and father expects us to keep the ranch in the family. Jake could easily survive without me since he already knows how to run everything, but I could never make it without him."

"Your determination is admirable, but you need to be very careful," she said. "Jake Johnson knows what women like, and he is not used to being put on hold."

"So you don't think I should go back to the ranch?"

"Once again, it is not my place to tell you what to do, although as your surrogate grandmother I would like to keep you safe by my side. I just want you to be happy, Brylee, but this thing with Jake is something only you can decide."

I talked to LeAnn for a few minutes before turning the Land Rover in the direction of the ranch but didn't mention what Emma and I had discussed. She had enough to worry about with Trevor and the new baby. Besides, I was no closer to knowing what I was going to do about Jake than I had been when we parted on Sunday morning. I only knew that I needed to see him again. It was an unrelenting obsession that refused to give up.

Chapter 20

"Jake," I called out as the screen door leading into the kitchen slammed shut. I had stopped at the market for a few groceries, and both of my hands were filled with plastic shopping bags.

When he didn't answer, I placed the bags on the counter and began sorting through them. I was exhausted and more than a little grateful I hadn't fallen asleep at the wheel while driving home. I could count the number of hours I had slept the past two nights on one hand. Between dreams of Jake and worrying about Trevor, I was dangerously close to sleep deprivation, and the conflict in my mind was only making my ability to think clearly worse.

Since it was too early to fix dinner, I headed up the stairs to my bedroom once the groceries were put away. I needed to change my clothes and make a list of the things I could do to make life at the ranch better. If I had something productive to do each day, perhaps it would keep me from dwelling on things that only brought pain.

My feelings for Jake had come on far too quickly and strongly after Ben and I broke up, but I figured they had fallen back into place once our bickering started again. This new onslaught of desire had only become a problem because I had admitted how I felt, but since I couldn't take that back I would simply have to work my way through it. No matter what happened to me, I couldn't drive him away. It would destroy everything for LeAnn and Trevor.

I hadn't been in my room for long when he knocked on my door to tell me that Uncle Ned was there and needed to talk to both of us. That news unnerved me even further because Uncle Ned never left his ranch when it was still light outside, unless there was something crucially important on his mind.

"You look exhausted," he said when I walked into the kitchen to join them at the table where they were drinking cold beer.

I never bought any when I went to the store, but there still seemed to be an endless supply of it in the house. It must be stockpiled somewhere. I slid into a chair and rested my chin on the palms of my hands.

"I hope you are not still worried about Trevor. He is in good hands both at school and with Emma. In fact, he will be a new little boy by the time you see him next weekend."

"That's what I am afraid of," I told him. "I don't want him to change, and it is so lonely here without him." I didn't look up at Jake even though I could feel his eyes on me.

"Change is never easy, honey. That's why I am here. One of those corporate guys by the name of Raymond Tucker came by the ranch again today. He heard about Jack's death and wanted to know if we were ready to reconsider his former offer. Old Mason sold out to him last week. There are only a few privately operated homesteads left in a two-hundred-mile radius that they haven't gobbled up by him yet."

I willed myself to be calm. I couldn't lose the ranch. It was all we had left.

"I hope you told him we weren't interested."

"I told him to 'buzz off' in no uncertain terms, but he is like vultures on a carcass. He will keep circling around until we are dead."

Tears filled my eyes as I thought about the graves of my parents and all of our ancestors. No one would take care of them if we were gone.

"We are not giving up, love, but it is time for us to work even more closely together if we want to survive."

I looked helplessly over at him. I had been trying so hard to keep everything of value together and hadn't spent over a few thousand dollars since my father's death—most of that going to pay Jake's salary and LeAnn's doctor bills. I still hadn't taken a penny for myself.

"I thought we were doing okay, Uncle Ned. You said we got a good price when the wool, sheep and cattle were sold, and we are certainly not in the red according to my records." I looked at Jake for support, but he just threw his hands in the air.

"Hey, I'm not family," he said. "I am just the bloody hired hand. You and LeAnn are the ones authorized to make decisions."

"Come on, Jake," Uncle Ned encouraged. "Why don't you tell her what we are really up against? We have some tough decisions to make whether you want to be part of them or not."

"What decisions?" I asked as my heart began to race. I might have been diligent with the ranch's finances on the computer, but I really had no idea what was going on outside my father's office. My world had revolved around LeAnn and Trevor for months, but letting other things slide must have been another horrible mistake.

"Listen, Brylee," Jake said. "We all had great hopes that things would work out, but you have no idea how bad things are out there, and I don't feel right about continuing to take a salary when my sister and her children are going to need some kind of livelihood for the rest of their lives."

I looked down at the worn, red and white-checkered oilcloth that covered the table. The plastic coating was beginning to yellow. I would have to take some cleanser to it and hope it didn't fall completely apart during a good cleaning.

"Did you hear what I said," Jake asked. "LeAnn won't be able to help out for months, and I need to be contributing something towards their futures, not taking it away."

"But you are contributing. This ranch won't make it without you."

"That is where you are wrong," he said, setting his bottle of beer on the table. "When your father was here, we had all these glorious plans for expansion. We were going to buy more cattle and make better use of all the land, not just the fraction of it we use for grazing."

"But we can still do that." I said, interrupting him.

"No, we can't, Brylee. Your father was a dreamer. That was one of the things I enjoyed most about him, but he had been sick for a long time."

"Are you saying my father didn't know what he was doing? I have been over the books. We are on solid ground financially."

"Only on paper," Uncle Ned interjected.

I thought I might become ill the knot in my stomach constricted so rapidly. My father was a good rancher. I didn't care what anyone else said.

"There isn't enough feed in the hills on your side of the ranch to handle the animals you already have. How can you expand?"

"But we had so much rain it caused a flood," I responded, trying up back up my beliefs.

"That rain didn't help us, love. It just washed away more of our best soil. I am not saying you won't make it . . . ."

"Then what are you saying?" I interrupted.

I was scared! No, I was terrified. Too many lives depended on us—LeAnn, Trevor, the new baby. Father wanted them to have this ranch as their home for always.

"Give Ned a chance to explain, Brylee," Jake said. "He is only here to help, not make things worse."

I took a deep breath and looked at my uncle, but I knew there was still a spark of defiance in my eyes. He looked both tired and upset but was trying to maintain control even harder than I was.

"You know this ranch was left to your father—in its entirety—because he was the oldest son and rightful heir."

"Yes, but he wanted you to have part of it," I said.

"So he gave me the most fertile part and kept all the hilly land for himself. Don't you see, Brylee? Your father was one of the most generous blokes on the face of the earth, and I loved him dearly. But I wouldn't have anything if he hadn't given it to me, and now I want to give back what is rightfully yours."

I looked at him in utter confusion. "You can't give what my father gave you back to us. I won't accept it. You have your own family and they need to be taken care of too."

"Just hear me out before you start jumping to any conclusions. NJ has been vacillating between taking over the ranch and staying in Sydney for the past two years. But the truth is, he is not coming back here to live. He will be graduating as a Marine Biologist soon and that is what he wants to do with his life."

"But what about his inheritance and Molly's? Your ranch will go to your children someday no matter what occupation they choose. No one, especially NJ, would walk away from it forever, and I would never fight my cousins for anything."

"NJ and Molly will be well proved for, but I know my children, and the allure of money and all it can buy will win out over family obligations after Nora and I are gone. Maybe we have done wrong as parents giving them everything they ever wanted and not expecting them to work for it, but the bottom line is that this ranch—in its entirety—is supposed to stay in the family. I don't want it sold to anyone else after I die just because my children are more interested in what it can provide for them than they are in a family legacy."

"NJ and Molly would never sell it. They know how much it means to you."

"You haven't been listening, Brylee. I love my children dearly, but they aren't going to come back out here to live—ever. Even if they don't sell the ranch, they will have someone else running it. I can't face my ancestors when I die knowing that my actions left the ranch they sacrificed their entire lives for to someone else. I'm getting old, and I need some help. Otherwise, I might be forced to sell to someone outside of the family myself."

"You would never do that," I countered, as my nostrils stung with unwelcome tears. "And what about Aunt Nora? She works as hard, if not harder, than any man I know."

"That she does," Uncle Ned admitted. "But neither of us are as young as we used to be. The flood taught us that."

"We should have been more helpful."

"You did everything you could, but Nora and I have lots of things we would like to do before we die—like spending more time in the city with our kids and our grandchild."

He gave me a funny, little look that made my heart sink. "Yes, I am going to a grandfather. I can't say that I am thrilled about the baby's father. I wish he was more like use, but he isn't. He is an only child and comes from a very affluent Sydney family."

"Molly is having a baby," I fiercely whispered as another sheet of darkness descended over me. I had seen her at the barbecue three days earlier and she hadn't said anything. In fact, she was still acting very possessive about Jake and drinking what I had assumed was a beer. Maybe she was just pretending to be pregnant to see what her parents would do.

"That was exactly the reaction I had when she dropped that bomb on us after you left Friday night, but she assured us it was true. The thing that concerns me most is that I am afraid she is more interested in what the bloke can give her than the kind of husband and father he will be. Nora already wants to spend all of her time in Sydney once the baby comes. She has even started knitting baby booties."

I looked across the table at Jake. He was every bit as surprised by Uncle Ned's news as I was, only he didn't say anything.

"Congratulations," I said, collecting my scattered emotions and walking around the table to where Uncle Ned was sitting. I gave him a hug, and then retraced my steps back to the chair I had been sitting on. "Tell Molly I am very happy for her. When is the baby due?"

I wanted to cry but wouldn't, at least not yet. Everyone had a life but me! I was the only one in my family who was trying to live by a set of standards higher than the ones the world valued, yet everyone else was getting the blessings I would have had if I'd never come home. How could Molly become a mother before me? She had even less homemaking skills than I did.

"She found out about the baby last week, but she is nearly three months along," Uncle Ned was saying. "They want to get married before the baby comes. His family is big on providing a rightful heir, not an illegitimate one, so I guess we will be planning a bloody, enormous wedding in the next few months. You know Molly, she'll want the best of everything."

My head was spinning so fast I couldn't even remember what we had been discussing before Uncle Ned's bombshell, but Jake did.

"So what's your plan, Ned?" he asked my uncle.

"Other than being a reluctant grandfather, I need help running the ranch since neither of my children have any interest in doing it. So here is what I am proposing, if you both agree."

I looked at Jake again, but he just shrugged his shoulders and gave me a speculative glance that told me we might as well listen to what my uncle had to say before jumping to any more conclusions.

"I want the ranch to stay in the family and for that to happen, I have to make sure it stays in the hands of people who love it as much as I do."

"I do love it, Uncle Ned, but my father gave that land to you." I said.

His hand went into the air before I could continue. "I am not just going to hand it over to you. I am still hoping that someday I will have a grandchild who might want to live out here, but that might not happen until long after I am gone."

I felt goose flesh cover my arms as I leaned back in my chair and folded my arms tightly across my chest. I was weary of talking about death and dying.

"Don't talk like that, Uncle Ned. I couldn't bear it if something happened to you."

"Not to worry, Brylee. I plan on waking up in the morning for a very long time, but I have to be practical. None of us knows what tomorrow will bring, and in light of this new development, I don't want to leave anything to chance. I have made some tentative decisions that I need to discuss with both of you."

I looked at the small stack of papers sitting on the table in front of him and wondered why I hadn't noticed them before.

"What about LeAnn?" Jake asked him. "She speaks for Trevor until he is old enough to do it for himself."

"There is no need to concern her about this right now since the plans are still in the preliminary stage, but this house will always belong to her just like our home will always belong to Nora. I have put the same kind of provisos on it that your father did. It can never be sold to anyone outside the family."

I tried to listen to what he was saying without questioning, but it was too much to absorb at one time. What he was saying made sense as long as there was a Hawkins who wanted to live in the outback, but what if the time came when no one in the family wanted what our ancestors had worked so tirelessly to provide for us? What would happen to it then?

Uncle Ned answered my questions as if he had overheard my thoughts. "I am leaving my land to the Aborigine Society just like your father did if no one in the family wants it. After all, we pretty much stole it from them in the first place, and they deserve to have it back."

I was on the verge of tears and frowned in bewilderment. No one had said anything about my father leaving the land to the Aborigines if no one in the family wanted it. I had assumed we were past the vicious habit of keeping secrets from each other, but apparently I was wrong.

"The lawyer didn't mention that when he read father's will," I said.

"I asked him not to, but it was in the codicil. I figured you had already read the complete document."

"Well, I haven't," I told him as I tried to control my mounting anger. Just when I thought things couldn't possibly get any worse, they did. "Why didn't you say something about it sooner?"

"I suppose I could have, but I didn't think you needed to worry about something that might not happen for generations, if ever, while you were in mourning. Buck Henry will explain everything the next time we are all together. It doesn't change anything we are talking about right now."

"But it does, Uncle Ned!" I insisted. "If NJ and Molly knew what might happen to your ranch, one of them would choose to stay out here and help out."

"That's just the point, they did know, Brylee! I laid everything out to them, just like I am doing to you, and they still chose to walk away. They have always had everything they ever wanted, including an education, but being in the city has changed both of them. They want to visit us occasionally naturally, but they definitely don't want to live and work out here."

I looked across the table at Jake, but he was an expert at hiding his emotions when he wanted to.

"So what do you want us to do, Uncle Ned?"

"Nothing at present, but my ultimate goal is to have the land revert back to the way it was in our parent's will when everything was left to your father."

I opened my mouth to object again, but Uncle Ned's firm hand on my arm stopped me.

"Hear me out before you start protesting again," he said. "I am not going to deed it back to you right now. What I am proposing is that Jake comes to work for me."

My mouth dropped open. Certainly Uncle Ned couldn't be serious. Our ranch would fail miserably without him.

"And I want you to work for me as well, Brylee. As I see it, you have spent four years learning how to run a business. If our ranches were united again we could form our own corporation. That way, we wouldn't be nearly as vulnerable to companies who want to claim everything out here."

"That actually makes sense," Jake said. "You and Jack have over 4,500 acres of some of the best and the worst land in the outback. If they were under the same management, the good could easily offset the bad."

I put my fingers to my head and pressed into my brow. An acute headache was forming, and I wasn't sure I would be able to stop it, not with the announcements my uncle's visit had brought.

"I'm not following all of this," I said.

Uncle Ned continued. "Think about it, Brylee. Your father deeded me the most fertile land where we raised hay and grain, while he kept all the mountain pasture. We have always just helped each other out, but there has never been anything in writing. If you became the head of the Hawkins' Corporation, we would be protecting ourselves. We could increase Jake's salary because he would be doing more work, and the shareholders—meaning Trevor, you and me—could divide the profits and share the losses."

"I don't know, Uncle Ned. I am still trying to get used to the way my father did things."

"Then you are all set because Nora and I run our ranch the way he did. Our cattle and sheep are all intermixed anyway because of the flood. The way I see it, you and Jake are the ones who will be saving this land for the coming generations, if you are willing to do it."

Jake's chair legs scraped across the worn linoleum floor as he rose to his feet and crossed the floor to the kitchen sink. "You can leave me out of this. Like I said earlier I am not a Hawkins, and while I would do anything for my family, I am not sure it is fair to ask Brylee to take on so much added responsibility. What if she decides to get married and leave the outback?"

"I am not going anywhere," I said, noticing that his eyes were narrowed as he looked at me. "You could just as easily decide to get married and leave."

He snorted his disapproval.

"And you honestly think I would ever desert my family, Brylee? Have you learned nothing about me in all the months you have been here? If I say I am going to do something, then I sure as hell will."

I bit the inside of my lip to keep from saying anything else. This proposal would make our working relationship permanent, and we would have to live with the consequences. But even knowing that one of us could leave or get involved with someone else could not deter me from the path I knew I must take. I had to give Uncle Ned's offer a chance for Trevor, LeAnn and the baby. They deserved a stable future.

"I have no problem with anything you are suggesting," I told Uncle Ned.

"Then I guess we are good," Jake replied without looking at me. "I will sign whatever you need me to."

"It's a gentleman's agreement until the paperwork is ready," Uncle Ned replied. "Unless you become a legal member of the family by marriage."

"Well, that is not going to happen," Jake said with a grunt of laughter. "Molly's got herself a rich young bloke, and Brylee wants someone who is a million times better than me."

"Things have a habit of changing," Uncle Ned said. "I remember when Nora gave me some ultimatums that made me so bloody mad I drove clear to Perth and stayed there for an entire month before I missed her so much I came straight back and told her a few things I have never regretted. Some women are just worth fighting for because life only makes sense when they are part of it."

His love for Aunt Nora was so evident I had to sniff back more tears, but I knew what he said was mostly directed at Jake and me. We had been in a pickle when I arrived home earlier today, but now we were stuck in a predicament we might not be able to extricate ourselves out of. We were both headstrong and determined, and we had never been much on compromise. What would happen to our family if we couldn't get along? We held their futures in the palms of our hands.

We talked details of the proposed arrangement until Uncle Ned cleared his throat, stood up and told us he would be back in a few days with Buck Henry and all the papers we needed to sign to make the arrangement legal.

I walked him to the door, and when I came back to the kitchen, Jake was waiting for me.

"I certainly didn't expect that, but it sounds like a reasonable solution since neither of his kids want to live out here," he said.

"I'm still not sure about that," I replied, looking at the door through which my uncle had just left. "NJ could easily change his mind once he has really thought things through."

Jake poured himself a cup of coffee. "I doubt it. I didn't want to say anything to Ned because I know how much he wants his children to love this land, but NJ has told me numerous times that he can never see himself being happy out here. He is far too enamored with the finer things of life."

"That is just so different than the NJ I used to know. He loved this land as much as Trevor does when he was a child. All he ever wanted was to be part of it."

"People change, Brylee, and so do priorities."

"But to walk away from everything."

Suddenly, I felt like the biggest hypocrite on the planet. Wasn't that exactly what I had done almost six years ago? But I had changed my mind and so could NJ or Molly. I just hoped Jake would be sensitive and not call me on it.

"I can understand the follies of youth," he said, resuming his seat at the table with his hands wrapped around his coffee mug.

Apparently our conversation with Uncle Ned was making him want to sober up in a hurry. There was no way of knowing how many beers either of them had consumed before my return.

"I would be a bloody liar if I said I hadn't run away from a whole lot of things myself but if I have learned one thing about human nature, it's that we have to make our own mistakes and then pay the consequences."

I swallowed hard. He wasn't just talking about wanting to hold on to a legacy. He was talking about us.

"You know my past well enough," I said. "I was pretty much like NJ until I came home and figured out what was really important."

"Like religion?" Jake asked, his eyes boring into mine.

"Like family," I replied. "I would do anything for Trevor, LeAnn and the baby."

"I understand your devotion to them because I feel the same way, but with your degree, you could get a job anywhere in the world. Why would you choose to be out here where the weather is awful, you will never meet anyone suitable, and it is a constant struggle for survival?"

"There are lots of reasons," I told him. "When I first got here, all I wanted was to hurry home to Ben where my life was safe and secure and where the weather is consistently nice. But somewhere along the way, I found my roots again, and this is where I want to be."

I looked down at my hands that had become so rough and sunburned from working outside in the scorching heat and caring for my family that I barely recognized them any more.

"Can you imagine me at a fancy party with these? People would think I was hired help no matter what I was wearing."

"Your hands are beautiful, just like you," Jake said, covering them with his own stronger and more sunburned ones.

I choked back a sob. Ben wouldn't even want me now. I seldom wore makeup unless I was going to town because the constant heat made it run. My hair was dry and brittle and almost always pulled back in a ponytail. And I smiled so seldom that I was beginning to get permanent frown lines between my eyes.

"You are awfully quiet," Jake said a few moments later. "Did I overstep the boundaries again without meaning to? You are a beautiful woman, even if you have gotten a little too much sun."

His honesty made me laugh.

"That's a first," he said. "What I say usually makes you barmy."

"I can't be too mad when you give me a compliment, even if it is an odd one."

"I guess I am just out of practice when it comes to flirting with a desirable woman."

"Is that what you are trying to do—flirt with me?"

"If you have to ask, I must be doing it badly. I know you have a lot of healing to do. I also understand why you are hesitant about getting involved with me. My track record isn't the greatest. Sometimes I think the world might be a much better place if more people set goals and actually worked towards reaching them. But in light of what Ned just proposed, I am willing to call a truce if you are. We can't bother LeAnn with all our petty differences. She needs as much tranquility as possible, and if that means hiding certain things from her for the time being then I am willing to do it."

"Then a truce it is," I said. "And for what it's worth, you were right when you said it was too soon for me to get involved again. Everything in my head is still jumbled up but I could fix something to eat if you are hungry."

Jake removed his hands from mine, stood up and stretched. "I had a big lunch at Ned's. Maybe after I have finished the chores."

"I could help you with them."

"No need to. It is a one-man job. Besides, you are tired. I know you were trying to rest when Ned came."

"I am wide awake now," I told him as I watched him put his mug in the sink and fill it with water. "Uncle Ned's proposal was more than a shock, and that doesn't even include the news about Molly's baby. Do you really think it is the best thing for us to do?"

"What I think doesn't really matter. People aren't selling because they no longer love it out here. They are selling because they cannot make it and don't want the bank to take everything. Ned needs our help, and we could certainly benefit by having a legal document that shows we are the same operation—tax benefits included."

"I suppose you're right." I said. It would take time getting used to the idea of incorporation, but if it could save the ranch, I was willing to give it my best try.

"Don't lose any sleep over it. Things always seem to work out," he said as he moved across the floor to the back door. "And just for the record, I am not trying to avoid another conversation about personal feelings by not having you help me with the chores. I just think it might be best to set them aside until we come to grips with this latest development. I will see you a little later."

But he didn't return to the house before I went to bed, and it was a very lonely evening without him.

Chapter 21

I talked to Trevor every afternoon. He would call the moment he got to Emma's. I awaited those conversations with nervous anticipation knowing how frightened and apprehensive he had been when I left him behind the red doors at the school. But after the new-student nervousness wore off, he started making friends. Emma packed him a lunch each morning, and he would sit outside underneath a tree to eat it with some of the kids in his class.

He liked his teacher. She was pretty and gave him extra help when he didn't understand something. He was learning to read short books and took a different one home each night to read to his mother. He was good at math—a testament to the work LeAnn had done with him at home.

It was all an adventure, and he seemed to be enjoying the public school experience except for physical education. He had never learned how to play dodge ball, basketball or any of the other games children his age were accustomed to. I promised him we would practice those activities when he came home for the weekend, even if it meant asking Jake to pick up a few things in town when he went to get Trevor on Friday.

I tried to make my time alone count but by Wednesday evening, I was so lonesome for him that I found myself counting the hours until the weekend. Jake spent the majority of his waking hours in the outback or with Uncle Ned, leaving me to wonder if he was avoiding me on purpose. It made sense if he was. We may have admitted our feelings for each other, but I wasn't ready to let go of the past, and he wasn't going to play second fiddle to my unresolved feelings for Ben.

On Thursday, desperate for some human contact, I saddled my father's horse, Thunder, and rode the few miles to talk to Aunt Nora. Thunder was a mustang and needed to be ridden often so he wouldn't revert to his natural wildness. We had a sort of symbiotic relationship. I wouldn't hold him back, and he wouldn't try to throw me.

My aunt was on the back porch separating cream from milk when I arrived.

"My goodness," she said when I approached, making just enough noise not to startle her. "It feels like an oven outside already, and it isn't even ten in the morning. I am beginning to see why the twins want to live in Sydney. It is so much cooler by the ocean. What brings you away from home this morning?"

"I wanted to tell you congratulations on becoming a grandmother in person. It was quite a surprise. I didn't know Molly was dating anyone seriously."

"Neither did we," she admitted, pushing a lock of faded red hair from her forehead. Maybe it was just the idea of thinking of her as a soon-to-be grandmother that made her appear older, but she looked more worn-down than she had when they had been rebuilding their home after the flood.

"Uncle Ned said she wanted a big wedding. I would be happy to help any way I can."

"I appreciate the offer, but I am pretty much in the dark about her plans. I just don't understand how this happened.

She was on birth control and is definitely not ready to be a mother, or a wife for that matter."

I shared her concern but didn't want to express it. Molly was going on twenty-one, but she still acted like a child. She had been all over Jake at the barbecue on Friday and that didn't say much about her readiness to stick with just one guy.

"As long as she has you to turn to, she will be fine," I said as a way to cover my unsettling thoughts.

"I wish I shared your optimism, but Ned and I are simple ranchers. How are we supposed to fit in with Bradley's parents who are multi-millionaires? Molly is looking at wedding dresses that cost more than we clear in a year. But I shouldn't be bothering you will all our troubles."

I put my arm around her shoulders. "You can talk to me about anything, Aunt Nora. And maybe it won't be as bad as you think. Motherhood has a way of making girls grow up in a hurry, and people with money can be really nice."

"I hope you're right," she said, putting a clean cloth over the clotted cream. "I love my daughter dearly, but sometimes I just don't know where her head is at. It seems like there is a different bloke in her life every week. Ned and I had never heard her mention a Bradley before she dropped this bomb on us. I just wanted her to get an education so she would be able to provide for herself if the need arose herself, and now she refuses to attend most of her classes because she claims she isn't feeling well. I just don't understand what she is thinking when she only has a little over a year and a half left."

"She can always finish her education after she's married. Lots of women do."

"Not my daughter! She has never wanted to work a day in her life. It was like pulling teeth to even get her to gather the eggs. I can only hope this wasn't planned so she wouldn't have to get a job when she graduates."

"I can't see Molly doing that. Maybe she really does love him, and it just happened. Birth control has been known to fail. Besides, I have heard that it is as easy to fall in love with a rich man as it is a poor one."

"Oh, my," she sighed. "Molly is no angel, but she is still my little girl and I want her to be happy."

"Then you have to believe this baby and wedding will make that happen."

"I'm trying! Ned tells me I need to relax and let everything be, but how am I supposed to do that when I have so many reservations? What if the family wants a paternity test and the baby isn't Bradley's? I want to believe Molly actually knows who the father is, but from some of the stories I have heard from NJ and others, I just can't be sure. Her idea of having a good time doesn't exactly jell with mine. What is going to happen to her if all of this blows up in her face?"

Poor Aunt Nora! I had been wondering some of those same things since Uncle Ned delivered the news, but Molly was the only one who could confirm or deny anything. And it was entirely possible that she really might not know.

"We will just have to cross that bridge if the time comes," I told her. "And we have to believe Molly knows what she is doing. After all, you gave her the best home possible and let her know that she was loved."

"Heaven knows I tried, but I didn't set a good example when it comes to marriage. Ned and I have been together for over thirty years, but we never made it official. I never considered that an issue until now, but how can we be introduced to Bradley's parents as a couple when we have no legal right to that title? I don't want them to think Molly was raised on the wrong side of the tracks."

"What they think doesn't matter."

"Oh, but it does, Brylee. I will have a grandchild in a few months that will spend most of its time with paternal grandparents because Bradley is going into the family business. I don't want my own grandchild to be ashamed of me."

"That's not going to happen. You will give him or her something money can't buy—all the love in the world. Nothing is more important than that."

"I wish that was true, but in polite society, NJ and Molly are illegitimate. It doesn't matter that Ned and I have been together far longer than most married couples, or that we have been faithful as the day is long. I don't want the lack of a simple sheet of paper to get in the way of Molly's happiness."

"Molly would never let that happen. She loves you and Uncle Ned."

"That may be, but I know my daughter and while she would never say anything hurtful on purpose, she hates confrontations. I'm afraid she would just remain silent if something unpleasant was said, and that would imply agreement."

I wished I could disagree so she would feel better, but like her I recognized Molly's need to be accepted by everyone. In ways, she reminded me of a chameleon—always adapting to the situation she found herself in. If she really wanted this marriage, I had no doubt that she would do or say whatever was necessary to make sure it happened.

We ate a lunch of cold cuts and potato salad. Uncle Ned and Jake were checking on the amount of free-range grass the sheep and cattle had left in the lower elevations and wouldn't be back until later. The cooler months were with us, but without more rain nothing was growing as it should.

Their absence from the meal gave us a chance to talk about Uncle Ned's proposal concerning the incorporation of the two ranches. I thought she might see things differently after she'd had more time to think about it, but she cleared up any doubts as we talked in the kitchen. She was drinking iced tea, and I was drinking lemonade made from frozen concentrate.

"I can't believe you have been able to give up both coffee and tea," she said, looking at me with what I knew was admiration. "Alcohol and tobacco I can understand, but nothing tastes better than hot coffee in the morning and iced tea in the afternoon."

"I guess my tastes have changed."

"Ned said he would like to see some of those things rub off on NJ. The boy drinks too much, but it is hard telling him to slow down when our own fridge is always stocked with our favorite brand. He reminds me so much of his father at that age, and to be quite frank, it scares me. How did you do it?"

"I'm not sure," I told her, wondering just how much I could say without becoming offensive again. She hadn't mentioned our conversation about religion since the day we had it, and she had enough concerns about Molly and her soon-to-be new husband and baby. "But when I heard about the Word of Wisdom it just sort of made sense."

"What's the *Word of Wisdom*?" she asked. "It sounds rather pretentious."

"It is sort of a principle with a promise," I told her, trying to choose my words carefully so as not to come off sounding judgmental again. Jake told me I sounded that way often enough, and I didn't want to damage any further relationships. "If we only take good things into our bodies we will be stronger, healthier and have more clarity of mind when making decisions."

I looked across the table at Aunt Nora who was staring at the coppery-colored liquid in her glass and wondered if my brief explanation had just instilled further confusion, but she put my mind at ease quite readily.

"It actually makes sense," she admitted. "I have known all my life that smoking can lead to cancer and emphysema and that alcohol destroys more than the liver, but no one thinks about stuff like that when they're young. Teenagers want to try everything. They think they are invincible and by the time they're twenty those habits have become a way of life. I suppose we fool ourselves into believing that bad things will only happen to someone else, but we learned that wasn't the truth with your father. Ned and I actually quit smoking for a couple of months once, but as they say some habits die hard, especially when one finds them enjoyable."

"I guess I've been lucky," I told her, clasping my hands tightly around the glass of lemonade she had given me to drink. It was the only way I could keep them from flailing around in the air.

"Luck has very little to do with it," she responded. "You never took up the habit in the first place. I would say that iss just being smart."

"But you can still quit," I told her. "You are an amazing woman, Aunt Nora. I have never known anyone as strong as you are."

I liked my Aunt Nora. She was down-to-earth and honest. How could anyone not see what a good person she was? And that included her children.

"Maybe I will now that I am going to be a grandmother, but I have an idea that talking about my daughter's upcoming nuptials and unexpected baby isn't the only reason you rode over to see me today. I have actually been waiting for you to come. I know what Ned and I are proposing must have come as a big surprise."

"It was more like an atomic explosion. Father gave that land to Uncle Ned for a reason, and the idea of consolidating the ranch again never crossed my mind."

"Your father was a wonderful man but not always a practical one. Ned suggested incorporating more than once, but it always came back to the same thing with Jack. He never felt right about having the entire property, although that was what his father intended."

"From what I have been told, my grandfather was a very stubborn man."

"That quality seems to runs in the family," she said with a shake of her head. "This ranch had been home for most of my life, and I love it dearly. It is where I raised my family, but the time has come when I have to accept that my children don't share my same dreams. As much as I would love for both NJ and Molly to move back home permanently, I know it will never happen."

"It does seem rather unlikely," I admitted.

"Then you have to agree that bringing the ranches together again is the best possible choice we could make. I would rather see this land go back to its original owners than have some huge corporation swallow it up because we can't make ends meet. That is not what your ancestors wanted. They built this little empire as a legacy for their family. I know that you and Trevor love it out here more than either of our children ever will."

"That could change, Aunt Nora. There is another generation of Hawkins on the way already with Molly's announcement."

"I am not going to kid myself into believing that my grandchild will want to become a rancher in the outback when the other side of the family lives in luxury, but even if that did happen, nothing is ever set in stone. At least that was what Buck Henry said."

By the time I walked outside to water my father's horse before the ride home, I was convinced that Uncle Ned and Aunt Nora were in complete agreement over the rejoining of the ranches. She loved her life in the outback, but with her children living in Sydney, she wanted to spend more time with them. That couldn't be done if she was tied to daily chores and the massive amounts of time it took to care for animals and plant and cultivate a garden, hay and grain.

Uncle Ned and Jake rode up just as I was saying goodbye

"You can't run off just when I am getting home," my uncle said, swinging his leg over the saddle and jumping to the ground. "As our new accountant, I think you need to be included in everything that goes on. Jake and I have made a few interesting discoveries today."

"Really, Ned," Aunt Nora shook her head at him. "You are going to drive the poor kids off if all you do is talk business. Everyone needs some down time."

"It's okay," I told her as she put her hand fondly on my arm. "I have never run a corporation before."

"Neither have I. Just don't let Ned scare you with all his talk. It is really just adding a few more columns to what you are already doing. You and I can have it hammered out in an afternoon once the papers have been drawn up and signed."

"See why I love this woman so much, Jake?" Uncle Ned said. "She is my voice of reason and just about the prettiest girl I ever saw."

He kissed Aunt Nora and suddenly changed his mind about more talking.

"Jake can fill you in on the ride home. I think Nora and I could use a little quiet time for ourselves."

Aunt Nora blushed. "You are a shameless old bloke, Ned Hawkins. There are animals to be fed, and I could use a strong arm churning that cream. It will make good butter."

Uncle Ned sighed as he put his arm fondly around her waist.

"I guess I spoke too soon. Nora's got a stubborn streak a mile wide, but I would be lost without her."

"Do you think Uncle Ned and Aunt Nora are acting a little strange?" I asked Jake as we headed our horses in the direction of our part of the ranch. We had stayed long enough for his horse, General, to cool down and drink plenty of water. It would be a few more weeks until we really noticed a change in the weather.

"They seem fine to me."

"That's just the problem. They almost seem too happy. I thought it would be much harder for them to relinquish control of their ranch."

"People change, Brylee, even you and me. The time always comes when money no longer dictates everything one does, and it certainly can't be taken along when you're gone."

"I suppose not. I'm just glad that doesn't apply to experiences and relationships," I replied, looking out over the dry brush that made up most of the Hawkins' brother's land. It always amazed me that anything could grow with so little water and so much sun, but the outback was teaming with life from the smallest insects to the tallest trees. Its beauty was mesmerizing, if one could just look beyond the obvious.

"There you go again," he said. "Always talking about having a family that lasts forever. I still don't believe that is going to happen."

I glanced in his direction and frowned. He was dressed in jeans and a long-sleeved, collared shirt. He looked relaxed and confident, but how much fuller his life would be if he could just accept what I had. There would be no more living just for the day. He would embrace life in a whole new way.

We shared a can of chili for dinner. Then Jake went to the bunkhouse while I retired to the den to look over the daily operating files Aunt Nora had sent home with me. I might have been offended by his lack of interest in the financial end of the ranch but knew he was just honoring the boundaries I had set while looking out for his own interests. Neither of us wanted to become the victim of a relationship that was doomed to failure.

Friday morning brought anticipation of better things to come—at least in one area of my life. Jake would fly into town and pick Trevor up after school, and he would be home with me before six. I wanted everything to be perfect when he arrived, so I drove over to Uncle Ned's in the Land Rover for fresh milk, eggs, cream and butter so I could bake a sour cream chocolate cake. I also made Snicker doodles he could take back to town with him on Sunday—even though I knew

Emma kept the cookie jar filled just for him. A roast was in the crock-pot with carrots, potatoes and onions from Aunt Nora's garden. I wanted to plant one of my own the next time spring came. That was something I had never learned how to do.

True to my promise, I had spent as much time as possible in the barn talking to Trevor's animals, and in many ways I had become as fond of them as he was. They were playful and attentive and seemed to understand his absence, but Copper was another story. At night, she would stand in his room and whimper until I picked her up and carried her to my room where she would sleep at the foot of my bed, or on my pillow if I was too tired to notice. And every time a door opened anywhere in the house, she went running to investigate with her tail wagging. I felt sorry for her because she didn't understand where Trevor had gone or when he would be back.

But as the week progressed, I soon discovered that a puppy was good company and began confiding in her the way Trevor did. She would wag her tail and climb into my lap whenever I sat down. At first, I found it annoying because she always wanted to lick my face, but after realizing that it was simply her way of communicating, I welcomed the little bundle of energy. With her around, I didn't feel quite so alone.

The minute I heard the engine from Jake's plane, I picked Copper up in my arms and ran to the landing strip behind the barn.

The puppy was so excited to see Trevor when he climbed to the ground that she jumped from my arms and ran straight into his, furiously licking his face, his neck and his hands as he fell down on the hard, barren soil laughing. There was no doubt that Copper knew who her best friend was.

Friday night went by amazingly fast. We ate dinner, played a few games and then it was time to read him a story and tuck him into bed. Naturally, Copper slept with him, and I felt oddly disjointed going to my room alone. Saturday was the same. I couldn't seem to get enough of his presence. I eagerly accepted his hugs and kisses. He was the only person I could shower with love and affection without further complicating my mostly miserable existence. I wanted desperately to say something to Jake about what was going on between us, but I hadn't changed my mind about anything and I doubted he had either.

We saddled our horses in the afternoon and rode over to Uncle Ned's so he could give them a picture he had painted at school. Aunt Nora cried when he handed it to her.

"This is a wonderful gift, Trevor," she said, looking at his simple replication of their barn right after the flood. The ground appeared to be covered with mud, and the murky water lines on the barn's exterior were visible. The trees had lost their leaves, and the fence surrounding the pasture was missing some of its boards.

"I tried to remember exactly what it looked like, Aunt Nora. I didn't want to forget."

She kissed his upturned cheek. "It looks exactly right to me, and I am going to have it framed and hung in the den so we can see it every day."

Trevor was visibly moved by her declaration of love and admiration.

"You don't have to hang it up," he said. "I am not a very good artist yet."

"But it's the perfect gift for me, Trevor. It will always remind me of how lucky we are to have a place to live and to be part of a wonderful family."

I wondered if NJ and Molly understood how really fortunate they were to have Aunt Nora for a mother. She was the epitome of warmth, acceptance and love, almost the exact opposite of my mother with her fearfulness and lack of affection for anyone but me.

She insisted we stay for a light supper. Uncle Ned joined us for meatloaf, potatoes and pie.

"So, how's school, Trevor?" Uncle Ned asked him as we sat down at the table together. "I hope you are learning lots of new things."

Trevor looked at me for direction.

"He has only been in school for five days." I said, rising to my little brother's defense.

"Plenty of time to gather new information," Uncle Ned replied, looking at me from over the rim of his coffee cup. "Your father was a whiz at math."

"I'm good at it too," Trevor said. "I got hundreds on all my papers."

"Now, that is what Ima talking about! You need to learn everything you can so you will be able to run the ranch someday."

"But what about Brylee and Uncle Jake?" he asked. "They know lots more than I do."

"There's enough work out here for anyone who wants to stay long enough to do it, and that includes people both in and out of the family."

It seemed to me that Uncle Ned was specifically driving home the fact that the ranch would someday belong to Trevor, if the people now running it ever moved away. It made me wonder just how much Jake had told him about our relationship during the time they spent together. I knew he would never reveal the details of our conversation on the beach or the kiss we had shared, but even a drongo whose lift didn't go to the top floor could tell that things were not right between us now. Maybe he really expected one of us to bail, and that was the main reason we hadn't signed the papers to incorporate yet.

When we got home, I drew a hopscotch board on the sidewalk leading up to the veranda while Trevor looked for the perfect pebbles in the driveway. I had never played the game but had looked up the rules on the Internet, and it seemed simple enough. But even the most straightforward childhood game can be challenging, and I had nearly as much trouble as Trevor did hopping on one foot and then on two as we progressed from one square to another. I was laughing so hard by the time I finished my first turn I had to sit down on the sparse grass to recover. Trevor plopped down beside me.

"This is fun," he said. "I thought you knew how to do everything, but you are having as much trouble as me."

I rolled onto my side and looked over at him. "You forget that I grew up out here too. Only I didn't go away to school until I was much older than you are. That meant I never learned how to play even the simplest games."

"I can teach you," he said. "We play all kinds of stuff during recess and gym."

"That would be very helpful," I told him.

I loved having him with me, especially since he seemed happier and more content than he had for a very long time. I couldn't bring myself to think about tomorrow when I would have to take him back to town.

It was a great temptation to tell him how much I missed having him around, but guilt was a horrible taskmaster and he felt enough of it already after the way his mother had left. So I kept my feelings to myself as we tried our hand at dribbling a basketball and throwing a baseball around.

We fixed something for Jake to eat when he got home. He had spent most of the day in the hills and looked tired, dusty and discouraged. I didn't ask him where he had been or what he had been doing, but I wished I could offer comfort when he looked so down. It was impossible not to think about him most all the time, and not in the negative way I had for the first few months after we met. I could now see past all the things I had once despised into his heart and was beginning to accept what I found there.

He was a good man who loved deeply and took his responsibilities seriously. He was protective of his family, honest, hard-working, and dependable, and he had never given me any reason to believe that he wouldn't be totally faithful to the woman he chose to spend his life with. But he had set the boundaries because I hadn't been able to do it, and they were good ones considering all that we could potentially lose.

"Can we go, Brylee?" Trevor's question broke into my thoughts as I watched Jake eat the last bite of chocolate cake on his plate.

"Go where?" I asked, totally oblivious to what they had been talking about.

"To see the cave and waterfall," he impatiently replied. "Uncle Jake said he would take us there tomorrow. It is way up in the hills, and you can walk right behind the water into the cave. Please say *yes*, I want to go exploring so desperately."

I bit my thumbnail. Tomorrow was the Sabbath—a day for worship—not a day to go sightseeing or exploring. I momentarily wondered if Jake's invitation was just another way to prove to himself, and to me, that the church I had joined wasn't worth the cost because it discouraged families from doing other things together when they were supposed to be attending meetings.

"Please, Brylee," Trevor pleaded, while I tried to make a decision. In all fairness to Jake, I had never explained Sabbath day observance to him. "I really want to go."

"It would be good for all of us," Jake interjected. "I haven't been able to spend any time with Trevor since he got home. I'm sure your God will understand if you don't make it to church for one Sunday. You said it yourself. Family is the most important thing of all."

Jake was right about that, only he didn't understand why. I wanted my family to love God as much as I did, and that would never happen if they didn't come to know him personally.

"Okay!" I relented as a lump of compromise stuck in my throat. I would have to get used to a little concession if I ever wanted Jake to understand that my rules were not arbitrary or only applicable to him. "I will even pack a lunch."

Trevor ran around the table to give me a hug and a kiss. It was unreal how much he wanted to please others. "We can go to church next week, Brylee. I like it there, but I also like doing special things with you and Uncle Jake."

"You don't have to sell me on the idea," I told him. "I would like to see more of the ranch myself, and your Uncle Jake is the perfect guide. I know we can trust him with anything."

Chapter 22

Trevor was up before I was on Sunday morning. We had played checkers together at the kitchen table while laughing and eating popcorn until after ten the night before. Jake had played with us after taking a shower and changing clothes. He was comfortable to be around, knowing exactly how to make my little brother laugh, even when he missed an obvious move and had to be reminded. I watched them interact when they were playing together and tried to keep my mind on the game when it was my turn to challenge Jake. I had disarming thoughts of us being a real family—not just one dictated by circumstances beyond our control. It had taken me hours to fall asleep after going to bed.

By the time Trevor came knocking on my door, he was showered and dressed and had his clean clothes packed in his duffle bag. That was one of the things I insisted on doing. Emma shouldn't have to worry about everything, and washing a couple of batches of laundry took no time at all.

I invited him in, but my stomach ached and I felt a bit of a headache coming on. I wasn't getting sick like having the flu, although I knew that could happen if I didn't stop all the circular thinking and second-guessing myself. Jake had been pleasant enough the night before, but I could tell that something was really bothering him. I hqd made it halfway to the bunkhouse to talk to him about it before turning around and practically running back to the house. Our personal issues could not be intermingled with other items of worry, and that would most surely happen in the dark of night with no one around to chaperone.

"You must really be excited," I said as I followed him down the stairs yawning a few minutes later. I had taken the time to get dressed and swallow enough Ibuprofen to stop the onslaught of a migraine, unless it became overly stubborn.

"I'm not the only one," he said with a mischievous smile. "Uncle Jake is packing a lunch, and we already have the horses saddled."

"Wow! You guys are amazing," I replied, almost tripping over him because he had stopped at the bottom of the stairs to turn around and give me a frown.

"Can I tell you a secret?" he asked.

"You can tell me anything, little brother," I said, resting my hand on the banister. I had never seen him look quite so serious.

"Uncle Jake really likes you," he whispered.

"Your Uncle Jake likes everyone," I replied, grateful that my sunburned face hid the sudden rush of color to my cheeks.

"Not like that," he insisted. "He thinks you are pretty and smart and work too hard."

"And how would you know that? Has he ever said anything about me to you?"

"No, but he always smiles when he sees you, and he watches you when you don't notice. He never does that with Molly."

"That's because cousin Molly flirts a lot. It makes some guys uncomfortable."

"Not Uncle Jake! He talks to girls all the time."

"Really?" I responded with a mixture of surprise and disbelief. The phone in the house seldom rang, and the one in the bunkhouse was an extension. But that didn't mean he wasn't calling them while I was doing something else. Trevor's assessment didn't prove anything.

"That's not all, Brylee," he continued. "He used to go into town every weekend. He doesn't do that anymore. That is how I know he really likes you."

I didn't want to believe what he was saying. If my little brother could see what   was going on between us then everyone else could too, and that made the problems we faced riskier than ever. People we both cared about could get seriously hurt if either one of us made a decision we weren't prepared to live with.

"There could be lots of reasons he doesn't go into town as much as he used to. He is been really busy out here, especially with your mother in bed."

But Trevor wasn't about to be dissuaded from what believed.

"So how come he got up early to fix our lunch. He even made breakfast and put flowers on the table."

"That was very thoughtful of him," I said as my head began to spin. Talk about indecisiveness! He had avoided me all week and now he was bringing me flowers. Maybe it was just his way of saying *thank you* because I had agreed to go with them, and maybe there was something new brewing in his handsome head.

"Good morning, sleepy-head," I heard him say as I followed Trevor into the kitchen. There was a stack of pancakes on the table next to a vase of wildflowers he had picked somewhere in the outback since there was nothing like them close to the house.

"The flowers are beautiful," I responded as a way of avoiding the possibility of making an erroneous assumption. "You shouldn't have gone to so much trouble."

"You deserve having nice things done for you," he said, without turning around to look at me. He was busy getting butter and syrup from the refrigerator. "You are always doing things for other people."

I slid into the nearest chair afraid my legs would no longer support the weight of my body. I had never had a guy do nice things for me, except Ben, and I was still trying to close the door on that chapter of my life.

"We didn't want you to do any work today," Trevor interjected, sliding into the chair next to me. "Isn't that right, Uncle Jake?"

"As right as rain," he answered, holding out the platter of pancakes so Trevor could put a small stack on his plate.

I slipped one onto my own plate when he offered them to me. Jake was certainly a man of contradictions, and he was a master at keeping a woman guessing. If this was the way he treated all of the women in his life, I wondered why they didn't search for someone else who was much easier to understand. It would be a boon to their mental health not having to wonder where they stood all the time.

It was a three-hour ride on horseback before we came to the waterfall Jake told us about. I was glad Trevor had not been allowed to ride Thunder. While the terrain wasn't unreasonably difficult, we had to walk our horses the last quarter mile or so up a fairly steep incline and then leave them tethered to Kangaroo Paw trees near the trickling water while we passed underneath low-hanging branches and walked through grass tall enough to hide large reptiles I had no desire to meet unexpectedly.

The last few yards were so rocky and overgrown with brush that it was difficult to navigate them at all, and I had to help Trevor so he wouldn't get caught up in something and fall. Jake carried the backpack that contained our lunch while we fought off as much of the insect population as we possibly could. Notwithstanding its longer duration, this trip wasn't nearly as arduous as our short hike up the hill behind the house when we had gone looking for the slide I'd played on as a child, but we would still have a few bites and scrapes to contend with once we got home.

I spent the majority of the time we walked and swatted insects wondering how Jake had found the cave when it was so far up the mountain and so far away from areas where animals usually pastured. Perhaps he had seen it from his plane. I had certainly never heard about it from my father or even the aborigines that had once worked for us, and they loved talking about their unity with nature and the beauties of their place of origin.

Perhaps it was one of the places they went to when they wandered off without making mention of when, or even if, they would be returning. The concept of walkabouts had confused me as a child, but it was all part of their culture and my father had never questioned their behavior.

"This is so cool, Uncle Jake," Trevor said when we finally came to a stop at the edge of a small stream that seemed to zigzag every few yards. Further up its banks was a true beauty of nature that almost made my jaw drop.

The waterfall Jake had brought us to see wasn't large when compared to some of the ones I had seen in both Australia and America. In fact, the water descending from above wasn't all that deep in the stream bed and the entrance to the cave was clearly visible behind it, even from where we were standing at the edge of the stream. The light spray being showered on us was refreshing after the heat generated by climbing.

I took a deep breath of air as I absorbed some of its splendor. Despite the small amount of water, this place wasn't dead-looking and dry like so many other places on the ranch.

It was spectacular with its green trees and broad-leafed plants and its wildflowers of purple, pink and crimson. There were corellas and galahs singing their songs in the air, and furry little rodents moving along the water's edge. It seemed almost magical, and I half-expected to see a fabled unicorn, leprechaun or some other mythological creature come out of the shadows.

"It's incredible," I whispered to Jake who had one knee on the ground and was opening the backpack he had been carrying. He needn't have spent his day bringing us here, but I was ever so glad he had. If there were more beauties like this on the ranch, I wanted to see every one of them.

"I was hoping you would like it. I wanted to share something extra special extra special."

I spun around, nearly bumping into him. "It's more than amazing, Jake. It is what the Garden of Eden must have looked like."

"I wouldn't know anything about that," he replied, and I hoped I hadn't spoiled what remained of the day. "But there is still more to see. Would you like to eat before we take a look inside?"

I was starving, but when I looked for Trevor, he was already balancing himself on a rock in the stream.

"I guess that means no," I told Jake as I made my way back to the water's edge.

"Not so fast," he said. "It's dark in the cave, and you will need light to see anything."

Trevor obediently returned when Jake called to him and took the flashlight he offered. I accepted a second one. If I was ever lucky enough to have children of my own, I hoped they would be just like my little half-brother—obedient, trusting and teachable.

"How did you find this cave?" I asked Jake as we stepped from one rock to another. Less than an inch of water glided over them, but I knew looks could be deceiving. The water had tempered them until they were as smooth as brightly colored glass. "I have never heard anyone mention it before, not even Asum and Keida."

"Who's that?" he asked, glancing back at me.

"The aborigines who worked for us when I was a child. They knew every inch of this ranch."

"That might explain part of what I found."

"Do tell," I said. "You know how much I hate secrets."

"Not just yet my inquisitive one. This is something you have to see to believe."

Now, I was more than intrigued. Jake was sharing something obviously important to him with us. I doubted that he had ever brought anyone else here. The climb alone would discourage most girls.

"You didn't answer my question about how you found this place," I continued, knowing he wouldn't share anything more until he was ready.

"I was just scouting things out in the plane, saw it below me and decided to take a closer look."

"But how? There are dozens of mountains that look just like this one from both above and beneath."

"Where there is a will, there is always a way, and a little GPS guidance helps."

"You're impossible." I said, looking up at him and almost sliding off the rock I was trying to get a foothold on.

"Be careful!" he cautioned, grabbing my arm so I wouldn't fall. His touch was electrifying, and when he looked into my eyes all I wanted to do was to melt into his arms for the rest of my life. "I forgot to tell you that some of the rocks have moss on them."

"I can see that," I responded as I watched his lips move, bringing back a keen awareness of the emotions his kiss could arouse. Perhaps there was more to him bringing me here than just seeing a beauty of nature.

We stood for a moment transfixed. I wished the spell we seemed to be under could last forever, but Jake knew the danger of festering feelings as well as I did and looked away from me far sooner than I wanted him to.

"I think we had better hurry because I can no longer see Trevor, and there is plenty of trouble a young bloke can get into in a place like this."

I had never been behind a waterfall before. In fact, I had never been inside a cave and an ominous thrill of the unknown descended instantaneously on me. It was cold and damp and the curtain of water masked the brilliance of the sun. I turned on my flashlight and looked at the rock formations that surrounded me on three sides. It was a small room, dark and foreboding, and there were passages leading to both the right and the left.

I was just about to ask Jake which way we were going when something flew over our heads and touched my hair. It startled me so completely I screamed.

Trevor, who had been standing close by, reached for my hand. "I want to go back, Brylee. I don't like this cave any more."

But Jake's laugh was reassuring. "It was just a wee batty. They are more scared of us than we are of them."

"Maybe Trevor's right," I replied as my heart began to slow, and I looked past the falling water to the sunlight on the other side. This was just the sort of place poisonous snakes and other undesirable creatures would inhabit. "We don't know what we will find, and it could be dangerous."

"Don't you trust me?" Jake asked.

For a moment I wasn't so sure, but he would never take Trevor to a place where he could be harmed. I knew that as surely as I knew the sun would rise in the morning, even if clouds obscured it.

"Of course, I do," I said.

"That's good because I checked it out yesterday to just to make sure."

So that was one of the reasons he had been gone all day and why he'd come home looking so hot and disheveled. He was keeping an eye out for our wellbeing like he always did.

I looked down at Trevor and smiled. "Why don't we go on just a little further? It would be sad to miss out on an opportunity like this."

"Besides," Jake said, lifting up the corner of his jacket so we could see his holster. "I have my gun, and I am an excellent shot."

With Trevor still holding my hand, we followed him down a passageway to the right. It was dark, dank and silent.

"This is what I really brought you here to see," he said as soon as we stepped into another small room. He shinned his light at the rocks surrounding us, and the white line drawings nearly leaped off the walls. They were crude, but they seemed to be telling a story—a story of the white man coming to Australia on their ships with their cannons and muskets and taking everything away from the aborigines. Was this cave the place where some of them had lived after they were driven from their land? The thought that my ancestors might have been even partially responsible for their mostly-lost civilization saddened me, but they had only been making a home for their own families like everyone else who made it out of the penal system alive.

I moved closer the rock wall and ran my fingers lightly over a few of the lines, not wishing to disturb anything. "These are amazing! Do you think we are the only white people who have seen them?"

"It wouldn't surprise me," Jake said, stepping up beside me. His nearness brought warmth and a feeling of safety. "There is no way of knowing for sure, of course, but this cave isn't on any bloody map I have been able to find."

"You've looked?"

"I haven't combed the deep recesses of Edna's only library, if that's what you are asking. But it is a place that can't be stumbled on, except by accident. I would never have come here myself if it hadn't been for idle curiosity and a little free time."

"Did you tell my father about it?"

"He was gone before I found it. Wouldn't he have been bloody surprised, though? A real spot of history right here on his own land. If I am reading their story correctly, these drawings have been here for over 200 years. Look at their representations of guns and canons. Those things didn't exist in the outback until the British sent our relatives out here for punishment."

"Do you think our ancestors drove them away?"

"Somebody's did, but we can't blame ourselves for what happened in the past. It had nothing to do with us."

"Maybe not," I responded, trying to read part of the story behind the line drawings for myself. "But it's still unfair that they were forced to relinquish everything they had ever known because someone else wanted what they had."

"That's the story of civilization, and there is nothing we can do to change it. I have no doubt that the very land we are standing on right now will belong to someone else one day. Even the hardiest of families have a breaking point where everything fades away."

I didn't want to think about that today. I just wanted to pay respect to those persons who had gone before us.

"Where do you think the majority of the aborigines went?" I asked.

Trevor had joined us at the wall.

"Further into the outback would be my guess. But I'm sure that a lot of the tribes simply died out from natural causes. The outback is relentlessly hostile to most every living thing."

"So finding this really is an important discovery—a historic record that should be preserved and shared with others."

"It is preserved, and I have thought about sharing it with others," Jake said. "I even flew into Edna after finding the cave to see if there was any precedence regarding it, but there isn't a record of it on any of the topographical or geological maps of the region. And I am not convinced that having a bunch of archeologists up here digging around is the right thing to do. Why should anyone be given recognition or monetary compensation for something that destroyed part of a civilization? Besides, these drawings aren't the only thing I found."

We followed him down another passage into an even smaller enclosure—one where Jake had to squat down in order to enter. Aborigines were small people, and he was well over six-feet tall.

"Shine your light on these walls and then tell me we ought to let the bloody government know about this cave."

I did as he instructed. It took a moment to catch a glimmer here and there among the craggy recesses. I looked from Jake to Trevor and back again.

"Is that what I think it is?" I asked him.

"I believe so, and there are several more caverns just like this one. I haven't even scratched the surface when it comes to finding out what is really here."

"How long have you known." I walked over to the wall and touched the golden deposits. They were rough and cooler than the rocks surrounding them.

"A few weeks, but I have been curious about its existence ever since I found the rock I made into your Christmas necklace. This cave lies almost directly above the clearing where we spent the second night herding sheep."

My fingers found the stone that lay slightly below my collarbone. I hadn't taken it off since he had fastened it around my neck.

"But why are you sharing this with us now?" I asked him. "It could have remained your secret until you decided what to do with it."

I looked around at Trevor. He was shinning his flashlight up and down the wall on the opposite side of the cave and appeared oblivious to what we were saying.

"First," Jake said. "I am not that kind of man. I would never take something that didn't belong to me. And second, we have no idea if this is a legitimate vein of gold or just a fluke. You would have to hire geologists to find out, and their presence on the ranch would tell the whole world what might be here. Can you imagine the gold fever that would arouse? Besides, it would cost a lot more than I have tucked away to get them out here to do a legitimate survey."

I looked at his profile. His jaw was set in a harsh line. I couldn't see his eyes, but I could feel his hurt at my doubting his devotion to his family, the land and his honesty as a man.

"I'm sorry. I know you would never do anything to hurt LeAnn or Trevor. This is just such a surprise."

"I would never hurt you either, Brylee."

The sincerity of his words caused chills to race up and down my spine.

"I just hope that someday you will believe that I really do care about you."

"I know you care," I replied, staring at the rock formations in front of me until they became nothing more than a blur. "And I care about you."

"But I'm not the right man for you," he finished for me. "I don't know how you can believe in a church or a God that keeps people who care about each other apart."

"It's not just the church, Jake. You and I are at very different places in our lives, both searching for something we have yet to find."

"I've found what I have bloody well been looking for, Brylee. It's you who can't make up your mind. Why do you think I have been absent so much this week? I couldn't bear being in the same room with you and knowing I had no right to take you into my arms. It is killing me inside."

"Me too," I whispered.

"Then take a chance. Give me a chance to prove that I am not some bloody bloke who is only out to use and hurt you. I know I said that I was a patient man and didn't want to be part of some rebound relationship, but I don't think I can do that anymore."

Oh, how I wanted to do just what he asked—throw everything aside and just allow myself to love him. I ran my hand down his cheek. There was a stubble of softness there. He hadn't taken the time to shave.

But how could I live with myself if I gave in to my ardent side without considering all the repercussions? God required more of me than he had a year and a half ago, and I required more of myself?

"You're silent again," he continued, as his hand covered mine and his eyes bored a hole in my heart.

It would be so easy to tell him that I had fallen completely and hopelessly in love with him and that what I believed no longer mattered, but it did!

"I'm sorry," I whispered as tears tickled my nose. "All I do is hurt you."

"You don't hurt me," he replied. "I hurt myself by wanting something I can't have. I'm well aware that I am not the best husband material, but that doesn't stop how I feel about you. Sometimes I think it would be better for everyone if I just disappeared."

My hand involuntarily slipped from his face and gripped his arm as a sob of horror escaped through my parted lips. We had been through this before, and the thought of him leaving was still as abhorrent as it had been the first time he mentioned it.

"I don't want you to leave, ever."

"Then give me a reason to stay!"

I should have kissed him then, but I didn't, and that one action cost both of us dearly.

"I just need a little more time," I said instead. "You know how I feel about you. Doesn't that count for anything?"

His fingers tightened over mine, but their warmth was far from comforting. "Maybe it should, but I want far more than you are willing to give right now. That might not be very magnanimous after what I have said before, but it's how I feel. Wanting you when you don't want me in return is pure torture."

"But I do want you," I admitted, wishing that loving him would make everything okay. "I just wish you could understand that I have made certain promises . . . ."

He interrupted before I could finish my thought.

"Then we are right back where we always end up, me wanting to give us a chance, and you being conflicted over religious mores. I keep hoping things will change, but they aren't going to, are they?"

"I want them to," I said as I felt his fingers move apart until they were no longer touching mine. "But what if we tried building a relationship and it didn't work out? We would never be able to work with each other again."

"Just another excuse," he said, backing completely away from me. "You have a ton of those, don't you, love?"

"Love!" The very way he said the word nearly turned my resolve to melted butter. I wanted to reach out and draw him back to me but knew I didn't have the right. Love, even if it were beginning to grow between us, would never be enough. But if he left me for someone else, I wasn't sure I would ever survive the pain.

"I think it is time for both of us to move on," he was saying when I forced my thoughts back to the horrid moment we were in. "We have been beating this dead horse for months now.

You already have your mind made up that I will never be worthy of you, and I might as well accept it."

"What are you saying, Jake?"

"I'll be damned if I know," he looked in Trevor's direction. "But I am a man, Brylee, and I am bloody tired of being pushed away."

"I don't mean to be that way."

"Maybe you don't, but that doesn't change the fact that I have told you how I feel and you can't reciprocate, and it isn't all your fault. I think you are right when you say that monster took something away from you when he stole your innocence and trust. Maybe you will get it back and maybe you won't. I am a patient bloke, Brylee, but I am not a fool. If you really cared about me, you would give me a chance."

I just stood there in stunned silence, unable to move or speak.

"Hey, Trevor," he said, turning his back on me and walking away. "It will be too late for your sister to drive you into town by the time we get back to the ranch, so why don't I fly you in instead. I haven't been with any of my friends for months now, and it is time to remedy that."

I couldn't eat our picnic lunch, and Trevor asked me if I was sick. I assured him that I was just tired and would be fine after a good night's rest. Jake didn't say a single word to me on the long ride home, but he chatted amicably with Trevor as they made plans to stop at Macca's before returning to Emma's.

I wished the entire day could be lived over again. I would refuse to go on the outing and head straight into town by myself. Trevor was never going to understand why I felt it was necessary to completely destroy my relationship with his uncle. There would be no more shared, special occasions or pleasant evenings. I would be lucky if Jake even spoke to me again.

That was why I had fought so hard not to become emotionally involved with him in the first place. The only consolation I found was in knowing that everything would be decidedly worse if we had given in to our passions.

Trevor didn't say anything about our silence. I packed up the cookies I had made and then walked with him out to the plane where I kissed him goodbye. If it weren't for him, I would pack my bags and never come back, but God expected more from me than caving in to a difficult situation. There were lessons I still needed to learn. Jake might be out of my life, but I doubted he would ever be out of my heart.

I stood in the field behind the barn and watched until the plane was out of sight. Then I went to the cemetery to talk to my parents. I knew they couldn't answer, but I needed to believe that someone still cared about me.

When Jake hadn't returned to the ranch by eleven, I knew he wouldn't be back before daylight. I missed him dreadfully and didn't want him to be with anyone else, but I had lost the right to say anything about the way he lived his life.

I learned that conclusively early the next morning when the phone rang.

"Hi, Brylee, this is Beth," a female voice said when I picked up the receiver at seven. "Is Jake there, yet?"

"I'm not sure," I told her as a hard knot of dread and sense of betrayal formed in the pit of my stomach. "I didn't wait up for him."

There was more than a small element of pride in her voice when she continued. "Oh, you didn't need to. He was with me until an hour ago. We had an amazing time."

Her implication didn't need explaining. Jake was her man now.

"Would you like me to give him a message?" I asked, biting the inside of my lower lip until I could taste blood. I wasn't going to cry, not now, anyway. I had made my bed by taking a stand and now I would have to sleep in it—alone, sad and miserable.

"Just tell him Beth called. I think we actually met at the diner a few months ago and saw each other again at your father's funeral. I am sorry for your loss. Anyway, Jake stopped by for coffee last night, and one thing lead to another, if you know what I mean."

I did know what she meant, but I wasn't about to comment on it. Without help from anyone else, I had destroyed my last chance for happiness.

"I will leave him the message. Is there anything else?"

"Nothing that can be repeated in polite society," she quipped. "He promised he would call later, but I just wanted to make sure he got home okay. He was awfully tired when he left."

I stood numbly with the phone still dangling in my hand after the call ended. How could Jake fall into bed with the first woman he saw after telling me that he was moving on? But I couldn't have it both ways any longer. If I didn't want him, there were plenty of women who did.

He got back around nine. I heard the back door slam shut because the kitchen lay directly below my bedroom where I had gone to reflect on the hodgepodge I had made of my life. He was whistling when he walked into the house, and that made my blood boil. But I felt even worse as I heard his laughter after the phone rang. He had never laughed like that with me, but then I had never given him a reason to. Sometimes sinning did bring happiness, at least to people who didn't believe like I did.

I thought he might try to find me, even though I was hiding, but he didn't. I stayed in my room all afternoon trying not to think about what had happened in town. I wanted him to be different like Ben, but he wasn't and never would be.

My convictions and lack of faith in who he could become with a little help from me, had sent him straight into the arms of another woman. The phone rang several times after that, but I was too disillusioned to answer it. I never wanted to talk to Jake or his waitress again.

It was dark before I realized I hadn't called Trevor. My sorry affairs of the heart were hurting him again, and that wasn't fair. He hadn't done anything but love me.

As for Jake, I found myself listening for any sound that might indicate he hadn't forgotten about me. I hadn't heard his plane take off or even the revving of his truck's engine, but that didn't mean he wasn't talking to his lover. I couldn't even bring myself to say her name.

Was this really the way it was going to end, a promise of passion, a declaration of love, and then nothing? Life couldn't be that cruel, but then history had a way of repeating itself unless people were willing to change. But I would have to think about that tomorrow. Tonight was a time for mourning.

To be continued . . . .

Enjoy this excerpt from

Betrayal

Indecision's Flame
Book Four

by JS Ririe

Morning dawned long before I was ready for it. I had slept fitfully—if at all. My eyes were rimmed with red, my stomach knotted and my head felt like it was being squeezed in a vice, but I had no one to blame but myself for the way things were turning out. I couldn't expect Jake to do all the changing when I wasn't willing to compromise or even give him a chance.

Defining why I felt as I did was impossible. Fear most certainly was part of it, but I had overcome that before by giving up my past way of life and allowing Ben in. I still loved him and the peaceful, fulfilling times we had shared. He was the polar opposite of Jake. With him, I had always known where I stood. There were no games or pretenses, and there had never been a harsh word between us.

But then he had insisted that I come home to face my father. It seemed as if my life had become one disaster after another since the moment I set foot on Australian soil, and every decision I avoided or made came crammed with consequences I did not want to face. Not only had I been forced to accept a new family and learn how to manage the financial affairs of a ranch, but every man who had been a real part of my life was gone—my father, Ben and now Jake.

Maybe I was doomed to spend mortality alone. It was a harsh veracity to face, but as long as I stayed where I was, there would be no happily ever after for me.

I pulled the covers over my head and settled in for another bout of self-pity and tears. Perhaps I had given up on my engagement too fast because, like my cousin Molly, confrontations were hard for me. I didn't want to be dumped so I had done the dumping before Ben's relationship with Jennifer progressed to the point where he would want her more than he wanted me. Everything had seemed so clear that night on the beach when he told me that he wasn't sure where our future would lead because I didn't really trust him. That was why I had released him from his promise, but the regrets had come hard and fast. My falling into Jake's arms for comfort was proof of that. And now I had even alienated him.

Oh, how I hated what I had done to my life. No matter how I sliced or diced it I came out on the bottom. I was still the prodigal daughter—home too late for anything except my father's funeral and the merry-go-round of complications set forth by the reading of his will.

It was too much to deal with, so I closed my eyes as tight as I could and tried to go back to sleep. I could stay right where I was and no one would come looking for me. Ben had Jennifer, LeAnn had Trevor and a baby on the way, and Jake had his waitress in town. All I had ever wanted, even when searching for something more, was to be a good person and show love towards others, but I couldn't even get that right. I had done nothing since coming home but offend and alienate people I cared about. Even Jake, the man who always had an answer for everything, had finally had enough of my platitudes and indecisiveness and had moved on with someone else.

I slept until noon and then crept down the stairs and into the kitchen to get something to eat and drink. It had been nearly thirty hours since I had learned of Jake's encounter in town, and the pain was still so raw I wondered if I would ever get over it, but I was pragmatic enough to understand that life would go on even if I didn't want to be part of it. I had promised my father I would not let his dream die, but doing that without seeing Jake again was impossible. If I could just get away from everybody and everything for a while maybe I could gain some perspective, but there was no place to go or anyone to turn to. I was on my own again and hated it.

Justifying my actions over the next few days was impossible, except to say that I was licking my wounds and couldn't bear to talk to anyone, especially my little brother. How could I pretend that everything was okay, and that Jake and I would be there for him—standing united—when he came home for the weekend? I didn't even know if Jake still planned on being there at all. He might already be making other plans.

I spent most of my time in my room or in the attic with Copper at my side. I loved that little dog. She sat curled up next to me while I cried and never complained when I hugged her too tightly. Jake came into the house several times, but I never went downstairs to talk to him, and he never came looking for me. He drove away from the ranch on Wednesday morning and didn't return that night or even the next day, but I still didn't leave the safety of the rooms I had designated as a safe haven, except to make sure the animals had enough to eat and drink.

My actions were mostly irrational, even to me, but I still made up excuses for why I couldn't see him. It wasn't as much for what we had lost as it was for what might have been if one of us had been willing to make more than minimal concessions. But as the hours wore endlessly on, I came to more fully understand that what had happened between us was as much my fault as it was his. I was rigid in everything I did, especially in my expectations about my future husband. Ben was everything I had dreamed of having, and I was constantly comparing Jake with him.

That wasn't fair, and it wasn't what the Savior would do. Jake had no idea where I was coming from because religion, or even the concept of spirituality, had never been part of his life. I had been much the same way when I first met Becky and Ben, and it had taken months for my heart to soften enough to do more than act resentful and contemptuous every time she talked about family and wanting to be with them forever. I hated my father and my mother was dead, so there seemed little point in even listening to anything she said. It just made me more angry and bitter.

Still, no matter how many times I replayed the issues and possible solutions to my predicament in my head as I slowly resumed simple household tasks, it always came back to the same thing. I might be falling hopelessly in love with Jake Johnson but was terrified of taking a risk because I knew what would happen if his heart didn't soften as mine had done. There would be an even worse ending to our relationship that could mean the loss of everything to our entire family.

The emotional turmoil of relentlessly hiding from him and yet wanting to run straight into his strong, protective arms was making me ill, so I called Emma on Thursday afternoon to see if she would cover for me with Trevor on his expected visit home for the weekend. It wasn't a lie that I was sick. I had lost my ability to move forward. I still wanted to be there for the people who needed me but, like LeAnn, I had experienced too much loss, and until I was able to replenish the emptiness inside, I would never be able to help anyone again.

"This isn't like you," she said, after listening to my short outburst of garbled feelings. "You have only talked to Trevor once this week and now you are asking me to make excuses for why he can't come to the ranch this weekend. He will never understand. All he talks about is you, Jake and his animals. I think you owe me an explanation since I am the one you expect to get in the middle of this with him. The last time we talked, you seemed more hopeful than you had in a long time."

"Well, I have lost all hope now," I responded. "All I do is destroy everything I touch. Even the heavens seem closed against me."

Her intake of breath was sharp. "You know that's not true, Brylee. God never leaves us to endure more than we can handle, and whether you believe it or not, you are not alone."

"But I feel alone, Emma," I sobbed as a floodgate of tears opened again. "There isn't one single person who would not survive just fine if I left and never came back."

"That is utter nonsense, and you know it," she protested. "There are a great many people who love you. Did something happen with Jake I should know about?"

"Yes," I retorted. "He has moved on with someone else because I couldn't, or wouldn't, let him into my life."

"Oh, my," she sighed. "I suppose we both knew that was a possibility once you took a firm stand . . . ."

"But he didn't have to sleep with a waitress just a few hours after telling me that if I didn't want him he would find someone who did?" I interrupted.

"So that is what has your knickers in such a knot. Jake is a passionate, attentive man who is used to getting what he wants. That is one of the things women love most about him."

"No kidding!" I replied with more anger than was necessary. "Beth called an hour after he left her. She wanted to make sure I knew they had spent the night together."

"Have you talked to Jake about it? She might only be trying to get you to stay away from him. It is pretty much obvious to everyone who sees the two of you together that there is more going on than simple friendship."

"Not anymore, and our relationship was never simple. I have avoided him since he flew Trevor into town on Sunday after what was supposed to be a very special day. I even missed church so he would know I was capable of making compromises. Now I can't bring myself to even look at him his betrayal hurts so much. That's why I need to put some distance between us before I fall completely apart."

"You can't run away from your problems, Brylee. They will still be there when you get back."

"Then maybe I won't come back!" I told her.

Her quick intake of breath was more than obvious. "You aren't planning on doing something foolish, are you?"

"No," I replied, sinking onto the stool that had been placed underneath the wall-mounted kitchen phone. "But I don't know what else to do. Jake and I can't even be in the same room right now, and I am not sure that will ever change."

"I am not trying to minimize your pain or concern, Brylee. There are some very serious issues that need resolution and it is doubtful that will happen overnight, but you cannot let your personal problems affect Trevor. He has been through so much the past few months. If you leave now, he will spend the rest of his life believing that you never really cared."

"But that's not true, Emma! Trevor means everything to me."

"Then maybe you will have to treat the situation with Jake like a less-than-amicable divorce until you can figure things out. He called here earlier today to say he would pick Trevor up after school tomorrow as planned. I don't know what he intends to do after that, but it gives you twenty-four hours to decide what your response is going to be. Can you be there for your little brother this weekend or not?"

The tears were flowing freely now. "How can I be there for him when my own life is such a muddle? What if Jake brings Beth with them, and what if he doesn't even bring Trevor back to the ranch?"

"You sound plumb loco right now. Jake is not the kind of man to throw any relationship in your face, but you are never going to know the truth about anything unless you are willing to talk to him. I know you feel that is impossible, but this situation is bigger than the two of you. There is a little boy to consider who needs both his sister and his uncle to provide some stability in his otherwise unsettled life. You simply can't let him down again."

"But what about me?" I cried out, hating the fact that I had allowed the darkness to enter my heart, but Satan was a cunning demon hitting below the belt when a person was already down. He could twist everything that was good until the truth was completely obliterated. "I can't see Jake again. It would tear me apart."

See Book Five: **Reawakening - Indecision's Flame** for more of Brylee's story.

Other Titles From Jan Hill Books:

Indecision's Flame - Book 1: by JS Ririe

Brylee Hawkins was prepared to enjoy a bright, hopeful future until her fiancé convinced her to return to the Australian Outback to confront the father that had driven her away. On her own again in a harsh and unforgiving land, she is forced to face a mottled and unsavory past and an even more disturbing and dangerous present. As unrelenting lies, secrets and cover-ups – including a family she never knew about - continue to unfold, Brylee soon learns that both decisions and indecision are bringing her closer to a point of no return. Will she find the strength to fight the darkness, or will it seep into her soul and take away everything she had come to treasure?

Lost - Indecision's Flame - Book 2: by JS Ririe

Torn between her family and the obligations of a promise made to her father, Brylee longs to return to the United States and to her fiancé who is patiently waiting for her, but fate seems to have other plans. Jake, the brother of her father's wife, decides to take her under his wing and teach her the ropes of running the ranch - mostly in an attempt to get rid of her. His mockery and ridicule are only enhanced when she learns of her father's legacy and the part she is to play if she wants to help keep it alive. Unable to make a decision about leaving, she is left to wonder if the outback will consume her before the next harsh blow comes.

About the Author

JS Ririe is the pen name for Jan Hill. She spent her youth in the country where she learned to appreciate solitude, making her own fun, and reading romance novels from some of the masters like the Bronte sisters, Louisa May Alcott, Victoria Holt and Phyllis Whitney. She penned her first novel as a teenager but never pursued what is now her greatest passion until becoming the lead witness in a federal case brought against the school district where she taught broadcasting and journalism. Writing Brylee's story as she waited two years to testify helped her through a terrifying time. She lives in Utah and has two children and two living grandchildren who help bring meaning and joy to her life.

A Note From Jan

Thank you so much for reading this novel. I'd love to stay in touch with you. Please consider joining my MAILING LIST so I can send you periodic newsletters about upcoming book releases, special offers and more. The link to sign up for my mailing list is: http://eepurl.com/dCPYVf . I promise that I will not spam you, will not sell your email information and will treat it with care.

One last favor: Your rating/review of this book helps me to keep writing. I would really appreciate it if you could leave a review. It shouldn't take more than a minute or two. You can reach the page directly at http://amzn.to/2BXNSdv

Thank you again,
JS Ririe

www.JanHillBooks.com
For contacting the author: JSRirie@JanHillBooks.com